William Michael Rossetti, Thomas Hood, Gustave Doré

The Poetical Works of Thomas Hood

William Michael Rossetti, Thomas Hood, Gustave Doré

The Poetical Works of Thomas Hood

ISBN/EAN: 9783337366506

Printed in Europe, USA, Canada, Australia, Japan

Cover: Foto ©Andreas Hilbeck / pixelio.de

More available books at **www.hansebooks.com**

THE

POETICAL WORKS

OF

THOMAS HOOD.

EDITED, WITH A CRITICAL MEMOIR,

BY

WILLIAM MICHAEL ROSSETTI.

ILLUSTRATED BY

GUSTAVE DORÉ.

NEW YORK:

GEORGE ROUTLEDGE & SONS,

416 BROOME STREET.

1873.

CONTENTS.

PREFATORY NOTICE.

THERE were scarcely any events in the life of Thomas Hood. One condition there was of too potent determining importance—lifelong ill-health; and one circumstance of moment—a commercial failure, and consequent expatriation. Beyond this, little presents itself for record in the outward facts of this upright and beneficial career, bright with genius and coruscating with wit, dark with the lengthening and deepening shadow of death.

The father of Thomas Hood was engaged in business as a publisher and bookseller in the Poultry, in the city of London,—a member of the firm of Vernor, Hood, and Sharpe. He was a Scotchman, and had come up to the capital early in life, to make his way. His interest in books was not solely confined to their saleable quality. He reprinted various old works with success; published Bloomfield's poems, and dealt handsomely with him; and was himself the author of two novels, which are stated to have

had some success in their day. For the sake of the son
rather than the father, one would like to see some account,
with adequate specimens, of these long-forgotten tales ; for
the queries which Thomas Hood asks concerning the
piteous woman of his *Bridge of Sighs* interest us all concerning a man of genius, and interest us moreover with
regard to the question of intellectual as well as natural
affinity :—

> " Who was his father
> Who was his mother?
> · Had he a sister,
> Had he a brother ?"

Another line of work in which the elder Hood is recorded
to have been active was the opening of the English book-
trade with America. He married a sister of the engraver
Mr. Sands, and had by her a large family : two sons and
four daughters survived the period of childhood. The
elder brother, James, who died early of consumption, drew
well, as did also one or two of the sisters. It would seem,
therefore, when we recall Thomas Hood's aptitudes and
frequent miscellaneous practice in the same line, that a
certain tendency towards fine art, as well as towards
literature, ran in the family. The consumption which
killed James appears to have been inherited from his
mother : she, and two of her daughters, died of the same
disease—and a pulmonary affection of a somewhat different
kind became, as we shall see, one of the poet's most invete-
rate persecutors. The death of the father, which was
sudden and unexpected, preceded that of the mother, but
not of James, and left the survivors in rather straitened circumstances.

Thomas, the second of the two sons, was born in the

Poultry, on or about the 23d of May 1799. He is stated to have been a retired child, with much quiet humour ; chuckling, we may guess, over his own quaint imaginings, which must have come in crowds, and of all conceivable or inconceivable sorts, to judge from the product of his after years ; keeping most of these fancies and surprises to himself, but every now and then letting some of them out, and giving homely or stolid bystanders an inkling of insight into the many-peopled crannies of his boyish brain. He received his education at Dr. Wanostrocht's school at Clapham. It is not very clear how far this education extended : * I should infer that it was just about enough, and not more than enough, to enable Hood to shift for himself in the career of authorship, without serious disadvantage from inadequate early training, and also without much aid thence derived—without, at any rate, any such rousing and refining of the literary sense as would warrant us in attributing to educational influences either the inclination to become an author, or the manipulative power over language and style which Hood displayed in his serious poems, not to speak of those of a lighter kind. We seem to see him sliding, as it were, into the profession of letters, simply through capacity and liking, and the course of events—not because he had resolutely made up his mind to be an author, nor because his natural faculty had been steadily or studiously cultivated. As to details, it may be remarked that his schooling included some amount—perhaps a fair

---

* The authority—I might almost say, the *one* authority—for the life of Hood, is the *Memorials* published by his son and daughter. Any point which is not clearly brought out in that affectionate and interesting record will naturally be equally or more indefinite in my brief summary, founded as it is on the *Memorials*.

average amount—of Latin. We find it stated that he had a Latin prize at school, but was not apt at the language in later years. He had, however, one kind of aptitude at it—being addicted to the use of familiar Latin quotations or phrases, cited with humorous verbal perversions.

In all the relations of family life, and the forms of family affection, Hood was simply exemplary. The deaths of his elder brother and of his father left him the principal reliance of his mother, herself destined soon to follow them to the tomb : he was an excellent and devoted son. His affection for one of his sisters, Anne, who also died shortly afterwards, is attested in the beautiful lines named *The Deathbed,*—

> "We watched her breathing through the night."

At a later date, the loves of a husband and a father seem to have absorbed by far the greater part of his nature and his thoughts : his letters to friends are steeped and drenched in "Jane," "Fanny," and "Tom junior." These letters are mostly divided between perpetual family details and perennial jocularity : a succession of witticisms, or at lowest of puns and whimsicalities, mounts up like so many squibs and crackers, fizzing through, sparkling amid, or ultimately extinguished by, the inevitable shower—the steady gush and downpour—of the home-affections. It may easily be inferred from this account that there are letters which one is inclined to read more thoroughly, and in greater number consecutively, than Hood's.

The vocation first selected for Hood, towards the age of fifteen, was one which he did not follow up for long—that of an engraver. He was apprenticed to his uncle Mr. Sands, and afterwards to one of the Le Keux family.

The occupation was ill-suited to his constantly ailing health, and this eventually conduced to his abandoning it. He then went to Scotland to recruit, remaining there among his relatives about five years.* According to a statement made by himself, he was in a merchant's office within this interval; it is uncertain, however, whether this assertion is to be accepted as genuine, or as made for some purpose of fun. His first published writing appeared in the *Dundee Advertiser* in 1814—his age being then, at the utmost, fifteen and a half; this was succeeded by some contribution to a local magazine. But as yet Hood had no idea of authorship as a profession.

Towards the middle of the year 1820, Hood was resettled in London, improved in health, and just come of age. At first he continued practising as an engraver; but in 1821 he began to act as a sort of sub-editor for the *London Magazine*, after the death of the editor, Mr. Scott, in a duel. He concocted fictitious and humorous answers to correspondents—a humble yet appropriate introduction to

---

* "Two years," according to the *Memorials;* but the dates for this early portion of Hood's life are not accurately given in that work. Hood completed the fifteenth year of his age in May 1814. It is certain, from the dates of his letters, that his sojourn in Scotland began not later than September 1815; and the writer of the *Memorials* himself affirms that Hood "returned to London about 1820," in or before July. If so, he was in Scotland about *five* years; and, from the fact that he had written in a Dundee newspaper in 1814, one might even surmise that the term of six years was nearer the mark. At any rate, as he had reached Scotland by September 1815, he was there soon after completing his sixteenth year: yet Mr. Hessey (*Memorials*, p. 23) says that he was articled to the engraving business "at the age of fifteen or sixteen," and his apprenticeship, according to Mr. Hood junior, lasted "some years" even *before* his transfer from Mr. Sands to Mr. Le Keux. The apprenticeship did not begin until after the father's death; but the year of that death is left unspecified, though the day and month are given. These dates, as the reader will readily perceive, are sometimes vague, and oftener contradictory. In the text of my notice, I have endeavoured to pick my way through their discrepancies.

the insatiable habit and faculty for out-of-the-way verbal
jocosity which differentiated his after career from that of
all other excellent poets. His first regular contribution to
the magazine, in July 1821, was a little poem _To Hope:_
even before this, as early at any rate as 1815, he was in the
frequent practice of writing correctly and at some length in
verse, as witnessed by selections, now in print, from what
he had composed for the amusement of his relatives. Soon
afterwards, a private literary society was the recipient of
other verses of the same order. The lines _To Hope_ were
followed, in the _London Magazine,_ by the _Ode to Dr.
Kitchener_ and some further poems, including the importan*
work _Lycus the Centaur_—after the publication of which,
there could not be much doubt of the genuine and uncom-
non powers of the new writer. The last contribution of
Hood to this magazine was the _Lines to a Cold Beauty._

By this time it may have become pretty clear to himself
and others that his proper vocation and destined profession
was literature. Through the _London Magazine,_ he got to
know John Hamilton Reynolds (author of the _Garden of
Florence_ and other poems, and a contributor to this serial
under the pseudonym of Edward Herbert), Charles Lamb,
Allan Cunningham, De Quincey, and other writers of reputation. To Hood the most directly important of all
these acquaintances was Mr. Reynolds; this gentleman
having a sister, Jane, to whom Hood was introduced. An
attachment ensued, and shortly terminated in marriage,
the wedding taking place on the 5th of May 1824. The
father of Miss Reynolds was the head writing-master at
Christ Hospital. She is stated to have had good manners,
a cultivated mind, and literary tastes, though a high educational standard is not always traceable in her letters. At

any rate, the marriage was a happy one ; Mrs. Hood being
a tender and attentive wife, unwearied in the cares which
her husband's precarious health demanded, and he being
(as I have said) a mirror of marital constancy and devotion,
distinguishable from a lover rather by his intense delight
in all domestic relations and details than by any cooling-
down in his fondness. It would appear that, in the later
years of Hood's life, he was not on entirely good terms with
some members of his wife's family, including his old friend
John Hamilton Reynolds. What may have caused this
I do not find specified : all that we know of the character
of Hood justifies us in thinking that he was little or not at
all to blame, for he appears throughout as a man of just,
honourable, and loving nature, and free besides from that
sort of self-assertion which invites a collision. Every one,
however, has his blemishes ; and we may perhaps discern
in Hood a certain over-readiness to think himself imposed
upon, and the fellow-creatures with whom he had immediately to do a generation of vipers—a state of feeling not
characteristic of a mind exalted and magnanimous by
habit, or "gentle" in the older and more significant meaning of the term

The time was now come for Hood to venture a volume
upon the world. Conjointly with Reynolds, he wrote, and
published in 1825, his *Odes and Addresses to Great People*.
The title page bore no author's name ; but the extraordinary
talent and point of the work could hardly fail to be noticed,
even apart from its appeal to immediate popularity, dealing
as it did so continually with the uppermost topics of the
day. It had what it deserved, a great success. This
volume was followed, in 1826, by the first series of *Whims
and Oddities*, which also met with a good sale ; the second

b

series appeared in 1827. Next came two volumes of *National Tales*, somewhat after the manner of Boccaccio (but how far different from his spirit may easily be surmised), which are now little known. The volume containing the *Plea of the Midsummer Fairies, Hero and Leander*, and some others of Hood's most finished and noticeable poems, came out in 1827. *The Midsummer Fairies* itself was one of the author's own favourite works, and certainly deserved to be so, as far as dainty elegance of motive and of execution is concerned : but the conception was a little too ingeniously remote for the public to ratify the author's predilection. In 1829 appeared the most famous of all Hood's poems of a narrative character—*The Dream of Eugene Aram :* it was published in the *Gem*, an annual which the poet was then editing. Besides this amount of literary activity, Hood continued writing in periodicals, sometimes under the signature of " Theodore M."

His excessive and immeasurable addiction to rollicking fun, to the perpetual " cracking of jokes " (for it amounts to that more definitely than to anything else in the domain of the Comic Muse), is a somewhat curious problem, taken in connection with his remarkable genius and accomplishment as a poet, and his personal character as a solid housekeeping citizen, bent chiefly upon rearing his family in respectability, and paying his way, or, as the Church Catechism has neat'y and unimprovably expressed it, upon " doing his duty in that state of life to which it had pleased God to call him." His almost constant ill-health, and, in a minor degree, the troubles which beset him in money matters, make the problem all the more noticeable. The influence of Charles Lamb may have had something to do with it,— probably not very much. Perhaps there was something in

the literary atmosphere or the national tone of the time which
gave comicality a turn of predominance after the subsiding
of the great poetic wave which filled the last years of the
eighteenth and the first quarter of the nineteenth century in
our country, in Burns, Scott, Coleridge, Wordsworth, Landor,
Byron, Keats, and, supreme among all, Shelley. Something
of the same transition may be noticed in the art of design :
the multifarious illustrator in the prior generation is
Stothard,—in the later, Cruikshank. At any rate, in
literature, Lamb, Hood, and then Dickens in his earliest
works, the *Sketches by Boz* and *Pickwick*, are uncommonly
characteristic and leading minds, and bent, with singular
inveteracy, upon being "funny,"—though not funny and
nothing else at all. But we should not force this considera-
tion too far : Hood is the central figure in the group and
the period, and the tendency of the time may be almost as
much due to him as he to the tendency. Mainly, we have
to fall back upon his own idiosyncrasy : he was born with
a boundlessly whimsical perception, which he trained into
an inimitable sleight-of-hand in the twisting of notions and
of words ; circumstances favoured his writing for fugitive
publications and skimming readers, rather than under
conditions of greater permanency ; and the result is as we
find it in his works. His son expresses the opinion that
part of Hood's success in comic writing arose from his
early reading of *Humphrey Clinker*, *Tristram Shandy*,
Tom Jones, and other works of that period, and imbuing
himself with their style : a remark, however, which applies
to his prose rather than his poetical works. Certain it is
that the appetite for all kinds of fun, verbal and other, was
a part of Hood's nature. We see it in the practical jokes
he was continually playing on his good-humoured wife—

such as altering into grotesque absurdity many of the words
contained in her letters to friends : we see it—the mere
animal love of jocularity, as it might be termed—in such a
small point as his frequently addressing his friend Philip
de Franck, in letters, by the words " Tim says he," instead
of any human appellative.* Hood reminds us very much
of one of Shakspeare's Fools (to use the word in no invidious
sense) transported into the nineteenth century,—the Fool in
King Lear, or Touchstone. For the occasional sallies of
coarseness or ribaldry, the spirit of the time has substituted
a *bourgeois* good-humour which respects the family circle,
and haunts the kitchen stairs ; for the biting jeer, intended
to make some victim uncomfortable, it gives the sarcastic
or sprightly banter, not unconscious of an effort at moral
amelioration ; for the sententious sagacity, and humorous
enjoyment of the nature of man, it gives bright thoughts
and a humanitarian sympathy. But, on the whole, the
intellectual personality is nearly the same : seeking by

---

* This " Tim says he " is a perfect *gag* in many of Hood's letters. It is
curious to learn what was the kind of joke which could assume so powerful an
ascendant over the mind and associations of this great humourist. Here it is,
as given in the Hood *Memorials* from *Sir Jonah Barrington's Memoirs* :—

    " ' Tim,' says he.—
    ' Sir,' says he.—
    ' Fetch me my hat,' says he ;
    ' That I may go,' says he,
    ' To Timahoe,' says he,
    ' And go the fair,' says he,
    ' And see all that's there,' says he.—
    ' First pay what you owe,' says he ;
    ' And then you may go,' says he,
    ' To Timahoe,' says he,
    ' And go to the fair,' says he,
    ' And see all that's there,' says he.—
    ' Now by this and by that,' says he,
    ' Tim, hang up my hat,' says he."

natural affinity, and enjoying to the uttermost, whatever tends to lightness of heart and to ridicule—thus dwelling indeed in the region of the common-place and the gross, but constantly informing it with some suggestion of poetry, some wise side-meaning, or some form of sweetness and grace. These observations relate of course to Hood's humorous poems : into his grave and pathetic poems he can import qualities still loftier than these—though even here it is not often that he utterly forswears quaintness and oddity. The risible, the fantastic, was his beacon-light ; sometimes as delicate as a dell of glow-worms ; sometimes as uproarious as a bonfire ; sometimes, it must be said (for he had to be perpetually writing, whether the inspiration came or not, or his inspiration was too liable to come from the very platitudes and pettinesses of everyday life), not much more brilliant than a rushlight, and hardly more aromatic than the snuff of a tallow candle.

We must now glance again at Hood's domestic affairs. His first child had no mundane existence worth calling such ; but has nevertheless lived longer than most human beings in the lines which Lamb wrote for the occasion, *On an Infant dying as soon as born.* A daughter followed, and in 1830 was born his son, the Thomas Hood of the present day whose writings are more distinguishable from those of his father upon perusal of the contents of a volume than upon inspection of its title page. The family was then living at Winchmore Hill ; thence they removed, about 1832, to the Lake House, Wanstead, a highly picturesque dwelling, but scanty in domestic comforts. The first of the *Comic Annual* series was brought out at Christmas 1830. In the following couple of years, Hood did some theatrical work ; writing the libretto for an English opera which (it is

believed) was performed at the Surrey Theatre. Its name
is now unknown, but it had a good run in its day : a similar
fate has befallen an entertainment which he wrote for
Mathews. He also composed a pantomime for the Adelphi ;
and, along with Reynolds, dramatised *Gil Blas.* This play
is understood to have been acted at Drury Lane. The
novel of *Tylney Hall,* and the poem of the *Epping Hunt,*
were written at Wanstead.

Born in comfortable mediocrity, and early inured to narrow fortunes, Hood had no doubt entered upon the literary
calling without expecting or caring to become rich. Hitherto, however, he seems to have prospered progressively, and
to have had no reason to regret, even in a worldly sense,
his choice of a profession. But towards the end of 1834
a disaster overtook him ; and thenceforward, to the end of
his days, he had nothing but tedious struggling and uphill
work. To a man of his buoyant temperament, and happy
in his home, this might have been of no extreme conse-
quence, if only sound health had blessed him : unfortunately,
the very reverse was the case. Sickly hitherto, he was soon
to become miserably and hopelessly diseased : he worked
on through everything bravely and uncomplainingly, but no
doubt with keen throbs of discomfort, and not without
detriment at times to the quality of his writings. The disaster adverted to was the failure of a firm with which
Hood was connected, entailing severe loss upon him. With
his accustomed probity, he refused to avail himself of any
legal immunities, and resolved to meet his engagements in
full eventually ; but it became requisite that he should withdraw from England. He proposed to settle down in some
one of the towns on the Rhine, and circumstances fixed his
choice on Coblentz. A great storm which overtook him

during the passage to Rotterdam told damagingly on his
already feeble health. Coblentz, which he reached in
March 1835, pleased him at first; though it was not long
before he found himself a good deal of an Englishman, and
his surroundings vexatiously German. After a while he
came to consider a German Jew and a Jew German nearly
convertible terms; and indulged at times in considerable
acrimony of comment, such as a reader of cosmopolitan
temper is not inclined to approve. He had, however, at
least one very agreeable acquaintance at Coblentz—Lieutenant Philip de Franck, an officer in the Prussian service,
of partly English parentage : the good-fellowship which he
kept up with this amiable gentleman, both in personal in-
tercourse and by letter, was (as we have seen) even boyishly
vivacious and exuberant. In the first instance Hood lived
at No. 372 Castor Hof, where his family joined him in the
spring of 1835 : about a year later, they removed to No.
752 Alten Graben. Spasms in the chest now began to be a
trying and alarming symptom of his ill health, which,
towards the end of 1836, took a turn for the worse; he
never afterwards rallied very effectually, though the fluctua-
tions were numerous—(in November 1838, for instance, he
fancied that a radical improvement had suddenly taken
place)—and at times the danger was imminent. The un-
favourable change in question was nearly simultaneous with
a visit which he made to Berlin, accompanying Lieutenant
de Franck and his regiment, on their transfer to Bromberg :
the rate of travelling was from fifteen to twenty English
miles per diem, for three days consecutively, and then one
day of rest. Hood liked the simple unextortionate Saxon
folk whom he encountered on the route, and contrasted
them with the Coblentzers, much to the disadvantage of the

latter. By the beginning of December he was back in his
Rhineland home ; but finally quitted it towards May 1837.
Several attacks of blood-spitting occurred in the interval ;
and at one time Hood proposed for himself the deadly-
lively epitaph, "Here lies one who spat more blood and
made more puns than any other man." About this time he
was engaged in writing *Up the Rhine;* performing, as was
his wont, the greater part of the work during the night-
hours.

The sojourn at Coblentz was succeeded by a sojourn at
Ostend ; in which city—besides the sea, which Hood always supremely delighted in—he found at first more comfort in the ordinary mode of living, including the general
readiness at speaking or understanding English. Gradually,
however, the climate, extremely damp and often cold,
proved highly unsuitable to him ; and, when he quitted
Ostend in the spring of 1840, at the close of nearly three
years' residence there, it was apparent that his stay had
already lasted too long. Within this period the publication
of *Hood's Own* had occurred, and put to a severe trial even
his unrivalled fertility in jest : one of his letters speaks
of the difficulty of being perfectly original in the jocose
vein, more especially with reference to the concurrent demands of *Hood's Own*, and of the *Comic Annual* of the
year. At the beginning of 1839, he paid a visit of about
three weeks to his often-regretted England, staying with
one of his oldest and most intimate friends, Mr. Dilke, then
editor of the *Athenæum*. Another of his best friends—one
indeed who continued to the end most unwearied and
affectionate in his professional and other attentions—Dr.
Elliot—now made a medical examination of Hood's con-

dition. He pronounced the lungs to be organically sound ;
the chief seat of disease being the liver, and the heart,
which was placed lower down than usual. At a later stage
of the disease, enlargement of the heart is mentioned, along
with hæmorrhage from the lungs consequent on that malady,
and recurring with terrible frequency : to these dropsy,
arising from extreme weakness, was eventually superadded.
Indeed, the catalogue of the illnesses of the unconquerably
hilarious Hood, and the detail of his sufferings, are painful
to read. They have at least the merit of giving a touch ot
adventitious but intimate pathos even to some of his wildest
extravagances of verbal fence,—and of enhancing our sympathy and admiration for the force and beauty of his personal character, which could produce work such as this out
of a torture of body and spirit such as that. During this
visit to London, Hood scrutinised his publishing and other
accounts, and found them sufficiently encouraging. The
first edition of *Up the Rhine*, consisting of 1500 copies, sold
off in a fortnight. Soon, however, some vexations with
publishers ensued : Hood felt it requisite to take legal pro-
ceedings, and the action lingered on throughout and beyond
the brief remainder of his life. Thus his prospects were
again blighted, and his means crippled when most they
needed to be unembarrassed.

The poet was back in England from Ostend in April
1840 ; and, under medical advice, he determined to prolong
his visit into a permanent re-settlement in his native
London. Here therefore he remained, and returned no
more to the continent. He took a house, with his family,
in Camberwell, not far from the Green ; removing afterwards to St. John's Wood, and finally to another house in

the same district, Devonshire Lodge, Finchley Road. He
wrote in the *New Monthly Magazine*, then edited by
Theodore Hook : his *Rhymes for the Times*, the celebrated
Miss Kilmansegg, and other compositions, first appeared
here. Hook dying in August 1841, Hood was invited to
succeed him as editor, and closed with the offer : this gave
him an annual salary of £300, besides the separate pay-
ments for any articles that he wrote. The *Song of the
Shirt*, which it would be futile to praise, or even to char-
acterise, came out, anonymously of course, in the Christmas
number of *Punch* for 1843 : it ran like wildfire, and rang
like a tocsin, through the land. Immediately afterwards,
in January 1844, Hood's connection with the *New Monthly*
closed, and he started a publication of his own, *Hood's
Magazine*, which was a considerable success : more than
half the first number was the actual handiwork of the
editor. Many troubles and cross purposes, however, beset
the new periodical ; difficulties with which Hood was ill
fitted, by his now rapidly and fatally worsening health, to
cope. They pestered him when he was most in need of
rest ; and he was in need of rest when most he was wanted
to control the enterprise. *The Haunted House*, and various
other excellent poems by Hood, were published in this
magazine.

His last days and final agonies were a little cheered by
the granting of a Government pension of £100, dating from
June 1844, which, with kindly but ominous foresight, was
conferred upon Mrs Hood, as likely to prove the survivor.
This was during the ministry of Sir Robert Peel, whose
courteous communications to the poet, and expressions of
direct personal interest in his writings, made the boon all

the more acceptable. Hood, indeed, had not been directly concerned in soliciting it. At a somewhat earlier date, January 1841, the Literary Society had, similarly unasked by him, voted him a sum of £50; but this he returned, although his circumstances were such as might have made it by no means unwelcome. From Christmas 1844 he was compelled to take to his bed, and was fated never to leave his room again. The ensuing spring, throughout which the poet lay seemingly almost at the last gasp day by day, was a lovely one. At times he was delirious; but mostly quite clear in mind, and full of gentleness and resignation. "Dying, dying," were his last words; and shortly before, "Lord, say 'Arise, take up thy cross, and follow me.'" On the 3d of May 1845 he lay dead.

Hood's funeral took place in Kensal Green Cemetery: it was a quiet one, but many friends attended. His faithful and loving wife would not be long divided from him. Eighteen months later she was laid beside him, dying of an illness first contracted from her constant tendance on his sick-bed. In the closing period of his life, Hood could hardly bear her being out of his sight, or even write when she was away. Some years afterwards, a public subscription was got up, and a monument erected to mark the grave of the good man and true poet who "sang the Song of the Shirt."

The face of Hood is best known by two busts and an oil portrait which have both been engraved from. It is the sort of face to which apparently a bust does more than justice, yet less than right. The features, being mostly by no means bad ones, look better, when thus reduced to the mere simple and abstract contour, than they probably showed in reality, for no one supposed Hood to be a fine-looking man ; on the other hand, the *value* of the face must have been in its shifting expression—keen, playful, or subtle—and this can be but barely suggested by the sculptor. The poet's visage was pallid, his figure slight, his voice feeble ; he always dressed in black, and is spoken of as presenting a generally clerical aspect. He was remarkably deficient in ear for music—not certainly for the true chime and varied resources of verse. His aptitude for the art of design was probably greater than might be inferred from the many comic woodcut drawings which he has left. These are irresistibly ludicrous—(who would not laugh over " The Spoiled Child "—" What next ? as the Frog said when his tail fell off"—and a host of others)—and all the more ludicrous and effective for being drawn more childishly and less artistically than was within Hood's compass. One may occasionally see some water-colour landscape-bit or the like from his hands pleasantly done ; and during his final residence in England he acted upon an idea he had long entertained, and produced some little in the way of oil-painting. He was also ingenious in any sort of light fancy-work—such, for instance, as carving the scenery for a child's theatre which formed the delight of his little son and daughter. His religious faith was, according to the writers of the *Memorials,* deep and sincere, though his opposition to sectarian narrowness and spite of all sorts was vigorous, and caused him sometimes to be regarded as anti-religious. A letter of his to a tract-giving and piously censorious lady who had troubled him (published in the same book) is absolutely fierce, and indeed hardly to be reconciled with the courtesy due to a woman, as a mere question of sex. It would be convenient, I may observe, to know more plainly what the biographers mean by such expressions as "religious faith," "Christian gentleman," and the like. They are not explained, for instance, by adding that Hood honoured the Bible too much to make it a task-book for his children. "Religious faith" covers many very serious differences of sentiment and conviction, between natural theology and historical Christianity; and, when we hear that a man possessed religious faith, one would like to learn which of the two extremes this faith was more nearly conversant with. In respect of political or social opinion, Hood appears to have been rather humane and philanthropic than democratic, or "liberal" in the distinct technical sense. His favourite theory of Government, as he said in a letter to Peel, was "an angel from heaven, and a despotism." He loved neither Whigs nor Tories, but was on the side of a national policy: war was his abhorrence, and so were the corn-laws. His private generosity, not the less true or hearty for the limits which a precarious and very moderate income necessarily imposed on it, was in accordance with the general sentiments of kindness which he was wont to express both in public and private : if he preached, he did not forget to practise.

It has been well said * that "the predominant characteristics of his genius are humorous fancies grafted upon melancholy impressions." Yet the term "grafted" seems hardly strong enough. Hood appears, by natural bent and permanent habit of mind, to have seen and sought for

* Horne's *New Spirit of the Age.*

ludicrousness under all conditions—it was the first thing that struck him as a matter of intellectual perception or choice. On the other hand, his nature being poetic, his sympathies acute, and the condition of his life morbid, he very frequently wrote in a tone of deep and indeed melancholy feeling, and was a master both of his own art and of the reader's emotion ; but, even in work of this sort, the intellectual exercitation, when it takes precedence of the general feeling, is continually fantastic, grotesque, or positively mirthful. And so again with those of his works—including rude designs along with finished or off-hand writing—which are professedly comical: the funny twist of thought is the essential thing, and the most gloomy or horrible subject-matter is often selected as the occasion for the horse-laugh. A man of such a faculty and such a habit of work could scarcely, in all instances, keep himself within the bounds of good taste—a term which people are far too ready to introduce into serious discussions, for the purpose of casting disparagement upon some work which transcends the ordinary standards of appreciation, but a term nevertheless which has its important meaning and its true place. Hood is too often like a man grinning awry, or interlarding serious and beautiful discourse with a nod, a wink, or a leer, neither requisite nor convenient as auxiliaries to his speech : and to do either of these things is to fail in perfect taste. Sometimes, not very often, we are allowed to reach the close of a poem of his without having our attention jogged and called off by a single interpolation of this kind ; and then we feel unalloyed—what we constantly feel also even under the contrary conditions—how exquisite a poetic sense and choice a cunning of hand were his. On the whole, we can pronounce him the finest English poet between the generation of Shelley and the generation of Tennyson.

W. M. ROSSETTI.

FAC SIMILE OF HOODS HANDWRITING

SONG OF THE SHIRT.

Work, work, work
speed,

That works for a daily feed —
Nor have a tear to shed,

A little weeping would ease my heart,
~~but to ease my heart with tears~~
To ~~ease my heart with~~ tears,
; only for time to think & weep —
But in spare being too
My tears must stop for every drop
Hinders needle & thread

O but
Then give the Soul sleeps
little
A leisure for love & hope
Or only time, for grief.

HOOD'S POETICAL WORKS.

THE BRIDGE OF SIGHS.

ONE more Unfortunate,
Weary of breath,
Rashly importunate,
Gone to her death!

Take her up tenderly,
Lift her with care;
Fashion'd so slenderly,
Young, and so fair!

Look at her garments
Clinging like cerements;
Whilst the wave constantly
Drips from her clothing;
Take her up instantly,
Loving, not loathing.—

Touch her not scornfully;
Think of her mournfully,
Gently and humanly;
Not of the stains of her,
All that remains of her
Now is pure womanly.

Make no deep scrutiny
Into her mutiny
Rash and undutiful ;
Past all dishonour,
Death has left on her
Only the beautiful.

Still, for all slips of hers,
One of Eve's family—
Wipe those poor lips of hers
Oozing so clammily.

Loop up her tresses
Escaped from the comb,
Her fair auburn tresses ;
Whilst wonderment guesses
Where was her home ?

Who was her father ?
Who was her mother ?
Had she a sister ?
Had she a brother ?
Or was there a dearer one
Still, and a nearer one
Yet, than all other ?

Alas ! for the rarity
Of Christian charity
Under the sun !
Oh ! it was pitiful !
Near a whole city full,
Home she had none.

Sisterly, brotherly,
Fatherly, motherly,
Feelings had changed :
Love, by harsh evidence,
Thrown from its eminence ;
Even God's providence
Seeming estranged.

Where the lamps quiver
So far in the river,
With many a light
From window and casement,
From garret to basement,
She stood, with amazement,
Houseless by night.

The bleak wind of March
Made her tremble and shiver;
But not the dark arch,
Or the black flowing river:
Mad from life's history,
Glad to death's mystery,
Swift to be hurl'd—
Any where, any where
Out of the world!

In she plunged boldly,
No matter how coldly
The rough river ran,—
Over the brink of it,
Picture it—think of it,
Dissolute Man!
Lave in it, drink of it,
Then, if you can!

Take her up tenderly,
Lift her with care ;
Fashion'd so slenderly,
Young, and so fair !

Ere her limbs frigidly
Stiffen too rigidly,
Decently,—kindly,—
Smoothe, and compose them
And her eyes, close them
Staring so blindly!

Dreadfully staring
Thro' muddy impurity,

As when with the daring
Last look of despairing
Fix'd on futurity.

Perishing gloomily,
Spurr'd by contumely,
Cold inhumanity,
Burning insanity,
Into her rest.—
Cross her hands humbly,
As if praying dumbly,
Over her breast !

Owning her weakness,
Her evil behaviour,
And leaving, with meekness,
Her sins to her Saviour !

THE PLEA OF THE MIDSUMMER FAIRIES.

'Twas in that mellow season of the year
When the hot sun singes the yellow leaves
Till they be gold,—and with a broader sphere
The Moon looks down on Ceres and her sheaves;
When more abundantly the spider weaves,
And the cold wind breathes from a chiller clime;—
That forth I fared, on one of those still eves,
Touch'd with the dewy sadness of the time,
To think how the bright months had spent their prime.

So that, wherever I address'd my way,
I seem'd to track the melancholy feet
Of him that is the Father of Decay,
And spoils at once the sour weed and the sweet;—
Wherefore regretfully I made retreat
To some unwasted regions of my brain,
Charm'd with the light of summer and the heat,
And bade that bounteous season bloom again,
And sprout fresh flowers in mine own domain.

It was a shady and sequester'd scene,
Like those famed gardens of Boccaccio,
Planted with his own laurels ever green,
And roses that for endless summer blow;
And there were fountain springs to overflow
Their marble basins,—and cool green arcades
Of tall o'erarching sycamores, to throw
Athwart the dappled path their dancing shades,—
With timid coneys cropping the green blades.

And there were crystal pools, peopled with fish,
Argent and gold; and some of Tyrian skin,
Some crimson-barr'd;—and ever at a wish
They rose obsequious till the wave grew thin
As glass upon their backs, and then dived in,
Quenching their ardent scales in watery gloom;
Whilst others with fresh hues row'd forth to win
My changeable regard,—for so we doom
Things born of thought to vanish or to bloom.

And there were many birds of many dyes,
From tree to tree still faring to and fro,
And stately peacocks with their splendid eyes,
And gorgeous pheasants with their golden glow,
Like Iris just bedabbled in her bow,
Besides some vocalists without a name,
That oft on fairy errands come and go,
With accents magical;—and all were tame,
And peckèd at my hand where'er I came.

And for my sylvan company, in lieu
Of Pampinea with her lively peers,
Sate Queen Titania with her pretty crew,
All in their liveries quaint, with elfin gears,
For she was gracious to my childish years,
And made me free of her enchanted round;
Wherefore this dreamy scene she still endears,
And plants her court upon a verdant mound,
Fenced with umbrageous woods and groves profound.

"Ah me," she cries, "was ever moonlight seen
So clear and tender for our midnight trips?
Go some one forth, and with a trump convene
My lieges all!"—Away the goblin skips
A pace or two apart, and deftly strips
The ruddy skin from a sweet rose's cheek,
Then blows the shuddering leaf between his lips,
Making it utter forth a shrill small shriek,
Like a fray'd bird in the grey owlet's beak.

And lo! upon my fix'd delighted ken
Appear'd the loyal Fays.—Some by degrees
Crept from the primrose buds that opened then,
And some from bell-shaped blossoms like the bees,
Some from the dewy meads, and rushy leas,
Flew up like chafers when the rustics pass;
Some from the rivers, others from tall trees
Dropp'd like shed blossoms, silent to the grass,
Spirits and elfins small, of every class.

Peri and Pixy, and quaint Puck the Antic,
Brought Robin Goodfellow, that merry swain,
And stealthy Mab, queen of old realms romantic,
Came too, from distance, in her tiny wain,
Fresh dripping from a cloud—some bloomy rain,
Then circling the bright Moon, had wash'd her car,
And still bedew'd it with a various stain:
Lastly came Ariel, shooting from a star,
Who bears all fairy embassies afar.

But Oberon, that night elsewhere exiled,
Was absent, whether some distemper'd spleen
Kept him and his fair mate unreconciled,
Or warfare with the Gnome (whose race had been
Sometime obnoxious), kept him from his queen,
And made her now peruse the starry skies
Prophetical, with such an absent mien;
Howbeit, the tears stole often to her eyes,
And oft the Moon was incensed with her sighs—

Which made the elves sport drearily, and soon
Their hushing dances languish'd to a stand,
Like midnight leaves, when, as the Zephyrs swoon,
All on their drooping stems they sink unfann'd,—
So into silence droop'd the fairy band,
To see their empress dear so pale and still
Crowding her softly round on either hand,
As pale as frosty snowdrops, and as chill,
To whom the sceptred dame reveals her ill.

"Alas," quoth she, "ye know our fairy lives
Are leased upon the fickle faith of men;
Not measured out against Fate's mortal knives,
Like human gossamers,—we perish when
We fade and are forgot in worldly ken—
Though poesy has thus prolong'd our date,
Thanks to the sweet Bard's auspicious pen
That rescued us so long!—howbeit of late
I feel some dark misgivings of our fate.

"And this dull day my melancholy sleep
Hath been so thronged with images of woe,
That even now I cannot choose but weep
To think this was some sad prophetic show
Of future horror to befall us so,—
Of mortal wreck and uttermost distress,—
Yea, our poor empire's fall and overthrow,—
For this was my long vision's dreadful stress,
And when I waked my trouble was not less.

"Whenever to the clouds I tried to seek,
Such leaden weight dragg'd these Icarian wings,
My faithless wand was wavering and weak,
And slimy toads had trespass'd in our rings—
The birds refused to sing for me—all things
Disown'd their old allegiance to our spells;
The rude bees prick'd me with their rebel stings;
And, when I pass'd, the valley-lily's bells
Rang out, methought, most melancholy knells.

"And ever on the faint and flagging air
A doleful spirit with a dreary note
Cried in my fearful ear, 'Prepare! prepare!'
Which soon I knew came from a raven's throat,
Perch'd on a cypress-bough not far remote,—
A cursed bird, too crafty to be shot,
That alway cometh with his soot-black coat
To make hearts dreary:—for he is a blot
Upon the book of life, as well ye wot!—

"Wherefore some while I bribed him to be mute,
With bitter acorns stuffing his foul maw,
Which barely I appeased, when some fresh bruit
Startled me all aheap!—and soon I saw
The horridest shape that ever raised my awe,—
A monstrous giant, very huge and tall,
Such as in elder times, devoid of law,
With wicked might grieved the primeval ball,
And this was sure the deadliest of them all!

"Gaunt was he as a wolf of Languedoc,
With bloody jaws, and frost upon his crown;
So from his barren poll one hoary lock
Over his wrinkled front fell far adown,
Well nigh to where his frosty brows did frown
Like jaggèd icicles at cottage eaves;
And for his coronal he wore some brown
And bristled ears gather'd from Ceres' sheaves,
Entwined with certain sere and russet leaves.

"And lo! upon a mast rear'd far aloft,
He bore a very bright and crescent blade,
The which he waved so dreadfully, and oft,
In meditative spite, that, sore dismay'd,
I crept into an acorn-cup for shade;
Meanwhile the horrid effigy went by:
I trow his look was dreadful, for it made
The trembling birds betake them to the sky,
For every leaf was lifted by his sigh.

"And ever, as he sigh'd, his foggy breath
Blurr'd out the landscape like a flight of smoke:
Thence knew I this was either dreary Death
Or Time who leads all creatures to his stroke.
Ah wretched me!"—Here, even as she spoke,
The melancholy Shape came gliding in,
And lean'd his back against an antique oak,
Folding his wings, that were so fine and thin,
They scarce were seen against the Dryad's skin.

Then what a fear seized all the little rout!
Look how a flock of panic'd sheep will stare—
And huddle close—and start and—wheel about,
Watching the roaming mongrel here and there, —
So did that sudden Apparition scare
All close aheap those small affrighted things;
Nor sought they now the safety of the air,
As if some leaden spell withheld their wings;
But who can fly that ancientest of Kings?

Whom now the Queen, with a forestalling tear
And previous sigh, beginneth to entreat,
Bidding him spare for love, her lieges dear;
"Alas!" quoth she, "is there no nodding wheat
Ripe for thy crooked weapon, and more meet,—
Or wither'd leaves to ravish from the tree,—
Or crumbling battlements for thy defeat?
Think but what vaunting monuments there be
Builded in spite and mockery of thee.

"O fret away the fabric walls of Fame,
And grind down marble Cæsars with the dust:
Make tombs inscriptionless—raze each high name,
And waste old armours of renown with rust:
Do all of this, and thy revenge is just:
Make such decays the trophies of thy prime,
And check Ambition's overweening lust,
That dares exterminating war with Time,—
But we are guiltless of that lofty crime.

"Frail feeble sprites!—the children of a dream!
Leased on the sufferance of fickle men,
Like motes dependent on the sunny beam,
Living but in the sun's indulgent ken,
And when that light withdraws, withdrawing then;—
So do we flutter in the glance of youth
And fervid fancy,—and so perish when
The eye of faith grows agèd ;—in sad truth,
Feeling thy sway, O Time! though not thy tooth !

"Where be those old divinities forlorn,
That dwelt in trees, or haunted in a stream ?
Alas ! their memories are dimm'd and torn,
Like the remainder tatters of a dream :
So will it fare with our poor thrones, I deem ;—
For us the same dark trench Oblivion delves,
That holds the wastes of every human scheme.
O spare us then,—and these our pretty elves,—
We soon, alas ! shall perish of ourselves !"

Now as she ended, with a sigh, to name
Those old Olympians, scattered by the whirl
Of Fortune's giddy wheel and brought to shame,
Methought a scornful and malignant curl
Show'd on the lips of that malicious churl,
To think what noble havocs he had made ;
So that I fear'd he all at once would hurl
The harmless fairies into endless shade,—
Howbeit he stopp'd awhile to whet his blade.

Pity it was to hear the elfins' wail
Rise up in concert from their mingled dread ;
Pity it was to see them, all so pale,
Gaze on the grass as for a dying bed ;—
But Puck was seated on a spider's thread,
That hung between two branches of a briar,
And 'gan to swing and gambol, heels o'er head,
Like any Southwark tumbler on a wire,
For him no present grief could long inspire.

Meanwhile the Queen with many piteous drops,
Falling like tiny sparks full fast and free,
Bedews a pathway from her throne;—and stops
Before the foot of her arch enemy,
And with her little arms enfolds his knee,
That shows more grisly from that fair embrace;
But she will ne'er depart.   "Alas!" quoth she,
"My painful fingers I will here enlace
Till I have gain'd your pity for our race.

"What have we ever done to earn this grudge,
And hate—(if not too humble for thy hating)?—
Look o'er our labours and our lives, and judge
If there be any ills of our creating;
For we are very kindly creatures, dating
With nature's charities still sweet and bland:—
O think this murder worthy of debating!"
Herewith she makes a signal with her hand,
To beckon some one from the Fairy band.

Anon I saw one of those elfin things,
Clad all in white like any chorister,
Come fluttering forth on his melodious wings,
That made soft music at each little stir,
But something louder than a bee's demur
Before he lights upon a bunch of broom,
And thus 'gan he with Saturn to confer,—
And oh his voice was sweet, touch'd with the gloom
Of that sad theme that argued of his doom!

Quoth he, " We make all melodies our care,
That no false discords may offend the Sun,
Music's great master—tuning everywhere
All pastoral sounds and melodies, each one
Duly to place and season, so that none
May harshly interfere.   We rouse at morn
The shrill sweet lark; and when the day is done,
Hush silent pauses for the bird forlorn,
That singeth with her breast against a thorn,

"We gather in loud choirs the twittering race,
That make a chorus with their single note ;
And tend on new-fledged birds in every place,
That duly they may get their tunes by rote ;
And oft, like echoes, answering remote,
We hide in thickets from the feather'd throng,
And strain in rivalship each throbbing throat,
Singing in shrill responses all day long,
Whilst the glad truant listens to our song.

"Wherefore, great King of Years, as thou dost love
The raining music from a morning cloud,
When vanish'd larks are carolling above,
To wake Apollo with their pipings loud ;—
If ever thou hast heard in leafy shroud
The sweet and plaintive Sappho of the dell,
Show thy sweet mercy on this little crowd,
And we will muffle up the sheepfold bell
Whene'er thou listenest to Philomel."

Then Saturn thus :—"Sweet is the merry lark,
That carols in man's ear so clear and strong ;
And youth must love to listen in the dark
That tuneful elegy of Tereus' wrong ;
But I have heard that ancient strain too long,
For sweet is sweet but when a little strange,
And I grow weary for some newer song ;
For wherefore had I wings, unless to range
Through all things mutable, from change to change ?

"But wouldst thou hear the melodies of Time,
Listen when sleep and drowsy darkness roll
Over hush'd cities, and the midnight chime
Sounds from their hundred clocks, and deep bells toll
Like a last knell over the dead world's soul,
Saying, 'Time shall be final of all things,
Whose late, last voice must elegise the whole, —
O then I clap aloft my brave broad wings,
And make the wide air tremble while it rings !"

Then next a fair Eve-Fay made meek address,
Saying, " We be the handmaids of the Spring ;
In sign whereof, May, the quaint broideress,
Hath wrought her samplers on our gauzy wing.
We tend upon buds' birth and blossoming,
And count the leafy tributes that they owe—
As, so much to the earth—so much to fling
In showers to the brook—so much to go
In whirlwinds to the clouds that made them grow.

" The pastoral Cowslips are our little pets,
And daisy stars, whose firmament is green ;
Pansies, and those veiled nuns, meek violets,
Sighing to that warm world from which they screen ;
And golden daffodils, pluck'd for May's Queen ;
And lonely harebells, quaking on the heath ;
And Hyacinth, long since a fair youth seen,
Whose tuneful voice, turn'd fragrance in his breath,
Kiss'd by sad Zephyr, guilty of his death.

" The widow'd primrose weeping to the moon
And Saffron crocus in whose chalice bright
A cool libation hoarded for the noon
Is kept—and she that purifies the light,
The virgin lily, faithful to her white,
Whereon Eve wept in Eden for her shame ;
And the most dainty rose, Aurora's spright,
Our every godchild, by whatever name—
Spare us our lives, for we did nurse the same ! "

Then that old Mower stamp'd his heel, and struck
His hurtful scythe against the harmless ground,
Saying, " Ye foolish imps, when am I stuck
With gaudy buds, or like a wooer crown'd
With flow'ry chaplets, save when they are found
Wither'd ?—Whenever have I pluck'd a rose,
Except to scatter its vain leaves around ?
For so all gloss of beauty I oppose,
And bring decay on every flow'r that blows,

"Or when am I so wroth as when I view
The wanton pride of summer;—how she decks
The birthday world with blossoms ever-new,
As if Time had not lived, and heap'd great wrecks
Of years on years?—O then I bravely vex
And catch the gay Months in their gaudy plight,
And slay them with the wreaths about their necks,
Like foolish heifers in the holy rite,
And raise great trophies to my ancient might."

Then saith another, "We are kindly things,
And like her offspring nestle with the dove,—
Witness these hearts embroider'd on our wings,
To show our constant patronage of love :—
We sit at even, in sweet bow'rs above
Lovers, and shake rich odours on the air,
To mingle with their sighs ; and still remove
The startling owl, and bid the bat forbear
Their privacy, and haunt some other where.

" And we are near the mother when she sits
Beside her infant in its wicker bed ;
And we are in the fairy scene that flits
Across its tender brain : sweet dreams we shed.
And whilst the little merry soul is fled
Away, to sport with our young elves, the while
We touch the dimpled cheek with roses red,
And tickle the soft lips until they smile,
So that their careful parents they beguile. ,

"O then, if ever thou hast breathed a vow
At Love's dear portal, or at pale moon-rise
Crush'd the dear curl on a regardful brow,
That did not frown thee from thy honey prize—
If ever thy sweet son sat on thy thighs,
And wooed thee from thy careful thoughts within
To watch the harmless beauty of his eyes,
Or glad thy fingers on his smooth soft skin,
For Love's dear sake, let us thy pity win !"

Then Saturn fiercely thus :—" What joy have I
In tender babes, that have devour'd mine own,
Whenever to the light I heard them cry,
Till foolish Rhea cheated me with stone ?
Whereon, till now, is my great hunger shown,
In monstrous dint of my enormous tooth ;
And—but the peopled world is too full grown
For hunger's edge—I would consume all youth
At one great meal, without delay or ruth !

" For I am well nigh crazed and wild to hear
How boastful fathers taunt me with their breed,
Saying, ' We shall not die nor disappear,
But, in these other selves, ourselves succeed
Ev'n as ripe flowers pass into their seed
Only to be renew'd from prime to prime,'
All of which boastings I am forced to read,
Besides a thousand challenges to Time,
Which bragging lovers have compiled in rhyme.

" Wherefore, when they are sweetly met o' nights,
There will I steal and with my hurried hand
Startle them suddenly from their delights
Before the next encounter had been plann'd,
Ravishing hours in little minutes spann'd ;
But when they say farewell, and grieve apart,
Then like a leaden statue I will stand,
Meanwhile their many tears encrust my dart,
And with a ragged edge cut heart from heart."

Then next a merry Woodsman clad in green,
Stept vanward from his mates, that idly stood
Each at his proper ease, as they had been
Nursed in the liberty of old Shérwood,
And wore the livery of Robin Hood,
Who wont in forest shades to dine and sup,—
So come this chief right frankly, and made good
His haunch against his axe, and thus spoke up,
Doffing his cap, which was an acorn's cup :—

"We be small foresters and gay, who tend
On trees, and all their furniture of green,
Training the young boughs airily to bend,
And show blue snatches of the sky between ;—
Or knit more close intricacies, to screen
Birds' crafty dwellings, as may hide them best,
But most the timid blackbird's—she that, seen,
Will bear black poisonous berries to her nest,
Lest man should cage the darlings of her breast.

"We bend each tree in proper attitude,
And founting willows train in silvery falls ;
We frame all shady roofs and arches rude,
And verdant aisles leading to Dryads' halls,
Or deep recesses where the Echo calls ;—
We shape all plumy trees against the sky,
And carve tall elms' Corinthian capitals,—
When sometimes, as our tiny hatchets ply,
Men say, the tapping woodpecker is nigh.

"Sometimes we scoup the squirrel's hollow cell,
And sometimes carve quaint letters on trees' rind,
That haply some lone musing wight may spell
Dainty Aminta,—Gentle Rosalind,—
Or chastest Laura,—sweetly call'd to mind
In sylvian solitudes, ere he lies down ;—
And sometimes we enrich grey stems with twined
And vagrant ivy,—or rich moss, whose brown
Burns into gold as the warm sun goes down.

"And, lastly, for mirth's sake and Christmas cheer,
We bear the seedling berries, for increase,
To graft the Druid oaks, from year to year,
Careful that mistletoe may never cease ;—
Wherefore, if thou dost prize the shady peace
Of sombre forests, or to see light break
Through sylvan cloisters, and in spring release
Thy spirit amongst leaves from careful ake,
Spare us our lives for the Green Dryad's sake."

Then Saturn with a frown :—" Go forth, and fell
Oak for your coffins, and thenceforth lay by
Your axes for the rust, and bid farewell
To all sweet birds, and the blue peeps of sky
Through tangled branches, for ye shall not spy
The next green generation of the tree ;
But hence with the dead leaves, whene'er they fly,—
Which in the bleak air I would rather see,
Than flights of the most tuneful birds that be.

" For I dislike all prime, and verdant pets,
Ivy except, that on the aged wall
Preys with its worm-like roots, and daily frets
The crumbled tower it seems to league withal,
King-like, worn down by its own coronal :—
Neither in forest haunts love I to won,
Before the golden plumage 'gins to fall,
And leaves the brown bleak limbs with few leaves on,
Or bare—like Nature in her skeleton.

" For then sit I amongst the crooked boughs,
Wooing dull Memory with kindred sighs ;
And there in rustling nuptials we espouse,
Smit by the sadness in each other's eyes ;—
But Hope must have green bowers and blue skies,
And must be courted with the gauds of Spring ;
Whilst Youth leans god-like on her lap, and cries,
' What shall we always do, but love and sing ?'-
And Time is reckon'd a discarded thing."

Here in my dream it made me fret to see
How Puck, the antic, all this dreary while
Had blithely jested with calamity,
With mis-timed mirth mocking the doleful style
Of his sad comrades, till it raised my bile
To see him so reflect their grief aside,
Turning their solemn looks to half a smile—
Like a straight stick shown crooked in the tide ; —
But soon a novel advocate I spied.

B

Quoth he—" We teach all natures to fulfil
Their fore-appointed crafts, and instincts meet,—
The bee's sweet alchemy,—the spider's skill,—
The pismire's care to garner up his wheat,—
And rustic masonry to swallows fleet,—
The lapwing's cunning to preserve her nest,—
But most, that lesser pelican, the sweet
And shrilly ruddock, with its bleeding breast,
Its tender pity of poor babes distrest.

" Sometimes we cast our shapes, and in sleek skins
Delve with the timid mole, that aptly delves
From our example ; so the spider spins,
And eke the silk-worm, pattern'd by ourselves:
Sometimes we travail on the summer shelves
Of early bees, and busy toils commence,
Watch'd of wise men, that know not we are elves,
But gaze and marvel at our stretch of sense,
And praise our human-like intelligence.

" Wherefore, by thy delight in that old tale,
And plaintive dirges the late robins sing,
What time the leaves are scattered by the gale,
Mindful of that old forest burying ;—
As thou dost love to watch each tiny thing.
For whom our craft most curiously contrives,
If thou hast caught a bee upon the wing,
To take his honey-bag,—spare us our lives,
And we will pay the ransom in full hives."

" Now by my glass," quoth Time, " ye do offend
In teaching the brown bees that careful lore,
And frugal ants, whose millions would have end,
But they lay up for need a timely store,
And travail with the seasons evermore ;
Whereas Great Mammoth long hath pass'd away,
And none but I can tell what hide he wore ;
Whilst purblind men, the creatures of a day,
In riddling wonder his great bones survey."

Then came an elf, right beauteous to behold,
Whose coat was like a brooklet that the sun
Hath all embroider'd with its crooked gold,
It was so quaintly wrought and overrun
With spangled traceries,—most meet for one
That was a warden of the pearly streams ;—
And as he stept out of the shadows dun,
His jewels sparkled in the pale moon's gleams.
And shot into the air their pointed beams.

Quoth he, —"We bear the gold and silver keys
Of bubbling springs and fountains, that below
Course thro' the veiny earth,—which when they freeze
Into hard crysolites, we bid to flow,
Creeping like subtle snakes, when, as they go,
We guide their windings to melodious falls,
At whose soft murmurings, so sweet and low,
Poets have tuned their smoothest madrigals,
To sing to ladies in their banquet-halls.

"And when the hot sun with his steadfast heat
Parches the river god,—whose dusty urn
Drips miserably, till soon his crystal feet
Against his pebbly floor wax faint and burn,
And languished fish, unpoised, grow sick and yearn,—
Then scoop we hollows in some sandy nook,
And little channels dig, wherein we turn
The thread-worn rivulet, that all forsook
The Naiad-lily, pining for her brook.

"Wherefore, by thy delight in cool green meads,
With living sapphires daintily inlaid,—
In all soft songs of waters and their reeds, —
And all reflections in a streamlet made,
Haply of thy own love, that, disarray'd,
Kills the fair lily with a livelier white, —
By silver trouts upspringing from green shade,
And winking stars reduplicate at night,
Spare us, poor ministers to such delight."

Howbeit his pleading and his gentle looks
Moved not the spiteful Shade :—Quoth he, "Your taste
Shoots wide of mine, for I despise the brooks
And slavish rivulets that run to waste
In noontide sweats, or, like poor vassals, haste
To swell the vast dominion of the sea,
In whose great presence I am held disgraced,
And neighbour'd with a king that rivals me
In ancient might and hoary majesty.

"Whereas I ruled in Chaos, and still keep
The awful secrets of that ancient dearth,
Before the briny fountains of the deep
Brimm'd up the hollow cavities of earth :—
I saw each trickling Sea-God at his birth,
Each pearly Naiad with her oozy locks,
And infant Titans of enormous girth,
Whose huge young feet yet stumbled on the rocks.
Stunning the early world with frequent shocks.

"Where now is Titan, with his cumbrous brood,
That scared the world?—By this sharp scythe they fell
And half the sky was curdled with their blood :
So have all primal giants sigh'd farewell.
No wardens now by sedgy fountains dwell,
Nor pearly Naiads.   All their days are done
That strove with Time, untimely, to excel ;
Wherefore I razed their progenies, and none
But my great shadow intercepts the sun !"

Then said the timid Fay—"Oh, mighty Time!
Well hast thou wrought the cruel Titans' fall,
For they were stain'd with many a bloody crime :
Great giants work great wrongs,—but we are small,
For love goes lowly ;—but Oppression's tall,
And with surpassing strides goes foremost still
Where love indeed can hardly reach at all ;
Like a poor dwarf o'erburthen'd with good will,
That labours to efface the tracks of ill.—

" Man even strives with Man, but we eschew
The guilty feud, and all fierce strifes abhor ;
Nay, we are gentle as the sweet heaven's dew
Beside the red and horrid drops of war,
Weeping the cruel hates men battle for,
Which worldly bosoms nourish in our spite :
For in the gentle breast we ne'er withdraw,
But only when all love hath taken flight,
And youth's warm gracious heart is harden'd quite.

" So are our gentle natures intertwined
With sweet humanities, and closely knit
In kindly sympathy with human kind.
Witness how we befriend, with elfin wit,
All hopeless maids and lovers,—nor omit
Magical succours unto hearts forlorn :—
We charm man's life, and do not perish it ;—
So judge us by the helps we showed this morn,
To one who held his wretched days in scorn.

" 'Twas nigh sweet Amwell ;—for the Queen had task'd
Our skill to-day amidst the silver Lea,
Whereon the noontide sun had not yet bask'd ;
Wherefore some patient man we thought to see,
Planted in moss-grown rushes to the knee,
Beside the cloudy margin cold and dim ;—
Howbeit no patient fisherman was he
That cast his sudden shadow from the brim,
Making us leave our toils to gaze on him.

" His face was ashy pale, and leaden care
Had sunk the levell'd arches of his brow,
Once bridges, for his joyous thoughts to fare
Over those melancholy springs and slow,
That from his piteous eyes began to flow,
And fell anon into the chilly stream ;
Which, as his mimick'd image showed below,
Wrinkled his face with many a needless seam,
Making grief sadder in its own esteem.

"And lo! upon the air we saw him stretch
His passionate arms! and, in a wayward strain,
He 'gan to elegise that fellow wretch
That with mute gestures answer'd him again,
Saying, 'Poor slave, how long wilt thou remain
Life's sad weak captive in a prison strong,
Hoping with tears to rust away thy chain,
In bitter servitude to worldly wrong?—
Thou wear'st that mortal livery too long!'

"This, with more spleenful speeches and some tears,
When he had spent upon the imaged wave,
Speedily I convened my elfin peers
Under the lily-cups, that we might save
This woeful mortal from a wilful grave
By shrewd diversions of his mind's regret,
Seeing he was mere melancholy's slave,
That sank wherever a dark cloud he met,
And straight was tangled in her secret net.

"Therefore, as still he watch'd the waters flow,
Daintily we transform'd, and with bright fins
Came glancing through the gloom; some from below
Rose like dim fancies when a dream begins,
Snatching the light upon their purple skins;
Then under the broad leaves made slow retire:
One like a golden galley bravely wins
Its radiant course,—another glows like fire.—
Making that wayward man our pranks admire.

"And so he banish'd thought, and quite forgot
All contemplation of that wretched face:
And so we wiled him from that lonely spot
Along the river's brink; till, by heaven's grace,
He met a gentle haunter of the place,
Full of sweet wisdom gather'd from the brooks,
Who there discuss'd his melancholy case
With wholesome texts learn'd from kind nature's books,
Meanwhile he newly trimm'd his lines and hooks."

Herewith the Fairy ceased.   Quoth Ariel now—
" Let me remember how I saved a man,
Whose fatal noose was fastened on a bough,
Intended to abridge his sad life's span ;
For haply I was by when he began
His stern soliloquy in life's dispraise,
And overheard his melancholy plan,
How he had made a vow to end his days,
And therefore follow'd him in all his ways,

" Through brake and tangled copse, for much he loathed
All populous haunts, and roam'd in forest rude,
To hide himself from man.   But I had clothed
My delicate limbs with plumes, and still pursued,
Where only foxes and wild cats intrude,
Till we were come beside an ancient tree
Late blasted by a storm.   Here he renew'd
His loud complaints,—choosing that spot to be
The scene of his last horrid tragedy.

" It was a wild and melancholy glen,
Made gloomy by tall firs and cypress dark,
Whose roots, like any bones of buried men,
Push'd through the rotten sod for fear's remark ;
A hundred horrid stems, jagged and stark,
Wrestled with crooked arms in hideous fray,
Besides sleek ashes with their dappled bark,
Like crafty serpents climbing for a prey,
With many blasted oaks moss-grown and grey.

" But here upon his final desperate clause
Suddenly I pronounced so sweet a strain,
Like a pang'd nightingale, it made him pause,
Till half the frenzy of his grief was slain,
The sad remainder oozing from his brain
In timely ecstasies of healing tears,
Which through his ardent eyes began to drain :—
Meanwhile the deadly Fates unclosed their shears :—
So pity me and all my fated peers ! "

Thus Ariel ended, and was some time hush'd :
When with the hoary shape a fresh tongue pleads,
And red as rose the gentle Fairy blush'd
To read the records of her own good deeds :—
"It chanced," quoth she, " in seeking through the meads
For honied cowslips, sweetest in the morn,
Whilst yet the buds were hung with dewy beads,
And Echo answer'd to the huntsman's horn,
We found a babe left in the swarths forlorn.

"A little, sorrowful, deserted thing,
Begot of love, and yet no love begetting ;
Guiltless of shame, and yet for shame to wring ;
And too soon banish'd from a mother's petting,
To churlish nurture and the wide world's fretting,
For alien pity and unnatural care ;—
Alas ! to see how the cold dew kept wetting
His childish coats, and dabbled all his hair,
Like gossamers across his forehead fair.

"His pretty pouting mouth, witless of speech,
Lay half-way open like a rose-lipp'd shell ;
And his young cheek was softer than a peach,
Whereon his tears, for roundness, could not dwell,
But quickly roll'd themselves to pearls, and fell,
Some on the grass, and some against his hand,
Or haply wander'd to the dimpled well,
Which love beside his mouth had sweetly plann'd,
Yet not for tears, but mirth and smilings bland.

"Pity it was to see those frequent tears
Falling regardless from his friendless eyes ;
There was such beauty in those twin blue spheres,
As any mother's heart might leap to prize ;
Blue were they, like the zenith of the skies
Soften'd betwixt two clouds, both clear and mild ;—
Just touch'd with thought, and yet not over wise,
They show'd the gentle spirit of a child,
Not yet by care or any craft defiled.

" Pity it was to see the ardent sun
Scorching his helpless limbs —it shone so warm ;
For kindly shade or shelter he had none,
Nor mother's gentle breast, come fair or storm.
Meanwhile I bade my pitying mates transform
Like grasshoppers, and then, with shrilly cries,
All round the infant noisily we swarm,
Haply some passing rustic to advise—
Whilst providential Heaven our care espies.

" And sends full soon a tender-hearted hind,
Who, wond'ring at our loud unusual note,
Strays curiously aside, and so doth find
The orphan child laid in the grass remote,
And laps the foundling in his russet coat,
Who thence was nurtured in his kindly cot :-
But how he prosper'd let proud London quote,
How wise, how rich, and how renown'd he got,
And chief of all her citizens, I wot.

" Witness his goodly vessels on the Thames,
Whose holds were fraught with costly merchandise.—
Jewels from Ind, and pearls from courtly dames,
And gorgeous silks that Samarcand supplies :
Witness that Royal Bourse he bade arise,
The mart of merchants from the East and West ;
Whose slender summit, pointing to the skies,
Still bears, in token of his grateful breast,
The tender grasshopper, his chosen crest—

" The tender grasshopper, his chosen crest,
That all the summer, with a tuneful wing,
Makes merry chirpings in its grassy nest,
Inspirited with dew to leap and sing :—
So let us also live, eternal King !
Partakers of the green and pleasant earth :—
Pity it is to slay the meanest thing,
That, like a mote, shines in the smile of mirth :
Enough there is of joy's decrease and dearth.

"Enough of pleasure, and delight, and beauty,
Perish'd and gone, and hasting to decay;—
Enough to sadden even thee, whose duty
Or spite it is to havoc and to slay:
Too many a lovely race razed quite away,
Hath left large gaps in life and human loving:—
Here then begin thy cruel war to stay,
And spare fresh sighs, and tears, and groans, reproving,
Thy desolating hand for our removing."

Now here I heard a shrill and sudden cry,
And, looking up, I saw the antic Puck
Grappling with Time, who clutch'd him like a fly,
Victim of his own sport,—the jester's luck!
He, whilst his fellows grieved, poor wight, had stuck
His freakish gauds upon the Ancient's brow,
And now his ear, and now his beard, would pluck;
Whereas the angry churl had snatch'd him now,
Crying "Thou impish mischief, who art thou?"

"Alas!" quoth Puck, "a little random elf,
Born in the sport of nature, like a weed,
For simple sweet enjoyment of myself,
But for no other purpose, worth, or need;
And yet withal of a most happy breed;
And there is Robin Goodfellow besides,
My partner dear in many a prankish deed
To make dame Laughter hold her jolly sides,
Like merry mummers twain on holy tides.

"'Tis we that bob the angler's idle cork,
Till e'en the patient man breathes half a curse;
We steal the morsel from the gossip's fork,
And curdling looks with secret straws disperse,
Or stop the sneezing chanter at mid verse:
And when an infant's beauty prospers ill,
We change, some mothers say, the child at nurse:
But any graver purpose to fulfil,
We have not wit enough and scarce the will.

"We never let the canker melancholy
To gather on our faces like a rust,
But gloss our features with some change of folly,
Taking life's fabled miseries on trust,
But only sorrowing when sorrow must :
We ruminate no sage's solemn cud,
But own ourselves a pinch of lively dust
To frisk upon a wind,—whereas the flood
Of tears would turn us into heavy mud.

"Beshrew those sad interpreters of nature,
Who gloze her lively universal law,
As if she had not form'd our cheerful feature
To be so tickled with the slightest straw !
So let them vex their mumping mouths, and draw
The corners downward, like a wat'ry moon,
And deal in gusty sighs and rainy flaw—
We will not woo foul weather all too soon,
Or nurse November on the lap of June.

"For ours are winging sprites, like any bird,
That shun all stagnant settlements of grief ;
And even in our rest our hearts are stirr'd,
Like insects settled on a dancing leaf :—
This is our small philosophy in brief,
Which thus to teach hath set me all agape :
But dost thou relish it ? O hoary chief !
Unclasp thy crooked fingers from my nape,
And I will show thee many a pleasant scrape."

Then Saturn thus :—shaking his crooked blade
O'erhead, which made aloft a lightning flash
In all the fairies' eyes, dismally fray'd !
His ensuing voice came like the thunder crash—
Meanwhile the bolt shatters some pine or ash—
"Thou feeble, wanton, foolish, fickle thing !
Whom nought can frighten, sadden, or abash,—
To hope my solemn countenance to wring
To idiot smiles !—but I will prune thy wing !

"Lo! this most awful handle of my scythe
Stood once a May-pole, with a flowery crown,
Which rustics danced around, and maidens blithe,
To wanton pipings ;—but I pluck'd it down,
And robed the May-Queen in a churchyard gown,
Turning her buds to rosemary and rue ;
And all their merry minstrelsy did drown,
And laid each lusty leaper in the dew ;—
So thou shalt fare—and every jovial crew !"

Here he lets go the struggling imp, to clutch
His mortal engine with each grisly hand,
Which frights the elfin progeny so much,
They huddle in a heap, and trembling stand
All round Titania, like the queen bee's band,
With sighs and tears and very shrieks of woe ! —
Meanwhile, some moving argument I plann'd,
To make the stern Shade merciful,—when lo !
He drops his fatal scythe without a blow !

For just at need, a timely Apparition
Steps in between, to bear the awful brunt ;
Making him change his horrible position,
To marvel at this comer, brave and blunt,
That dares Time's irresistible affront,
Whose strokes have scarr'd even the gods of old : ·
Whereas this seem'd a mortal, at mere hunt
For coneys, lighted by the moonshine cold,
Or stalker of stray deer, stealthy and bold.

Who, turning to the small assembled fays,
Doffs to the lily queen his courteous cap,
And holds her beauty for a while in gaze,
With bright eyes kindling at this pleasant hap ;
And thence upon the fair moon's silver map,
As if in question of this magic chance,
Laid like a dream upon the green earth's lap ;
And then upon old Saturn turns askance,
Exclaiming, with a glad and kindly glance : ·

"Oh, these be Fancy's revellers by night!
Stealthy companions of the downy moth
Diana's motes, that flit in her pale light.
Shunners of sunbeams in diurnal sloth ;
These be the feasters on night's silver cloth ;—
The gnat with shrilly trump is their convener,
Forth from their flowery chambers, nothing loth,
With lulling tunes to charm the air screner,
Or dance upon the grass to make it greener.

"These be the pretty genii of the flow'rs,
Daintily fed with honey and pure dew—
Midsummer's phantoms in her dreaming hours,
King Oberon, and all his merry crew,
The darling puppets of Romance's view ;
Fairies, and sprites, and goblin elves we call them,
Famous for patronage of lovers true ;—
No harm they act, neither shall harm befall them,
So do not thus with crabbed frowns appal them."

O what a cry was Saturn's then !—it made
The fairies quake. "What care I for their pranks,
However they may lovers choose to aid,
Or dance their roundelays on flow'ry banks ?—
Long must they dance before they earn my thanks, —
So step aside, to some far safer spot,
Whilst with my hungry scythe I mow their ranks,
And leave them in the sun, like weeds, to rot,
And with the next day's sun to be forgot."

Anon, he raised afresh his weapon keen ;
But still the gracious Shade disarm'd his aim,
Stepping with brave alacrity between,
And made his sere arm powerless and tame.
His be perpetual glory for the shame
Of hoary Saturn in that grand defeat !—
But I must tell how here Titania came
With all her kneeling lieges, to entreat
His kindly succour, in sad tones, but sweet

Saying, "Thou seest a wretched queen before thee,
The fading power of a failing land,
Who for a kingdom kneeleth to implore thee,
Now menaced by this tyrant's spoiling hand ;
No one but thee can hopefully withstand
That crooked blade, he longeth so to lift.
I pray thee blind him with his own vile sand,
Which only times all ruins by its drift,
Or prune his eagle wings that are so swift.

"Or take him by that sole and grizzled tuft,
That hangs upon his bald and barren crown ;
And we will sing to see him so rebuff'd,
And lend our little mights to pull him down,
And make brave sport of his malicious frown,
For all his boastful mockery o'er men.
For thou wast born I know for this renown,
By my most magical and inward ken,
That readeth ev'n at Fate's forestalling pen.

"Nay, by the golden lustre of thine eye,
And by thy brow's most fair and ample span,
Thought's glorious palace, framed for fancies high,
And by thy cheek thus passionately wan,
I know the signs of an immortal man, —
Nature's chief darling, and illustrious mate,
Destined to foil old Death's oblivious plan,
And shine untarnish'd by the fogs of Fate,
Time's famous rival till the final date !

"O shield us then from this usurping Time,
And we will visit thee in moonlight dreams :
And teach thee tunes, to wed unto thy rhyme,
And dance about thee in all midnight gleams,
Giving thee glimpses of our magic schemes,
Such as no mortal's eye hath ever seen ;
And, for thy love to us in our extremes,
Will ever keep thy chaplet fresh and green,
Such as no poet's wreath hath ever been!

"And we'll distil the aromatic dews,
To charm thy sense, when there shall be no flow'rs,
And flavour'd syrups in thy drinks infuse,
And teach the nightingale to haunt thy bow'rs,
And with our games divert thy weariest hours,
With all that elfin wits can e'er devise.
And, this churl dead, there'll be no hasting hours
To rob thee of thy joys, as now joy flies:"—
Here she was stopp'd by Saturn's furious cries.

Whom, therefore, the kind Shade rebukes anew.
Saying, "Thou haggard Sin, go forth, and scoop
Thy hollow coffin in some churchyard yew,
Or make th' autumnal flow'rs turn pale, and droop;
Or fell the bearded corn, till gleaners stoop
Under fat sheaves,—or blast the piny grove;—
But here thou shalt not harm this pretty group,
Whose lives are not so frail and feebly wove,
But leased on Nature's loveliness and love.

"'Tis these that free the small entangled fly,
Caught in the venom'd spider's crafty snare:—
These be the petty surgeons that apply
The healing balsams to the wounded hare,
Bedded in bloody fern, no creature's care! —
These be providers for the orphan brood,
Whose tender mother hath been slain in air,
Quitting with gaping bill her darling's food,
Hard by the verge of her domestic wood.

"'Tis these befriend the timid trembling stag,
When, with a bursting heart beset with fears,
He feels his saving speed begin to flag;
For then they quench the fatal taint with tears,
And prompt fresh shifts in his alarum'd ears,
So piteously they view all bloody morts;
Or if the gunner, with his arm, appears,
Like noisy pyes and jays, with harsh reports,
They warn the wild fowl of his deadly sports.

" For these are kindly ministers of nature,
To soothe all covert hurts and dumb distress;
Pretty they be, and very small of stature,—
For mercy still consorts with littleness ;—
Wherefore the sum of good is still the less,
And mischief grossest in this world of wrong ;—
So do these charitable dwarfs redress
The tenfold ravages of giants strong,
To whom great malice and great might belong.

" Likewise to them are Poets much beholden
For secret favours in the midnight glooms;
Brave Spenser quaff'd out of their goblets golden.
And saw their tables spread of prompt mushrooms,
And heard their horns of honeysuckle blooms
Sounding upon the air most soothing soft.
Like humming bees busy about the brooms,—
And glanced this fair queen's witchery full oft,
And in her magic wain soar'd far aloft.

"Nay I myself, though mortal, once was nursed
By fairy gossips, friendly at my birth,
And in my childish ear glib Mab rehearsed
Her breezy travels round our planet's girth,
Telling me wonders of the moon and earth;
My gramarye at her grave lay I conn'd,
Where Puck hath been convened to make me mirth ;
I have had from Queen Titania tokens fond,
And toy'd with Oberon's permitted wand.

" With figs and plums and Persian dates they fed me,
And delicate cates after my sunset meal,
And took me by my childish hand, and led me
By craggy rocks crested with keeps of steel,
Whose awful bases deep dark woods conceal,
Staining some dead lake with their verdant dyes:
And when the West sparkled at Phœbus' wheel,
With fairy euphrasy they purged mine eyes,
To let me see their cities in the skies.

"'Twas they first school'd my young imagination
To take its flights like any new-fledged bird,
And show'd the span of winged meditation
Stretch'd wider than things grossly seen or heard.
With sweet swift Ariel how I soar'd and stirr'd
The fragrant blooms of spiritual bow'rs!
'Twas they endear'd what I have still preferr'd,
Nature's blest attributes and balmy pow'rs
Her hills and vales and brooks, sweet birds and flow'rs!

" Wherefore with all true royalty and duty
Will I regard them in my honouring rhyme,
With love for love, and homages to beauty,
And magic thoughts gather'd in night's cool clime,
With studious verse trancing the dragon Time,
Strong as old Merlin's necromantic spells;
So these dear monarchs of the summer's prime
Shall live unstartled by his dreadful yells,
Till shrill larks warn them to their flowery cells."

Look how a poison'd man turns livid black,
Drugg'd with a cup of deadly hellebore,
That sets his horrid features all at rack,
So seem'd these words into the ear to pour
Of ghastly Saturn, answering with a roar
Of mortal pain and spite and utmost rage,
Wherewith his grisly arm he raised once more,
And bade the cluster'd sinews all engage,
As if at one fell stroke to wreck an age.

Whereas the blade flash'd on the dinted ground,
Down through his steadfast foe, yet made no scar
On that immortal Shade, or death-like wound;
But Time was long benumb'd, and stood a-jar,
And then with baffled rage took flight afar,
To weep his hurt in some Cimmerian gloom,
Or meaner fames (like mine) to mock and mar,
Or sharp his scythe for royal strokes of doom,
Whetting its age on some old Cæsar's tomb.

C

Howbeit he vanish'd in the forest shade,
Distinctly heard as if some grumbling pard,
And, like Nymph Echo, to a sound decay'd;—
Meanwhile the fays cluster'd the gracious Bard,
The darling centre of their dear regard :
Besides of sundry dances on the green,
Never was mortal man so brightly starr'd,
Or won such pretty homages, I ween.
"Nod to him, Elves !" cries the melodious queen.

"Nod to him, Elves, and flutter round about him,
And quite enclose him with your pretty crowd,
And touch him lovingly, for that, without him,
The silk-worm now had spun our dreary shroud ;—
But he hath all dispersed Death's tearful cloud,
And Time's dread effigy scared quite away :
Bow to him then, as though to me ye bow'd,
And his dear wishes prosper and obey
Wherever love and wit can find a way !

"'Noint him with fairy dew of magic savours,
Shaken from orient buds still pearly wet,
Roses and spicy pinks,—and, of all favours,
Plant in his walks the purple violet,
And meadow-sweet under the edges set,
To mingle breaths with dainty eglantine
And honeysuckles sweet,—nor yet forget
Some pastoral flowery chaplets to entwine,
To vie the thoughts about his brow benign !

"Let no wild things astonish him or fear him,
But tell them all how mild he is of heart,
Till e'en the timid hares go frankly near him,
And eke the dappled does, yet never start ;
Nor shall their fawns into the thickets dart,
Nor wrens forsake their nests among the leaves,
Nor speckled thrushes flutter far apart ;—
But bid the sacred swallow haunt his eaves,
To guard his roof from lightning and from thieves.

"Or when he goes the nimble squirrel's visitor,
Let the brown hermit bring his hoarded nuts,
For, tell him, this is Nature's kind Inquisitor,—
Though man keeps cautious doors that conscience shuts,
For conscious wrong all curious quest rebuts,—
Nor yet shall bees uncase their jealous stings,
However he may watch their straw-built huts;—
So let him learn the crafts of all small things,
Which he will hint most aptly when he sings."

Here she leaves off, and with a graceful hand
Waves thrice three splendid circles round his head;
Which, though deserted by the radiant wand,
Wears still the glory which her waving shed,
Such as erst crown'd the old Apostle's head,
To show the thoughts, there harbour'd, were divine,
And on immortal contemplations fed:—
Goodly it was to see that glory shine
Around a brow so lofty and benign!—

Goodly it was to see the elfin brood
Contend for kisses of his gentle hand,
That had their mortal enemy withstood,
And stay'd their lives, fast ebbing with the sand.
Long while this strife engaged the pretty band;
But now bold Chanticleer, from farm to farm,
Challenged the dawn creeping o'er eastern land,
And well the fairies knew that shrill alarm,
Which sounds the knell of every selfish charm.

And soon the rolling mist, that 'gan arise
From plashy mead and undiscover'd stream,
Earth's morning incense to the early skies,
Crept o'er the failing landscape of my dream.
Soon faded then the Phantom of my theme—
A shapeless shade, that fancy disavow'd,
And shrank to nothing in the mist extreme.
Then flew Titania,—and her little crowd,
Like flocking linnets, vanish'd in a crowd.

BIANCA'S DREAM.

A VENETIAN STORY.

BIANCA !—fair Bianca !—who could dwell
  With safety on her dark and hazel gaze,
Nor find there lurk'd in it a witching spell,
  Fatal to balmy nights and blessed days?
The peaceful breath that made the bosom swell,
  She turn'd to gas, and set it in a blaze ;
Each eye of hers had Love's Eupyrion in it,
That he could light his link at in a minute.

So that, wherever in her charms she shone,
  A thousand breasts were kindled into flame ;
Maidens who cursed her looks forgot their own,
  And beaux were turned to flambeaux where she came ;
All hearts indeed were conquer'd but her own,
  Which none could ever temper down or tame :
In short, to take our haberdasher's hints,
She might have written over it,—"From Flints."

She was, in truth, the wonder of her sex,
  At least in Venice—where with eyes of brown
Tenderly languid, ladies seldom vex
  An amorous gentle with a needless frown ;

Where gondolas convey guitars by pecks,
    And Love at casements climbeth up and down,
Whom for his tricks and custom in that kind,
Some have considered a Venetian blind.

Howbeit, this difference was quickly taught,
    Amongst more youths who had this cruel jailor,
To hapless Julio—all in vain he sought
    With each new moon his hatter and his tailor ;
In vain the richest padusoy he bought,
    And went in bran new beaver to assail her—
As if to show that Love had made him *smart*
All over—and not merely round his heart.

In vain he labour'd thro' the sylvan park
    Bianca haunted in—that where she came,
Her learned eyes in wandering might mark
    The twisted cypher of her maiden name,
Wholesomely going thro' a course of bark :
    No one was touch'd or troubled by his flame,
Except the Dryads, those old maids that grow
In trees,—like wooden dolls in embryo.

In vain complaining elegies he writ,
    And taught his tuneful instrument to grieve,
And sang in quavers how his heart was split,
    Constant beneath her lattice with each eve ;
She mock'd his wooing with her wicked wit,
    And slashed his suit so that it match'd his sleeve,
Till he grew silent at the vesper star,
And quite despairing hamstringed his guitar.

Bianca's heart was coldly frosted o'er
    With snows unmelting—an eternal sheet,
But his was red within him, like the core
    Of old Vesuvius, with perpetual heat ;
And oft he long'd internally to pour
    His flames and glowing lava at her feet,
But when his burnings he began to spout,
She stopp'd his mouth,—and put the *crater* out.

Meanwhile he wasted in the eyes of men,
  So thin, he seem'd a sort of skeleton-key
Suspended at death's door—so pale—and then
  He turn'd as nervous as an aspen tree ;
The life of man is three-score years and ten,
  But he was perishing at twenty-three,
For people truly said as grief grew stronger,
"It could not shorten his poor life—much longer."

For why, he neither slept, nor drank, nor fed,
  Nor relish'd any kind of mirth below—
Fire in his heart, and frenzy in his head,
  Love had become his universal foe,
Salt in his sugar—nightmare in his bed ;
  At last, no wonder wretched Julio,
O sorrow-ridden thing, in utter dearth
Of hope,—made up his mind to cut her girth !

For hapless lovers always died of old,
  Sooner than chew reflection's bitter cud ;
So Thisbe stuck herself, what time 'tis told,
  The tender-hearted mulberries wept blood ;
And so poor Sappho, when her boy was cold,
  Drown'd her salt tear-drops in a salter flood,
Their fame still breathing, tho' their death be past,
For those old *suitors* lived beyond their last.

So Julio went to drown,—when life was dull,
  But took his corks, and merely had a bath ;
And once, he pull'd a trigger at his skull,
  But merely broke a window in his wrath ;
And once, his hopeless being to annul,
  He tied a pack-thread to a beam of lath —
A line so ample, 'twas a query whether
Twas meant to be a halter or a tether.

Smile not in scorn, that Julio did not thrust
  His sorrows through—'tis horrible to die
And come down with our little all of dust,
  That Dun of all the duns to satisfy ;

To leave life's pleasant city as we must,
   In Death's most dreary spunging-house to lie,
Where even all our personals must go
To pay the debt of Nature that we owe!

So Julio lived :—'twas nothing but a pet
   He took at life—a momentary spite;
Besides, he hoped that Time would some day get
   The better of Love's flame, however bright;
A thing that Time has never compass'd yet,
   For Love, we know, is an immortal light;
Like that old fire, that, quite beyond a doubt,
Was always in,—for none have found it out.

Meanwhile, Bianca dream'd—'twas once when Night
   Along the darken'd plain began to creep,
Like a young Hottentot, whose eyes are bright,
   Altho' in skin as sooty as a sweep;
The flow'rs had shut their eyes—the zephyr light
   Was gone, for it had rock'd the leaves to sleep,
And all the little birds had laid their heads
Under their wings—sleeping in feather beds.

Lone in her chamber sate the dark-eyed maid,
   By easy stages jaunting through her prayers,
But list'ning side-long to a serenade,
   That robb'd the saints a little of their shares;
For Julio underneath the lattice play'd
   His Deh Vieni, and such amorous airs,
Born only underneath Italian skies,
Where every fiddle has a Bridge of Sighs.

Sweet was the tune—the words were even sweeter—
   Praising her eyes, her lips, her nose, her hair,
With all the common tropes wherewith in metre
   The hackney poets "overcharge their fair."
Her shape was like Diana's, but completer;
   Her brow with Grecian Helen's might compare:
Cupid, alas! was cruel Sagittarius,
Julio—the weeping water-man Aquarius.

Now, after listing to such laudings rare,
　　'Twas very natural indeed to go—
What if she did postpone one little pray'r—
　　To ask her mirror "if it was not so?"
'Twas a large mirror, none the worse for wear,
　　Reflecting her at once from top to toe :
And there she gazed upon that glossy track
That show'd her front face though it "gave her back."

And long her lovely eyes were held in thrall,
　　By that dear page where first the woman reads:
That Julio was no flatt'rer, none at all,
　　She told herself—and then she told her beads ;
Meanwhile, the nerves insensibly let fall
　　Two curtains fairer than the lily breeds ;
For sleep had crept and kiss'd her unawares,
Just at the half-way milestone of her pray'rs.

Then like a drooping rose so bended she,
　　Till her bow'd head upon her hand reposed ;
But still she plainly saw, or seem'd to see,
　　That fair reflection, tho' her eyes were closed,
A beauty bright as it was wont to be,
　　A portrait Fancy painted while she dozed :
'Tis very natural, some people say,
To dream of what we dwell on in the day.

Still shone her face—yet not, alas ! the same,
　　But 'gan some dreary touches to assume,
And sadder thoughts, with sadder changes came—
　　Her eyes resign'd their light, her lips their bloom,
Her teeth fell out, her tresses did the same,
　　Her cheeks were tinged with bile, her eyes with rheum :
There was a throbbing at her heart within,
For, oh ! there was a shooting in her chin.

And lo ! upon her sad desponding brow,
　　The cruel trenches of besieging age,
With seams, but most unseemly, 'gan to show
　　Her place was booking for the seventh stage ;

And where her raven tresses used to flow,
  Some locks that Time had left her in his rage,
And some mock ringlets, made her forehead shady,
A compound (like our Psalms) of *Tate* and Braidy.

Then for her shape—alas! how Saturn wrecks,
  And bends, and corkscrews all the frame about,
Doubles the hams, and crooks the straightest necks,
  Draws in the nape, and pushes forth the snout,
Makes backs and stomachs concave or convex:
  Witness those pensioners call'd In and Out,
Who all day watching first and second rater,
Quaintly unbend themselves—but grow no straighter.

So Time with fair Bianca dealt, and made
  Her shape a bow, that once was like an arrow;
His iron hand upon her spine he laid,
  And twisted all awry her "winsome marrow."
In truth it was a change!—she had obey'd
  The holy Pope before her chest grew narrow,
But spectacles and palsy seem'd to make her
Something between a Glassite and a Quaker.

Her grief and gall meanwhile were quite extreme,
  And she had ample reason for her trouble;
For what sad maiden can endure to seem
  Set in for singleness, though growing double?
The fancy madden'd her; but now the dream,
  Grown thin by getting bigger, like a bubble,
Burst,—but still left some fragments of its size,
That like the soapsuds, smarted in her eyes.

And here—just here—as she began to heed
  The real world, her clock chimed out its score;
A clock it was of the Venetian breed,
  That cried the hour from one to twenty-four;
The works moreover standing in some need
  Of workmanship, it struck some dozen more;
A warning voice that clench'd Bianca's fears,
Such strokes referring doubtless to her years.

At fifteen chimes she was but half a nun,
    By twenty she had quite renounced the veil ;
She thought of Julio just at twenty-one,
    And thirty made her very sad and pale,
To paint that ruin where her charms would run ;
    At forty all the maid began to fail,
And thought no higher, as the late dream cross'd her,
Of single blessedness, than single Gloster.

And so Bianca changed ; the next sweet even,
    With Julio in a black Venetian bark,
Row'd slow and stealthily—the hour, eleven,
    Just sounding from the tower of old St. Mark ;
She sate with eyes turn'd quietly to heav'n,
    Perchance rejoicing in the grateful dark
That veil'd her blushing cheek,—for Julio brought her,
Of course, to break the ice upon the water.

But what a puzzle is one's serious mind
    To open ;—oysters, when the ice is thick,
Are not so difficult and disinclined ;
    And Julio felt the declaration stick
About his throat in a most awful kind ;
    However, he contrived by bits to pick
His trouble forth,—much like a rotten cork
Groped from a long-neck'd bottle with a fork.

But love is still the quickest of all readers ;
    And Julio spent besides those signs profuse,
That English telegraphs and foreign pleaders,
    In help of language are so apt to use : —
Arms, shoulders, fingers, all were interceders,
    Nods, shrugs, and bends,—Bianca could not choose
But soften to his suit with more facility,
He told his story with so much agility.

"Be thou my park, and I will be thy dear,"
    (So he began at last to speak or quote ;)
"Be thou my bark, and I thy gondolier,"
    (For passion takes this figurative note ;)

"Be thou my light, and I thy chandelier ;
  Be thou my dove, and I will be thy cote ;
My lily be, and I will be thy river ;
Be thou my life—and I will be thy liver."

This, with more tender logic of the kind,
  He pour'd into her small and shell-like ear,
That timidly against his lips inclined ;
  Meanwhile her eyes glanced on the silver sphere
That even now began to steal behind
  A dewy vapour, which was lingering near,
Wherein the dull moon crept all dim and pale,
Just like a virgin putting on the veil :—

Bidding adieu to all her sparks—the stars,
  That erst had woo'd and worshipp'd in her train,
Saturn and Hesperus, and gallant Mars—
  Never to flirt with heavenly eyes again.
Meanwhile, remindful of the convent bars,
  Bianca did not watch these signs in vain,
But turn'd to Julio at the dark eclipse,
With words, like verbal kisses, on her lips.

He took the hint full speedily, and back'd
  By love, and night, and the occasion's meetness,
Bestow'd a something on her cheek that smack'd
  (Though quite in silence) of ambrosial sweetness ;
That made her think all other kisses lack'd
  Till then, but what she knew not, of completeness :
Being used but sisterly salutes to feel,
Insipid things—like sandwiches of veal.

He took her hand, and soon she felt him wring
  The pretty fingers all instead of one ;
Anon his stealthy arm began to cling
  About her waist that had been clasp'd by none :
Their dear confessions I forbear to sing,
  Since cold description would but be outrun ;
For bliss and Irish watches have the power,
In twenty minutes, to lose half an hour !

ODE TO RAE WILSON, ESQ.

A WANDERER, Wilson, from my native land,
Remote, O Rae, from godliness and thee,
Where rolls between us the eternal sea,
Besides some furlongs of a foreign sand,—
Beyond the broadest Scotch of London Wall;
Beyond the loudest Saint that has a call;
Across the wavy waste between us stretch'd,
A friendly missive warns me of a stricture,
Wherein my likeness you have darkly etch'd,
And though I have not seen the shadow sketch'd,
Thus I remark prophetic on the picture.

I guess the features:—in a line to paint
Their moral ugliness, I'm not a saint.
Not one of those self-constituted saints,
Quacks—not physicians—in the cure of souls,
Censors who sniff out mortal taints,
And call the devil over his own coals—
Those pseudo Privy Councillors of God,
Who write down judgments with a pen hard-nibb'd,
    Ushers of Beelzebub's Black Rod,
Commending sinners, not to ice thick-ribb'd,
But endless flames, to scorch them up like flax—
Yet sure of heaven themselves, as if they'd cribb'd
Th' impression of St. Peter's keys in wax!

Of such a character no single trace
Exists, I know, in my fictitious face;
There wants a certain cast about the eye;
A certain lifting of the nose's tip;
A certain curling of the nether lip,
In scorn of all that is, beneath the sky;
In brief it is an aspect deleterious,
A face decidedly not serious,
A face profane, that would not do at all
To make a face at Exeter Hall,—
That Hall where bigots rant, and cant, and pray,
And laud each other face to face,

Till ev'ry farthing-candle *ray*
Conceives itself a great gas-light of grace.

Well!—be the graceless lineaments confest!
I do enjoy this bounteous beauteous earth;
    And dote upon a jest
" Within the limits of becoming mirth ;"—
No solemn sanctimonious face I pull,
Nor think I'm pious when I'm only bilious—
Nor study in my sanctum supercilious
To frame a Sabbath Bill or forge a Bull.
I pray for grace—repent each sinful act—
Peruse, but underneath the rose, my Bible:
And love my neighbour far too well, in fact,
To call and twit him with a godly tract
That's turn'd by application to a libel.
My heart ferments not with the bigot's leaven,
All creeds I view with toleration thorough,
And have a horror of regarding heaven
    As anybody's rotten borough.

What else? no part I take in party fray,
With tropes from Billingsgate's slang-whanging tartars,
I fear no Pope—and let great Ernest play
At Fox and Goose with Fox's Martyrs!
I own I laugh at over-righteous men,
I own I shake my sides at ranters,
And treat sham-Abr'am saints with wicked banters.
I even own, that there are times—but then
It's when I've got my wine—I say d—— canters !

I've no ambition to enact the spy
On fellow souls, a Spiritual Pry—
'Tis said that people ought to guard their noses,
Who thrust them into matters none of theirs ;
And tho' no delicacy discomposes
Your Saint, yet I consider faith and pray'rs
Amongst the privatest of men's affairs.

I do not hash the Gospel in my books,
And thus upon the public mind intrude it,

As if I thought, like Otaheitan cooks,
No food was fit to eat till I had chew'd it.
On Bible stilts I don't affect to stalk ;
Nor lard with Scripture my familiar talk,—
     For man may pious texts repeat,
And yet religion have no inward seat ;
'Tis not so plain as the old Hill of Howth,
A man has got his belly full of meat
Because he talks with victuals in his mouth !

Mere verbiage,—it is not worth a carrot !
Why, Socrates—or Plato—where's the odds ?—
Once taught a jay to supplicate the Gods,
And made a Polly-theist of a Parrot !

A mere professor, spite of all his cant, is
     Not a whit better than a Mantis,—
An insect, of what clime I can't determine,
That lifts its paws most parson-like, and thence,
By simple savages—thro' sheer pretence—
Is reckon'd quite a saint amongst the vermin.

But where's the reverence, or where the *nous,*
To ride on one's religion thro' the lobby,
     Whether a stalking-horse or hobby,
To show its pious paces to "the House?"

I honestly confess that I would hinder
The Scottish member's legislative rigs,
     That spiritual Pinder,
Who looks on erring souls as straying pigs,
That must be lash'd by law, wherever found,
And driven to church, as to the parish pound.
I do confess, without reserve or wheedle,
I view that grovelling idea as one
Worthy some parish clerk's ambitious son,
A charity-boy, who longs to be a beadle.

On such a vital topic sure 'tis odd
How much a man can differ from his neighbour :

One wishes worship freely giv'n to God,
Another wants to make it statute-labour—
The broad distinction in a line to draw,
As means to lead us to the skies above,
You say—Sir Andrew and his love of law,
And I—the Saviour with his law of love.

Spontaneously to God should tend the soul,
Like the magnetic needle to the Pole ;
But what were that intrinsic virtue worth,
Suppose some fellow, with more zeal than knowledge,
    Fresh from St. Andrew's College,
Should nail the conscious needle to the north?

I do confess that I abhor and shrink
From schemes, with a religious willy-nilly,
That frown upon St. Giles's sins, but blink
The peccadilloes of all Piccadilly—
My soul revolts at such a bare hypocrisy,
And will not, dare not, fancy in accord
The Lord of Hosts with an Exclusive Lord
    Of this world's aristocracy.
It will not own a notion so unholy,
As thinking that the rich by easy trips
May go to heav'n, whereas the poor and lowly
Must work their passage as they do in ships.

One place there is—beneath the burial sod
Where all mankind are equalised by death ;
Another place there is—the Fane of God,
Where all are equal, who draw living breath;
Juggle who will *elsewhere* with his own soul,
Playing the Judas with a temporal dole—
He who can come beneath that awful cope,
In the dread presence of a Maker just,
Who metes to ev'ry pinch of human dust
One even measure of immortal hope—
He who can stand within that holy door,
With soul unbow'd by that pure spirit-level,
And frame unequal laws for rich and poor,—
Might sit for Hell and represent the Devil !

Such are the solemn sentiments, O Rae,
In your last Journey-Work, perchance you ravage,
Seeming, but in more courtly terms, to say
I'm but a heedless, creedless, godless savage ;
A very Guy, deserving fire and faggots,—
     A Scoffer, always on the grin,
And sadly given to the mortal sin
Of liking Mawworms less than merry maggots !

The humble records of my life to search,
I have not herded with mere pagan beasts ;
But sometimes I have "sat at good men's feasts,"
And I have been "where bells have knoll'd to church."
Dear bells ! how sweet the sounds of village bells
When on the undulating air they swim !
Now loud as welcomes ! faint, now, as farewells !
And trembling all about the breezy dells
As flutter'd by the wings of Cherubim.
Meanwhile the bees are chanting a low hymn ;
And lost to sight th' ecstatic lark above
Sings, like a soul beatified, of love,—
With, now and then, the coo of the wild pigeon ;—
O Pagans, Heathens, Infidels, and Doubters !
If such sweet sounds can't woo you to religion,
Will the harsh voices of church cads and touters?

A man may cry "Church ! Church !" at ev'ry word,
With no more piety than other people—
A daw's not reckon'd a religious bird
Because it keeps a-cawing from a steeple.
The Temple is a good, a holy place,
But quacking only gives it an ill savour ;
While saintly mountebanks the porch disgrace,
And bring religion's self into disfavour !

Behold yon servitor of God and Mammon,
Who, binding up his Bible with his Ledger,
     Blends Gospel texts with trading gammon,
A black-leg saint, a spiritual hedger,
Who backs his rigid Sabbath, so to speak,
Against the wicked remnant of the week,

A saving bet against his sinful bias—
"Rogue that I am," he whispers to himself,
"I lie—I cheat—do anything for pelf,
But who on earth can say I am not pious?"

In proof how over-righteousness re-acts,
Accept an anecdote well based on facts.
One Sunday morning (at the day don't fret)—
In riding with a friend to Ponder's End
Outside the stage, we happen'd to commend
A certain mansion that we saw To Let.
"Ay," cried our coachman, with our talk to grapple,
"You're right! no house along the road comes nigh it.
'Twas built by the same man as built yon chapel,
      And master wanted once to buy it,—
But t'other driv the bargain much too hard—
      He ax'd sure-*ly* a sum purdigious!
But being so particular religious,
Why, *that*, you see, put master on his guard!"

      Church is "a little heav'n below,
        I have been there and still would go,"—
Yet I am none of those who think it odd
      A man can pray unbidden from the cassock,
        And, passing by the customary hassock,
Kneel down remote upon the simple sod,
And sue *in formâ pauperis* to God.
As for the rest, intolerant to none,
Whatever shape the pious rite may bear,
Ev'n the poor Pagan's homage to the Sun
I would not harshly scorn, lest even there
I spurn'd some elements of Christian pray'r—
An aim, tho' erring, at a "world ayont"—
      Acknowledgment of good—of man's futility,
A sense of need, and weakness, and indeed
That very thing so many Christian's want—
          Humility.
Such, unto Papists, Jews, or turban'd Turks,
Such is my spirit—(I don't mean my wraith!)
Such, may it please you, is my humble faith;

I know, full well, you do not like my *works!*
I have not sought, 'tis true, the Holy Land,
As full of texts as Cuddie Headrigg's mother.
  The Bible in one hand,
And my own common-place-book in the other—
But you have been to Palestine—alas !
Some minds improve by travel, others, rather,
  Resemble copper wire, or brass,
Which gets the narrower by going farther !
Worthless are all such Pilgrimages—very !
If Palmers at the Holy Tomb contrive
The human heats and rancour to revive
That at the Sepulchre they ought to bury,
A sorry sight it is to rest the eye on,
To see a Christian creature graze at Sion,
Then homeward, of the saintly pasture full,
Rush bellowing, and breathing fire and smoke,
At crippled Papistry to butt and poke,
Exactly as a skittish Scottish bull
Hunts an old woman in a scarlet cloak !

Why leave a serious, moral, pious home,
Scotland, renown'd for sanctity of old,
Far distant Catholics to rate and scold
For—doing as the Romans do at Rome ?
With such a bristling spirit wherefore quit
The Land of Cakes for any land of wafers,
About the graceless images to flit,
And buzz and chafe importunate as chafers,
Longing to carve the carvers to Scotch collops?—
People who hold such absolute opinions
Should stay at home, in Protestant dominions,
  Not travel like male Mrs. Trollopes.

 Gifted with noble tendency to climb,
  Yet weak at the same time,
Faith is a kind of parasitic plant,
That grasps the nearest stem with tendril-rings ;
And as the climate and the soil may grant,
So is the sort of tree to which it clings.

Consider then, before, like Hurlothrumbo,
You aim your club at any creed on earth,
That, by the simple accident of birth,
You might have been High Priest to Mumbo Jumbo.
For me—thro' heathen ignorance perchance,
Not having knelt in Palestine,—I feel
None of that griffinish excess of zeal,
Some travellers would blaze with here in France.
Dolls I can see in Virgin-like array,
Nor for a scuffle with the idols hanker
Like crazy Quixote at the puppet's play,
If their "offence be rank," should mine be *rancour?*
Mild light, and by degrees, should be the plan
To cure the dark and erring mind;
But who would rush at a benighted man,
And give him two black eyes for being blind?

Suppose the tender but luxuriant hop
Around a canker'd stem should twine,
What Kentish boor would tear away the prop
So roughly as to wound, nay, kill the bine?
The images, 'tis true, are strangely dress'd,
With gauds and toys extremely out of season;
The carving nothing of the very best,
The whole repugnant to the eye of reason,
Shocking to taste, and to Fine Arts a treason—
Yet ne'er o'erlook in bigotry of sect
One truly *Catholic*, one common form,
    At which uncheck'd
  All Christian hearts may kindle or keep warm
Say, was it to my spirit's gain or loss,
One bright and balmy morning, as I went
From Liege's lovely environs to Ghent,
If hard by the wayside I found a cross,
That made me breathe a pray'r upon the spot—
While Nature of herself, as if to trace
The emblem's use, had trail'd around its base
The blue significant Forget-me-not?
Methought, the claims of Charity to urge
More forcibly, along with Faith and Hope,
The pious choice had pitch'd upon the verge

Of a delicious slope,
Giving the eye much variegated scope ;—
"Look round," it whisper'd, "on that prospect rare,
Those vales so verdant, and those hills so blue ;
Enjoy the sunny world, so fresh, and fair,
But "—(how the simple legend pierced me thro' !)
   "PRIEZ POUR LES MALHEUREUX."

With sweet kind natures, as in honey'd cells,
Religion lives, and feels herself at home ;
But only on a formal visit dwells
Where wasps instead of bees have formed the comb.
Shun pride, O Rae !—whatever sort beside
You take in lieu, shun spiritual pride !
A pride there is of rank—a pride of birth,
A pride of learning, and a pride of purse,
A London pride—in short, there be on earth
A host of prides, some better and some worse ;
But of all prides, since Lucifer's attaint,
The proudest swells a self-elected Saint.

To picture that cold pride so harsh and hard,
Fancy a peacock in a poultry yard.
Behold him in conceited circles sail,
Strutting and dancing, and now planted stiff,
In all his pomp of pageantry, as if
He felt "the eyes of Europe" on his tail !
As for the humble breed retain'd by man,
   He scorns the whole domestic clan—
   He bows, he bridles,
   He wheels, he sidles,
At last, with stately dodgings in a corner
He pens a simple russet hen, to scorn her
Full in the blaze of his resplendent fan !
   "Look here," he cries (to give him words)
   "Thou feather'd clay—thou scum of birds !"
Flirting the rustling plumage in her eyes,—
"Look here, thou vile predestined sinner,
   Doom'd to be roasted for a dinner,
Behold these lovely variegated dyes !
These are the rainbow colours of the skies

That Heav'n has shed upon me *con amore*—
A Bird of Paradise?—a pretty story!
I am that Saintly Fowl, thou paltry chick!
    Look at my crown of glory!
Thou dingy, dirty, drabbled, draggled jill!"
And off goes Partlet, wriggling from a kick,
With bleeding scalp laid open by his bill!
That little simile exactly paints
How sinners are despised by saints.
By saints!—the Hypocrites that ope heav'n's door
Obsequious to the sinful man of riches—
But put the wicked, naked, barelegg'd poor,
    In parish stocks instead of breeches.

The Saints!—the Bigots that in public spout.
Spread phosphorus of zeal on scraps of fustian,
And go like walking "Lucifers" about
    Mere living bundles of combustion.

The Saints!—the aping Fanatics that talk
All cant and rant, and rhapsodies highflown—
    That bid you baulk
    A Sunday walk,
And shun God's work as you should shun your own.

The Saints!—the Formalists, the extra pious,
Who think the mortal husk can save the soul,
By trundling with a mere mechanic bias,
To church, just like a lignum-vitæ bowl!

The Saints!—The Pharisees, whose beadle stands
    Beside a stern coercive kirk.
    A piece of human mason-work,
Calling all sermons contrabands,
In that great Temple that's not made with hands.
Thrice blessed, rather, is the man, with whom
The gracious prodigality of nature,
The balm, the bliss, the beauty, and the bloom,
The bounteous providence in ev'ry feature,
Recall the good Creator to his creature,
Making all earth a fane, all heav'n its dome!

To *his* tuned spirit the wild heather-bells
    Ring Sabbath knells;
The jubilate of the soaring lark
    Is chant of clerk;
For choir, the thrush and the gregarious linnet;
The sod's a cushion for his pious want;
And, consecrated by the heav'n within it,
    The sky-blue pool, a font.
Each cloud-capp'd mountain is a holy altar;
    An organ breathes in every grove;
    And the full heart's a Psalter,
Rich in deep hymns of gratitude and love!

Sufficiently by stern necessitarians
Poor Nature, with her face begrimed by dust,
Is stoked, coked, smoked, and almost choked; but must
Religion have its own Utilitarians,
Labell'd with evangelical phylacteries,
To make the road to heav'n a railway trust,
And churches—that's the naked fact—mere factories?

Oh! simply open wide the Temple door,
And let the solemn, swelling, organ greet,
    With *Voluntaries* meet,
The willing advent of the rich and poor!
And while to God the loud Hosannas soar,
With rich vibrations from the vocal throng—
From quiet shades that to the woods belong,
    And brooks with music of their own,
Voices may come to swell the choral song
With notes of praise they learn'd in musings lone.

How strange it is while on all vital questions,
That occupy the House and public mind,
We always meet with some humane suggestions
Of gentle measures of a healing kind,
Instead of harsh severity and vigour,
The Saint alone his preference retains
    For bills of penalties and pains,
And marks his narrow code with legal rigour!
Why shun, as worthless of affiliation,

What men of all political persuasion
Extol—and even use upon occasion—
That Christian principle, Conciliation?
But possibly the men who make such fuss
With Sunday pippins and old Trots infirm,
Attach some other meaning to the term,
As thus :

One market morning, in my usual rambles,
Passing along Whitechapel's ancient shambles,
Where meat was hung in many a joint and quarter,
I had to halt awhile, like other folks,
To let a killing butcher coax
A score of lambs and fatted sheep to slaughter.

A sturdy man he look'd to fell an ox,
Bull-fronted, ruddy, with a formal streak
Of well-greased hair down either cheek,
As if he dee-dash-dee'd some other flocks
Beside those woolly-headed stubborn blocks
That stood before him, in vexatious huddle—
Poor little lambs, with bleating wethers group'd,
While, now and then, a thirsty creature stoop'd
And meekly snuff'd, but did not taste the puddle.

Fierce bark'd the dog, and many a blow was dealt,
That loin, and chump, and scrag and saddle felt,
Yet still, that fatal step they all declined it,—
And shunn'd the tainted door as if they smelt
Onions, mint sauce, and lemon juice behind it.

At last there came a pause of brutal force,
The cur was silent, for his jaws were full
Of tangled locks of tarry wool,
The man had whoop'd and hallo'd till dead hoarse.
The time was ripe for mild expostulation,
And thus it stammer'd from a stander-by—
"Zounds!—my good fellow,—it quite makes me—why
It really—my dear fellow—do just try
Conciliation !"

Stringing his nerves like flint,
The sturdy butcher seized upon the hint,—
At least he seized upon the foremost wether,—
And hugg'd and lugg'd and tugg'd him neck and crop
Just *nolens volens* thro' the open shop—
If tails come off he didn't care a feather,—
Then walking to the door and smiling grim,
He rubb'd his forehead and his sleeve together—
    "There !—I've *con*ciliated him !"
Again—good-humouredly to end our quarrel—
    (Good humour should prevail !)—
    I'll fit you with a tale,
    Whereto is tied a moral.

Once on a time a certain English lass
Was seized with symptoms of such deep decline
Cough, hectic flushes, ev'ry evil sign,
That, as their wont is at such desperate pass,
The Doctors gave her over—to an ass.
Accordingly, the grisly Shade to bilk,
Each morn the patient quaffed a frothy bowl
    Of asinine new milk,
Robbing a shaggy suckling of a foal
Which got proportionably spare and skinny—
Meanwhile the neighbours cried "Poor Mary Ann !
She can't get over it ! she never can !"
When lo ! to prove each prophet was a ninny,
The one that died was the poor wetnurse Jenny.

    To aggravate the case,
There were but two grown donkeys in the place;
And most unluckily for Eve's sick daughter,
The other long-ear'd creature was a male,
Who never in his life had given a pail
    Of milk, or even chalk and water.
No matter: at the usual hour of eight
Down trots a donkey to the wicket-gate,
With Mister Simon Gubbins on its back,—
"Your sarvant, Miss,—a werry spring-like day,—
Bad time for hasses tho' ! good lack ! good lack !

Jenny be dead, Miss,—but I'ze brought ye Jack,
He doesn't give no milk—but he can bray."
    So runs the story,
  And, in vain self-glory,
Some Saints would sneer at Gubbins for his blindness—
But what the better are their pious saws
To ailing souls, than dry hee-haws,
    Without the milk of human kindness?

ODE TO MELANCHOLY.

Come, let us set our careful breasts,
Like Philomel, against the thorn,
To aggravate the inward grief,
That makes her accents so forlorn;
The world has many cruel points,
Whereby our bosoms have been torn,
And there are dainty themes of grief,
In sadness to outlast the morn,—
True honour's dearth, affection's death,
Neglectful pride, and cankering scorn,
With all the piteous tales that tears
Have water'd since the world was born.

The world!—it is a wilderness,
Where tears are hung on every tree;
For thus my gloomy phantasy
Makes all things weep with me!
Come let us sit and watch the sky,
And fancy clouds, where no clouds be;
Grief is enough to blot the eye,
And make heaven black with misery.

Why should birds sing such merry notes,
Unless they were more blest than we?
No sorrow ever chokes their throats,
Except sweet nightingale; for she
Was born to pain our hearts the more
With her sad melody.
Why shines the Sun, except that he

Makes gloomy nooks for Grief to hide,
And pensive shades for Melancholy,
When all the earth is bright beside?
Let clay wear smiles, and green grass wave,
Mirth shall not win us back again,
Whilst man is made of his own grave,
And fairest clouds but gilded rain!

I saw my mother in her shroud,
Her cheek was cold and very pale;
And ever since I've look'd on all
As creatures doom'd to fail!
Why do buds ope except to die?
Ay, let us watch the roses wither,
And think of our loves' cheeks;
And oh! how quickly time doth fly
To bring death's winter hither!
Minutes, hours, days, and weeks,
Months, years, and ages, shrink to nought,
An age past is but a thought!

Ay, let us think of him awhile
That, with a coffin for a boat,
Rows daily o'er the Stygian moat,
And for our table choose a tomb:
There's dark enough in any skull
To charge with black a raven plume;
And for the saddest funeral thoughts
A winding-sheet hath ample room,
Where Death, with his keen-pointed style,
Hath writ the common doom.
How wide the yew-tree spreads its gloom,
And o'er the dead lets fall its dew,
As if in tears it wept for them,
The many human families
That sleep around its stem!

How cold the dead have made these stones,
With natural drops kept ever wet!
Lo! here the best—the worst—the world
Doth now remember or forget,

Are in one common ruin hurl'd,
And love and hate are calmly met;
The loveliest eyes that ever shone,
The fairest hands, and locks of jet.
Is't not enough to vex our souls,
And fill our eyes, that we have set
Our love upon a rose's leaf,
Our hearts upon a violet?
Blue eyes, red cheeks, are frailer yet,
And sometimes at their swift decay
Beforehand we must fret.
The roses bud and bloom again;
But Love may haunt the grave of Love,
And watch the mould in vain.

O clasp me, sweet, whilst thou art mine,
And do not take my tears amiss;
For tears must flow to wash away
A thought that shows so stern as this:
Forgive, if somewhile I forget,
In woe to come, the present bliss;
As frighted Proserpine let fall
Her flowers at the sight of Dis:
Ev'n so the dark and bright will kiss—
The sunniest things throw sternest shade,
And there is ev'n a happiness
That makes the heart afraid!

Now let us with a spell invoke
The full-orb'd moon to grieve our eyes;
Not bright, not bright, but, with a cloud
Lapp'd all about her, let her rise
All pale and dim, as if from rest
The ghost of the late-buried sun
Had crept into the skies.
The Moon! she is the source of sighs,
The very face to make us sad;
If but to think in other times
The same calm quiet look she had,
As if the world held nothing base,

Of vile and mean, of fierce and bad ;
The same fair light that shone in streams,
The fairy lamp that charm'd the lad ;
For so it is, with spent delights
She taunts men's brains, and makes them mad.

All things are touch'd with Melancholy,
Born of the secret soul's mistrust,
To feel her fair ethereal wings
Weigh'd down with vile degraded dust ;
Even the bright extremes of joy
Bring on conclusions of disgust,
Like the sweet blossoms of the May,
Whose fragrance ends in must.
O give her, then, her tribute just,
Her sighs and tears, and musings holy;
There is no music in the life
That sounds with idiot laughter solely;
There's not a string attuned to mirth,
But has its chord in Melancholy.

LYCUS THE CENTAUR.[*]

FROM AN UNROLLED MANUSCRIPT OF APOLLONIUS CURIUS.

THE ARGUMENT.

Lycus, detained by Circe in her magical dominion is beloved by a Water
Nymph, who, desiring to render him immortal, has recourse to the Sorceress. Circe gives her an incantation to pronounce, which should turn
Lycus into a horse ; but the horrible effect of the charm causing her to
break off in the midst, he becomes a Centaur.

Who hath ever been lured and bound by a spell
To wander, fore-damn'd, in that circle of hell

----

[*] When this poem was republished in "The Plea of the Midsummer Fairies,"
the following dedication was added to it :—

TO J. H. REYNOLDS, ESQ.

My dear Reynolds,

    You will remember "Lycus."—It was written in the pleasant spring-
time of our friendship, and I am glad to maintain that association by connecting
your name with the poem. It will gratify me to find that you regard it with
the old partiality for the writings of each other, which prevailed with us in those
days. For my own sake, I must regret that your pen goes now into far other
records than those which used to delight me.

               Your true friend and brother,

                         T. Hood.

Where Witchery works with her will like a god,
Works more than the wonders of time at a nod, —
At a word,—at a touch,—at a flash of the eye,
But each form is a cheat, and each sound is a lie,
Things born of a wish—to endure for a thought,
Or last for long ages—to vanish to nought,
Or put on new semblance? O Jove, I had given
The throne of a kingdom to know if that heaven,
And the earth and its streams were of Circe, or whether
They kept the world's birthday and brighten'd together!
For I loved them in terror, and constantly dreaded
That the earth where I trod, and the cave where I bedded
The face I might dote on, should live out the lease
Of the charm that created, and suddenly cease:
And I gave me to slumber, as if from one dream
To another—each horrid, and drank of the stream
Like a first taste of blood, lest as water I quaff'd
Swift poison, and never should breathe from the draft,—
Such drink as her own monarch husband drain'd up
When he pledged her, and Fate closed his eyes in the cup.
And I pluck'd of the fruit with held breath, and a fear
That the branch would start back and scream out in my ear;
For once, at my suppering, I pluck'd in the dusk
An apple, juice gushing and fragrant of musk;
But by daylight my fingers were crimson'd with gore,
And the half-eaten fragment was flesh at the core;
And once—only once—for the love of its blush,
I broke a bloom bough, but there came such a gush
On my hand, that it fainted away in weak fright,
While the leaf-hidden woodpecker shriek'd at the sight
And oh! such an agony thrill'd in that note,
That my soul, startling up, beat its wings in my throat,
As it long'd to be free of a body whose hand
Was doom'd to work torments a Fury had plann'd!

There I stood without stir, yet how willing to flee,
As if rooted and horror-turn'd into a tree,—
Oh! for innocent death,—and to suddenly win it,
I drank of the stream, but no poison was in it;
I plunged in its waters, but ere I could sink,
Some invisible fate pull'd me back to the brink;

I sprang from the rock, from its pinnacle height,
But fell on the grass with a grasshopper's flight;
I ran at my fears—they were fears and no more,
For the bear would not mangle my limbs, nor the boar,
But moan'd—all their brutalised flesh could not smother
The horrible truth,—we were kin to each other!

They were mournfully gentle, and group'd for relief,
All foes in their skin, but all friends in their grief:
The leopard was there,—baby-mild in its feature;
And the tiger, black-barr'd, with the gaze of a creature
That knew gentle pity; the bristle-back'd boar,
His innocent tusks stain'd with mulberry gore;
And the laughing hyena—but laughing no more;
And the snake, not with magical orbs to devise
Strange death, but with woman's attraction of eyes;
The tall ugly ape, that still bore a dim shine
Through his hairy eclipse of a manhood divine;
And the elephant stately, with more than its reason,
How thoughtful in sadness! but this is no season
To reckon them up from the lag-bellied toad
To the mammoth, whose sobs shook his ponderous load.
There were woes of all shapes, wretched forms, when I came,
That hung down their heads with a human-like shame;
The elephant hid in the boughs, and the bear
Shed over his eyes the dark veil of his hair;
And the womanly soul turning sick with disgust,
Tried to vomit herself from her serpentine crust;
While all groan'd their groans into one at their lot,
As I brought them the image of what they were not.

Then rose a wild sound of the human voice choking
Through vile brutal organs—low tremulous croaking;
Cries swallow'd abruptly—deep animal tones
Attuned to strange passion, and full-utter'd groans;
All shuddering weaker, till hush'd in a pause
Of tongues in mute motion and wide yawning jaws;
And I guess'd that those horrors mere meant to tell o'er
The tale of their woes; but the silence told more,
That writhed on their tongues; and I knelt on the sod,
And prayed with my voice to the cloud-stirring god,

For the sad congregation of supplicants there,
That upturn'd to his heaven brute faces of prayer;
And I ceased and they utter'd a moaning so deep,
That I wept for my heart-ease,—but they could not weep,
And gazed with red eyeballs, all wistfully dry,
At the comfort of tears in a stag's human eye.
Then I motion'd them round, and, to soothe their distress,
I caress'd, and they bent them to meet my caress,
Their necks to my arm, and their heads to my palm,
And with poor grateful eyes suffer'd meekly and calm
Those tokens of kindness, withheld by hard fate
From returns that might chill the warm pity to hate;
So they passively bow'd—save the serpent, that leapt
To my breast like a sister, and pressingly crept
In embrace of my neck, and with close kisses blister'd
My lips in rash love,—then drew backward, and glister'd
Her eyes in my face, and loud hissing affright,
Dropt down, and swift started away from my sight!

This sorrow was theirs, but thrice wretched my lot,
Turn'd brute in my soul, though my body was not,
When I fled from the sorrow of womanly faces,
That shrouded their woe in the shade of lone places,
And dash'd off bright tears, till their fingers were wet,
And then wiped their lids with long tresses of jet:
But I fled—though they stretch'd out their hands, all entangled
With hair, and blood-stain'd of the breasts they had mangled,—
Though they call'd—and perchance but to ask, had I seen ·
Their loves, or to tell the vile wrongs that had been;
But I stay'd not to hear, lest the story should hold
Some hell form of words, some enchantment, once told,
Might translate me in flesh to a brute; and I dreaded
To gaze on their charms, lest my faith should be wedded
With some pity,—and love in that pity perchance—
To a thing not all lovely; for once at a glance,
Methought, where one sat, I descried a bright wonder
That flow'd like a long silver rivulet under
The long fenny grass,—with so lovely a breast,
Could it be a snake-tail made the charm of the rest?

So I roam'd in that circle of horrors, and Fear
Walk'd with me, by hills, and in valleys, and near

Cluster'd trees for their gloom—not to shelter from heat—
But lest a brute-shadow should grow at my feet;
And besides that full oft in the sunshiny place
Dark shadows would gather like clouds on its face
In the horrible likeness of demons (that none
Could see, like invisible flames in the sun);
But grew to one monster that seized on the light,
Like the dragon that strangles the moon in the night;
Fierce sphinxes, long serpents, and asps of the south;
Wild birds of huge beak, and all horrors that drouth
Engenders of slime in the land of the pest,
Vile shapes without shape, and foul bats of the West,
Bringing Night on their wings; and the bodies wherein
Great Brahma imprisons the spirits of sin,
Many-handed, that blent in one phantom of fight
Like a Titan, and threatfully warr'd with the light;
I have heard the wild shriek that gave signal to close,
When they rush'd on that shadowy Python of foes,
That met with sharp beaks and wide gaping of jaws,
With flappings of wings, and fierce grasping of claws,
And whirls of long tails;—I have seen the quick flutter
Of fragments dissever'd—and necks stretch'd to utter
Long screamings of pain,—the swift motion of blows,
And wrestling of arms—to the flight at the close,
When the dust of the earth startled upwards in rings,
And flew on the whirlwind that follow'd their wings.

Thus they fled—not forgotten—but often to grow
Like fears in my eyes, when I walk'd to and fro
In the shadows, and felt from some beings unseen
The warm touch of kisses, but clean or unclean
I knew not, nor whether the love I had won
Was of heaven or hell—till one day in the sun,
In its very noon-blaze, I could fancy a thing
Of beauty, but faint as the cloud-mirrors fling
On the gaze of the shepherd that watches the sky,
Half-seen and half-dream'd, in the soul of his eye.
And when in my musings I gazed on the stream,
In motionless trances of thought, there would seem
A face like that face, looking upward through mine;
With its eyes full of love, and the dim drownèd shine

Of limbs and fair garments, like clouds in that blue
Serene:—there I stood for long hours but to view
Those fond earnest eyes that were ever uplifted
Towards me, and wink'd as the water-weed drifted
Between; but the fish knew that presence, and plied
Their long curvy tails, and swift darted aside.

There I gazed for lost time, and forgot all the things
That once had been wonders—the fishes with wings,
And the glimmer of magnified eyes that look'd up
From the glooms of the bottom like pearls in a cup,
And the huge endless serpent of silvery gleam,
Slow winding along like a tide in the stream.
Some maid of the waters, some Naiad, methought
Held me dear in the pearl of her eye— and I brought
My wish to that fancy; and often I dash'd
My limbs in the water, and suddenly splash'd
The cool drops around me, yet clung to the brink,
Chill'd by watery fears, how that beauty might sink
With my life in her arms to her garden and bind me
With its long tangled grasses, or cruelly wind me
In some eddy to hum out my life in her ear,
Like a spider-caught bee,—and in aid of that fear
Came the tardy remembrance—Oh falsest of men!
Why was not that beauty remembered till then?
My love, my safe love, whose glad life would have run
Into mine—like a drop—that our fate might be one,
That now, even now,—may be,—clasp'd in a dream,
That form which I gave to some jilt of the stream,
And gazed with fond eyes that her tears tried to smother
On a mock of those eyes that I gave to another!

Then I rose from the stream, but the eyes of my mind,
Still full of the tempter, kept gazing behind
On her crystalline face, while I painfully leapt
To the bank, and shook off the curst waters, and wept
With my brow in the reeds; and the reeds to my ear
Bow'd, bent by no wind, and in whispers of fear,
Growing small with large secrets, foretold me of one
That loved me,—but oh to fly from her, and shun

E

Her love like a pest—though her love was as true
To mine as her stream to the heavenly blue ;
For why should I love her with love that would bring
All misfortune, like hate, on so joyous a thing?
Because of her rival,—even Her whose witch-face
I had slighted, and therefore was doom'd in that place
To roam, and had roam'd, where all horrors grew rank,
Nine days ere I wept with my brow on that bank ;
Her name be not named, but her spite would not fail
To our love like a blight ; and they told me the tale
Of Scylla,—and Picus, imprison'd to speak
His shrill-screaming woe through a woodpecker's beak.

    Then they ceased—I had heard as the voice of my star
That told me the truth of my fortunes—thus far
I had read of my sorrow, and lay in the hush
Of deep meditation,—when lo ! a light crush
Of the reeds, and I turn'd and look'd round in the night
Of new sunshine, and saw, as I sipp'd of the light
Narrow-winking, the realised nymph of the stream,
Rising up from the wave with the bend and the gleam
Of a fountain, and o'er her white arms she kept throwing
Bright torrents of hair, that went flowing and flowing
In falls to her feet, and the blue waters roll'd
Down her limbs like a garment, in many a fold,
Sun-spangled, gold-broider'd, and fled far behind,
Like an infinite train. So she came and reclined
In the reeds, and I hunger'd to see her unseal
The buds of her eyes that would ope and reveal
The blue that was in them ;—they oped and she raised
Two orbs of pure crystal, and timidly gazed
With her eyes on my eyes ; but their colour and shine
Was of that which they look'd on, and mostly of mine—
For she loved me,—except when she blush'd, and they sank,
Shame-humbled, to number the stones on the bank,
Or her play-idle fingers while lisping she told me
How she put on her veil, and in love to behold me
Would wing through the sun till she fainted away
Like a mist, and then flew to her waters and lay
In love-patience long hours, and sore dazzled her eyes
In watching for mine 'gainst the midsummer skies.

But now they were healed,—O my heart it still dances
When I think of the charm of her changeable glances,
And my image how small when it sank in the deep
Of her eyes where her soul was,—Alas! now they weep,
And none knoweth where.   In what stream do her eyes
Shed invisible tears?   Who beholds where her sighs
Flow in eddies, or sees the ascent of the leaf
She has pluck'd with her tresses?   Who listens her grief
Like a far fall of waters, or hears where her feet
Grow emphatic among the loose pebbles, and beat
Them together?   Ah! surely her flowers float adown
To the sea unaccepted, and little ones drown
For need of her mercy,—even he whose twin-brother
Will miss him for ever; and the sorrowful mother
Imploreth in vain for his body to kiss
And cling to, all dripping and cold as it is.
Because that soft pity is lost in hard pain!
We loved, how we loved!—for I thought not again
Of the woes that were whisper'd like fears in that place
If I gave me to beauty.   Her face was the face
Far away, and her eyes were the eyes that were drown'd
For my absence,—her arms were the arms that sought round
And claspt me to nought; for I gazed and became
Only true to my falsehood, and had but one name
For two loves, and call'd ever on Ægle, sweet maid
Of the sky-loving waters,—and was not afraid
Of the sight of her skin;—for it never could be,
Her beauty and love were misfortunes to me!

Thus our bliss had endured for a time-shorten'd space,
Like a day made of three, and the smile of her face
Had been with me for joy,—when she told me indeed
Her love was self-tax'd with a work that would need
Some short hours, for in truth 'twas the veriest pity
Our love should not last, and then sang me a ditty,
Of one with warm lips that should love her, and love her
When suns were burnt dim and long ages past over.
So she fled with her voice, and I patiently nested
My limbs in the reeds, in still quiet, and rested
Till my thoughts grew extinct, and I sank in a sleep
Of dreams,—but their meaning was hidden too deep

To be read what their woe was ;—but still it was woe
That was writ on all faces that swam to and fro
In that river of night ;—and the gaze of their eyes
Was sad,—and the bend of their brows,—and their cries
Were seen, but I heard not.　The warm touch of tears
Travell'd down my cold cheeks, and I shook till my fears
Awaked me, and lo! I was couch'd in a bower,
The growth of long summers rear'd up in an hour!
Then I said, in the fear of my dream, I will fly
From this magic, but could not, because that my eye
Grew love-idle among the rich blooms; and the earth
Held me down with its coolness of touch, and the mirth
Of some bird was above me,—who, even in fear,
Would startle the thrush? and methought there drew near
A form as of Ægle,—but it was not the face
Hope made, and I knew the witch-Queen of that place,
Even Circe the Cruel, that came like a Death
Which I fear'd, and yet fled not, for want of my breath.
There was thought in her face, and her eyes were not raised
From the grass at her foot, but I saw, as I gazed,
Her spite—and her countenance changed with her mind
As she plann'd how to thrall me with beauty, and bind
My soul to her charms,—and her long tresses play'd
From shade into shine and from shine into shade,
Like a day in mid-autumn,—first fair, O how fair !
With long snaky locks of the adder-black hair
That clung round her neck,—those dark locks that I prize.
For the sake of a maid that once loved me with eyes
Of that fathomless hue,—but they changed as they roll'd,
And brighten'd, and suddenly blazed into gold
That she comb'd into flames, and the locks that fell down
Turn'd dark as they fell, but I slighted their brown,
Nor loved, till I saw the light ringlets shed wild,
That innocence wears when she is but a child ;
And her eyes,—Oh I ne'er had been witch'd with their shine,
Had they been any other, my Ægle, than thine !

Then I gave me to magic, and gazed till I madden'd
In the full of their light,—but I sadden'd and sadden'd
The deeper I look'd,—till I sank on the snow
Of her bosom, a thing made of terror and woe,

And answer'd its throb with the shudder of fears,
And hid my cold eyes from her eyes with my tears,
And strain'd her white arms with the still languid weight
Of a fainting distress.   There she sat like the Fate
That is nurse unto Death, and bent over in shame
To hide me from her—the true Ægle—that came
With the words on her lips the false witch had forgiven
To make me immortal—for now I was even
At the portals of Death, who but waited the hush
Of worlds-sounds in my ear to cry welcome, and rush
With my soul to the banks of his black flowing river.
Oh, would it had flown for my body for ever,
Ere I listen'd those words, when I felt with a start,
The life-blood rush back in one throb to my heart,
And saw the pale lips where the rest of that spell
Had perish'd in horror—and heard the farewell
Of that voice that was drown'd in the dash of the stream!
How fain had I follow'd and plunged with that scream
Into death, but my being indignantly lagg'd
Through the brutalised flesh that I painfully dragg'd
Behind me :—" O Circe ! O mother of spite !
Speak the last of that curse? and imprison me quite
In the husk of a brute,—that no pity may name
The man that I was,—that no kindred may claim
The monster I am ! Let me utterly be
Brute-buried, and Nature's dishonour with me
Uninscribed !"—But she listen'd my prayer, that was praise
To her malice, with smiles, and advised me to gaze
On the river for love,—and perchance she would make
In pity a maid without eyes for my sake,
And she left me like Scorn.   Then I ask'd of the wave,
What monster I was, and it trembled and gave
The true shape of my grief, and I turn'd with my face
From all waters for ever, and fled through that place,
Till with horror more strong than all magic I pass'd
Its bounds, and the world was before me at last.

　　There I wander'd in sorrow, and shunn'd the abodes
Of men, that stood up in the likeness of Gods,
But I saw from afar the warm shine of the sun
On their cities, where man was a million, not one ;

And I saw the white smoke of their altars ascending,
That show'd where the hearts of the many were blending,
And the wind in my face brought shrill voices that came
From the trumpets that gather'd whole bands in one fame
As a chorus of man,—and they streamed from the gates
Like a dusky libation poured out to the Fates.
But at times there were gentler processions of peace
That I watch'd with my soul in my eyes till their cease,
There were women! there men! but to me a third sex
I saw them all dots—yet I loved them as specks:
And oft to assuage a sad yearning of eyes
I stole near the city, but stole covert-wise
Like a wild beast of love, and perchance to be smitten
By some hand that I rather had wept on than bitten!
Oh, I once had a haunt near a cot where a mother
Daily sat in the shade with her child, and would smother
Its eyelids in kisses, and then in its sleep
Sang dreams in its ear of its manhood, while deep
In a thicket of willows I gazed o'er the brooks
That murmur'd between us and kiss'd them with looks;
But the willows unbosom'd their secret, and never
I return'd to a spot I had startled for ever,
Though I oft long'd to know, but could ask it of none,
Was the mother still fair, and how big was her son?

For the haunters of fields they all shunn'd me by flight,
The men in their horror, the women in fright ;
None ever remain'd save a child once that sported
Among the wild bluebells, and playfully courted
The breeze ; and beside him a speckled snake lay
Tight strangled, because it had hiss'd him away
From the flower at his finger; he rose and drew near
Like a Son of Immortals, one born to no fear,
But with strength of black locks and with eyes azure bright
To grow to large manhood of merciful might.
He came, with his face of bold wonder, to feel,
The hair of my side, and to lift up my heel,
And question'd my face with wide eyes ; but when under
My lids he saw tears,—for I wept for his wonder,
He stroked me, and utter'd such kindliness then,
That the once love of women, the friendship of men

In past sorrow, no kindness e'er came like a kiss
On my heart in its desolate day such as this !
And I yearn'd at his cheeks in my love, and down bent,
And lifted him up with my arms with intent
To kiss him,—but he cruel-kindly, alas !
Held out to my lips a pluck'd handfull of grass !
Then I dropt him in horror, but felt as I fled
The stone he indignantly hurl'd at my head,
That dissever'd my ear,—but I felt not, whose fate
Was to meet more distress in his love than his hate !

    Thus I wander'd companion'd of grief and forlorn
Till I wish'd for that land where my being was born,
But what was that land with its love, where my home
Was self-shut against me for why should I come
Like an after-distress to my grey-bearded father,
With a blight to the last of his sight ?—let him rather
Lament for me dead, and shed tears in the urn
Where I was not, and still in fond memory turn
To his son even such as he left him.   Oh, how
Could I walk with the youth once my fellows, but now
Like Gods to my humbled estate ?—or how bear
The steeds once the pride of my eyes and the care
Of my hands ? Then I turn'd me self-banish'd, and came
Into Thessaly here, where I met with the same
As myself.   I have heard how they met by a stream
In games, and were suddenly changed by a scream
That made wretches of many, as she roll'd her wild eyes
Against heaven, and so vanish'd.—The gentle and wise
Lose their thoughts in deep studies, and others their ill
In the mirth of mankind where they mingle them still.*

---

* Although "Lycus" has never met with very warm admirers, owing, perhaps, to its classical origin and style (indeed, in a letter I have of his, simple
John Clare confesses he does not understand a word of it), I incline to hold
with the following opinion from a letter written to my father by Hartley Coleridge, in 1831.

"I wish you would write a little more in the style of ' Lycus the Centaur,' or
' Eugene Aram's Dream.' In whatever you attempt you excel. Then why not
exert your best and noblest talent, as well as that wit, which I would never wish
to be dormant ? I am not a graduate in the Academy of Compliment, but I
think ' Lycus' a work absolutely unique in its line, such as no man has written,
or could have written, but yourself."

THE EPPING HUNT,

"HUNT'S ROASTED ——."

"On Monday they began to hunt."—Chevy Chase.

JOHN HUGGINS was as bold a man
    As trade did ever know,
A warehouse good he had, that stood
    Hard by the church of Bow.

There people bought Dutch cheeses round
    And single Glos'ter flat ;
And English butter in a lump,
    And Irish—in a *pat.*

Six days a week beheld him stand,
    His business next his heart,
At *counter*, with his apron tied
    About his *counter-part.*

The seventh, in a Sluice-house box
    He took his pipe and pot ;
On Sundays, for *eel-piety*,
    A very noted spot.

Ah, blest if he had never gone
    Beyond its rural shed !
One Easter-tide, some evil guide
    Put Epping in his head !

Epping, for butter justly famed,
    And pork in sausage popp'd ;
Where, winter time or summer time,
    Pig's flesh is always *chopp'd.*

But famous more as annals tell,
    Because of Easter chase ;
There every year, 'twixt dog and deer,
    There is a gallant race.

With Monday's sun John Huggins rose,
    And slapped his leather thigh,
And sang the burden of the song,
    "This day a stag must die."

For all the live-long day before,
    And all the night in bed,
Like Beckford, he had nourished "Thoughts
    On Hunting" in his head.

Of horn and morn, and hark and bark,
    And echo's answering sounds,
All poets' wit hath every writ
    In *dog*-rel verse of *hounds.*

Alas ! there was no warning voice
    To whisper in his ear,
Thou art a fool in leaving *Cheap*
    To go and hunt the *dear.*

No thought he had of twisted spine,
    Or broken arms or legs ;
Not *chicken-hearted* he, although
    'Twas whispered of his *eggs!*

Ride out he would, and hunt he would,
   Nor dreamt of ending ill ;
Mayhap with Dr. *Ridout's* fee,
   And Surgeon *Hunter's* bill.

So he drew on his Sunday boots,
   Of lustre superfine ;
The liquid black they wore that day
   Was *Warren*-ted to shine.

His yellow buckskins fitted close,
   As erst upon a stag ;
Thus well equipped he gayly skipped,
   At once upon his nag.

But first to him that held the rein
   A crown he nimbly flung;
For holding of the horse !—why, no,
   For holding of his tongue.

To say the horse was Huggins' own
   Would only be a brag;
His neighbour Fig and he went halves,
   Like Centaurs, in a nag.

And he that day had got the gray,
   Unknown to brother cit ;
The horse he knew would never tell,
   Although it was a *tit.*

A well-bred horse he was, I wis,
   As he began to show,
By quickly " rearing up within
   The way he ought to go."

But Huggins, like a wary man.
   Was ne'er from saddle cast ;
Resolved, by going very slow,
   On sitting very fast.

And so he jogged to Tot'n'am Cross,
  An ancient town well known,
Where Edward wept for Eleanor
  In mortar and in stone.

A royal game of fox and goose,
  To play on such a loss ;
Wherever she set down her *orts*,
  Thereby he put a *cross.*

Now Huggins had a crony here,
  That lived beside the way ;
One that had promised sure to be
  His comrade for the day.

Whereas the man had changed his mind
  Meanwhile upon the case !
And meaning not to hunt at all,
  Had gone to Enfield Chase !

For why, his spouse had made him vow
  To let a game alone,
Where folks that ride a bit of blood,
  May break a bit of bone.

"Now, be his wife a plague for life !
  A coward sure is he !"
Then Huggins turned his horse's head,
  And crossed the bridge of Lea.

Thence slowly on through Laytonstone,
  Past many a Quaker's box—
No Friends to hunters after deer,
  Though followers of a *Fox.*

And many a score behind—before—
  The self-same rout inclined ;
And, minded all to march one way,
  Made one great march of mind.

Gentle and simple, he and she,
   And swell, and blood, and prig;
And some had carts, and some a chaise,
   According to their gig.

Some long-eared jacks, some knacker's hacks
   (However odd it sounds),
Let out that day to *hunt*, instead
   Of going to the hounds!

And some had horses of their own,
   And some were forced to job it;
And some, while they inclined to *Hunt*,
   Betook themselves to *Cob-it*.

All sorts of vehicles and vans,
   Bad, middling, and the smart;
Here rolled along the gay barouche,
   And there a dirty cart!

And lo! a cart that held a squad
   Of costermonger line;
With one poor hack, like Pegasus,
   That slaved for all the Nine!

Yet marvel not at any load
   That any horse might drag;
When all, that morn, at once were drawn
   Together by a stag.

Now when they saw John Huggins go
   At such a sober pace;
"Hallo!" cried they; "come trot away,
   You'll never see the chase!"

But John, as grave as any judge,
   Made answer quite as blunt;
"It will be time enough to trot,
   When I begin to hunt!"

And so he paced to Woodford Wells,
  Where many a horseman met,
And letting go the *reins* of course,
  Prepared for *heavy wet.*

And lo! within the crowded door,
  Stood Rounding, jovial elf;
Here shall the Muse frame no excuse,
  But frame the man himself.

A snow-white head, a merry eye,
  A cheek of jolly blush;
A claret tint laid on by health,
  With master Reynard's brush;

A hearty frame, a courteous bow,
  The prince he learned it from
His age about threescore and ten,
  And there you have Old Tom.

In merriest key I trow was he,
  So many guests to boast;
So certain congregations meet,
  And elevate the host.

"Now welcome lads," quoth he, "and prads.
  You're all in glorious luck:
Old Robin has a run to-day,
  A noted forest buck.

"Fair Mead's the place, where Bob and Tom,
  In red already ride;
'Tis but a *step*, and on a horse,
  You soon may go *a-stride.*"

So off they scampered, man and horse,
  As time and temper pressed—
But Huggins, hitching on a tree,
  Branched off from all the rest.

Howbeit he tumbled down in time
    To join with Tom and Bob,
All in Fair Mead, which held that day
    Its own fair meed of mob.

Idlers to wit—no Guardians some,
    Of Tattlers in a squeeze ;
Ramblers in heavy carts and vans,
    Spectators up in trees.

Butchers on backs of butchers' hacks,
    That *shambled* to and fro !
Bakers intent upon a buck,
    Neglectful of the *dough!*

Change Alley Bears to speculate,
    As usual for a fall ;
And green and scarlet runners, such
    As never climbed a wall !

'Twas strange to think what difference
    A single creature made ;
A single stag had caused a whole
    *Stag*nation in their trade.

Now Huggins from his saddle rose,
    And in the stirrups stood ;
And lo ! a little cart that came
    Hard by a little wood.

In shape like half a hearse—though not
    For corpses in the least ;
For this contained the *deer alive*,
    And not the *dear deceased!*

And now began a sudden stir,
    And then a sudden shout,
The prison doors were opened wide,
    And Robin bounded out !

His antlered head shone blue and red,
  Bedecked with ribbons fine ;
Like other bucks that come to 'list
  The hawbucks in the line.

One curious gaze of wild amaze,
  He turned and shortly took:
Then gently ran adown the mead,
  And bounded o'er the brook.

Now Huggins, standing far aloof,
  Had never seen the deer,
Till all at once he saw the beast
  Come charging in his rear.

Away he went, and many a score
  Of riders did the same,
On horse and ass—like High and Low
  And Jack pursuing game !

Good Lord ! to see the riders now,
  Thrown off with sudden whirl,
A score within the purling brook,
  Enjoyed their "early purl."

A score were sprawling on the grass,
  And beavers fell in showers ;
There was another *Floorer* there,
  Beside the Queen of Flowers !

Some lost their stirrups, some their whips,
  Some had no caps to show :
But few, like Charles at Charing Cross
  Rode on in *Statue* quo.

"O dear ! O dear !" now might you hear,
  " I've surely broke a bone ;"
"My head is sore"—with many more
  Such Speeches from the *Thrown.*

Howbeit their wailings never moved
   The wide Satanic clan,
Who grinned, as once the Devil grinned,
   To see the fall of Man.

And hunters good that understood.
   Their laughter knew no bounds,
To see the horses "throwing off"
   So long before the hounds.

For deer must have due course of law,
   Like men the Courts among;
Before those Barristers the dogs
   Proceed to "giving tongue."

But now Old Robin's foes were set
   That fatal taint to find,
'That always is scent after him,
   Yet always left behind.

And here observe how dog and man
   A different temper shows :
What hound resents that he is sent
   To follow his own nose?

Towler and Jowler—howlers all,
   No single tongue was mute;
The stag had led a hart, and lo!
   The whole pack followed suit.

No spur he lacked; fear stuck a knife
   And fork in either haunch;
And every dog he knew had got
   An eye-tooth to his paunch !

Away, away! he scudded like
   A ship before the gale ;
Now flew to hills we know not of,
   Now, nun-like, took the vale.

Another squadron charging now,
    Went off at furious pitch ;—
A perfect Tam O'Shanter mob,
    Without a single witch.

But who was he with flying skirts,
    A hunter did endorse,
And, like a poet, seemed to ride
    Upon a wingèd horse ?

A whipper-in? no whipper-in :
    A huntsman? no such soul :
A connoisseur, or amateur?
    Why, yes—a horse patrol.

A member of police, for whom
    The county found a nag,
And, like Actæon in the tale,
    He found himself in stag !

Away they went, then, dog and deer,
    And hunters all away ;
The maddest horses never knew
    Mad staggers such as they !

Some gave a shout, some rolled about,
    And anticked as they rode ;
And butchers whistled on their curs,
    And milkmen *Tally-ho'd!*

About two score there were, or more,
    That galloped in the race ;
The rest, alas ! lay on the grass,
    As once in Chevy Chase !

But even those that galloped on
    Were fewer every minute ;
The field kept getting more select,
    Each thicket served to thin it.

F

For some pulled up, and left the hunt,
    Some fell in miry bogs,
And vainly rose and "ran a muck,"
    To overtake the dogs.

And some, in charging hurdle stakes,
    Were left bereft of sense ;
What else could be premised of blades
    That never learned to fence ?

But Roundings, Tom and Bob, no gate,
    Nor hedge, nor ditch could stay ;
O'er all they went, and did the work
    Of leap-years in a day !

And by their side see Huggins ride,
    As fast as he could speed ;
For, like Mazeppa, he was quite
    At mercy of his steed.

No means he had, by timely check,
    The gallop to remit,
For firm and fast, between his teeth,
    The biter held the bit.

Trees raced along, all Essex fled
    Beneath him as he sate ;
He never saw a county go
    At such a county rate !

"Hold hard ! hold hard ! you'll lame the dogs !",
    Quoth Huggins, "so I do ;
I've got the saddle well in hand,
    And hold as hard as you !"

Good Lord ! to see him ride along,
    And throw his arms about,
As if with stitches in the side
    That he was drawing out !

And now he bounded up and down,
　Now like a jelly shook ;
Till bumped and galled—yet not where Gall
　For bumps did ever look !

And rowing with his legs the while,
　As tars are apt to ride ;
With every kick he gave a prick
　Deep in the horse's side !

But soon the horse was well avenged
　For cruel smart of spurs,
For, riding through a moor, he pitched
　His master in a furze !

Where, sharper set than hunger is,
　He squatted all forlorn;
And, like a bird, was singing out
　While sitting on a thorn !

Right glad was he, as well might be,
　Such cushion to resign :
" Possession is nine points," but his
　Seems more than ninety-nine.

Yet worse than all the prickly points
　That entered in his skin,
His nag was running off the while
　The thorns were running in !

Now had a Papist seen his sport,
　Thus laid upon the shelf,
Although no horse he had to cross,
　He might have crossed himself.

Yet surely still the wind is ill
　That none can say is fair;
A jolly wight there was, that rode
　Upon a sorry mare !

A sorry mare, that surely came
    Of pagan blood and bone ;
For down upon her knees she went
    To many a stock and stone !

Now seeing Huggins' nag adrift,
    This farmer, shrewd and sage,
Resolved, by changing horses here,
    To hunt another stage !

Though felony, yet who would let
    Another's horse alone,
Whose neck is placed in jeopardy
    By riding on his own?

And yet the conduct of the man
    Seemed honest-like and fair ;
For he seemed willing, horse and all,
    To go before the *mare!*

So up on Huggins' horse he got,
    And swiftly rode away,
While Huggins mounted on the mare ,
    Done brown upon a bay !

And off they set in double chase,
    For such was fortune's whim,
The farmer rode to hunt the stag,
    And Huggins hunted him !

Alas ! with one that rode so well
    In vain it was to strive ;
A dab was he, as dabs should be—
    All leaping and alive.

And here of Nature's kindly care
    Behold a curious proof,
As nags are meant to leap, she puts
    A frog in every hoof !

Whereas the mare, although her share
  She had of hoof and frog,
On coming to a gate stopped short
  As stiff as any log ;

While Huggins in the stirrup stood
  With neck like neck of crane,
As sings the Scottish song—" to see
  The *gate* his *hart* had gane."

And, lo ! the dim and distant hunt
  Diminished in a trice :
The steeds, like Cinderella's team,
  Seemed dwindling into mice ;

And, far remote, each scarlet coat
  Soon flitted like a spark—
Though still the forest murmured back
  An echo of the bark !

But sad at soul John Huggins turned :
  No comfort could he find ;
While thus the " Hunting Chorus " sped,
  To stay five bars behind.

For though by dint of spur he got
  A leap in spite of fate
Howbeit there was no toll at all—
  They could not clear the gate.

And like Fitzjames, he cursed the hunt,
  And sorely cursed the day,
And mused a New Gray's elegy
  On his departed gray.

Now many a sign at Woodford town
  Its Inn-vitation tells :
But Huggins, full of ills, of course
  Betook him to the Wells.

Where Rounding tried to cheer him up
  With many a merry laugh :
But Huggins thought of neighbour Fig,
  And called for half-and-half.

Yet, spite of drink, he could not blink
  Remembrance of his loss;
To drown a care like his, required
  Enough to drown a horse.

When thus forlorn, a merry horn
  Struck up without the door—
The mounted mob were all returned;
  The Epping Hunt was o'er !

And many a horse was taken out
  Of saddle, and of shaft ;
And men, by dint of drink, became
  The only *"beasts of draught."*

For now begun a harder run
  On wine, and gin, and beer;
And overtaken men discussed
  The overtaken deer.

How far he ran, and eke how fast.
  And how at bay he stood,
Deerlike, resolved to sell his life
  As dearly as he could :—

And how the hunters stood aloof,
  Regardful of their lives,
And shunned a beast, whose very horns
  They knew could *handle* knives !

How Huggins stood when he was rubbed
  By help and ostler kind,
And when they cleaned the clay before,
  How worse "remained behind."

And one, how he had found a horse
    Adrift—a goodly gray!
And kindly rode the nag, for fear
    The nag should go astray;

Now Huggins, when he heard the tale,
    Jumped up with sudden glee;
"A goodly gray! why, then, I say,
    That gray belongs to me!

"Let me endorse again my horse,
    Delivered safe and sound;
And gladly I will give the man
    A bottle and a pound!"

The wine was drunk—the money paid,
    Though not without remorse,
To pay another man so much
    For riding on his horse ;—

And let the chase again take place
    For many a long, long year—
John Huggins will not ride again
    To hunt the Epping Deer!

MORAL.

Thus pleasure oft eludes our grasp
    Just when we think to grip her:
And hunting after Happiness,
    We only hunt the slipper.

JACK HALL.

'Tis very hard when men forsake
This melancholy world, and make
A bed of turf, they cannot take
    A quiet doze,
But certain rogues will come and break
    Their "bone" repose.

'Tis hard we can't give up our breath,
And to the earth our earth bequeath,
Without Death-Fetches after death,
⁏   Who thus exhume us ;
And snatch us from our homes beneath,
                    And hearths posthumous.

The tender lover comes to rear
The mournful urn, and shed his tear—
Her glorious dust, he cries, is here !
                    Alack ! Alack !
The while his Sacharissa dear
                    Is in a sack !

'Tis hard one cannot lie amid
The mould, beneath a coffin-lid,
But thus the Faculty will bid
                    Their rogues break through it,
If they don't want us there, why did
                    They send us to it ?

One of these sacrilegious knaves,
Who crave as hungry vulture craves,
Behaving as the goul behaves,
                    'Neath church-yard wall—
Mayhap because he fed on graves,
                    Was nam'd Jack Hall.

By day it was his trade to go
Tending the black coach to and fro ;
And sometimes at the door of woe,
                    With emblems suitable,
He stood with brother Mute, to show
                    That life is mutable.

But long before they pass'd the ferry,
The dead that he had help'd to bury,
He sack'd—(he had a sack to carry
                    The bodies off in)
In fact, he let them have a very
                    Short fit of coffin.

Night after night, with crow and spade,
He drove this dead but thriving trade,
Meanwhile his conscience never weigh'd
  A single horsehair;
On corses of all kinds he prey'd,
  A perfect corsair!

At last—it may be, Death took spite,
Or, jesting only, meant to fright—
He sought for Jack night after night
  The churchyards round;
And soon they met, the man and sprite,
  In Pancras' ground.

Jack, by the glimpses of the moon,
Perceiv'd the bony knacker soon,
An awful shape to meet at noon
  Of night and lonely;
But Jack's tough courage did but swoon
  A minute only.

Anon he gave his spade a swing
Aloft, and kept it brandishing,
Ready for what mishaps might spring
  From this conjunction;
Funking indeed was quite a thing
  Beside his function.

"Hollo!" cried Death, "d'ye wish your sands
Run out? the stoutest never stands
A chance with me,—to my commands
  The strongest truckles;
But I'm your friend—so let's shake hands,
  I should say—knuckles."

Jack, glad to see th' old sprite so sprightly
And meaning nothing but uprightly,
Shook hands at once, and, bowing slightly,
  His mull did proffer:
But Death, who had no nose, politely
  Declin'd the offer.

Then sitting down upon a bank,
Leg over leg, shank over shank,
Like friends for conversation frank,
      That had no check on:
Quoth Jack unto the Lean and Lank,
      "You're Death, I reckon."

The Jaw-bone grinn'd :—"I am that same,
You've hit exactly on my name ;
In truth it has some little fame
      Where burial sod is."
Quoth Jack, (and wink'd), "of course ye came
      Here after bodies."

Death grinn'd again and shook his head ;—
"I've little business with the dead ;
When they are fairly sent to bed
      I've done my turn :
Whether or not the worms are fed
      Is your concern.

"My errand here, in meeting you,
Is nothing but a 'how-d'ye-do ;'
I've done what jobs I had—a few
      Along this way ;
If I can serve a crony too,
      I beg you'll say."

Quoth Jack, "Your Honour's very kind :
And now I call the thing to mind,
This parish very strict I find ;
      But in the next 'un
There lives a very well-inclined
      Old sort of sexton."

Death took the hint, and gave a wink
As well as eyelet holes can blink ;
Then stretching out his arm to link
      The other's arm,—
"Suppose," says he, "we have a drink
      Of something warm."

Jack nothing loth, with friendly ease
Spoke up at once :—" Why, what ye please ;
Hard by there is the Cheshire Cheese,
        A famous tap."
But this suggestion seem'd to tease
        The bony chap.

" No, no—your mortal drinks are heady,
And only make my hand unsteady ;
I do not even care for Deady,
        And loathe your rum ;
But I've some glorious brewage ready,
        My drink is—Mum !"

And off they set, each right content—
Who knows the dreary way they went?
But Jack felt rather faint and spent,
        And out of breath ;
At last he saw, quite evident,
        The Door of Death.

All other men had been unmann'd
To see a coffin on each hand,
That served a skeleton to stand
        By way of sentry ;
In fact, Death has a very grand
        And awful entry.

Throughout his dismal sign prevails,
His name is writ in coffin nails ;
The mortal darts make area rails ;
        A skull that mocketh.
Grins on the gloomy gate, and quails
        Whoever knocketh.

And lo ! on either side, arise
Two monstrous pillars—bones of thighs ;
A monumental slab supplies
        The step of stone,
Where waiting for his master lies
        A dog of bone.

The dog leapt up, but gave no yell,
The wire was pull'd, but woke no bell,
The ghastly knocker rose and fell,
        But caused no riot ;
The ways of Death, we all know well
        Are very quiet.

Old Bones stept in; Jack stepp'd behind ;
Quoth Death, "I really hope you'll find
The entertainment to your mind,
        As I shall treat ye—
A friend or two of goblin kind,
        I've asked to meet ye."

And lo ! a crowd of spectres tall,
Like jack-a-lanterns on a wall,
Were standing—every ghastly ball—
        An eager watcher.
"My friend," says Death—"friends, Mr. Hall,
        The body-snatcher."

Lord, what a tumult it produced,
When Mr. Hall was introduced!
Jack even, who had long been used
        To frightful things,
Felt just as if his back was sluic'd
        With freezing springs !

Each goblin face began to make
Some horrid mouth—ape—gorgon—snake ;
And then a spectre-hag would shake
        An airy thigh-bone ;
And cried, (or seem'd to cry,) I'll break
        Your bone, with *my* bone!

Some ground their teeth—some seem'd to spit—
(Nothing, but nothing came of it,)
A hundred awful brows were knit
        In dreadful spite.
Thought Jack—"I'm sure I'd better quit
        Without good-night."

One skip and hop and he was clear,
And running like a hunted deer,
As fleet as people run by fear
        Well spurr'd and whipp'd,
Death, ghosts, and all in that career
        Were quite outstripp'd.

But those who live by death must die;
Jack's soul at last prepared to fly;
And when his latter end drew nigh.
        Oh! what a swarm
Of doctors came,—but not to try
        To keep him warm.

No ravens ever scented prey
So early where a dead horse lay,
Nor vultures sniff'd so far away
        A last convulse:
A dozen "guests" day after day
        Were "at his pulse."

'Twas strange, altho' they got no fees,
How still they watch'd by twos and threes.
But Jack a very little ease
        Obtain'd from them;
In fact he did not find M. D.'s
        Worth one D—M.

The passing bell with hollow toll
Was in his thought—the dreary hole!
Jack gave his eyes a horrid roll,
        And then a cough:—
"There's something weighing on my soul
        I wish was off;

"All night it roves about my brains,
All day it adds to all my pains,
It is concerning my remains
        When I am dead:"
Twelve wigs and twelve gold-headed canes
        Drew near his bed.

"Alas!" he sigh'd, "I'm sore afraid
A dozen pangs my heart invade;
But when I drove a certain trade
    In flesh and bone,
There was a little bargain made
    About my own."

Twelve suits of black began to close,
Twelve pair of sleek and sable hose,
Twelve flowing cambric frills in rows,
    At once drew round;
Twelve noses turn'd against his nose,
    Twelve snubs profound.

"Ten guineas did not quite suffice,
And so I sold my body twice;
Twice did not do—I sold it thrice,
    Forgive my crimes!
In short I have received its price
    A dozen times!

Twelve brows got very grim and black,
Twelve wishes stretched him on the rack,
Twelve pair of hands for fierce attack
    Took up position,
Ready to share the dying Jack
    By long division.

Twelve angry doctors wrangled so,
That twelve had struck an hour ago,
Before they had an eye to throw
    On the departed;
Twelve heads turn'd round at once, and lo!
    Twelve doctors started.

Whether some comrade of the dead,
Or Satan took it in his head
To steal the corpse—the corpse had fled!
    'Tis only written,
That "*there was nothing in the bed,*
    But twelve were bitten!"

THE HAUNTED HOUSE.

A ROMANCE.

PART I.

SOME dreams we have are nothing else but dreams,
Unnatural, and full of contradictions ;
Yet others of our most romantic schemes
Are something more than fictions.

It might be only on enchanted ground ;
It might be merely by a thought's expansion ;
But, in the spirit or the flesh, I found
An old deserted Mansion.

A residence for woman, child, and man,
A dwelling-place,—and yet no habitation ;
A House,—but under some prodigious ban
Of Excommunication.

Unhinged the iron gates half open hung,
Jarr'd by the gusty gales of many winters,
That from its crumbled pedestal had flung
One marble globe in splinters.

No dog was at the threshold, great or small ;
No pigeon on the roof no household creature—
No cat demurely dozing on the wall—
Not one domestic feature.

No human figure stirr'd, to go or come,
No face look'd forth from shut or open casement ;
No chimney smoked—there was no sign of Home
From parapet to basement.

With shatter'd panes the grassy court was starr'd ;
The time-worn coping-stone had tumbled after !
And thro' the ragged roof the sky shone, barr'd
With naked beam and rafter.

O'er all there hung a shadow and a fear;
A sense of mystery the spirit daunted,
And said, as plain as whisper in the ear,
The place is Haunted!

The flow'r grew wild and rankly as the weed,
Roses with thistles struggled for espial,
And vagrant plants of parasitic breed
Had overgrown the Dial.

But gay or gloomy, steadfast or infirm,
No heart was there to heed the hour's duration;
All times and tides were lost in one long term
Of stagnant desolation.

The wren had built within the Porch, she found
Its quiet loneliness so sure and thorough;
And on the lawn,—within its turfy mound,--
The rabbit made his burrow.

The rabbit wild and gray, that flitted thro'
The shrubby clumps, and frisk'd, and sat, and vanished
But leisurely and bold, as if he knew
His enemy was banish'd.

The wary crow,—the pheasant from the woods—
Lull'd by the still and everlasting sameness,
Close to the mansion, like domestic broods,
Fed with a " shocking tameness."

The coot was swimming in the reedy pond,
Beside the water-hen, so soon affrighted;
And in the weedy moat the heron, fond
Of solitude, alighted.

The moping heron, motionless and stiff,
That on a stone, as silently and stilly,
Stood, an apparent sentinel, as if
To guard the water-lily.

No sound was heard except, from far away,
The ringing of the witwall's shrilly laughter,
Or, now and then, the chatter of the jay,
That Echo murmur'd after.

But Echo never mock'd the human tongue ;
Some weighty crime, that Heaven could not pardon,
A secret curse on that old Building hung
And its deserted Garden.

The beds were all untouch'd by hand or tool ;
No footstep mark'd the damp and mossy gravel,
Each walk as green as is the mantled pool,
For want of human travel.

The vine unpruned, and the neglected peach,
Droop'd from the wall with which they used to grapple ;
And on the kanker'd tree, in easy reach,
Rotted the golden apple.

But awfully the truant shunn'd the ground,
The vagrant kept aloof, and daring Poacher,
In spite of gaps that thro' the fences round
Invited the encroacher.

For over all there hung a cloud of fear,
A sense of mystery the spirit daunted,
And said, as plain as whisper in the ear,
The place is Haunted !

The pear and quince lay squander'd on the grass :
The mould was purple with unheeded showers
Of bloomy plums—a Wilderness it was
Of fruits, and weeds, and flowers !

The marigold amidst the nettles blew,
The gourd embraced the rose bush in its ramble,
The thistle and the stock together grew,
The holly-hock and bramble

S

The bear-bine with the lilac interlaced,
The sturdy bur-dock choked its slender neighbour,
The spicy pink.   All tokens were effaced
Of human care and labour.

The very yew Formality had train'd
To such a rigid pyramidal stature,
For want of trimming had almost regain'd
The raggedness of nature.

The Fountain was a-dry—neglect and time
Had marr'd the work of artisan and mason,
And efts and croaking frogs, begot of slime,
Sprawl'd in the ruin'd bason.

The Statue, fallen from its marble base,
Amidst the refuse leaves, and herbage rotten,
Lay like the Idol of some by-gone race,
Its name and rites forgotten.

On ev'ry side the aspect was the same,
All ruin'd, desolate, forlorn and savage :
No hand or foot within the precinct came
To rectify or ravage.

For over all there hung a cloud of fear.
A sense of mystery the spirit daunted,
And said, as plain as whisper in the ear,
The place is Haunted !

———

PART II.

O, VERY gloomy is the House of Woe,
Where tears are falling while the bell is knelling,
With all the dark solemnities which show
That Death is in the dwelling.

O very, very dreary is the room
Where Love, domestic Love, no longer nestles,
But, smitten by the common stroke of doom,
The Corpse lies on the trestles !

But House of Woe, and hearse, and sable pall,
The narrow home of the departed mortal,
Ne'er look'd so gloomy as that Ghostly Hall,
With its deserted portal !

The centipede along the threshold crept,
The cobweb hung across in mazy tangle,
And in its winding-sheet the maggot slept,
At every nook and angle.

The keyhole lodged the earwig and her brood,
The emmets of the steps had old possession,
And marched in search of their diurnal food
In undisturbed procession.

As undisturb'd as the prehensile cell
Of moth or maggot, or the spider's tissue.
For never foot upon that threshold fell,
To enter or to issue.

O'er all there hung the shadow of a fear.
A sense of mystery the spirit daunted,
And said, as plain as whisper in the ear,
The place is Haunted !

Howbeit, the door I push'd—or so I dream'd—
Which slowly, slowly gaped,—the hinges creaking
With such a rusty eloquence, it seemed
That Time himself was speaking.

But Time was dumb within that Mansion old,
Or left his tale to the heraldic banners,
That hung from the corroded walls, and told
Of former men and manners :—

Those tatter'd flags, that with the open'd door,
Seem'd the old wave of battle to remember,
While fallen fragments danced upon the floor,
Like dead leaves in December.

The startled bats flew out,—bird after bird,
The screech-owl overhead began to flutter,
And seemed to mock the cry that she had heard
Some dying victim utter !

A shriek that echo'd from the joisted roof,
And up the stair, and further still and further,
Till in some ringing chamber far aloof
It ceased its tale of murther !

Meanwhile the rusty armour rattled round,
The banner shudder'd, and the ragged streamer ;
All things the horrid tenor of the sound
Acknowledged with a tremor.

The antlers, where the helmet hung, and belt,
Stirr'd as the tempest stirs the forest branches,
Or as the stag had trembled when he felt
The blood-hound at his haunches.

The window jingled in its crumbled frame,
And thro' its many gaps of destitution
Dolorous moans and hollow sighings came,
Like those of dissolution.

The wood-louse dropped, and rolled into a ball,
Touched by some impulse occult or mechanic ;
And nameless beetles ran along the wall
In universal panic.

The subtle spider, that from overhead
Hung like a spy on human guilt and error,
Suddenly turn'd and up its slender thread
Ran with a nimble terror.

The very stains and fractures on the wall
Assuming features solemn and terrific,
Hinted some Tragedy of that old Hall,
Lock'd up in hieroglyphic.

Some tale that might, perchance, have solved the doubt,
Wherefore amongst those flags so dull and livid,
The banner of the Bloody Hand shone out
So ominously vivid.

Some key to that inscrutable appeal,
Which made the very frame of Nature quiver;
And every thrilling nerve and fibre feel
So ague-like a shiver.

For over all there hung a cloud of fear;
A sense of mystery the spirit daunted,
And said, as plain as whisper in the ear,
The place is Haunted!

If but a rat had linger'd in the house,
To lure the thought into a social channel!
But not a rat remain'd, or tiny mouse,
To squeak behind the panel.

Huge drops rolled down the walls, as if they wept;
And where the cricket used to chirp so shrilly,
The toad was squatting, and the lizard crept
On that damp hearth and chilly.

For years no cheerful blaze had sparkled there,
Or glanced on coat of buff or knightly metal;
The slug was crawling on the vacant chair,—
The snail upon the settle.

The floor was redolent of mould and must,
The fungus in the rotten seams had quicken'd;
While on the oaken table coats of dust
Perennially had thicken'd.

No mark of leathern jack or metal can,
No cup—no horn—no hospitable token,—
All social ties between that board and Man
Had long ago been broken.

There was so foul a rumour in the air,
The shadow of a presence so atrocious ;
No human creature could have feasted there,
Even the most ferocious.

For over all there hung a cloud of fear,
A sense of mystery the spirit daunted,
And said, as plain as whisper in the ear,
The place is Haunted !

PART III.

'Tis hard for human actions to account,
Whether from reason or from impulse only—
But some internal prompting bade me mount
The gloomy stairs and lonely.

Those gloomy stairs, so dark, and damp, and cold,
With odours as from bones and relics carnal,
Deprived of rite, and consecrated mould,
The chapel vault or charnel.

Those dreary stairs, where with the sounding stress
Of ev'ry step so many echoes blended,
The mind, with dark misgivings, feared to guess
How many feet ascended.

The tempest with its spoils had drifted in,
Till each unwholesome stone was darkly spotted,
As thickly as the leopard's dappled skin,
With leaves that rankly rotted.

The air was thick—and in the upper gloom
The bat—or something in its shape—was winging,
And on the wall, as chilly as a tomb,
The Death's-Head moth was clinging.

That mystic moth, which, with a sense profound
Of all unholy presence, augurs truly;
And with a grim significance flits round
The taper burning bluely.

Such omens in the place there seem'd to be,
At ev'ry crooked turn, or on the landing,
The straining eyeball was prepared to see
Some Apparition standing.

For over all there hung a cloud of fear,
A sense of mystery the spirit daunted,
And said, as plain as whisper in the ear,
The place is Haunted!

Yet no portentous Shape the sight amazed;
Each object plain, and tangible, and valid;
But from their tarnish'd frames dark Figures gazed,
And Faces spectre-pallid.

Not merely with the mimic life that lies
Within the compass of Art's simulation;
Their souls were looking thro' their painted eyes
With awful speculation.

On ev'ry lip a speechless horror dwelt;
On ev'ry brow the burthen of affliction;
The old Ancestral Spirits knew and felt
The House's malediction.

Such earnest woe their features overcast,
They might have stirr'd, or sigh'd, or wept, or spoken,
But, save the hollow moaning of the blast,
The stillness was unbroken.

No other sound or stir of life was there,
Except my steps in solitary clamber,
From flight to flight, from humid stair to stair,
From chamber into chamber.

Deserted rooms of luxury and state,
That old magnificence had richly furnish'd
With pictures, cabinets of ancient date,
And carvings gilt and burnish'd.

Rich hangings, storied by the needle's art
With scripture history, or classic fable ;
But all had faded, save one ragged part,
Where Cain was slaying Abel.

The silent waste of mildew and the moth
Had marr'd the tissue with a partial ravage ;
But undecaying frown'd upon the cloth
Each feature stern and savage.

The sky was pale ; the cloud a thing of doubt ;
Some hues were fresh, and some decay'd and duller ;
But still the Bloody Hand shone strangely out
With vehemence of colour !

The Bloody Hand that with a lurid stain
Shone on the dusty floor, a dismal token,
Projected from the casement's painted pane,
Where all beside was broken.

The Bloody Hand significant of crime,
That glaring on the old heraldic banner,
Had kept its crimson unimpaired by time,
In such a wondrous manner.

O'er all there hung the shadow of a fear,
A sense of mystery the spirit daunted,
And said, as plain as whisper in the ear,
The place is Haunted !

The Death Watch tick'd behind the panel'd oak,
Inexplicable tremors shook the arras,
And echoes strange and mystical awoke,
The fancy to embarrass.

Prophetic hints that fill'd the soul with dread,
But thro' one gloomy entrance pointing mostly,
The while some secret inspiration said,
That Chamber is the Ghostly!

Across the door no gossamer festoon
Swung pendulous— no web— no dusty fringes,
No silk chrysalis or white cocoon
About its nooks and hinges.

The spider shunn'd the interdicted room,
The moth, the beetle, and the fly were banish'd,
And where the sunbeam fell athwart the gloom,
The very midge had vanish'd.

One lonely ray that glanced upon a Bed,
As if with awful aim direct and certain,
To show the Bloody Hand in burning red
Embroidered on the curtain.

And yet no gory stain was on the quilt—
The pillow in its place had slowly rotted;
The floor alone retain'd the trace of guilt,
Those boards obscurely spotted.

Obscurely spotted to the door, and thence
With mazy doubles to the grated casement—
Oh what a tale they told of fear intense,
Of horror and amazement!

What human creature in the dead of night
Had coursed like hunted hare that cruel distance?
Had sought the door, the window in his flight,
Striving for dear existence?

What shrieking Spirit in that bloody room
Its mortal frame had violently quitted?—
Across the sunbeam, with a sudden gloom,
A ghostly Shadow flitted.

Across the sunbeam, and along the wall,
But painted on the air so very dimly,
It hardly veil'd the tapestry at all,
Or portrait frowning grimly.

O'er all there hung the shadow of a fear,
A sense of mystery the spirit daunted,
And said, as plain as whisper in the ear,
The place is Haunted!

MISS KILMANSEGG AND HER PRECIOUS LEG.

A GOLDEN LEGEND.

HER PEDIGREE.

To trace the Kilmansegg pedigree
To the very root of the family tree
   Were a task as rash as ridiculous :
Through antediluvian mists as thick
As London fog such a line to pick
Were enough, in truth, to puzzle old Nick.—
   Not to name Sir Harris Nicolas.

It wouldn't require much verbal strain
To trace the Kill-man, perchance, to Cain,
   But, waiving all such digressions,
Suffice it, according to family lore,
A Patriarch Kilmansegg lived of yore,
   Who was famed for his great possessions.

Tradition said he feather'd his nest
Through an Agricultural Interest
   In the Golden Age of farming ;
When golden eggs were laid by the geese,
And Colchian sheep wore a golden fleece,
And golden pippins—the sterling kind
Of Hesperus—now so hard to find—
   Made Horticulture quite charming !

A Lord of Land, on his own estate,
He lived at a very lively rate,
   But his income would bear carousing ;
Such acres he had of pasture and heath,
With herbage so rich from the ore beneath,
The very ewe's and lambkin's teeth
   Were turn'd into gold by browsing.

He gave, without any extra thrift,
A flock of sheep for a birthday gift
   To each son of his loins, or daughter :
And his debts—if debts he had—at will
He liquidated by giving each bill
   A dip in Pactolian water.

'Twas said that even his pigs of lead,
By crossing with some by Midas bred,
   Made a perfect mine of his piggery.
And as for cattle, one yearling bull
Was worth all Smithfield-market full
   Of the Golden Bulls of Pope Gregory.

The high-bred horses within his stud,
Like human creatures of birth and blood,
   Had their Golden Cups and flagons :
And as for the common husbandry nags,
Their noses were tied in money-bags,
   When they stopp'd with the carts and waggons.

Moreover, he had a Golden Ass,
Sometimes at stall, and sometimes at grass,
  That was worth his own weight in money—
And a golden hive, on a Golden Bank,
Where golden bees, by alchemical prank,
  Gather'd gold instead of honey.

Gold! and gold! and gold without end!
He had gold to lay by, and gold to spend,
Gold to give, and gold to lend,
  And reversions of gold *in futuro.*
In wealth the family revell'd and roll'd,
Himself and wife and sons so bold;—
And his daughters sang to their harps of gold
  "O bella eta del' oro!"

Such was the tale of the Kilmansegg Kin,
In golden text on a vellum skin,
Though certain people would wink and grin,
  And declare the whole story a parable—
That the Ancestor rich was one Jacob Ghrimes,
Who held a long lease, in prosperous times,
  Of acres, pasture and arable.

That as money makes money, his golden bees
Were the Five per Cents., or which you please
  When his cash was more than plenty—
That the golden cups were racing affairs;
And his daughters, who sang Italian airs,
  Had their golden harps of Clementi.

That the Golden Ass, or Golden Bull,
Was English John, with his pockets full,
  Then at war by land and water:
While beef, and mutton, and other meat,
Were almost as dear as money to eat,
And Farmers reaped Golden Harvests of wheat
  At the Lord knows what per quarter!

HER BIRTH.

WHAT different dooms our birthdays bring
For instance, one little manikin thing
   Survives to wear many a wrinkle;
While Death forbids another to wake,
And a son that it took nine moons to make
   Expires without even a twinkle!

Into this world we come like ships,
Launch'd from the docks, and stocks, and slips,
   For fortune fair or fatal ;
And one little craft is cast away
In its very first trip in Babbicome Bay,
   While another rides safe at Port Natal.

What different lots our stars accord !
This babe to be hail'd and woo'd as a Lord !
   And that to be shunn'd like a leper !
One, to the world's wine, honey, and corn,
Another, like Colchester native, born
   To its vinegar, only, and pepper.

One is litter'd under a roof
Neither wind nor water proof—
   That's the prose of Love in a Cottage—
A puny, naked, shivering wretch,
   The whole of whose birthright would not fetch,
Though Robins himself drew up the sketch
   The bid of "a mess of pottage."

Born of Fortunatus's kin,
Another comes tenderly ushered in
   To a prospect all bright and burnish'd :
No tenant he for life's back slums—
He comes to the world, as a gentleman comes
   To a lodging ready furnish'd.

And the other sex—the tender—the fair—
What wide reverses of fate are there !
Whilst Margaret, charm'd by the Bulbul rare,
   In a garden of Gul reposes—
Poor Peggy hawks nosegays from street to street
Till—think of that, who find life so sweet !—
   She hates the smell of roses !

Not so with the infant Kilmansegg !
She was not born to steal or beg,
   Or gather cresses in ditches ;
To plait the straw, or bind the shoe,
Or sit all day to hem and sew,
As females must—and not a few—
   To fill their insides with stitches !

She was not doom'd, for bread to eat,
To be put to her hands as well as her feet—
   To carry home linen from mangles—
Or heavy-hearted, and weary-limb'd,
To dance on a rope in a jacket trimm'd
   With as many blows as spangles.

She was one of those who by Fortune's boon
Are born, as they say, with a silver spoon
   In her mouth, not a wooden ladle :
To speak according to poet's wont,
Plutus as sponsor stood at her font,
   And Midas rock'd the cradle.

At her first *debut* she found her head
On a pillow of down, in a downy bed,
   With a damask canopy over.
For although, by the vulgar popular saw,
All mothers are said to be "in the straw,"
   Some children are born in clover.

Her very first draught of vital air,
It was not the common chameleon fare
  Of plebeian lungs and noses,—
    No—her earliest sniff
    Of this world was a whiff
  Of the genuine Otto of Roses !

When she saw the light, it was no mere ray
Of that light so common—so everyday—
  That the sun each morning launches—
But six wax tapers dazzled her eyes,
From a thing—a gooseberry bush for size—
  With a golden stem and branches.

She was born exactly at half-past two,
As witness'd a time-piece in or-molu
  That stood on a marble table—
Showing at once the time of day,
And a team of *Gildings* running away
  As fast as they were able,
With a golden God, with a golden Star,
And a golden Spear, in a golden Car,
  According to Grecian table.

Like other babes, at her birth she cried ;
Which made a sensation far and wide—
  Ay, for twenty miles around her :
For though to the ear 'twas nothing more
Than an infant's squall, it was really the roar
  Of a Fifty-thousand Pounder !
    It shook the next heir
    In his library chair,
  And made him cry, " Confound her !"

Of signs and omens there was no dearth,
Any more than at Owen Glendower's birth,

Or the advent of other great people :
   Two bullocks dropp'd dead,
   As if knock'd on the head,
   And barrels of stout
   And ale ran about,
And the village-bells such a peal rang out,
  That they crack'd the village-steeple.

In no time at all, like mushroom spawn,
Tables sprang up all over the lawn ;
  Not furnish'd scantly or shabbily,
   But on scale as vast
   As that huge repast,
   With its loads and cargoes
   Of drink and botargoes,
  At the birth of the Babe in Rabelais.

Hundreds of men were turn'd into beasts,
Like the guests at Circe's horrible feasts,
  By the magic of ale and cider :
And each country lass, and each country lad,
Began to caper and dance like mad,
And ev'n some old ones appear'd to have had
  A bite from the Naples Spider.

  Then as night came on,
  It had scared King John
Who considered such signs not risible,
  To have seen the maroons,
  And the whirling moons,
  And the serpents of flame,
  And wheels of the same,
That according to some were " whizzable."

Oh, happy Hope of the Kilmanseggs !
Thrice happy in head, and body, and legs.

That her parents had such full pockets !
For had she been born of Want and Thrift,
For care and nursing all adrift,
It's ten to one she had had to make shift
  With rickets instead of rockets !

And how was the precious baby drest?
In a robe of the East, with lace of the West.
  Like one of Crœsus's issue—
    Her best bibs were made
    Of rich gold brocade,
  And the others of silver tissue.

And when the Baby inclined to nap
She was lull'd on a Gros de Naples lap,
By a nurse in a modish Paris cap,
  Of notions so exalted,
She drank nothing lower than Curaçoa,
Maraschino, or pink Noyau,
  And on principle never malted.

From a golden boat, with a golden spoon,
The babe was fed night, morning, and noon ;
  And altho' the tale seems fabulous,
'Tis said her tops and bottoms were gilt,
Like the oats in that Stable-yard Palace built
  For the Horse of Heliogabalus.

And when she took to squall and kick—
For pain will ring, and pins will prick,
  E'en the wealthiest nabob's daughter—
They gave her no vulgar Dalby or gin,
But a liquor with leaf of gold therein,
  Videlicet,—Dantzic Water.

In short, she was born, and bred, and nurst,
And drest in the best from the very first,
　To please the genteelest censor—
And then, as soon as strength would allow
Was vaccinated, as babes are now,
With virus ta'en from the best-bred cow
　Of Lord Althorpe's—now Earl Spencer.

HER CHRISTENING.

THOUGH Shakespeare asks us, "What's in a name?"
(As if cognomens were much the same),
　There's really a very great scope in it.
A name?—why, wasn't there Doctor Dodd,
That servant at once of Mammon and God,
Who found four thousand pounds and odd,
　A prison—a cart—and a rope in it?

A name?—if the party had a voice,
What mortal would be a Bugg by choice?
As a Hogg, a Grubb, or a Chubb rejoice?
　Or any such nauseous blazon?
Not to mention many a vulgar name,
That would make a door-plate blush for shame,
　If door-plates were not so brazen !

A name?—it has more than nominal worth,
And belongs to good or bad luck at birth –
　As dames of a certain degree know.
In spite of his Page's hat and hose,
His Page's jacket, and buttons in rows
Bob only sounds like a page in prose
　Till turned into Rupertino.

Now to christen the infant Kilmansegg,
For days and days it was quite a plague,

To hunt the list in the Lexicon :
And scores were tried, like coin, by the ring,
Ere names were found just the proper thing
    For a minor rich as a Mexican.

Then cards were sent the presence to beg
Of all the kin of Kilmansegg,
    White, yellow, and brown relations :
Brothers, Wardens of City Halls,
And Uncles—rich as three Golden Balls
    From taking pledges of nations.

Nephews, whom Fortune seem'd to bewitch,
    Rising in life like rockets—
Nieces, whose doweries knew no hitch—
Aunts, as certain of dying rich
    As candles in golden sockets—
Cousins German and Cousins' sons,
All thriving and opulent—some had tons
    'Of Kentish hops in their pockets !

For money had stuck to the race through life
(As it did to the bushel when cash so rife
Posed Ali Baba's brother's wife)—
    And down to the Cousins and Coz-lings,
The fortunate brood of the Kilmanseggs,
As if they had come out of golden eggs,
    Were all as wealthy as "Goslings."

It would fill a Court Gazette to name
What East and West End people came
    To the rite of Christianity :
The lofty Lord, and the titled Dame,
    All di'monds, plumes, and urbanity :
His Lordship the May'r with his golden chain,
And two Gold Sticks, and the Sheriffs twain,

Nine foreign Counts, and other great men
With their orders and stars, to help " M. or N."
　　To renounce all pomp and vanity.

To paint the maternal Kilmansegg
The pen of an Eastern Poet would beg,
　　And need an elaborate sonnet ;
How she sparkled with gems whenever she stirr'd,
And her head niddle-noddled at every word,
And seem'd so happy, a Paradise Bird
　　Had nidificated upon it.

And Sir Jacob the Father strutted and bow'd,
And smiled to himself, and laugh'd aloud,
　　To think of his heiress and daughter—
And then in his pockets he made a grope,
And then, in the fulness of joy and hope,
Seem'd washing his hands with invisible soap
　　In imperceptible water.

He had roll'd in money like pigs in mud,
Till it seem'd to have enter'd into his blood
　　By some occult projection :
And his cheeks instead of a healthy hue.
As yellow as any guinea grew,
Making the common phrase seem true,
　　About a rich complexion.

And now came the nurse, and during a pause,
Her dead-leaf satin would fitly cause
　　A very autumnal rustle—
So full of figure, so full of fuss,
As she carried about the babe to buss,
　　She seem'd to be nothing but bustle.

A wealthy Nabob was Godpapa,
And an Indian Begum was Godmamma,
   Whose jewels a Queen might covet—
And the Priest was a Vicar, and Dean withal
Of that Temple we see with a Golden Ball,
   And a Golden Cross above it.

The Font was a bowl of American gold,
Won by Raleigh in days of old,
   In spite of Spanish bravado ;
And the Book of Pray'r was so overrun
With gilt devices, it shone in the sun
Like a copy—a presentation one—
   Of Humboldt's "El Dorado."

Gold ! and gold ! and nothing but gold !
The same auriferous shine behold
   Wherever the eye could settle !
On the walls—the sideboard—the ceiling-sky
On the gorgeous footmen standing by,
In coats to delight a miner's eye
   With seams of the precious metal.

Gold ! and gold ! and besides the gold,
The very robe of the infant told
A tale of wealth in every fold,
   It lapp'd her like a vapour !
So fine ! so thin ! the mind at a loss
Could compare it to nothing except a cross
   Of cobweb with bank-note paper.

Then her pearls—'twas a perfect sight, forsooth,
To see them, like " the dew of her youth,"
   In such a plentiful sprinkle.
Meanwhile, the Vicar read through the form,
And gave her another, not overwarm,
   That made her little eyes twinkle.

Then the babe was cross'd and bless'd amain !
But instead of the Kate, or Ann, or Jane,
   Which the humbler female endorses—
Instead of one name, as some people prefix,
Kilmansegg went at the tails of six,
   Like a carriage of state with its horses.

Oh, then the kisses she got and hugs !
The golden mugs and the golden jugs
   That lent fresh rays to the midges !
The golden knives, and the golden spoons,
The gems that sparkled like fairy boons,
It was one of the Kilmansegg's own saloons,
   But look'd like Rundell and Bridge's !

Gold ! and gold ! the new and the old,
The company ate and drank from gold,
   They revell'd, they sang, and were merry ;
And one of the Gold Sticks rose from his chair,
And toasted "the Lass with the golden hair"
   In a bumper of Golden Sherry.

Gold ! still gold ! it rain'd on the nurse,
Who—un-like Danäe—was none the worse !
   There was nothing but guineas glistening !
   Fifty were given to Doctor James,
   For calling the little Baby names,
   And for saying, Amen !
   The Clerk had ten,
   And that was the end of the Christening.

HER CHILDHOOD.

Our youth ! our childhood ! that spring of springs !
'Tis surely one of the blessedest things

That nature ever invented !
When the rich are wealthy beyond their wealth,
And the poor are rich in spirits and health,
    And all with their lots contented !

There's little Phelim, he sings like a thrush,
In the selfsame pair of patchwork plush,
    With the selfsame empty pockets,
That tempted his daddy so often to cut
His throat, or jump in the water-butt—
But what cares Phelim? an empty nut
    Would sooner bring tears to their sockets.

Give him a collar without a skirt,
(That's the Irish linen for shirt)
And a slice of bread with a taste of dirt,
    (That's Poverty's Irish butter),
And what does he lack to make him blest ?
Some oyster-shells, or a sparrow's nest,
    A candle-end, and a gutter.

But to leave the happy Phelim alone,
Gnawing, perchance, a marrowless bone,
    For which no dog would quarrel—
Turn we to little Miss Kilmansegg
Cutting her first little toothy-peg
    With a fifty-guinea coral—
        A peg up n which
        About poor and rich
    Reflection might hang a moral.

Born in wealth, and wealthily nursed,
Capp'd, papp'd, napp'd, and lapp'd from the first
    On the knees of Prodigality,
Her childhood was one eternal round
Of the game of going on Tickler's ground
    Picking up gold—in reality.

With extempore cartes she never play'd,
Or the odds and ends of a Tinker's trade,
Or little dirt pies and puddings made,
　　Like children happy and squalid ;
The very puppet she had to pet,
Like a bait for the " Nix my Dolly" set,
　　Was a Dolly of gold—and solid !

Gold ! and gold ! 'twas the burden still !
To gain the Heiress's early goodwill
　　There was much corruption and bribery—
The yearly cost of her golden toys
Would have given half London's Charity Boys
And Charity Girls the annual joys
　　Of a holiday dinner at Highbury.

Bon-bons she ate from the gilt *cornet;*
And gilded queens on St. Bartlemy's day ;
　　Till her fancy was tinged by her presents—
And first a Goldfinch excited her wish,
Then a spherical bowl with its Golden fish,
　　And then two Golden Pheasants.

Nay, once she squall'd and scream'd like wild—
And it shows how the bias we give to a child
　　Is a thing most weighty and solemn :—
But whence was wonder or blame to spring
If little Miss K.—after such a swing—
Made a dust for the flaming gilded thing
　　On the top of the Fish Street column?

———

HER EDUCATION.

ACCORDING to metaphysical creed,
To the earliest books that children read

For much good or much bad they are debtors—
But before with their A B C they start,
There are things in morals, as well as art,
That play a very important part—
  "Impressions before the letters."

Dame Education begins the pile,
Mayhap in the graceful Corinthian style,
  But alas for the elevation !
If the Lady's maid or Gossip the Nurse
With a load of rubbish, or something worse,
  Have made a rotten foundation.

Even thus with little Miss Kilmansegg,
Before she learnt her E for egg,
  Ere her Governess came, or her masters—
Teachers of quite a different kind
Had "cramm'd" her beforehand, and put her mind
  In a go-cart on golden castors.

Long before her A B and C,
They had taught her by heart her L. S. D.
  And as how she was born a great Heiress;
And as sure as London is built of bricks,
My Lord would ask her the day to fix,
To ride in a fine gilt coach and six,
  Like Her Worship the Lady May'ress.

Instead of stories from Edgeworth's page,
The true golden lore for our golden age,
  Or lessons from Barbauld and Trimmer,
Teaching the worth of Virtue and Health,
All that she knew was the Virtue of Wealth,
Provided by vulgar nursery stealth
  With a Book of Leaf Gold for a Primer.

The very metal of merit they told,
And praised her for being as " good as gold !"
　　Till she grew as a peacock haughty ;
Of money they talk'd the whole day round,
And weigh'd desert, like grapes, by the pound,
Till she had an idea from the very sound
　　That people with nought were naughty.

They praised—poor children with nothing at all !
Lord ! how you twaddle and waddle and squall
　　Like common-bred geese and ganders !
What sad little bad little figures you make
To the rich Miss K., whose plainest seed-cake
　　Was stuff'd with corianders !

They praised her falls, as well as her walk,
Flatterers make cream cheese of chalk,
They praised—how they praised—her very small talk,
　　As if it fell from a Solon ;
Or the girl who at each pretty phrase let drop
A ruby comma, or pearl full-stop,
　　Or an emerald semi-colon.

They praised her spirit, and now and then
The Nurse brought her own little " nevy " Ben,
　　To play with the future May'ress,
And when he got raps, and taps, and slaps,
Scratches, and pinches, snips, and snaps,
　　As if from a Tigress, or Bearess,
They told him how Lords would court that hand,
And always gave him to understand,
　　　While he rubb'd, poor soul,
　　　His carroty poll,
　　That his hair had been pull'd by " a *Hairess.*"

Such were the lessons from maid and nurse,
A Governess help'd to make still worse,

Giving an appetite so perverse
  Fresh diet whereon to batten—
Beginning with A B C to hold
Like a royal playbill printed in gold
  On a square of pearl-white satin.

The books to teach the verbs and nouns,
And those about countries, cities, and towns,
Instead of their sober drabs and browns,
  Were in crimson silk, with gilt edges ;—
Her Butler, and Enfield, and Entick—in short
Her " Early Lessons " of every sort,
  Look'd like Souvenirs, Keepsakes, and Pledges.

Old Johnson shone out in as fine array
As he did one night when he went to the play ;
Chambaud like a beau of King Charles's day—
  Lindley Murray in like conditions—
Each weary, unwelcome, irksome task,
Appear'd in a fancy dress and a mask ;—
If you wish for similar copies, ask
  For Howell and James's Editions.

Novels she read to amuse her mind,
But always the affluent match-making kind
  That ends with Promessi Sposi,
And a father-in-law so wealthy and grand,
He could give cheque-mate to Coutts in the Strand ;
  So, along with a ring and posy,
He endows the Bride with Golconda off hand,
  And gives the Groom Potosi.

Plays she perused—but she liked the best
Those comedy gentlefolks always possess'd
  Of fortunes so truly romantic—
Of money so ready that right or wrong

It always is ready to go for a song,
 Throwing it, going it, pitching it strong—
They ought to have purses as green and long
 As the cucumber call'd the Gigantic.

Then Eastern Tales she loved for the sake
Of the Purse of Oriental make,
 And the thousand pieces they put in it—
But Pastoral scenes on her heart fell cold,
For Nature with her had lost its hold,
No field but the Field of the Cloth of Gold
 Would ever have caught her foot in it.

What more? She learnt to sing, and dance,
To sit on a horse, although he should prance,
And to speak a French not spoken in France
 Any more than at Babel's building—
And she painted shells, and flowers, and Turks,
But her great delight was in Fancy Works
 That are done with gold or gilding.

Gold! still gold!—the bright and the dead,
With golden beads, and gold lace, and gold thread
She work'd in gold, as if for her bread;
 The metal had so undermined her,
Gold ran in her thoughts and fill'd her brain,
She was golden-headed as Peter's cane
 With which he walk'd behind her.

—

HER ACCIDENT.

THE horse that carried Miss Kilmansegg,
And a better never lifted leg,
 Was a very rich bay, call'd Banker—

A horse of a breed and a mettle so rare,—
By Bullion out of an Ingot mare,—
That for action, the best of figures, and air,
    It made many good judges hanker.

And when she took a ride in the Park,
Equestrian Lord, or pedestrian Clerk,
    Was thrown in an amorous fever,
To see the Heiress how well she sat,
With her groom behind her, Bob or Nat,
In green, half smother'd with gold, and a hat
    With more gold lace than beaver.

And then when Banker obtain'd a pat,
To see how he arch'd his neck at that !
    He snorted with pride and pleasure !
Like the Steed in the fable so lofty and grand,
Who gave the poor Ass to understand,
That *he* didn't carry a bag of sand,
    But a burden of golden treasure.

A load of treasure?—alas ! alas !
Had her horse but been fed upon English grass,
    And shelter'd in Yorkshire spinneys,
Had he scour'd the sand with the Desert Ass,
    Or where the American whinnies—
But a hunter from Erin's turf and gorse,
A regular thorough-bred Irish horse,
Why, he ran away, as a matter of course,
    With a girl worth her weight in guineas !

Mayhap 'tis the trick of such pamper'd nags
To shy at the sight of a beggar in rags,—
    But away, like the bolt of a rabbit,—
Away went the horse in the madness of fright,
And away went the horsewoman mocking the sight—
Was yonder blue flash a flash of blue light,
    Or only the skirt of her habit ?

Away she flies, with the groom behind,—
It looks like a race of the Calmuck kind,
   When Hymen himself is the starter,
And the Maid rides first in the fourfooted strife,
Riding, striding, as if for her life,
While the Lover rides after to catch him a wife,
   Although it's catching a Tartar.

But the Groom has lost his glittering hat !
Though he does not sigh and pull up for that—
Alas ! his horse is a tit for Tat
   To sell to a very low bidder—
His wind is ruin'd, his shoulder is sprung,
Things, though a horse be handsome and young,
   A purchaser *will* consider.

But still flies the Heiress through stones and dust,
Oh, for a fall, if fall she must,
   On the gentle lap of Flora !
But still, thank Heaven ! she clings to her seat —
Away! away ! she could ride a dead heat
With the Dead who ride so fast and fleet,
   In the Ballad of Leonora !

Away she gallops,—it's awful work !
It's faster than Turpin's ride to York,
   On Bess that notable clipper !
She has circled the Ring !—she crosses the Park !
Mazeppa, although he was stripp'd so stark,
   Mazeppa couldn't outstrip her !

The fields seem running away with the folks !
The Elms are having a race for the Oaks
   At a pace that all Jockeys disparages !
All, all is racing ! the Serpentine
Seems rushing past like the "arrowy Rhine,"
The houses have got on a railway line,
   And are off like the first-class carriages !

She'll lose her life! she is losing her breath!
A cruel chase, she is chasing Death,
  As female shriekings forewarn her :
And now—as gratis as blood of Guelph—
She clears that gate, which has clear'd itself
  Since then, at Hyde Park Corner!

Alas! for the hope of the Kilmanseggs!
For her head, her brains, her body, and legs,
  Her life's not worth a copper!
      Willy-nilly,
      In Piccadilly,
  A hundred hearts turn sick and chilly,
  A hundred voices cry, "Stop her!"
And one old gentleman stares and stands,
Shakes his head and lifts his hands,
  And says, "How very improper!"

On and on!—what a perilous run!
The iron rails seem all mingling in one,
  To shut out the Green Park scenery!
And now the Cellar its dangers reveals,
She shudders—she shrieks—she's doom'd, she feels,
To be torn by powers of horses and wheels,
  Like a spinner by steam machinery!

Sick with horror she shuts her eyes,
But the very stones seem uttering cries,
  As they did to that Persian daughter,
When she climb'd up the steep vociferous hill,
Her little silver flagon to fill
  With the magical Golden Water!

"Batter her! shatter her!
  Throw and scatter her!"
Shouts each stony-hearted chatterer!
  "Dash at the heavy Dover!

Spill her! kill her! tear and tatter her!
Smash her! crash her!" (the stones didn't flatter her!)
"Kick her brains out! let her blood spatter her!
  Roll on her over and over!"

For so she gather'd the awful sense
Of the street in its past unmacadamized tense,
  As the wild horse overran it,—
His four heels making the clatter of six,
Like a Devil's tattoo, play'd with iron sticks
  On a kettle-drum of granite!

On! still on! she's dazzled with hints
Of oranges, ribbons, and colour'd prints,
A Kaleidoscope jumble of shapes and tints,
  And human faces all flashing,
Bright and brief as the sparks from the flints,
  That the desperate hoof keeps dashing!

On and on! still frightfully fast!
Dover-street, Bond-street, all are past!
But—yes—no—yes!—they're down at last!
  The Furies and Fates have found them!
Down they go with sparkle and crash,
Like a Bark that's struck by the lightning flash—
    There's a shriek—and a sob—
    And the dense dark mob
Like a billow closes around them!

"She breathes!"
"She don't!"
"She'll recover!"
"She won't!"

" She's stirring ! she's living, by Nemesis ! "
Gold, still gold ! on counter and shelf !
Golden dishes as plenty as delf ;
Miss Kilmansegg's coming again to herself
    On an opulent Goldsmith's premises !

Gold ! fine gold !—both yellow and red,
Beaten, and molten—polish'd, and dead—
To see the gold with profusion spread
    In all forms of its manufacture !
But what avails gold to Miss Kilmansegg,
When the femoral bone of her dexter leg
    Has met with a compound fracture ?

Gold may soothe Adversity's smart ;
Nay, help to bind up a broken heart ;
But to try it on any other part
    Were as certain a disappointment,
As if one should rub the dish and plate,
Taken out of a Staffordshire crate—
In the hope of a Golden Service of State—
    With Singleton's " Golden Ointment."

HER PRECIOUS LEG.

" As the twig is bent, the tree's inclined,"
Is an adage often recall'd to mind,
    Referring to juvenile bias :
And never so well is the verity seen,
As when to the weak, warp'd side we lean,
    While Life's tempests and hurricanes try us.

Even thus with Miss K. and her broken limb :
By a very, very remarkable whim,
    She show'd her early tuition :

While the buds of character came into blow
With a certain tinge that served to show
The nursery culture long ago,
   As the graft is known by fruition !

For the King's Physician, who nursed the case,
His verdict gave with an awful face,
   And three others concurr'd to egg it ;
That the Patient to give old Death the slip,
Like the Pope, instead of a personal trip,
   Must send her Leg as a Legate.

The limb was doom'd—it couldn't be saved !
And like other people the patient behaved,
Nay, bravely that cruel parting braved,
   Which makes some persons so falter,
They rather would part, without a groan,
With the flesh of their flesh, and bone of their bone,
   They obtain'd at St. George's altar.

But when it came to fitting the stump
With a proxy limb—then flatly and plump
   She spoke, in the spirit olden ;
She couldn't—she shouldn't—she wouldn't have wood
Nor a leg of cork, if she never stood,
And she swore an oath, or something as good,
   The proxy limb should be golden !

A wooden leg ! what, a sort of peg,
   For your common Jockeys and Jennies !
No, no, her mother might worry and plague—
Weep, go down on her knees, and beg,
But nothing would move Miss Kilmansegg !
She could—she would have a Golden Leg,
   If it cost ten thousand guineas !

Wood indeed, in Forest or Park,
With its sylvan honours and feudal bark,
  Is an aristocratic article :
But split and sawn, and hack'd about town,
Serving all needs of pauper or clown,
Trod on! stagger'd on! Wood cut down
  Is vulgar—fibre and particle.

And Cork!—when the noble Cork Tree shades
A lovely group of Castilian maids,
  'Tis a thing for a song or sonnet !—
But cork, as it stops the bottle of gin,
Or bungs the beer—the *small* beer—in,
It pierced her heart like a corking-pin,
  To think of standing upon it !

A Leg of Gold—solid gold throughout,'
Nothing else, whether slim or stout,
  Should ever support her, God willing !
She must—she could—she would have her whim,
Her father, she turn'd a deaf ear to him—
  He might kill her—she didn't mind killing!
He was welcome to cut off her other limb—
  He might cut her all off with a shilling !

All other promised gifts were in vain,
Golden Girdle, or Golden Chain,
She writhed with impatience more than pain.
  And utter'd "pshaws !" and "pishes !"
But a Leg of Gold as she lay in bed,
It danced before her—it ran in her head !
  It jump'd with her dearest wishes !

"Gold—gold—gold! Oh, let it be gold !"
Asleep or awake that tale she told,

And when she grew delirious:
Till her parents resolved to grant her wish,
If they melted down plate, and goblet, and dish,
  The case was getting so serious.

So a Leg was made in a comely mould,
Of Gold, fine virgin glittering gold,
  As solid as man could make it—
Solid in foot, and calf, and shank,
A prodigious sum of money it sank;
In fact 'twas a Branch of the family Bank,
  And no easy matter to break it.

All sterling metal—not half-and-half,
The Goldsmith's mark was stamp'd on the calf—
  'Twas pure as from Mexican barter!
And to make it more costly, just over the knee,
Where another ligature used to be,
Was a circle of jewels, worth shillings to see,
  A new-fangled Badge of the Garter!

'Twas a splendid, brilliant, beautiful Leg,
Fit for the Court of Scander-Beg,
That Precious Leg of Miss Kilmansegg!
  For, thanks to parental bounty,
Secure from Mortification's touch,
She stood on a Member that cost as much
  As a Member for all the County!

HER FAME.

To gratify stern ambition's whims,
What hundreds and thousands of precious limbs
  On a field of battle we scatter!

Sever'd by sword, or bullet, or saw,
Off they go, all bleeding and raw,—
But the public seems to get the lock-jaw
　So little is said on the matter!

Legs, the tightest that ever were seen,
The tightest, the lightest, that danced on the green,
　Cutting capers to sweet Kitty Clover;
Shatter'd, scatter'd, cut, and bowl'd down,
Off they go, worse off for renown,
A line in the *Times*, or a talk about town,
　Than the leg that a fly runs over!

But the Precious Leg of Miss Kilmansegg,
That gowden, goolden, golden leg,
　Was the theme of all conversation!
Had it been a Pillar of Church and State,
Or a prop to support the whole Dead Weight,
It could not have furnish'd more debate
　To the heads and tails of the nation!

East and west, and north and south,
Though useless for either hunger or drouth,—
The Leg was in everybody's mouth,
　To use a poetical figure,
Rumour, in taking her ravenous swim,
Saw, and seized on the tempting limb,
　Like a shark on the leg of a nigger.

Wilful murder fell very dead;
Debates in the House were hardly read;
In vain the Police Reports were fed
　With Irish riots and *rumpuses*—
The Leg! the Leg! was the great event,
Through every circle in life it went,
　Like the leg of a pair of compasses.

The last new Novel seem'd tame and flat,
The Leg, a novelty newer than that,
   Had tripp'd up the heels of Fiction !
It Burked the very essays of Burke,
And, alas ! how Wealth over Wit plays the Turk!
As a regular piece of goldsmith's work,
   Got the better of Goldsmith's diction.

"A leg of gold ! what of solid gold !"
Cried rich and poor, and young and old,—
   And Master and Miss and Madam—
'Twas the talk of 'Change—the Alley—the Bank-
And with men of scientific rank,
It made as much stir as the fossil shank
   Of a Lizard coeval with Adam !

Of course with Greenwich and Chelsea elves,
Men who had lost a limb themselves,
   Its interest did not dwindle—
But Bill, and Ben, and Jack, and Tom
Could hardly have spun more yarns therefrom.
   If the leg had been a spindle.

Meanwhile the story went to and fro,
Till, gathering like the ball of snow.
By the time it got to Stratford-le-Bow.
   Through Exaggeration's touches,
The Heiress and Hope of the Kilmanseggs
Was propp'd on *two* fine Golden Legs,
   And a pair of Golden Crutches !

Never had Leg so great a run !
'Twas the "go" and the "Kick" thrown into one !
The mode—the new thing under the sun,
   The rage—the fancy—the passion !
Bonnets were named, and hats were worn,

A la Golden Leg instead of Leghorn,
　　And stockings and shoes,
　　　　Of golden hues,
　　Took the lead in the walks of fashion!

The Golden Leg had a vast career,
It was sung and danced—and to show how near
　　Low folly to lofty approaches,
Down to society's very dregs,
The Belles of Wapping wore "Kilmanseggs,"
And St. Giles's Beaux sported Golden Legs
　　In their pinchbeck pins and brooches!

Her First Step.

SUPPOSING the Trunk and Limbs of Man
Shared, on the allegorical plan,
　　By the Passions that mark Humanity,
Whichever might claim the head, or heart,
The stomach, or any other part,
　　The Legs would be seized by Vanity.

There's Bardus, a six-foot column of fop,
A lighthouse without any light atop,
　　Whose height would attract beholders
If he had not lost some inches clear
By looking down at his kerseymere,
Ogling the limbs he holds so dear,
　　Till he got a stoop in his shoulders.

Talk of Art, of Science, or Books,
And down go the everlasting looks,
　　To his crural beauties so wedded!
Try him, wherever you will, you find
His mind in his legs, and his legs in his mind,
All prongs and folly—in short a kind
　　Of fork—that is fiddle-headed.

What wonder, then, if Miss Kilmansegg,
With a splendid, brilliant, beautiful leg,
Fit for the court of Scander-Beg,
Disdain'd to hide it like Joan or Meg,
  In petticoats stuff'd or quilted?
Not she ! 'twas her convalescent whim
To dazzle the world with her precious limb,—
  Nay, to go a little high-kilted.

So cards were sent for that sort of mob
Where Tartars and Africans hob-and-nob,
And the Cherokee talks of his cab and cob
  To Polish or Lapland lovers—
Cards like that hieroglyphical call
To a geographical Fancy Ball
  On the recent Post-Office covers.

For if Lion-hunters—and great ones too—
Would mob a savage from Latakoo,
Or squeeze for a glimpse of Prince Lee Boo,
  That unfortunate Sandwich scion—
Hundreds of first-rate people, no doubt,
Would gladly, madly, rush to a rout,
  That promised a Golden Lion !

. ———

HER FANCY BALL.

OF all the spirits of evil fame,
That hurt the soul or injure the frame,
  And poison what's honest and hearty,
There's none more needs a Matthew to preach
A cooling antiphlogistic speech,
    To praise and enforce
    A temperate course,
  Than the Evil Spirit of Party.

Go to the House of Commons, or Lords,
And they seem to be busy with simple words
   In their popular sense or pedantic—
But, alas ! with their cheers, and sneers, and jeers,
They're really busy, whatever appears,
Putting peas in each other's ears,
   To drive their enemies frantic !

Thus Tories like to worry the Whigs,
Who treat them in turn like Schwalbach pigs,
Giving them lashes, thrashes, and digs,
   With their writhing and pain delighted—
But after all that's said, and more,
The malice and spite of Party are poor
To the malice and spite of a party next door,
   To a party not invited.

On with the cap and out with the light,
Weariness bids the world good night,
   At least for the usual season ;
But hark ! a clatter of horses' heels !
And Sleep and Silence are broken on wheels,
   Like Wilful Murder and Treason !

Another crash—and the carriage goes—
Again poor Weariness seeks the repose
   That Nature demands, imperious ;
But Echo takes up the burden now,
With a rattling chorus of row-de-dow-dow,
Till Silence herself seems making a row,
   Like a Quaker gone delirious !

'Tis night—a winter night—and the stars
Are shining like winkin'—Venus and Mars
Are rolling along in their golden cars
   Through the sky's serene expansion—
But vainly the stars dispense their rays,
Venus and Mars are lost in the blaze
   Of the Kilmanseggs' luminous mansion !

Up jumps Fear in a terrible fright !
His bedchamber windows look so bright,—
  With light all the Square is glutted !
Up he jumps, like a sole from the pan,
And a tremor sickens his inward man,
For he feels as only a gentleman can,
  Who thinks he's being "gutted."

Again Fear settles, all snug and warm,
But only to dream of a dreadful storm
  From Autumn's sulphurous locker ;
But the only electrical body that falls,
Wears a negative coat, and positive smalls,
And draws the peal that so appals
  From the Kilmanseggs' brazen knocker !

'Tis Curiosity's Benefit night—
And perchance 'tis the English-Second-Sight,
  But whatever it be, so be it—
As the friends and guests of Miss Kilmansegg
Crowd in to look at her Golden Leg,
    As many more
    Mob round the door,
  To see them going to see it !

In they go—in jackets, and cloaks,
Plumes, and bonnets, turbans, and toques,
  As if to a Congress of Nations :
Greeks and Malays, with daggers and dirks,
Spaniards, Jews, Chinese, and Turks—
Some like original foreign works,
  But mostly like bad translations.

In they go, and to work like a pack,
Juan, Moses, and Shacabac—
Tom, and Jerry, and Springheel'd Jack,—
  For some of low Fancy are lovers—

Skirting, zigzagging, casting about,
Here and there, and in and out,
With a crush, and a rush, for a full-bodied rout
　　In one of the stiffest of covers.

In they went, and hunted about,
Open-mouth'd like chub and trout,
And some with the upper lip thrust out,
　　Like that fish for routing, a barbel—
While Sir Jacob stood to welcome the crowd,
And rubb'd his hands, and smiled aloud,
And bow'd, and bow'd, and bow'd, and bow'd,
　　Like a man who is sawing marble.

For Princes were there, and Noble Peers ;
Dukes descended from Norman spears ;
Earls that dated from early years ;
　　And Lords in vast variety—
Besides the Gentry both new and old—
For people who stand on legs of gold,
　　Are sure to stand well with society.

"But where—where—where?" with one accord
Cried Moses and Mufti, Jack and my Lord,
　　Wang-Fong and Il Bondocani—
When slow, and heavy, and dead as a dump,
　　They heard a foot begin to stump,
　　　　Thump ! lump !
　　　　Lump ! thump !
　　Like the Spectre in "Don Giovanni !"

And lo ! the Heiress, Miss Kilmansegg,
With her splendid, brilliant, beautiful leg,
　　In the garb of a Goddess olden—
Like chaste Diana going to hunt,
With a golden spear—which of course was blunt,
And a tunic loop'd up to a gem in front,
　　To show the Leg that was Golden !

Gold ! still gold ; her Crescent behold,
That should be silver, but would be gold ;
   And her robe's auriferous spangles !
Her golden stomacher—how she would melt !
Her golden quiver, and golden belt,
   Where a golden bugle dangles !

And her jewell'd Garter ! Oh, Sin, oh, Shame !
Let Pride and Vanity bear the blame,
That bring such blots on female fame !
   But to be a true recorder,
Besides its thin transparent stuff,
The tunic was loop'd quite high enough
   To give a glimpse of the Order !

But what have sin or shame to do
With a Golden Leg—and a stout one too ?
   Away with all Prudery's panics !
That the precious metal, by thick and thin,
Will cover square acres of land or sin,
     Is a fact made plain
     Again and again,
  In Morals as well as Mechanics.

A few, indeed, of her proper sex,
Who seem'd to feel her foot on their necks,
And fear'd their charms would meet with checks
   From so rare and splendid a blazon—
A few cried "fie !"—and "forward "—and "bold !"
And said of the Leg it might be gold,
   But to them it look'd like brazen !

'Twas hard they hinted for flesh and blood,
Virtue and Beauty, and all that's good,
   To strike to mere dross their topgallants—
But what were Beauty, or Virtue, or Worth,
Gentle manners, or gentle birth,
Nay, what the most talented head on earth
   To a Leg worth fifty Talents !

But the men sang quite another hymn
Of glory and praise to the precious Limb—
Age, sordid Age, admired the whim,
   And its indecorum pardon'd—
While half of the young—ay, more than half—
Bow'd down and worshipp'd the Golden Calf,
   Like the Jews when their hearts were harden'd.

A Golden Leg !—what fancies it fired !
What golden wishes and hopes inspired !
   To give but a mere abridgment—
What a leg to leg-bail Embarrassment's serf
What a leg for a Leg to take on the turf !
   What a leg for a marching regiment !

A golden Leg !—whatever Love sings,
'Twas worth a bushel of " Plain Gold Rings "
   With which the Romantic wheedles.
'Twas worth all the legs in stockings and socks—
'Twas a leg that might be put in the Stocks,
   N.B.—Not the parish beadle's !

And Lady K. nid-nodded her head,
Lapp'd in a turban fancy-bred,
Just like a love-apple, huge and red,
   Some Mussul-womanish mystery ;
     But whatever she meant
       To represent,
   She talk'd like the Muse of History.

She told how the filial leg was lost ;
And then how much the gold one cost,
   With its weight to a Trojan fraction:
And how it took off, and how it put on ;
And call'd on Devil, Duke, and Don,
Mahomet, Moses, and Prester John,
   To notice its beautiful action.

And then of the Leg she went in quest ;
And led it where the light was best ;
And made it lay itself up to rest
   In postures for painter's studies .
It cost more tricks and trouble by half,
Than it takes to exhibit a six-legg'd Calf
   To a boothful of country Cuddies.

Nor yet did the Heiress herself omit
The arts that help to make a hit,
   And preserve a prominent station,
She talk'd and laugh'd far more than her share ;
And took a part in "Rich and Rare
Were the gems she wore"—and the gems were there
   Like a Song with an Illustration.

She even stood up with a Count of France
To dance—alas !—the measures we dance
   When Vanity plays the Piper !
Vanity, Vanity, apt to betray,
And lead all sorts of legs astray,
Wood, or metal, or human clay,—
   Since Satan first play'd the Viper !

But first she doff'd her hunting gear,
And favour'd Tom Tug with her golden spear
   To row with down the river—
A Bonze had her golden bow to hold ;
A Hermit her belt and bugle of gold ;
   And an Abbot her golden quiver.

And then a space was clear'd on the floor,
And she walk'd the Minuet de la Cour,
With all the pomp of a Pompadour,
   But although she began *andante*,
Conceive the faces of all the Rout,
When she finished off with a whirligig bout,
And the Precious Leg stuck stiffly out
   Like the leg of a *Figurante.*

So the courtly dance was goldenly done,
And golden opinions, of course, it won
From all different sorts of people—
Chiming, ding-dong, with flattering phrase,
In one vociferous peal of praise,
Like the peal that rings on Royal days
From Loyalty's parish-steeple.

And yet, had the leg been one of those
That danced for bread in flesh-colour'd hose,
With Rosina's pastoral bevy,
The jeers it had met,—the shouts! the scoff!
The cutting advice to "take itself off,"
For sounding but half so heavy.

Had it been a leg like those, perchance,
That teach little girls and boys to dance,
To set, poussette, recede, and advance,
With the steps and figures most proper,—
Had it hopp'd for a weekly or quarterly sum,
How little of praise or grist would have come
To a mill with such a hopper!

But the Leg was none of those limbs forlorn—
Bartering capers and hops for corn—
That meet with public hisses and scorn,
Or the morning journal denounces—
Had it pleased to caper from morn till dusk,
There was all the music of "Money Musk"
In its ponderous bangs and bounces.

But hark ;—as slow as the strokes of a pump,
Lump, thump!
Thump, lump!
As the Giant of Castle Otranto might stump,
To a lower room from an upper—

Down she goes with a noisy dint,
For taking the crimson turban's hint,
A noble Lord at the Head of the Mint
  Is leading the Leg to supper!

But the supper, alas! must rest untold,
With its blaze of light and its glitter of gold,
  For to paint that scene of glamour,
It would need the Great Enchanter's charm,
Who waves over Palace, and Cot, and Farm.
An arm like the Goldbeater's Golden Arm
  That wields a Golden Hammer.

He—only He—could fitly state
The Massive Service of Golden Plate,
  With the proper phrase and expansion—
The Rare Selection of Foreign Wines—
The Alps of Ice and Mountains of Pines,
The punch in Oceans and sugary shrines,
The Temple of Taste from Gunter's Designs—
In short, all that Wealth with A Feast combines,
  In a Splendid Family Mansion.

Suffice it each mask'd outlandish guest
Ate and drank of the very best,
  According to critical conners—
And then they pledged the Hostess and Host,
But the Golden Leg was the standing toast,
    And as somebody swore,
    Walk'd off with more
Than its share of the " Hips !" and honours!

    " Miss Kilmansegg !—
    Full glasses I beg !—
Miss Kilmansegg and her Precious Leg !"
  And away went the bottle careering !

K

Wine in bumpers ! and shouts in peals !
Till the clown didn't know his head from his heels
The Mussulman's eyes danced two-some reels,
 And the Quaker was hoarse with cheering !

HER DREAM.

MISS KILMANSEGG took off her leg,
And laid it down like a cribbage-peg,
 For the Rout was done and the riot :
The Square was hush'd ; not a sound was heard ;
The sky was gray, and no creature stirr'd,
Except one little precocious bird,
 That chirp'd—and then was quiet.

So still without,—so still within ;—
 It had been a sin
 To drop a pin—
So intense is silence after a din,
 It seem'd like Death's rehearsal !
To stir the air no eddy came ;
And the taper burnt with as still a flame,
As to flicker had been a burning shame,
 In a calm so universal.

The time for sleep had come at last ;
And there was the bed, so soft, so vast,
 Quite a field of Bedfordshire clover ;
Softer, cooler, and calmer, no doubt,
From the piece of work just ravell'd out,
For one of the pleasures of having a rout
 Is the pleasure of having it over.

No sordid pallet, or truckle mean,
Of straw, and rug, and tatters unclean ;

But a splendid, gilded, carved machine,
   That was fit for a Royal Chamber.
On the top was a gorgeous golden wreath ;
And the damask curtains hung beneath,
   Like clouds of crimson and amber ;

Curtains, held up by two little plump things,
With golden bodies and golden wings,—
   Mere fins for such solidities—
      Two Cupids, in short,
      Of the regular sort,
But the housemaid call'd them "Cupidities."

No patchwork quilt, all seams and scars,
But velvet, powder'd with golden stars,
   A fit mantle for *Night*-Commanders !
And the pillow, as white as snow undimm'd
And as cool as the pool that the breeze has skimm'd,
Was cased in the finest cambric, and trimm'd
   With the costliest lace of Flanders.

And the bed—of the Eider's softest down,
'Twas a place to revel, to smother, to drown
   In a bliss inferr'd by the Poet ;
For if Ignorance be indeed a bliss,
What blessed ignorance equals this,
   To sleep—and not to know it ?

Oh, bed ! oh, bed ! delicious bed !
That heaven upon earth to the weary head ;
But a place that to name would be ill-bred,
   To the head with a wakeful trouble—
Tis held by such a different lease !
To one, a place of comfort and peace,
All stuff'd with the down of stubble geese,
   To another with only the stubble !

To one, a perfect Halcyon nest,
All calm, and balm and quiet, and rest,
    And soft as the fur of the cony—
To another, so restless for body and head,
That the bed seems borrow'd from Nettlebed,
    And the pillow from Stratford the Stony !

To the happy, a first-class carriage of ease,
To the Land of Nod, or where you please ;
    But alas ! for the watchers and weepers,
Who turn, and turn, and turn again,
But turn, and turn, and turn in vain,
        With an anxious brain,
        And thoughts in a train,
    That does not run upon *sleepers !*

Wide awake as the mousing owl,
Night-hawk, or other nocturnal fowl,—
    But more profitless vigils keeping,—
Wide awake in the dark they stare,
Filling with phantoms the vacant air,
As if that Crook-back'd Tyrant Care
    Had plotted to kill them sleeping.

And oh ! when the blessed diurnal light
Is quench'd by the providential night,
    To render our slumber more certain !
Pity, pity the wretches that weep,
For they must be wretched, who cannot sleep
    When God himself draws the curtain !

The careful Betty the pillow beats,
And airs the blankets, and smooths the sheets,
    And gives the mattress a shaking—
But vainly Betty performs her part,
If a ruffled head and a rumpled heart,
    As well as the couch, want making.

There's Morbid, all bile, and verjuice, and nerves,
Where other people would make preserves,
   He turns his fruits into pickles :
Jealous, envious, and fretful by day,
At night, to his own sharp fancies a prey,
He lies like a hedgehog roll'd up the wrong way,
   Tormenting himself with his prickles.

But a child—that bids the world good night,
In downright earnest and cuts it quite—
   A Cherub no Art can copy,—
'Tis a perfect picture to see him lie
As if he had supp'd on a dormouse pie,
(An ancient classical dish, by the by)
   With a sauce of syrup of poppy.

Oh, bed ! bed ! bed ! delicious bed !
That heaven upon earth to the weary head,
   Whether lofty or low its condition !
But instead of putting our plagues on shelves,
In our blankets how often we toss ourselves,
Or are toss'd by such allegorical elves
   As Pride, Hate, Greed, and Ambition !

The independent Miss Kilmansegg
Took off her independent Leg
   And laid it beneath her pillow,
And then on the bed her frame she cast,
The time for repose had come at last,
But long, long, after the storm is past
   Rolls the turbid, turbulent billow.

No part she had in vulgar cares
That belong to common household affairs —
Nocturnal annoyances such as theirs,
   Who lie with a shrewd surmising,
That while they are couchant (a bitter cup !)
Their bread and butter are getting up,
   And the coals, confound them, are rising.

No fear she had her sleep to postpone,
Like the crippled Widow who weeps alone
And cannot make a doze her own,
　　For the dread that mayhap on the morrow,
The true and Christian reading to baulk,
A broker will take up her bed and walk
　　By way of curing her sorrow.

No cause like these she had to bewail,
But the breath of applause had blown a gale,
And winds from that quarter seldom fail
　　To cause some human commotion ;
But whenever such breezes coincide
　　　　With the very spring-tide
　　　　Of human pride,
　　There's no such swell on the ocean !

Peace, and ease, and slumber lost,
She turn'd, and roll'd, and tumbled and toss'd
　　With a tumult that would not settle :
A common case, indeed, with such
As have too little, or think too much,
　　Of the precious and glittering metal.

Gold !—she saw at her golden foot
The Peer whose tree had an olden root,
The Proud, the Great, the Learned to boot,
　　The handsome, the gay, and the witty—
The Man of Science—of Arms—of Art,
The man who deals but at Pleasure's mart,
　　And the man who deals in the City.

Gold, still gold—and true to the mould !
In the very scheme of her dream it told ;
　　For, by magical transmutation,
From her Leg through her body it seem'd to go,
Till, gold above, and gold below,
She was gold, all gold, from her little gold toe
　　To her organ of Veneration !

And still she retain'd through Fancy's art,
The Golden Bow, and Golden Dart,
With which she had play'd a Goddess's part
   In her recent glorification :
And still, like one of the self-same brood,
On a Plinth of the self-same metal she stood
   For the whole world's adoration.

And hymns and incense around her roll'd,
From Golden Harps and Censers of Gold, –
For Fancy in dreams is as uncontroll'd
   As a horse without a bridle :
What wonder, then, from all checks exempt,
If, inspired by the Golden Leg, she dreamt
   She was turn'd to a Golden Idol?

HER COURTSHIP.

WHEN leaving Eden's happy land
The grieving Angel led by the hand
   Our banish'd Father and Mother,
Forgotten amid their awful doom,
The tears, the fears, and the future's gloom,
On each brow was a wreath of Paradise bloom,
   That our Parents had twined for each other.

It was only while sitting like figures of stone,
For the grieving Angel had skyward flown,
As they sat, those Two in the world alone,
   With disconsolate hearts nigh cloven,
That scenting the gust of happier hours,
They look'd around for the precious flow'rs,
And lo !—a last relic of Eden's dear bow'rs—
   The chaplet that Love had woven !

And still, when a pair of Lovers meet,
There's a sweetness in air, unearthly sweet,
That savours still of that happy retreat
    Where Eve by Adam was courted :
Whilst the joyous Thrush, and the gentle Dove,
Woo'd their mates in the boughs above,
    And the Serpent, as yet, only sported.

Who hath not felt that breath in the air,
A perfume and freshness strange and rare,
A warmth in the light, and a bliss everywhere,
    When young hearts yearn together ?
All sweets below, and all sunny above,
Oh ! there's nothing in life like making love,
    Save making hay in fine weather !

Who hath not found amongst his flow'rs
A blossom too bright for this world of ours,
    Like a rose among snows of Sweden ?
But to turn again to Miss Kilmansegg.
Where must Love have gone to beg,
If such a thing as a Golden Leg
    Had put its foot in Eden !

And yet—to tell the rigid truth—
Her favour was sought by Age and Youth—
    For the prey will find a prowler !
She was follow'd, flatter'd, courted, address'd,
Woo'd, and coo'd, and wheedled, and press'd,
By suitors from North, South, East, and West,
    Like that Heiress, in song, Tibbie Fowler !

But, alas ! alas ! for the Woman's fate,
Who has from a mob to choose a mate !
    'Tis a strange and painful mystery !
But the more the eggs, the worse the hatch ;
The more the fish, the worse the catch ;
The more the sparks, the worse the match ;
    Is a fact in Woman's history.

Give her between a brace to pick,
And mayhap, with luck to help the trick,
She will take the Faustus, and leave the Old Nick—
    But her future bliss to baffle,
Amongst a score let her have a voice,
And she'll have as little cause to rejoice,
As if she had won the " Man of her choice '
    In a matrimonial raffle !

Thus, even thus, with the Heiress and Hope,
Fulfilling the adage of too much rope,
    With so ample a competition,
She chose the least worthy of all the group,
Just as the vulture makes a stoop,
And singles out from the herd or troop
    The beast of the worst condition.

A Foreign Count—who came incog.,
Not under a cloud, but under a fog,
    In a Calais packet's fore-cabin,
To charm some lady British-born,
With his eyes as black as the fruit of the thorn,
And his hooky nose, and his beard half-shorn,
    Like a half-converted Rabbin.

And because the Sex confess a charm
In the man who has slash'd a head or arm,
    Or has been a throat's undoing,
He was dress'd like one of the glorious trade,
At least when Glory is off parade,
With a stock, and a frock, well trimm'd with braid,
    And frogs—that went a-wooing.

Moreover, as Counts are apt to do,
On the left-hand side of his dark surtout,
At one of those holes that buttons go through,
    (To be a precise recorder,)

A ribbon he wore, or rather a scrap,
About an inch of ribbon mayhap,
That one of his rivals, whimsical chap,
    Described as his " Retail Order."

And then—and much it help'd his chance—
He could sing, and play first fiddle, and dance,
Perform charades, and Proverbs of France—
    Act the tender, and do the cruel ;
For amongst his other killing part,
He had broken a brace of female hearts,
    And murder'd three men in duel !

Savage at heart, and false of tongue,
Subtle with age, and smooth to the young,
    Like a snake in his coiling and curling—
Such was the Count—to give him a niche—
Who came to court that Heiress rich,
And knelt at her foot—one needn't say which—
    Besieging her castle of *Sterling*.

With pray'rs and vows he open'd his trench,
And plied her with English, Spanish, and French,
    In phrases the most sentimental :
And quoted poems in High and Low Dutch,
With now and then an Italian touch,
Till she yielded, without resisting much,
    To homage so continental.

And then—the sordid bargain to close—
With a miniature sketch of his hooky nose,
And his dear dark eyes, as black as sloes,
And his beard and whiskers as black as those,
    The lady's consent he requited—
And instead of the lock that lovers beg,
The count received from Miss Kilmansegg
A model, in small, of her Precious leg—
    And so the couple were plighted !

But, oh ! the love that gold must crown !
Better—better, the love of the clown,
Who admires his lass in her Sunday gown,
   As if all the fairies had dress'd her !
Whose brain to no crooked thought gives birth,
Except that he never will part on earth
   With his true love's crooked tester !

Alas ! for the love that's linked with gold !
Better—better a thousand times told—
   More honest, happy, and laudable,
The downright loving of pretty Cis,
Who wipes her lips, though there's nothing amiss,
And takes a kiss, and gives a kiss,
   In which her heart is audible !

Pretty Cis, so smiling and bright,
Who loves—as she labours—with all her might,
   And without any sordid leaven !
Who blushes as red as haws and hips,
Down to her very finger-tips,
For Roger's blue ribbons—to her, like strips
   Cut out of the azure of Heaven !

HER MARRIAGE.

'TWAS morn—a most auspicious one !
From the Golden East, the Golden Sun
Came forth his glorious race to run,
   Through clouds of most splendid tinges ;
Clouds that lately slept in shade,
    But now seem'd made
    Of gold brocade,
  With magnificent golden fringes.

Gold above, and gold below,
The earth reflected the golden glow,
    From river, and hill, and valley
Gilt by the golden light of morn,
The Thames—it look'd like the Golden Horn,
And the Barge, that carried coal or corn,
        Like Cleopatra's Galley !

Bright as clusters of Golden-rod,
Suburban poplars began to nod,
    With extempore splendour furnish'd ;
While London was bright with glittering clocks,
Golden dragons, and Golden cocks,
        And above them all,
        The dome of St. Paul,
With its Golden Cross and its Golden Ball,
    Shone out as if newly burnish'd !

And lo ! for Golden Hours and Joys,
Troops of glittering Golden Boys
Danced along with a jocund noise,
    And their gilded emblems carried !
In short, 'twas the year's most Golden Day,
By mortals call'd the First of May,
        When Miss Kilmansegg,
        Of the Golden Leg,
    With a Golden Ring was married !

And thousands of children, women, and men,
Counted the clock from eight till ten.
    From St. James's sonorous steeple ;
For next to that interesting job,
The hanging of Jack, or Bill, or Bob,
There's nothing so draws a London mob
    As the noosing of very rich people.

And a treat it was for the mob to behold
The Bridal Carriage that blazed with gold !

And the Footman tall and the Coachman bold,
   In liveries so resplendent—
Coats you wonder'd to see in place,
They seem'd so rich with golden lace,
   That they might have been independent.

Coats, that made those menials proud
Gaze with scorn on the dingy crowd,
   From their gilded elevations:
Not to forget that saucy lad
(Ostentation's favourite cad),
The Page, who look'd so splendidly clad,
   Like a Page of the " Wealth of Nations."

But the Coachman carried off the state,
With what was a Lancashire body of late
   Turn'd into a Dresden Figure ;
With a bridal Nosegay of early bloom,
About the size of a birchen broom,
And so huge a White Favour, had Gog been Groom,
   He need not have worn a bigger.

And then to see the Groom ! the Count !
With Foreign Orders to such an amount,
   And whiskers so wild—nay, bestial ;
He seem'd to have borrow'd the shaggy hair
As well as the Stars of the Polar Bear,
   To make him look celestial !

And then—Great Jove !—the struggle, the crush,
The screams, the heaving, the awful rush,
   The swearing, the tearing, and fighting,—
The hats and bonnets smash'd like an egg—
To catch a glimpse of the Golden Leg,
Which between the steps and Miss Kilmansegg
   Was fully display'd in alighting !

From the Golden Ankle up to the Knee
There it was for the mob to see !
A shocking act had it chanced to be
  A crooked leg or a skinny:
But although a magnificent veil she wore,
Such as never was seen before,
In case of blushes, she blush'd no more
  Than George the First on a guinea !

Another step, and lo ! she was launched !
All in white, as Brides are *blanched*
  With a wreath of most wonderful splendour—
Diamonds, and pearls, so rich in device,
That, according to calculation nice,
Her head was worth as royal a price,
  As the head of the Young Pretender.

Bravely she shone—and shone the more
As she sail'd through the crowd of squalid and poor,
  Thief, beggar, and tatterdemalion—
Led by the Count, with his sloe-black eyes
Bright with triumph, and some surprise,
Like Anson on making sure of his prize
  The famous Mexican Galleon !

Anon came Lady K., with her face
Quite made up to act with grace,
  But she cut the performance shorter ;
For instead of pacing stately and stiff,
At the stare of the vulgar she took a miff,
And ran, full speed, into Church, as if
  To get married before her daughter.

But Sir Jacob walk'd more slowly, and bow'd
Right and left to the gaping crowd,
  Wherever a glance was seizable :

For Sir Jacob thought he bow'd like a Guelph,
And therefore bow'd to imp and elf,
And would gladly have made a bow to himself,
  Had such a bow been feasible.

And last—and not the least of the sight,
Six "Handsome Fortunes," all in white,
Came to help in the marriage rite,—
  And rehearse their own hymeneals ;
And then the bright procession to close,
They were followed by just as many Beaux
  Quite fine enough for Ideals.

Glittering men, and splendid dames,
Thus they enter'd the porch of St. James'.
  Pursued by a thunder of laughter ;
For the Beadle was forced to intervene,
For Jim the Crow, and his Mayday Queen,
With her gilded ladle, and Jack i' the Green,
  Would fain have follow'd after !

Beadle-like he hush'd the shout ;
But the temple was full "inside and out,"
And a buzz kept buzzing all round about
  Like bees when the day is sunny—
A buzz universal, that interfered
With the right that ought to have been revered.
As if the couple already were smear'd
  With Wedlock's treacle and honey!

Yet Wedlock's a very awful thing !
'Tis something like that feat in the ring,
  Which requires good nerve to do it—
When one of a "Grand Equestrian Troop"
Makes a jump at a gilded hoop,
    Not certain at all
    Of what may befall
After his getting through it !

But the count he felt the nervous work
No more than any polygamous Turk,
  Or bold piratical skipper,
Who, during his buccaneering search,
Would as soon engage a hand in church
  As a hand on board his clipper !

And how did the Bride perform her part?
Like any bride who is cold at heart,
  Mere snow with the ice's glitter ;
What but a life of winter for her !
Bright but chilly, alive without stir,
So splendidly comfortless,—just like a Fir
  When the frost is severe and bitter.

Such were the future man and wife !
Whose bale or bliss to the end of life
  A few short words were to settle—
    "Wilt thou have this woman?"
      "I will"—and then,
    "Wilt thou have this man?"
      "I will," and "Amen"—
And those Two were one Flesh, in the Angels' ken,
  Except one Leg—that was metal.

Then the names were sign'd—and kiss'd the kiss :
And the Bride, who came from her coach a Miss,
  As a Countess walk'd to her carriage—
Whilst Hymen preen'd his plumes like a dove,
And Cupid flutter'd his wings above,
In the shape of a fly—as little a Love
  As ever look'd in at a marriage !

Another crash—and away they dash'd,
And the gilded carriage and footman flash'd
  From the eyes of the gaping people—

Who turn'd to gaze at the toe-and-heel
Of the Golden Boys beginning a reel,
To the merry sound of a wedding-peal
   From St. James's musical steeple.

Those wedding-bells ! those wedding-bells !
How sweetly they sound in pastoral dells
   From a tow'r in an ivy-green jacket !
But town-made joys how dearly they cost ;
And after all are tumbled and tost,
Like a peal from a London steeple, and lost
   In town-made riot and racket.

The wedding-peal, how sweetly it peals
With grass or heather beneath our heels,—
   For bells are Music's laughter !—
But a London peal, well mingled, be sure,
With vulgar noises and voices impure, —
What a harsh and discordant overture
   To the Harmony meant to come after !

But hence with Discord—perchance, too soon
To cloud the face of the honeymoon
   With a dismal occultation!—
Whatever Fate's concerted trick,
The Countess and Count, at the present nick,
Have a chicken, and not a crow, to pick
   At a sumptuous Cold Collation.

A Breakfast—no unsubstantial mess,
But one in the style of Good Queen Bess,
   Who,—hearty as hippocampus,—
Broke her fast with ale and beef,
Instead of toast and the Chinese leaf,
   And—in lieu of anchovy—grampus.

A breakfast of fowl, and fish, and flesh,
Whatever was sweet, or salt, or fresh ;
    With wines the most rare and curious—
Wines, of the richest flavour and hue ;
With fruits from the worlds both Old and New ;
And fruits obtain'd before they were due
    At a discount most usurious.

For wealthy palates there be, that scout
What is *in* season, for what is *out,*
    And prefer all precocious savour :
For instance, early green peas, of the sort
That costs some four or five guineas a quart ;
    Where the *Mint* is the principal flavour.

And many a wealthy man was there,
Such as the wealthy City could spare,
    To put in a portly appearance—
Men, whom their father's had help'd to gild :
And men, who had had their fortunes to build,
And—much to their credit—had richly fill'd
    Their purses by *pursy-verance.*

Men, by popular rumour at least,
Not the last to enjoy a feast !
    And truly they were not idle !
Luckier far than the chestnut tits,
Which, down at the door, stood champing their bits,
    At a different sort of bridle.

For the time was come—and the whisker'd Count
Help'd his Bride in the carriage to mount,
    And fain would the Muse deny it,
But the crowd, including two butchers in blue,
(The regular killing Whitechapel hue,)
Of her Precious Calf had as ample a view
    As if they had come to buy it !

Then away ! away ! with all the speed
That golden spurs can give to the steed,—
Both Yellow Boys and Guineas, indeed,
   Concurr'd to urge the cattle—
Away they went, with favours white,
Yellow jackets, and panels bright,
And left the mob, like a mob at night,
   Agape at the sound of a rattle.

Away ! away ! they rattled and roll'd,
The Count, and his Bride, and her Leg of Gold—
   That faded charm to the charmer !
Away, through old Brentford rang the din,
Of wheels and heels, on their way to win
That hill, named after one of her kin,
   The Hill of the Golden Farmer !

Gold, still gold—it flew like dust !
It tipp'd the post-boy, and paid the trust ;
In each open palm it was freely thrust ;
   There was nothing but giving and taking !
And if gold could ensure the future hour,
What hopes attended that Bride to her bow'r,
But alas ! even hearts with a four-horse pow'r
   Of opulence end in breaking !

HER HONEYMOON.

THE moon—the moon, so silver and cold,
Her fickle temper has oft been told,
   Now shady—now bright and sunny—
But of all the lunar things that change,
The one that shows most fickle and strange,
And takes the most eccentric range
   Is the moon—so call'd—of honey !

To some a full-grown orb reveal'd,
As big and as round as Norval's shield,
    And as bright as a burner Bude-lighted ;
To others as dull, and dingy, and damp,
As any oleaginous lamp,
Of the regular old parochial stamp,
    In a London fog benighted.

To the loving, a bright and constant sphere,
That makes earth's commonest things appear
    All poetic, romantic, and tender :
Hanging with jewels a cabbage-stump,
And investing a common post, or a pump,
A currant-bush or a gooseberry-clump,
    With a halo of dreamlike splendour.

A sphere such as shone from Italian skies,
In Juliet's dear, dark liquid eyes,
    Tipping trees, with its argent braveries—
And to couples not favour'd with Fortune's boons
One of the most delightful of moons,
For it brightens their pewter platters and spoons
    Like a silver service of Savory's !

For all is bright, and beauteous, and clear,
And the meanest thing most precious and dear
    When the magic of love is present :
Love, that lends a sweetness and grace,
To the humblest spot and the plainest face—
That turns Wilderness Row into Paradise Place,
    And Garlick Hill to Mount Pleasant !

Love that sweetens sugarless tea,
And makes contentment and joy agree
    With the coarsest boarding and bedding :
Love, that no golden ties can attach,

But nestles under the humblest thatch,
And will fly away from an Emperor's match
  To dance at a Penny Wedding !

Oh, happy, happy, thrice happy state,
When such a bright Planet governs the fate
  Of a pair of united lovers !
'Tis theirs, in spite of the Serpent's hiss,
To enjoy the pure primeval kiss,
With as much of the old original bliss
  As mortality ever recovers !

Their's strength in double joints, no doubt,
In double X Ale, and Dublin Stout,
That the single sorts know nothing about—
  And the fist is strongest when doubled—
And double aqua-fortis of course,
And double soda-water, perforce,
  Are the strongest that ever bubbled !

There's double beauty whenever a Swan
Swims on a Lake with her double thereon ;
And ask the gardener, Luke or John,
  Of the beauty of double-blowing—
A double dahlia delights the eye ;
And it's far the loveliest sight in the sky
  When a double rainbow is glowing !

There's warmth in a pair of double soles ;
As well as a double allowance of coals—
  In a coat that is double-breasted—
In double windows and double doors ;
And a double U wind is blest by scores
  For its warmth to the tender-chested.

There's a twofold sweetness in double pipes ;
And a double barrel and double snipes

Give the sportsman a duplicate pleasure :
There's double safety in double locks ;
And double letters bring cash for the box ;
And all the world knows that double knocks
　　Are gentility's double measure.

There's double sweetness in double rhymes,
And a double at Whist and a double Times
　　In profit are certainly double—
By doubling, the Hare contrives to escape ;
And all seamen delight in a doubled Cape,
　　And a double-reef'd topsail in trouble.

There's a double chuck at a double chin,
And of course there's a double pleasure therein,
　　If the parties were brought to telling :
And however our Dennises take offence,
A double meaning shows double sense ;
　　　　And if proverbs tell truth,
　　　　A double tooth
　　Is Wisdom's adopted dwelling !

But double wisdom, and pleasure, and sense,
Beauty, respect, strength, comfort and thence
　　Through whatever the list discovers,
They are all in the double blessedness summ'd,
Of what was formerly double-drumm'd,
　　The Marriage of two true Lovers !

Now the Kilmansegg Moon, it must be told—
Though instead of silver it tipp'd with gold—
Shone rather wan, and distant, and cold,
　　And before its days were at thirty,
Such gloomy clouds began to collect,
With an ominous ring of ill effect,
As gave but too much cause to expect
　　Such weather as seamen call dirty !

And yet the moon was the "Young May Moon,"
And the scented hawthorn had blossom'd soon,
   And the thrush and the blackbird were singing—
The snow-white lambs were skipping in play,
And the bee was humming a tune all day
To flowers, as welcome as flowers in May,
   And the trout in the stream was springing!

But what were the hues of the blooming earth,
Its scents—its sounds—or the music and mirth
   Of its furr'd or its feather'd creatures,
To a Pair in the world's last sordid stage,
Who had never look'd into Nature's page,
And had strange ideas of a Golden Age,
   Without any Arcadian features?

And what were joys of the pastoral kind
To a Bride—town-made—with a heart and a mind
   With simplicity ever at battle?
A bride of an ostentatious race,
Who, thrown in the Golden Farmer's place,
Would have trimm'd her shepherds with golden lace,
   And gilt the horns of her cattle.

She could not please the pigs with her whim,
And the sheep wouldn't cast their eyes at a limb
   For which she had been such a martyr:
The deer in the park, and the colts at grass,
And the cows unheeded let it pass;
And the ass on the common was such an ass,
    That he wouldn't have swapp'd
    The thistle he cropp'd
For her Leg, including the Garter!

She hated lanes and she hated fields—
She hated all that the country yields—

And barely knew turnips from clover ;
She hated walking in any shape,
And a country stile was an awkward scrape,
Without the bribe of a mob to gape
      At the Leg in clambering over !

O blessed nature, "O rus ! O rus !"
Who cannot sigh for the country thus,
      Absorb'd in a worldly torpor—
Who does not yearn for its meadow-sweet breath,
Untainted by care, and crime, and death,
And to stand sometimes upon grass or heath—
      That soul, spite of gold, is a pauper !

But to hail the pearly advent of morn,
And relish the odour fresh from the thorn,
      She was far too pamper'd a madam,
Or to joy in the daylight waxing strong,
While, after ages of sorrow and wrong,
The scorn of the proud, the misrule of the strong,
And all the woes that to man belong,
The Lark still carols the self-same song
      That he did to the uncurst Adam !

The Lark ! she had given all Leipsic's flocks
For a Vauxhall tune in a musical box ;
      And as for the birds in the thicket,
Thrush or ousel in leafy niche,
The linnet or finch, she was far too rich
To care for a Morning Concert, to which
      She was welcome without any ticket.

Gold, still gold, her standard of old,
All pastoral joys were tried by gold,
      Or by fancies golden and crural—
Till ere she had pass'd one week unblest,

As her agricultural Uncle's guest,
Her mind was made up, and fully imprest,
  That felicity could not be rural !

And the Count ?—to the snow-white lambs at play
And all the scents and the sights of May,
  And the birds that warbled their passion,
His ears and dark eyes, and decided nose,
Were as deaf and as blind and as dull as those
That overlooked the Bouquet de Rose,
    The Huille Antique,
    And Parfum Unique,
In a Barber's Temple of Fashion.

To tell, indeed, the true extent
Of his rural bias so far it went
  As to covet estates in ring fences—
And for rural lore he had learn'd in town
That the country was green, turn'd up with brown,
And garnish'd with trees that a man might cut down
  Instead of his own expenses.

And yet had that fault been his only one,
The Pair might have had few quarrels or none,
  For their tastes thus far were in common ;
But faults he had that a haughty bride
With a Golden Leg could hardly abide—
Faults that would even have roused the pride
  Of a far less metalsome woman !

It was early days indeed for a wife,
In the very spring of her married life,
  To be chill'd by its wintry weather—
But instead of sitting as Love-Birds do,
On Hymen's turtles that bill and coo—
Enjoying their "moon and honey for two "
  They were scarcely seen together ?

In vain she sat with her Precious Leg
A little exposed, *à la* Kilmansegg,
    And roll'd her eyes in their sockets !
He left her in spite of her tender regards,
And those loving murmurs described by bards,
For the rattling of dice and the shuffling of cards,
    And the poking of balls into pockets !

Moreover he loved the deepest stake
And the heaviest bets the players would make;
    And he drank—the reverse of sparely,—
And he used strange curses that made her fret;
And when he play'd with herself at piquet,
        She found, to her cost,
        For she always lost,
    That the Count did not count quite fairly.

And then came dark mistrust and doubt,
Gather'd by worming his secrets out,
    And slips in his conversations—
Fears, which all her peace destroy'd,
That his title was null—his coffers were void—
And his French Château was in Spain, or enjoy'd
    The most airy of situations.

But still his heart—if he had such a part—
She—only she—might possess his heart,
    And hold his affections in fetters—
Alas ! that hope, like a crazy ship,
Was forced its anchor and cable to slip
When, seduced by her fears, she took a dip
    In his private papers and letters.

Letters that told of dangerous leagues ;
And notes that hinted as many intrigues
    As the Count's in the " Barber of Seville "—
In short such mysteries came to light,

That the Countess-Bride, on the thirtieth night,
Woke and started up in affright,
And kick'd and scream'd with all her might,
And finally fainted away outright,
   For she dreamt she had married the Devil!

HER MISERY.

Who hath not met with home-made bread,
A heavy compound of putty and lead—
And home-made wines that rack the head,
   And home-made liqueurs and waters?
Home-made pop that will not foam,
And home-made dishes that drive one from home,
     Not to name each mess,
     For the face or dress,
  Home-made by the homely daughters?

Home-made physic that sickens the sick;
Thick for thin and thin for thick;—
In short each homogeneous trick
   For poisoning domesticity?
And since our Parents, call'd the First,
A little family squabble nurst,
Of all our evils the worst of the worst
   Is home-made infelicity.

There's a Golden Bird that claps its wings,
And dances for joy on its perch, and sings
   With a Persian exultation:
For the Sun is shining into the room,
And brightens up the carpet-bloom,
As if it were new, bran new, from the loom,
   Or the lone Nun's fabrication.

And thence the glorious radiance flames
On pictures in massy gilded frames—
Enshrining, however, no painted Dames,
   But portraits of colts and fillies—
Pictures hanging on walls, which shine,
In spite of the bard's familiar line,
 , With clusters of "Gilded lilies."

And still the flooding sunlight shares
Its lustre with gilded sofas and chairs,
   That shine as if freshly burnish'd—
And gilded tables, with glittering stocks
Of gilded china, and golden clocks,
Toy, and trinket, and musical box,
   That Peace and Paris have furnish'd.

And lo ! with the brightest gleam of all
The glowing sunbeam is seen to fall
   On an object as rare as splendid—
The golden foot of the Golden Leg
Of the Countess—once Miss Kilmansegg—
   But there all sunshine is ended.

Her cheek is pale, and her eye is dim,
And downward cast, yet not at the limb,
   Once the centre of all speculation ;
But downward drooping in comfort's dearth,
As gloomy thoughts are drawn to the earth—
Whence human sorrows derive their birth —
   By a moral gravitation.

Her golden hair is out of its braids,
And her sighs betray the gloomy shades
   That her evil planet revolves in—
And tears are falling that catch a gleam
So bright as they drop in the sunny beam,
That tears of *aqua regia* they seem,
   The water that gold dissolves in ;

Yet, not filial grief were shed
  Those tears for a mother's insanity;
Nor yet because her father was dead,
For the bowing Sir Jacob had bow'd his head
  To Death—with his usual urbanity;
The waters that down her visage rill'd
Were drops of unrectified spirit distill'd
  From the limbeck of Pride and Vanity.

Tears that fell alone and uncheckt,
Without relief, and without respect,
Like the fabled pearls that the pigs neglect,
  When pigs have that opportunity—
And of all the griefs that mortals share,
The one that seems the hardest to bear
  Is the grief without community.

How bless'd the heart that has a friend
A sympathising ear to lend
  To troubles too great to smother !
For as ale and porter, when flat, are restored
Till a sparkling bubbling head they afford,
So sorrow is cheer'd by being pour'd
  From one vessel into another

But friend or gossip she had not one
To hear the vile deeds that the Count had done,
  How night after night he rambled ;
And how she had learnt by sad degrees
That he drank, and smoked, and worse than these,
  That he "swindled, intrigued, and gambled."

How he kiss'd the maids, and sparr'd with John !
And came to bed with his garments on ;
  With other offences as heinous—
And brought *strange* gentlemen home to dine,

That he said were in the Fancy Line,
And they fancied spirits instead of wine.
And call'd her lap-dog " Wenus."

Of "making a book" how he made a stir,
But never had written a line to her,
　　Once his idol and Cara Sposa :
And how he had storm'd, and treated her ill,
Because she refused to go down to a mill,
She didn't know where, but remember'd still
　　That the Miller's name was Mendoza.

How often he waked her up at night,
And oftener still by the morning light,
　　Reeling home from his haunts unlawful ;
Singing songs that shouldn't be sung,
Except by beggars and thieves unhung—
Or volleying oaths that a foreign tongue
　　Made still more horrid and awful !

How oft, instead of otto of rose,
With vulgar smells he offended her nose,
　　From gin, tobacco, and onion!
And then how wildly he used to stare !
And shake his fist at nothing, and swear,—
And pluck by the handful his shaggy hair,
Till he look'd like a study of Giant Despair
　　For a new Edition of Bunyan !

For dice will run the contrary way,
As well is known to all who play,
　　And cards will conspire as in treason:
And what with keeping a hunting-box,
　　　　Following fox—
　　　　Friends in flocks,
　　　　Burgundies, Hocks,
　　　　From London Docks;

Stultz's frocks,
Manton and Nock's
Barrels and locks,
Shooting blue rocks,
Trainers and jocks,
Buskins and socks,
Pugilistical knocks,
And fighting-cocks.
If he found himself short in funds and stocks
These rhymes will furnish the reason !

His friends, indeed, were falling away —
Friends who insist on play or pay—
And he fear'd at no very distant day
    To be cut by Lord and by cadger,
As one, who has gone, or is going, to smash,
For his checks no longer drew the cash,
Because, as his comrades explain'd in flash,
    " He had overdrawn his badger."

Gold, gold—alas ! for the gold
Spent where souls are bought and sold.
    In Vice's Walpurgis revel !
Alas ! for muffles, and bulldogs, and guns,
The leg that walks, and the leg that runs, —
All real evils, though Fancy ones,
When they lead to debt, dishonour, and duns,
    Nay, to death, and perchance the devil !

Alas ! for the last of a Golden race !
Had she cried her wrongs in the market-place,
    She had warrant for all her clamour—
For the worst of rogues, and brutes, and rakes,
Was breaking her heart by constant aches.
With as little remorse as the Pauper, who breaks
    A flint with a parish hammer !

———

HER LAST WILL.

Now the Precious Leg while cash was flush,
Or the Count's acceptance worth a rush,
   Had never excited dissension ;
But no sooner the stocks began to fall,
Than, without any ossification at all,
The limb became what people call
   A perfect bone of contention.

For alter'd days brought alter'd ways,
And instead of the complimentary phrase,
   So current before her bridal—
The Countess heard, in language low,
That her Precious Leg was precious slow,
A good 'un to look at but bad to go,
   And kept quite a sum lying idle.

That instead of playing musical airs,
Like Colin's foot in going up-stairs—
As the wife in the Scottish ballad declares—
   It made an infernal stumping.
Whereas a member of cork, or wood,
Would be lighter and cheaper and quite as good,
   Without the unbearable thumping.

P'rhaps she thought it a decent thing
To show her calf to cobbler and king,
   But nothing could be absurder—
While none but the crazy would advertise
Their gold before their servants' eyes,
Who of course some night would make it a prize,
   By a Shocking and Barbarous Murder.

But spite of hint, and threat, and scoff,
   The Leg kept its situation.

For legs are not to be taken off,
　By a verbal amputation.
And mortals when they take a whim,
The greater the folly the stiffer the limb
　That stand upon it or by it—
So the Countess, then Miss Kilmansegg,
At her marriage refused to stir a peg,
Till the Lawyers had fasten'd on her Leg
　As fast as the Law could tie it.

Firmly then—and more firmly yet—
With scorn for scorn, and with threat for threat,
　The Proud One confronted the Cruel :
And loud and bitter the quarrel arose
Fierce and merciless—one of those,
With spoken daggers, and looks like blows,
　In all but the bloodshed a duel !

Rash, and wild, and wretched, and wrong,
Were the words that came from Weak and Strong,
　Till madden'd for desperate matters,
Fierce as tigress escaped from her den,
She flew to her desk—'twas open'd—and then,
In the time it takes to try a pen,
Or the clerk to utter his slow Amen,
　Her Will was in fifty tatters !

But the Count, instead of curses wild,
Only nodded his head and smiled,
As if at the spleen of an angry child ;
　But the calm was deceitful and sinister !
A lull like the lull of the treacherous sea—·
For Hate in that moment had sworn to be
The Golden Leg's sole Legatee,
　And that very night to administer !

HER DEATH.

'Tis a stern and startling thing to think
How often mortality stands on the brink
   Of its grave without any misgiving
And yet in this slippery world of strife,
In the stir of human bustle so rife,
There are daily sounds to tell us that Life
   Is dying, and Death is living !

Ay, Beauty the Girl, and Love the Boy,
Bright as they are with hope and joy,
   How their souls would sadden instanter,
To remember that one of those wedding bells,
Which ring so merrily through the dells,
     Is the same that knells
     Our last farewells,
  Only broken into a canter !

But breath and blood set doom at nought—
How little the wretched Countess thought,
   When at night she unloosed her sandal,
That the Fates had woven her burial-cloth,
And that Death, in the shape of a Death's Head Moth,
   Was fluttering round her candle !

As she look'd at her clock of or-molu,
For the hours she had gone so wearily through
   At the end of a day of trial—
How little she saw in her pride of prime
The dart of Death in the Hand of Time—
   That hand which moved on the dial !

As she went with her taper up the stair,
How little her swollen eye was aware

That the Shadow which follow'd was double !
Or when she closed her chamber door,
It was shutting out, and for evermore,
  The world—and its worldly trouble.

Little she dreamt, as she laid aside
Her jewels—after one glance of pride—
  They were solemn bequests to Vanity—
Or when her robes she began to doff,
That she stood so near to the putting off
  Of the flesh that clothes humanity,

And when she quench'd the taper's light,
How little she thought as the smoke took flight,
That her day was done—and merged in a night
  Of dreams and duration uncertain —
      Or along with her own,
      That a Hand of Bone
Was closing mortality's curtain !

But life is sweet, and mortality blind,
And youth is hopeful, and Fate is kind
  In concealing the day of sorrow ;
And enough is the present tense of toil—
For this world is, to all, a stiffish soil—
And the mind flies back with a glad recoil
  From the debts not due till to-morrow.

Wherefore else does the Spirit fly
And bid its daily cares good-bye,
  Along with its daily clothing ?
Just as the felon condemn'd to die—
  With a very natural loathing—
Leaving the Sheriff to dream of ropes,
From his gloomy cell in a vision elopes
To a caper on sunny gleams and slopes,
  Instead of the dance upon nothing.

Thus, even thus, the Countess slept,
While Death still nearer and nearer crept,
  Like the Thane who smote the sleeping—
But her mind was busy with early joys,
Her golden treasures and golden toys ·
      That flash'd a bright
      And golden light
  Under lids still red with weeping.

The golden doll that she used to hug !
Her coral of gold, and the golden mug !
  Her godfather's golden presents !
The golden service she had at her meals,
The golden watch, and chain, and seals,
Her golden scissors, and thread, and reels,
  And her golden fishes and pheasants !

The golden guineas in silken purse—
And the Golden Legends she heard from her nurse
  Of the Mayor in his gilded carriage—
And London streets that were paved with gold—
And the Golden Eggs that were laid of old—
      With each golden thing
      To the golden ring
  At her own auriferous Marriage ?

And still the golden light of the sun
Through her golden dream appear'd to run,
Though the night, that roared without, was one
  To terrify seamen or gipsies—
While the moon, as if in malicious mirth,
Kept peeping down at the ruffled earth,
As though she enjoy'd the tempest's birth,
  In revenge of her old eclipses.

But vainly, vainly, the thunder fell,
For the soul of the Sleeper was under a spell

That time had lately embitter'd—
The Count, as once at her foot he knelt—
    That foot, which now he wanted to melt !
But—hush !—'twas a stir at her pillow she felt—
    And some object before her glitter'd.

'Twas the Golden Leg !—she knew its gleam !
And up she started and tried to scream,—
    But ev'n in the moment she started—
Down came the limb with a frightful smash,
And, lost in the universal flash
That her eyeballs made at so mortal a crash,
    The Spark, call'd Vital, departed !

.   .   .   .

Gold, still gold ! hard, hard yellow, and cold,
For gold she had lived, and she died for gold—
    By a golden weapon—not oaken ;
In the morning they found her all alone—
Stiff, and bloody, and cold as stone—
But her Leg, the Golden Leg, was gone,
    And the " Golden Bowl was broken !"

Gold—still gold ! it haunted her yet—
At the Golden Lion the Inquest met—
    Its foreman, a carver and gilder—
And the Jury debated from twelve till three
What the Verdict ought to be,
And they brought it in as Felo de Se,
    " Because her own Leg had kill'd her !"

HER MORAL.

GOLD ! Gold ! Gold ! Gold !
Bright and yellow, hard and cold,

Molten, graven, hammer'd and roll'd;
Heavy to get, and light to hold;
Hoarded, barter'd, bought, and sold,
Stolen, borrow'd, squander'd, doled:
Spurn'd by the young, but hugg'd by the old
To the very verge of the churchyard mould;
Price of many a crime untold;
Gold! Gold! Gold! Gold!
Good or bad a thousand-fold!
    How widely its agencies vary—
To save—to ruin—to curse—to bless—
As even its minted coins express,
Now stamp'd with the image of Good Queen Bess,
    And now of a Bloody Mary.

With painted letters, red as blood I wis,
Thus written,
   "CHILDREN TAKEN IN TO BATE,"
And oft, indeed, the inward of that gate,
Most ventriloque, doth utter tender squeak,
And moans of infants that bemoan their fate,
 In midst of sounds of Latin, French, and Greek,
Which, all i' the Irish tongue, he teacheth them to speak.

IV.

For some are meant to right illegal wrongs,
And some for Doctors of Divinitie,
Whom he doth teach to murder the dead tongues,
And soe win academical degree ;
But some are bred for service of the sea,
Howbeit, their store of learning is but small,
For mickle waste he counteth it would be
To stock a head with bookish wares at all,
Only to be knocked off by ruthless cannon ball.

V.

Six babes he sways,—some little and some big,
Divided into classes six ;—alsoe,
He keeps a parlour boarder of a pig,
That in the College fareth to and fro,
And picketh up the urchins' crumbs below,—
And eke the learned rudiments they scan,
And thus his A, B, C, doth wisely know,—
Hereafter to be shown in caravan,
And raise the wonderment of many a learned man.

VI.

Alsoe, he schools some tame familiar fowls,
Whereof, above his head, some two or three
Sit darkly squatting, like Minerva's owls,
But on the branches of no living tree,

And overlook the learned family ;
While, sometimes, Partlet from her gloomy perch,
Drops feather on the nose of Dominie,
Meanwhile, with serious eye, he makes research,
In leaves of that sour tree of knowledge—now a birch.

VII.

No chair he hath, the awful Pedagogue,
Such as would magisterial hams imbed,
But sitteth lowly on a beechen log,
Secure in high authority and dread :
Large, as a dome for learning, seems his head,
And like Apollo's, all beset with rays,
Because his locks are so unkempt and red,
And stand abroad in many several ways :—
No laurel crown he wears, howbeit his cap is baize,

VIII.

And, underneath, a pair of shaggy brows
O'erhang as many eyes of gizzard hue,
That inward giblet of a fowl, which shows
A mongrel tint, that is ne brown ne blue ;
His nose,—it is a coral to the view ;
Well nourish'd with Pierian Potheen,—
For much he loves his native mountain dew ;—
But to depict the dye would lack, I ween,
A bottle-red, in terms, as well as bottle-green.

IX.

As for his coat, 'tis such a jerkin short
As Spencer had, ere he composed his Tales ;
But underneath he hath no vest, nor aught,
So that the wind his airy breast assails ;
Below, he wears the nether garb of males,

Of crimson plush, but non-plushed at the knee ;—
Thence further down the native red prevails,
Of his own naked fleecy hosierie :—
Two sandals, without soles, complete his cap-a-pee.

X.

Nathless, for dignity, he now doth lap
His function in a magisterial gown,
That shows more countries in it than a map,—
Blue tinct, and red, and green, and russet brown,
Besides some blots, standing for country-town ;
And eke some rents, for streams and rivers wide ,
But, sometimes, bashful when he looks adown,
He turns the garment of the other side,
Hopeful that so the holes may never be espied !

XI.

And soe he sits, amidst the little pack,
That look for shady or for sunny noon,
Within his visage, like an almanack,—
His quiet smile foretelling gracious boon :
But when his mouth droops down, like rainy moon,
With horrid chill each little heart unwarms,
Knowing, that infant show'rs will follow soon,
And with forebodings of near wrath and storms
They sit, like timid hares, all trembling on their forms.

XII.

Ah ! luckless wight, who cannot then repeat
"Corduroy Colloquy,"—or " Ki, Kæ, Kod," –
Full soon his tears shall make his turfy seat
More sodden, tho' already made of sod,
For Dan shall whip him with the word of God, –
Severe by rule, and not by nature mild,
He never spoils the child and spares the rod,
But spoils the rod and never spares the child,
And soe with holy rule deems he is reconcil'd.

XIII.

But, surely, the just sky will never wink
At men who take delight in childish throe,
And stripe the nether-urchin like a pink
Or tender hyacinth, inscribed with woe ;
Such bloody Pedagogues, when they shall know,
By useless birches, that forlorn recess,
Which is no holiday, in Pit below,
Will hell not seem designed for their distress,—
A melancholy place, that is all bottomlesse?

XIV.

Yet would the Muse not chide the wholesome use
Of needful discipline, in due degree.
Devoid of sway, what wrongs will time produce,
Whene'er the twig untrain'd grows up a tree,
This shall a Carder, that a Whiteboy be,
Ferocious leaders of atrocious bands,
And Learning's help be used for infamie,
By lawless clerks, that, with their bloody hands,
In murder'd English write Rock's murderous commands.

XV.

But ah ! what shrilly cry doth now alarm,
The sooty fowls that doz'd upon the beam,
All sudden fluttering from the brandish'd arm,
And cackling chorus with the human scream ;
Meanwhile, the scourge plies that unkindly seam
In Phelim's brogues, which bares his naked skin,
Like traitor gap in warlike fort, I deem,
That falsely lets the fierce besieger in,
Nor seeks the Pedagogue by other course to win.

XVI.

No parent dear he hath to heed his cries ;— '
Alas ! his parent dear is far aloof,

And deep his Seven-Dial cellar lies,
Killed by kind cudgel-play, or gin of proof,
Or climbeth, catwise, on some London roof,
Singing, perchance, a lay of Erin's Isle,
Or, whilst he labours, weaves a fancy-woof,
Dreaming he sees his home,—his Phelim smile;
Ah me! that luckless imp, who weepeth all the while!

XVII.

Ah! who can paint that hard and heavy time,
When first the scholar lists in learning's train,
And mounts her rugged steep, enforc'd to climb,
Like sooty imp, by sharp posterior pain,
From bloody twig, and eke that Indian cane,
Wherein, alas! no sugar'd juices dwell?
For this, the while one stripling's sluices drain,
Another weepeth over chilblains fell,
Always upon the heel, yet never to be well!

XVIII.

Anon a third, for his delicious root,
Late ravish'd from his tooth by elder chit,
So soon is human violence afoot,
So hardly is the harmless biter bit!
Meanwhile, the tyrant, with untimely wit
And mouthing face, derides the small one's moan,
Who, all lamenting for his loss, doth sit,
Alack,—mischance comes seldom times alone,
But aye the worried dog must rue more curs than one.

XIX.

For lo! the Pedagogue, with sudden drub,
Smites his scald head, that is already sore,—
Superfluous wound,—such is Misfortune's rub!
Who straight makes answer with redoubled roar,
And sheds salt tears twice faster than before,

That still, with backward fist, he strives to dry;
Washing, with brackish moisture, o'er and o'er,
His muddy cheek, that grows more foul thereby,
Till all his rainy face looks grim as rainy sky.

XX.

So Dan, by dint of noise, obtains a peace,
And with his natural untender knack,
By new distress, bids former grievance cease,
Like tears dried up with rugged huckaback,
That sets the mournful visage all awrack ;
Yet soon the childish countenance will shine
Even as thorough storms the soonest slack,
For grief and beef in adverse ways incline,
This keeps, and that decays, when duly soak'd in brine.

XXI.

Now all is hushed, and, with a look profound,
The Dominie lays ope the learned page ;
(So be it called) although he doth expound
Without a book, both Greek and Latin sage ;
Now telleth he of Rome's rude infant age,
How Romulus was bred in savage wood,
By wet-nurse wolf, devoid of wolfish rage ;
And laid foundation-stone of walls of mud,
But watered it, alas ! with warm fraternal blood.

XXII.

Anon, he turns to that Homeric war,
How Troy was sieged like Londonderry town ;
And stout Achilles, at his jaunting-car,
Dragged mighty Hector with a bloody crown :
And eke the bard, that sung of their renown,
In garb of Greece most beggar-like and torn,
He paints, with colly, wand'ring up and down :
Because, at once, in seven cities born ;
And so, of parish rights, was, all his days, forlorn.

XXIII.

Anon, through old Mythology he goes,
Of gods defunct, and all their pedigrees,
But shuns their scandalous amours, and shows
How Plato wise, and clear-ey'd Socrates,
Confess'd not to those heathen hes and shes ;
But thro' the clouds of the Olympic cope
Beheld St. Peter, with his holy keys,
And own'd their love was naught, and bow'd to Pope,
Whilst all their purblind race in Pagan mist did grope.

XXIV.

From such quaint themes he turns, at last, aside,
To new philosophies, that still are green,
And shows what rail-roads have been track'd to guide
The wheels of great political machine ;
If English corn should grow abroad, I ween,
And gold be made of gold, or paper sheet ;
How many pigs be born to each spalpeen ;
And ah ! how man shall thrive beyond his meat,—
With twenty souls alive, to one square rod of peat !

XXV.

Here, he makes end ; and all the fry of youth,
That stood around with serious look intense,
Close up again their gaping eyes and mouth,
Which they had opened to his eloquence,
As if their hearing were a threefold sense ;
But now the current of his words is done,
And whether any fruits shall spring from thence,
In future time, with any mother's son !
It is a thing, God wot ! that can be told by none.

XXVI.

Now by the creeping shadows of the noon,
The hour is come to lay aside their lore ;

N

The cheerful Pedagogue perceives it soon,
And cries, " Begone !" unto the imps,—and four
Snatch their two hats, and struggle for the door,
Like ardent spirits vented from a cask,
All blythe and boisterous,—but leave two more,
With Reading made Uneasy for a task,
To weep, whilst all their mates in merry sunshine bask.

XXVII

Like sportive Elfins, on the verdant sod,
With tender moss so sleckly overgrown,
That doth not hurt, but kiss, the sole unshod,
So soothly kind is Erin to her own !
And one, at Hare and Hound, plays all alone,—
For Phelim's gone to tend his step-dame's cow;
Ah ! Phelim's step-dame is a canker'd crone !
Whilst other twain play at an Irish row,
And, with shillelah small, break one another's brow !

XXVIII

But careful Dominie, with ceaseless thrift,
Now changeth ferula for rural hoe ;
But, first of all, with tender hand doth shift
His college gown, because of solar glow,
And hangs it on a bush, to scare the crow :
Meanwhile, he plants in earth the dappled bean,
Or trains the young potatoes all a-row,
Or plucks the fragrant leek for pottage green,
With that crisp curly herb, call'd Kale in Aberdeen.

XXIX.

And so he wisely spends the fruitful hours,
Link'd each to each by labour, like a bee;
Or rules in Learning's hall, or trims her bow'rs ;—
Would there were many more such wights as he,
To sway each capital academie

Of Cam and Isis; for, alack ! at each
There dwells, I wot, some dronish Dominie,
That does no garden work, nor yet doth teach,
But wears a floury head, and talks in flow'ry speech !

TO A FALSE FRIEND.

OUR hands have met, but not our hearts :
Our hands will never meet again.
Friends, if we have ever been,
Friends we cannot now remain :
I only know I loved you once,
I only know I loved in vain ;
Our hands have met, but not our hearts ;
Our hands will never meet again !

Then farewell to heart and hand !
I would our hands had never met :
Even the outward form of love
Must be resign'd with some regret.
Friends, we still might seem to be,
If I my wrong could e'er forget ;
Our hands have join'd, but not our hearts ;
I would our hands had never met !

ODE

AUTUMN.

I SAW old Autumn in the misty morn
Stand shadowless like Silence, listening
To silence, for no lonely bird would sing
Into his hollow ear from woods forlorn,

Nor lowly hedge nor solitary thorn ;
Shaking his languid locks all dewy bright
With tangled gossamer that fell by night,
    Pearling his coronet of golden corn.

Where are the songs of Summer?—With the sun,
Oping the dusky eyelids of the south,
Till shade and silence waken up as one,
And Morning sings with a warm odorous mouth.
Where are the merry birds?—Away, away,
On panting wings through the inclement skies,
    Lest owls should prey
    Undazzled at noon-day,
And tear with horny beak their lustrous eyes.

Where are the blooms of Summer?—In the west,
Blushing their last to the last sunny hours,
When the mild Eve by sudden Night is prest
Like tearful Proserpine, snatch'd from her flow'rs
    To a most gloomy breast.
Where is the pride of Summer,—the green prime,—
The many, many leaves all twinkling ?—Three
On the moss'd elm ; three on the naked lime
Trembling,—and one upon the old oak tree !
    Where is the Dryad's immortality ?—
Gone into mournful cypress and dark yew,
Or wearing the long gloomy Winter through
    In the smooth holly's green eternity.

The squirrel gloats o'er his accomplish'd hoard,
The ants have brimm'd their garners with ripe grain,
    And honey bees have stored
The sweets of summer in their luscious cells ;
The swallows all have wing'd across the main ;
But here the Autumn melancholy dwells,
    And sighs her tearful spells
Amongst the sunless shadows of the plain.

Alone, alone,
Upon a mossy stone,
She sits and reckons up the dead and gone,
With the last leaves for a love-rosary;
Whilst all the wither'd world looks drearily,
Like a dim picture of the drownèd past
In the hush'd mind's mysterious far-away,
Doubtful what ghostly thing will steal the last
Into that distance, grey upon the grey.

O go and sit with her, and be o'ershaded
Under the languid downfall of her hair;   .
She wears a coronal of flowers faded
Upon her forehead, and a face of care;—
There is enough of wither'd everywhere
To make her bower,—and enough of gloom;
There is enough of sadness to invite,
If only for the rose that died, whose doom
Is Beauty's,—she that with the living bloom
Of conscious cheeks most beautifies the light;
There is enough of sorrowing, and quite
Enough of bitter fruits the earth doth bear,—
Enough of chilly droppings from her bowl;
Enough of fear and shadowy despair,
To frame her cloudy prison for the soul!

————

SONNET.

DEATH.

It is not death, that—sometime—in a sigh
This eloquent breath shall take its speechless flight;
That—sometime—these bright stars, that now reply
In sunlight to the sun, shall set in night;
That this warm conscious flesh shall perish quite,
And all life's ruddy springs forget to flow;
That thoughts shall cease, and the immortal sprite

Be lapp'd in alien clay and laid below;
It is not death to know this,—but to know
That pious thoughts, which visit at new graves
In tender pilgrimage, will cease to go
So duly and so oft,—and when grass waves
Over the past-away, there may be then
No resurrection in the minds of men.

SONNET.

SILENCE.

THERE is a silence where hath been no sound,
There is a silence where no sound may be,
In the cold grave—under the deep deep sea,
Or in wide desert where no life is found,
Which hath been mute, and still must sleep profound;
No voice is hush'd—no life treads silently,
But clouds and cloudy shadows wander free,
That never spoke, over the idle ground:
But in green ruins, in the desolate walls
Of antique palaces, where Man hath been,
Though the dun fox, or wild hyæna, calls,
And owls, that flit continually between,
Shriek to the echo, and the low winds moan,——
There the true Silence is, self-conscious and alone.

SONNET.

LOVE, I am jealous of a worthless man
Whom—for his merits—thou dost hold too dear:
No better than myself, he lies as near
And precious to thy bosom.　He may span
Thy sacred waist and with thy sweet breath fan

His happy cheek, and thy most willing ear
Invade with words and call his love sincere
And true as mine, and prove it—if he can :—
Not that I hate him for such deeds as this—
He were a devil to adore thee less,
Who wears thy favour,—I am ill at ease
Rather lest he should e'er too coldly press
Thy gentle hand :—This is my jealousy
Making myself suspect but never thee !

SONNET.

LOVE, see thy lover humbled at thy feet,
Not in servility, but homage sweet,
Gladly inclined :—and with my bended knee
Think that my inward spirit bows to thee—
More proud indeed than when I stand or climb
Elsewhere:—there is no statue so sublime
As Love's in all the world, and e'en to kiss
The pedestal is still a better bliss
Than all ambitions.   O ! Love's lowest base
Is far above the reaching of disgrace
To shame this posture.   Let me then draw nigh
Feet that have fared so nearly to the sky,
And when this duteous homage has been given
I will rise up and clasp the heart in Heaven.

THE FORSAKEN.

THE dead are in their silent graves,
And the dew is cold above,
And the living weep and sigh,
Over dust that once was love.

Once I only wept the dead,
But now the living cause my pain:
How couldst thou steal me from my tears,
To leave me to my tears again?

My Mother rests beneath the sod,—
Her rest is calm and very deep:
I wish'd that she could see our loves,—
But now I gladden in her sleep.

Last night unbound my raven locks,
The morning saw them turn'd to grey,
Once they were black and well beloved,
But thou art changed,—and so are they !

The useless lock I gave thee once,
To gaze upon and think of me,
Was ta'en with smiles,—but this was torn
In sorrow that I send to thee !

———

SONG.

THE stars are with the voyager
　　Wherever he may sail ;
The moon is constant to her time ;
　　The sun will never fail ;
But follow, follow round the world,
　　The green earth and the sea,
So love is with the lover's heart,
　　Wherever he may be.

Wherever he may be, the stars
　　Must daily lose their light ;

The moon will veil her in the shade ;
  The sun will set at night.
The sun may set, but constant love
  Will shine when he's away ;
So that dull night is never night,
  And day is brighter day,

SONG.

O Lady, leave thy silken thread
  And flowery tapestrie :
There's living roses on the bush,
  And blossoms on the tree ;
Stoop where thou wilt, thy careless hand
  Some random bud will meet ;
Thou canst not tread, but thou wilt find
  The daisy at thy feet.

'Tis like the birthday of the world,
  When earth was born in bloom ;
The light is made of many dyes,
  The air is all perfume ;
There's crimson buds, and white and blue—
  The very rainbow showers
Have turn'd to blossoms where they fell,
  And sown the earth with flowers.

There's fairy tulips in the east,
  The garden of the sun ;
The very streams reflect the hues,
  And blossoms as they run :
While Morn opes like a crimson rose,
  Still wet with pearly showers ;
Then, lady, leave the silken thread
  Thou twinest into flowers !

BIRTHDAY VERSES.

GOOD morrow to the golden morning
   Good morrow to the world's delight —
I've come to bless thy life's beginning,
   Since it makes my own so bright !

I have brought no roses, sweetest,
   I could find no flowers, dear, —
It was when all sweets were over
   Thou wert born to bless the year.*

But I've brought thee jewels, dearest,
   In thy bonny locks to shine, —
And if love shows in their glances,
   They have learned that look of mine !

I LOVE THEE.

I LOVE thee—I love thee !
   'Tis all that I can say ;—
It is my vision in the night,
   My dreaming in the day ;
The very echo of my heart,
   The blessing when I pray :
I love thee—I love thee !
   Is all that I can say.

I love thee—I love thee !
   Is ever on my tongue ;
In all my proudest poesy
   That chorus still is sung ;

---

* My mother's birthday was the 6th November.

It is the verdict of my eyes,
   Amidst the gay and young :
I love thee—I love thee !
   A thousand maids among.

I love thee—I love thee !
   Thy bright and hazel glance,
The mellow lute upon those lips,
   Whose tender tones entrance ;
But most, dear heart of hearts, thy proofs
   That still these words enhance,
I love thee—I love thee !
   Whatever be thy chance.

LINES.

LET us make a leap, my dear,
In our love, of many a year
And date it very far away,
On a bright clear summer day,
When the heart was like a sun
To itself, and falsehood none ;
And the rosy lips a part
Of the very loving heart,
And the shining of the eye
But a sign to know it by ;—
When my faults were all forgiven,
And my life deserved of Heaven.
Dearest, let us reckon so,
And love for all that long ago ;
Each absence count a year complete,
And keep a birthday when we meet.

FALSE POETS AND TRUE.

TO WORDSWORTH.

LOOK how the lark soars upward and is gone,
Turning a spirit as he nears the sky!
IIis voice is heard, but body there is none *
To fix the vague excursions of the eye.
So, poets' songs are with us, tho' they die
Obscured, and hid by death's oblivious shroud,
And Earth inherits the rich melody
Like raining music from the morning cloud.
Yet, few there be who pipe so sweet and loud
Their voices reach us through the lapse of space:
The noisy day is deafen'd by a crowd
Of undistinguish'd birds, a twittering race;
But only lark and nightingale forlorn
Fill up the silences of night and morn.

FRAGMENT.

"FAREWELL—Farewell"—it is an awful word
When that the quick do speak it to the dead;
For though 'tis brief upon the speaker's lips,
'Tis more than death can answer to, and hath
No living echo on the living ear.

. . . . .

'Tis awful to behold the midnight stars
They say do rule the destinies of men,

---

* These lines are repeated in the fourth verse of "Hero and Leander."

Gazing upon us from that point of space,
Where they were set even from their lustrous birth,
With a most sure foreknowledge of our doom
Watching its consummation.

.   .   .   .   .   .

.

THE TWO SWANS.

A FAIRY TALE.

IMMORTAL Imogen, crown'd queen above
The lilies of thy sex, vouchsafe to hear
A fairy dream in honour of true love—
True above ills, and frailty, and all fear—
Perchance a shadow of his own career
Whose youth was darkly prison'd and long-twined
By serpent-sorrow, till white Love drew near,
And sweetly sang him free, and round his mind
A bright horizon threw, wherein no grief may wind.

I saw a tower builded on a lake,
Mock'd by its inverse shadow, dark and deep—
That seem'd a still intenser night to make,
Wherein the quiet waters sank to sleep,—
And, whatsoe'er was prison'd in that keep,
A monstrous Snake was warden :—round and round
In sable ringlets I beheld him creep,
Blackest amid black shadows, to the ground
Whilst his enormous head the topmast turret crown'd.

From whence he shot fierce light against the stars,
Making the pale moon paler with affright ;

And with his ruby eye out-threaten'd Mars—
That blazed in the mid-heavens, hot and bright—
Nor slept, nor wink'd, but with a steadfast spite
Watch'd their wan looks and tremblings in the skies ;
And that he might not slumber in the night,
The curtain-lids were pluck'd from his large eyes,
So he might never drowse, but watch his secret prize.

Prince or princess in dismal durance pent,
Victims of old Enchantment's love or hate,
Their lives must all in painful sighs be spent,
Watching the lonely waters soon and late,
And clouds that pass and leave them to their fate.
Or company their grief with heavy tears :—
Meanwhile that Hope can spy no golden gate
For sweet escapement, but in darksome fears
They weep and pine away as if immortal years.

No gentle bird with gold upon its wing
Will perch upon the grate—the gentle bird
Is safe in leafy dell, and will not bring
Freedom's sweet key-note and commission-word
Learn'd of a fairy's lips, for pity stirr'd—
Lest while he trembling sings, untimely guest !
Watch'd by that cruel Snake and darkly heard,
He leave a widow on her lonely nest,
To press in silent grief the darlings of her breast.

No gallant knight, adventurous, in his bark,
Will seek the fruitful perils of the place,
To rouse with dipping oar the waters dark
That bear that serpent-image on their face.
And Love, brave Love! though he attempt the base,
Nerved to his loyal death, he may not win
His captive lady from the strict embrace
Of that foul Serpent, clasping her within
His sable folds—like Eve enthrall'd by the old Sin.

But there is none—no knight in panoply,
Nor Love, intrench'd in his strong steely coat :
No little speck—no sail—no helper nigh,
No sign—no whispering—no plash of boat :—
The distant shores show dimly and remote,
Made of a deeper mist,—serene and grey,—
And slow and mute the cloudy shadows float
Over the gloomy wave, and pass away,
Chased by the silver beams that on their marges play.

And bright and silvery the willows sleep
Over the shady verge—no mad winds tease
Their hoary heads ; but quietly they weep
Their sprinkling leaves—half fountains and half trees :
There lilies be—and fairer than all these,
A solitary Swan her breast of snow
Launches against the wave that seems to freeze
Into a chaste reflection, still below
Twin-shadow of herself wherever she may go.

And forth she paddles in the very noon
Of solemn midnight like an elfin thing,
Charm'd into being by the argent moon—
Whose silver light for love of her fair wing
Goes with her in the shade, still worshipping
Her dainty plumage :—all around her grew
A radiant circlet, like a fairy ring ;
And all behind, a tiny little clue
Of light, to guide her back across the waters blue.

And sure she is no meaner than a fay
Redeem'd from sleepy death, for beauty's sake,
By old ordainment :—silent as she lay,
Touch'd by a moonlight wand I saw her wake,
And cut her leafy slough, and so forsake

The verdant prison of her lily peers,
That slept amidst the stars upon the lake—
A breathing shape—restored to human fears,
And new-born love and grief—self-conscious of her tears.

And now she clasps her wings around her heart,
And near that lonely isle begins to glide,
Pale as her fears, and oft-times with a start
Turns her impatient head from side to side
In universal terrors—all too wide
To watch ; and often to that marble keep
Upturns her pearly eyes, as if she spied
Some foe, and crouches in the shadows steep
That in the gloomy wave go diving fathoms deep.

And well she may, to spy that fearful thing
All down the dusky walls in circlets wound
Alas ! for what rare prize, with many a ring
Girding the marble casket round and round?
His folded tail, lost in the gloom profound,
Terribly darkeneth the rocky base ;
But on the top his monstrous head is crown'd
With prickly spears, and on his doubtful face
Gleam his unwearied eyes, red watchers of the place.

Alas ! of the hot fires that nightly fall,
No one will scorch him in those orbs of spite,
So he may never see beneath the wall
That timid little creature, all too bright,
That stretches her fair neck, slender and white,
Invoking the pale moon, and vainly tries
Her throbbing throat, as if to charm the night
With song—but, hush—it perishes in sighs,
And there will be no dirge sad-swelling, though she dies!

She droops—she sinks—she leans upon the lake,
Fainting again into a lifeless flower ;

But soon the chilly springs anoint and wake
Her spirit from its death, and with new power
She sheds her stifled sorrows in a shower
Of tender song, timed to her falling tears—
That wins the shady summit of that tower,
And, trembling all the sweeter for its fears,
Fills with imploring moan that cruel monster's ears.

And, lo! the scaly beast is all deprest,
Subdued like Argus by the might of sound—
What time Apollo his sweet lute addrest
To magic converse with the air, and bound
The many monster eyes, all slumber-drown'd :—
So on the turret-top that watchful Snake
Pillows his giant head, and lists profound,
As if his wrathful spite would never wake,
Charm'd into sudden sleep for Love and Beauty's sake.

His prickly crest lies prone upon his crown,
And thirsty lip from lip disparted flies,
To drink that dainty flood of music down—
His scaly throat is big with pent-up sighs—
And whilst his hollow ear entrancèd lies,
His looks for envy of the charmed sense
Are fain to listen, till his steadfast eyes,
Stung into pain by their own impotence,
Distil enormous tears into the lake immense.

Oh, tuneful Swan! oh, melancholy bird!
Sweet was that midnight miracle of song,
Rich with ripe sorrow, needful of no word
To tell of pain, and love, and love's deep wrong—
Hinting a piteous tale—perchance how long
Thy unknown tears were mingled with the lake,
What time disguised thy leafy mates among—
And no eye knew what human love and ache
Dwelt in those dewy leaves, and heart so nigh to break.

Therefore no poet will ungently touch
The water-lily, on whose eyelids dew
Trembles like tears ; but ever hold it such
As human pain may wander through and through,
Turning the pale leaf paler in its hue—
Wherein life dwells, transfigured, not entomb'd.
By magic spells.   Alas ! who ever knew
Sorrow in all its shapes, leafy and plumed,
Or in gross husks of brutes eternally inhumed?

And now the winged song has scaled the height
Of that dark dwelling, builded for despair,
And soon a little casement flashing bright
Widens self-open'd into the cool air—
That music like a bird may enter there
And soothe the captive in his stony cage ;
For there is nought of grief, or painful care,
But plaintive song may happily engage
From sense of its own ill, and tenderly assuage

And forth into the light, small and remote,
A creature, like the fair son of a king,
Draws to the lattice in his jewell'd coat
Against the silver moonlight glistening,
And leans upon his white hand listening
To that sweet music that with tenderer tone
Salutes him, wondering what kindly thing
Is come to soothe him with so tuneful moan,
Singing beneath the walls as if for him alone.

And while he listens, the mysterious song,
Woven with timid particles of speech,
Twines into passionate words that grieve along
The melancholy notes, and softly teach
The secrets of true love,—that trembling reach
His earnest ear, and through the shadows dun
He missions like replies, and each to each

Their silver voices mingle into one,
Like blended streams that make one music as they run.

"Ah ! Love, my hope is swooning in my heart,—"
"Ay, sweet, my cage is strong and hung full high—"
"Alas ! our lips are held so far apart,
Thy words come faint,—they have so far to fly !—"
"If I may only shun that serpent-eye,—"
"Ah me ! that serpent-eye doth never sleep ;—"
"Then, nearer thee, Love's martyr, I will die !—"
"Alas, alas ! that word has made we weep !
For pity's sake remain safe in thy marble keep !"

"My marble keep ! it is my marble tomb—"
"Nay, sweet ! but thou hast there thy living breath—"
"Aye to expend in sighs for this hard doom ;—"
"But I will come to thee and sing beneath,
And nightly so beguile this serpent wreath ;—"
"Nay, I will find a path from these despairs,"
"Ah, needs then thou must tread the back of death,
Making his stony ribs thy stony stairs.—
Behold his ruby eye, how fearfully it glares !"

Full sudden at these words, the princely youth
Leaps on the scaly back that slumbers, still
Unconscious of his foot, yet not for ruth,
But numb'd to dulness by the fairy skill
Of that sweet music (all more wild and shrill
For intense fear) that charm'd him as he lay—
Meanwhile the lover nerves his desperate will,
Held some short throbs by natural dismay,
Then down the serpent-track begins his darksome way.

Now dimly seen—now toiling out of sight,
Eclipsed and cover'd by the envious wall ;

Now fair and spangled in the sudden light,
And clinging with wide arms for fear of fall ;
Now dark and shelter'd by a kindly pall
Of dusky shadow from his wakeful foe;
Slowly he winds adown—dimly and small,
Watch'd by the gentle Swan that sings below,
Her hope increasing, still, the larger he doth grow.

But nine times nine the serpent folds embrace
The marble walls about—which he must tread
Before his anxious foot may touch the base :
Long is the dreary path, and must be sped !
But Love, that holds the mastery of dread,
Braces his spirit, and with constant toil
He wins his way, and now, with arms outspread
Impatient plunges from the last long coil :
So may all gentle Love ungentle Malice foil !

The song is hush'd, the charm is all complete,
And two fair Swans are swimming on the lake :
But scarce their tender bills have time to meet,
When fiercely drops adown that cruel Snake—
His steely scales a fearful rustling make,
Like autumn leaves that tremble and foretell
The sable storm ;—the plumy lovers quake—
And feel the troubled waters pant and swell,
Heaved by the giant bulk of their pursuer fell.

His jaws, wide yawning like the gates of Death,
Hiss horrible pursuit—his red eyes glare
The waters into blood—his eager breath
Grows hot upon their plumes:—now, minstrel fair !
She drops her ring into the waves, and there
It widens all around, a fairy ring
Wrought of the silver light—the fearful pair
Swim in the very midst, and pant and cling
The closer for their fears, and tremble wing to wing.

Bending their course over the pale grey lake,
Against the pallid East, wherein light play'd
In tender flushes, still the baffled Snake
Circled them round continually, and bay'd
Hoarsely and loud, forbidden to invade
The sanctuary ring—his sable mail
Roll'd darkly through the flood, and writhed and made
A shining track over the waters pale,
Lash'd into boiling foam by his enormous tail.

And so they sail'd into the distance dim,
Into the very distance—small and white,
Like snowy blossoms of the spring that swim
Over the brooklets—follow'd by the spite
Of that huge Serpent, that with wild affright
Worried them on their course, and sore annoy,
Till on the grassy marge I saw them 'light,
And change, anon, a gentle girl and boy,
Lock'd in embrace of sweet unutterable joy!

Then came the Morn, and with her pearly showers
Wept on them, like a mother, in whose eyes
Tears are no grief ; and from his rosy bowers
The Oriental sun began to rise,
Chasing the darksome shadows from the skies ;
Wherewith that sable Serpent far away
Fled, like a part of night—delicious sighs
From waking blossoms purified the day,
And little birds were singing sweetly from each spray.

———

STANZAS TO TOM WOODGATE, OF HASTINGS.

Tom ;—are you still within this land
Of livers—still on Hastings' sand,
   Or roaming on the waves?
Or has some billow o'er you rolled,
Jealous that earth should lap so bold
   A seaman in her graves?

On land the rushlight lives of men
Go out but slowly; nine in ten,
   By tedious long decline—
Not so the jolly sailor sinks,
Who founders in the wave, and drinks
   The apoplectic brine !

Ay, while I write, mayhap your head
Is sleeping on an oyster-bed—
   I hope 'tis far from truth !—
With periwinkle eyes ;—your bone
Beset with mussels, not your own,
   And corals at your tooth !

Still does the Chance pursue the chance
The main affords—the Aidant dance
   In safety on the tide?
Still flies that sign of my good-will *
A little *bunting* thing—but still
   To thee a flag of pride?

Does that hard, honest hand now clasp
The tiller in its careful grasp—

---

* My father made Woodgate a present, in the shape of a small flag.

With every summer breeze
When ladies sail, in lady-fear—
Or, tug the oar, a gondolier
   On smooth Macadam seas?

Or are you where the flounders keep,
Some dozen briny fathoms deep,
   Where sand and shells abound—
With some old Triton on your chest,
And twelve brave mermen for a 'quest,
   To find that you are—drown'd?

Swift is the wave, and apt to bring
A sudden doom—perchance I sing
   A mere funereal strain;
You have endured the utter strife—
And are—the same in death or life—
   A good man "in the main!"

Oh, no—I hope the old brown eye
Still watches ebb, and flood, and sky;
   That still the brown old shoes
Are sucking brine up—pumps indeed!—
Your tooth still full of ocean weed,
   Or Indian—which you choose.

I like you, Tom! and in these lays
Give honest worth its honest praise,
   No puff at honour's cost;
For though you met these words of mine,
All letter-learning was a line
   You, somehow, never cross'd!

Mayhap we ne'er shall meet again,
Except on that Pacific main,

Beyond this planet's brink ;
Yet, as we erst have braved the weather,
Still may we float awhile together,
    As comrades on this ink !

Many a scudding gale we've had
Together, and, my gallant lad,
    Some perils we have pass'd ;
When huge and black the wave career'd,
And oft the giant surge appear'd
    The master of our mast ;—

'Twas thy example taught me how
To climb the billow's hoary brow,
    Or cleave the raging heap—
To bound along the ocean wild,
With danger—only as a child
    The waters rock'd to sleep.

Oh, who can tell that brave delight,
To see the hissing wave in might
    Come rampant like a snake !
To leap his horrid crest, and feast
One's eyes upon the briny beast,
    Left couchant in the wake !

The simple shepherd's love is still
To bask upon a sunny hill,
    The herdsman roams the vale—
With both their fancies I agree ;
Be mine the swelling, scooping sea,
    That is both hill and dale !

I yearn for that brisk spray—I yearn
To feel the wave from stem to stern

Uplift the plunging keel ;
That merry step we used to dance
On board the Aidant or the Chance,
The ocean " toe and heel."

I long to feel the steady gale
That fills the broad distended sail—
The seas on either hand !
My thought, like any hollow shell,
Keeps mocking at my ear the swell
Of waves against the land.

It is no fable—that old strain
Of syrens !—so the witching main
Is singing—and I sigh !
My heart is all at once inclined
To seaward—and I seem to find
The waters in my eye !

Methinks I see the shining beach ;
The merry waves, each after each,
Rebounding o'er the flints ;
I spy the grim preventive spy !
The jolly boatmen standing nigh !
The maids in morning chintz !

And there they float—the sailing craft !
The sail is up—the wind abaft—
The ballast trim and neat.
Alas ! 'tis all a dream—a lie !
A printer's imp is standing by
To haul my mizen sheet !

My tiller dwindles to a pen—
My craft is that of bookish men—

My sail—let Longman tell !
Adieu, the wave, the wind, the spray !
Men—maidens—chintzes—fade away !
Tom Woodgate, fare thee well !

—

TIME, HOPE, AND MEMORY.

I HEARD a gentle maiden, in the spring,
Set her sweet sighs to music, and thus sing :
"Fly through the world, and I will follow thee,
Only for looks that may turn back on me ;

"Only for roses that your chance may throw—
Though wither'd—I will wear them on my brow,
To be a thoughtful fragrance to my brain,—
Warm'd with such love, that they will bloom again.

"Thy love before thee, I must tread behind,
Kissing thy foot-prints, though to me unkind ;
But trust not all her fondness, though it seem,
Lest thy true love should rest on a false dream.

"Her face is smiling, and her voice is sweet ;
But smiles betray, and music sings deceit ;
And words speak false ;—yet, if they welcome prove,
I'll be their echo, and repeat their love.

"Only if waken'd to sad truth, at last,
The bitterness to come, and sweetness past ;
When thou art vext, then turn again, and see
Thou hast loved Hope, but Memory loved thee."

FLOWERS.

I WILL not have the maid Clytie
Whose head is turn'd by the sun;
The tulip is a courtly quean,
Whom, therefore, I will shun;
The cowslip is a country wench,
The violet is a nun;—
But I will woo the dainty rose,
The queen of every one.

The pea is but a wanton witch,
In too much haste to wed,
And clasps her rings on every hand;
The wolfsbane I should dread;
Nor will I dreary rosemarye,
That always mourns the dead;—
But I will woo the dainty rose,
With her cheeks of tender red.

The lily is all in white, like a saint,
And so is no mate for me—
And the daisy's cheek is tipp'd with a blush,
She is of such low degree;
Jasmine is sweet, and has many loves,
And the broom's betroth'd to the bee;—
But I will plight with the dainty rose,
For fairest of all is she.

BALLAD.

SHE's up and gone, the graceless girl,
And robb'd my failing years!
My blood before was thin and cold,
But now 'tis turn'd to tears;—

My shadow falls upon my grave,
   So near the brink I stand,
She might have stay'd a little yet,
   And led me by the hand !

Aye, call her on the barren moor,
   And call her on the hill :
'Tis nothing but the heron's cry,
   And plover's answer shrill ;
My child is flown on wilder wings
   Than they have ever spread,
And I may even walk a waste
   That widen'd when she fled.

Full many a thankless child has been,
   But never one like mine ;
Her meat was served on plates of gold,
   Her drink was rosy wine ,
But now she'll share the robin's food,
   And sup the common rill,
Before her feet will turn again
   To meet her father's will !

THE TWO PEACOCKS OF BEDFONT.

ALAS! That breathing Vanity should go
   Where Pride is buried,—like its very ghost,
Uprisen from the naked bones below,
   In novel flesh, clad in the silent boast
Of gaudy silk that flutters to and fro,
   Shedding its chilling superstition most
On young and ignorant natures—as it wont
To haunt the peaceful churchyard of Bedfont!

Each Sabbath morning, at the hour of prayer,
   Behold two maidens, up the quiet green
Shining far distant, in the summer air
   That flaunts their dewy robes and breathes between
Their downy plumes,—sailing as if they were
   Two far-off ships,—until they brush between
The churchyard's humble walls, and watch and wait
On either side of the wide open'd gate.

And there they stand—with haughty necks before
   God's holy house, that points towards the skies—
Frowning reluctant duty from the poor,
   And tempting homage from unthoughtful eyes :

And Youth looks lingering from the temple door,
  Breathing its wishes in unfruitful sighs,
With pouting lips,—forgetful of the grace,
Of health, and smiles, on the heart-conscious face ;—

Because that Wealth, which has no bliss beside,
  May wear the happiness of rich attire ;
And those two sisters, in their silly pride,
  May change the soul's warm glances for the fire
Of lifeless diamonds ;—and for health denied,—
  With art, that blushes at itself, inspire
Their languid cheeks—and flourish in a glory
That has no life in life, nor after-story.

The aged priest goes shaking his grey hair
  In meekest censuring, and turns his eye
Earthward in grief, and heavenward in pray'r,
  And sighs, and clasps his hands, and passes by,
Good-hearted man ! what sullen soul would wear
  Thy sorrow for a garb, and constantly
Put on thy censure, that might win the praise
Of one so grey in goodness and in days ?

Also the solemn clerk partakes the shame
  Of this ungodly shine of human pride,
And sadly blends his reverence and blame
  In one grave bow, and passes with a stride
Impatient :—many a red-hooded dame
  Turns her pain'd head, but not her glance, aside
From wanton dress, and marvels o'er again,
That heaven hath no wet judgments for the vain.

"I have a lily in the bloom at home,"
  Quoth one, "and by the blessed Sabbath day
I'll pluck my lily in its pride, and come
  And read a lesson upon vain array ;—'

And when stiff silks are rustling up, and some
   Give place, I'll shake it in proud eyes and say—
Making my reverence,—' Ladies, an you please
King Solomon's not half so fine as these.' "

Then her meek partner, who has nearly run
   His earthly course,—" Nay, Goody, let your text
Grow in the garden.—We have only one—
   Who knows that these dim eyes may see the next?
Summer will come again, and summer sun,
   And lilies too,—but I were sorely vext
To mar my garden, and cut short the blow
Of the last lily I may live to grow."

" The last!" quoth she, " and though the last it were—
   Lo! those two wantons, where they stand so proud
With waving plumes, and jewels in their hair,
   And painted cheeks, like Dagons to be bow'd
And curtsey'd to!—last Sabbath after pray'r,
   I heard the little Tomkins ask aloud
If they were angels—but I made him know
   God's bright ones better, with a bitter blow!"

So speaking, they pursue the pebbly walk
   That leads to the white porch the Sunday throng,
Hand-coupled urchins in restrainèd talk,
   And anxious pedagogue that chastens wrong,
And posied churchwarden with solemn stalk,
   And gold-bedizen'd beadle flames along,
And gentle peasant clad in buff and green,
Like a meek cowslip in the spring serene;

And blushing maiden—modestly array'd
   In spotless white,—still conscious of the glass;
And she, the lonely widow, that hath made
   A sable covenant with grief,—alas!

She veils her tears under the deep, deep shade,
  While the poor kindly-hearted, as they pass,
Bend to unclouded childhood, and caress
Her boy,—so rosy!—and so fatherless!

Thus, as good Christians ought, they all draw near
  The fair white temple, to the timely call
Of pleasant bells that tremble in the ear.—
  Now the last frock, and scarlet hood, and shawl
Fade into dusk, in the dim atmosphere
  Of.the low porch, and heav'n has won them all,
—Saving those two, that turn aside and pass,
In velvet blossom, where all flesh is grass.

Ah me! to see their silken manors trail'd
  In purple luxuries—with restless gold,—
Flaunting the grass where widowhood has wail'd
  In blotted black,—over the heapy mould
Panting wave-wantonly! They never quail'd
  How the warm vanity abused the cold;
Nor saw the solemn faces of the gone
Sadly uplooking through transparent stone:

But swept their dwellings with unquiet light,
  Shocking the awful presence of the dead;
Where gracious natures would their eyes benight
  Nor wear their being with a lip too red,
Nor move too rudely in the summer bright
  Of sun, but put staid sorrow in their tread,
Meting it into steps, with inward breath,
In very pity to bereaved death.

Now in the church, time-sober'd minds resign
  To solemn pray'r, and the loud chaunted hymn,—
With glowing picturings of joys divine
  Painting the mist-light where the roof is dim,

P

But youth looks upward to the window shine,
  Warming with rose and purple and the swim
Of gold, as if thought-tinted by the stains
  Of gorgeous light through many-colour'd panes ;

Soiling the virgin snow wherein God hath
  Enrobed his angels,—and with absent eyes
Hearing of Heav'n, and its directed path,
  Thoughtful of slippers,—and the glorious skies
Clouding with satin,—till the preacher's wrath
  Consumes his pity, and he glows, and cries
With a deep voice that trembles in its might,
And earnest eyes grown eloquent in light :

"Oh, that the vacant eye would learn to look
  On very beauty, and the heart embrace
True loveliness, and from this holy book
  Drink the warm-breathing tenderness and grace
Of love indeed !   Oh, that the young soul took
  Its virgin passion from the glorious face
Of fair religion, and address'd its strife,
To win the riches of eternal life !

"Doth the vain heart love glory that is none,
  And the poor excellence of vain attire ?
Oh go, and drown your eyes against the sun,
  The visible ruler of the starry quire,
Till boiling gold in giddy eddies run,
  Dazzling the brain with orbs of living fire ;
And the faint soul down-darkens into night,
  And dies a burning martyrdom to light.

"Oh go, and gaze,—when the low winds of ev'n
  Breathe hymns, and Nature's many forests nod
Their gold-crown'd heads ; and the rich blooms of heav'n
  Sun-ripen'd give their blushes up to God ;

And mountain-rocks and cloudy steeps are riv'n
  By founts of fire, as smitten by the rod
Of heavenly Moses,—that your thirsty sense
May quench its longings of magnificence !

"Yet suns shall perish—stars shall fade away—
  Day into darkness—darkness into death—
Death into silence; the warm light of day,
  The blooms of summer, the rich glowing breath
Of even—all shall wither and decay,
  Like the frail furniture of dreams beneath
The touch of morn—or bubbles of rich dyes
That break and vanish in the aching eyes."

They hear, soul-blushing, and repentant shed
  Unwholesome thoughts in wholesome tears, and pour
Their sin to earth,—and with low drooping head
  Receive the solemn blessing, and implore
Its grace—then soberly with chasten'd tread,
  They meekly press towards the gusty door,
With humbled eyes that go to graze upon
The lowly grass—like him of Babylon.

The lowly grass !—O water-constant mind !
  Fast-ebbing holiness !—soon-fading grace
Of serious thought, as if the gushing wind
  Through the low porch had wash'd it from the face
For ever !—How they lift their eyes to find
  Old vanities !—Pride wins the very place
Of meekness, like a bird, and flutters now
With idle wings on the curl-conscious brow !

And lo ! with eager looks they seek the way
  Of old temptation at the lowly gate ;
To feast on feathers, and on vain array,
  And painted cheeks, and the rich glistering state

Of jewel-sprinkled locks.—But where are they,
    The graceless haughty ones that used to wait
With lofty neck, and nods, and stiffen'd eye ?—
None challenge the old homage bending by.

In vain they look for the ungracious bloom
    Of rich apparel where it glow'd before,—
For Vanity has faded all to gloom,
    And lofty Pride has stiffen'd to the core,
For impious Life to tremble at its doom,—
    Set for a warning token evermore,
Whereon, as now, the giddy and the wise
Shall gaze with lifted hands and wond'ring eyes.

The aged priest goes on each Sabbath morn,
    But shakes not sorrow under his grey hair ;
The solemn clerk goes lavender'd and shorn,
    Nor stoops his back to the ungodly pair ;—
And ancient lips that pucker'd up in scorn,
    Go smoothly breathing to the house of pray'r ;
And in the garden-plot, from day to day,
The lily blooms its long white life away.

And where two haughty maidens used to be,
    In pride of plume, where plumy Death had trod,
Trailing their gorgeous velvets wantonly,
    Most unmeet pall, over the holy sod ;—
There, gentle stranger, thou may'st only see
    Two sombre Peacocks.——Age, with sapient nod
Marking the spot, still tarries to declare
How they once lived, and wherefore they are there.

THE DEPARTURE OF SUMMER.

SUMMER is gone on swallow's wings,
And Earth has buried all her flowers :
No more the lark,—the linnet—sings,
But Silence sits in faded bowers.
There is a shadow on the plain
Of Winter ere he comes again,—
There is in woods a solemn sound
Of hollow warnings whisper'd round,
As Echo in her deep recess
For once had turn'd a prophetess.
Shuddering Autumn stops to list,
And breathes his fear in sudden sighs,
With clouded face, and hazel eyes
That quench themselves, and hide in mist.

Yes, Summer's gone like pageant bright ;
Its glorious days of golden light
Are gone—the mimic suns that quiver,
Then melt in Time's dark-flowing river ;
Gone the sweetly-scented breeze
That spoke in music to the trees ;
Gone—for damp and chilly breath,
As if fresh blown o'er marble seas,
Or newly from the lungs of Death.
Gone its virgin roses' blushes,
Warm as when Aurora rushes
Freshly from the god's embrace,
With all her shame upon her face.
Old Time hath laid them in the mould :
Sure he is blind as well as old,
Whose hand relentless never spares
Young cheeks so beauty-bright as theirs !
Gone are the flame-eyed lovers now
From where so blushing-blest they tarried
Under the hawthorn's blossom-bough,
Gone ; for Day and Night are married.

All the light of love is fled :—
Alas! that negro breasts should hide
The lips that were so rosy red,
At morning and at even-tide!

Delightful Summer! then adieu
Till thou shalt visit us anew:
But who without regretful sigh
Can say, adieu, and see thee fly?
Not he that e'er hath felt thy pow'r,
His joy expanding like a flow'r,
That cometh after rain and snow,
Looks up at heaven, and learns to glow:—
Not he that fled from Babel-strife
To the green sabbath-land of life,
To dodge dull Care 'mid cluster'd trees,
And cool his forehead in the breeze,—
Whose spirit, weary-worn, perchance,
Shook from its wings a weight of grief,
And perch'd upon an aspen leaf,
For every breath to make it dance.

Farewell !—on wings of sombre stain,
That blacken in the last blue skies,
Thou fly'st; but thou wilt come again
On the gay wings of butterflies.
Spring at thy approach will sprout
Her new Corinthian beauties out,
Leaf-woven homes, where twitter-words
Will grow to songs, and eggs to birds;
Ambitious buds shall swell to flowers,
And April smiles to sunny hours.
Bright days shall be, and gentle nights
Full of soft breath and echo-lights
As if the god of sun-time kept
His eyes half-open while he slept,
Roses shall be where roses were,
Not shadows, but reality;

As if they never perish'd there,
But slept in immortality :
Nature shall thrill with new delight,
And Time's relumined river run
Warm as young blood, and dazzling bright,
As if its source were in the sun !

But say, hath Winter then no charms?
Is there no joy, no gladness warms
His aged heart? no happy wiles
To cheat the hoary one to smiles?
Onward he comes—the cruel North
Pours his furious whirlwind forth
Before him—and we breathe the breath
Of famish'd bears that howl to death.
Onward he comes from rocks that blanch
O'er solid streams that never flow :
His tears all ice, his locks all snow,
Just crept from some huge avalanche—
A thing half-breathing and half-warm,
As if one spark began to glow
Within some statue's marble form,
Or pilgrim stiffen'd in the storm.
Oh ! will not Mirth's light arrows fail
To pierce that frozen coat of mail ?
Oh ! will not joy but strive in vain
To light up those glazed eyes again?

No ! take him in, and blaze the oak,
And pour the wine, and warm the ale ;
His sides shall shake to many a joke,
His tongue shall thaw in many a tale,
His eyes grow bright, his heart be gay,
And even his palsy charm'd away.
What heeds he then the boisterous shout
Of angry winds that scold without,
Like shrewish wives at tavern door ?
What heeds he then the wild uproar
Of billows bursting on the shore ?

In dashing waves, in howling breeze,
There is a music that can charm him ;
When safe, and shelter'd, and at ease,
He hears the storm that cannot harm him.

But hark ! those shouts ! that sudden din
Of little hearts that laugh within.
Oh ! take him where the youngsters play,
And he will grow as young as they !
They come ! they come ! each blue-eyed Sport,
The Twelfth-Night King and all his court—
'Tis Mirth fresh crown'd with misletoe !
Music with her merry fiddles,
Joy "on light fantastic toe,"
Wit with all his jests and riddles,
Singing and dancing as they go.
And Love, young Love, among the rest,
A welcome—nor unbidden guest.

But still for Summer dost thou grieve ?
Then read our Poets—they shall weave
A garden of green fancies still,
Where thy wish may rove at will.
They have kept for after-treats
The essences of summer sweets,
And echoes of its songs that wind
In endless music through the mind :
They have stamp'd in visible traces
The "thoughts that breathe," in words that shine—
The flights of soul in sunny places—
To greet and company with thine.
These shall wing thee on to flow'rs—
The past or future, that shall seem
All the brighter in thy dream
For blowing in such desert hours.
The summer never shines so bright
As thought-of in a winter's night ;
And the sweetest, loveliest rose
Is in the bud before it blows ;

The dear one of the lover's heart
Is painted to his longing eyes,
In charms she ne'er can realise—
But when she turns again to part.
Dream thou then, and bind thy brow
With wreath of fancy roses now,
And drink of Summer in the cup
Where the Muse hath mix'd it up ;
The "dance, and song, and sun-burnt mirth,"
With the warm nectar of the earth :
Drink ! 'twill glow in every vein,
And thou shalt dream the winter through :
Then waken to the sun again,
And find thy Summer Vision true !

A LEGEND OF NAVARRE.

'Twas in the reign of Lewis, call'd the Great,
  As one may read on his triumphal arches,
The thing befel I'm going to relate,
  In course of one of those "pomposo" marches
He lov'd to make, like any gorgeous Persian,
Partly for war, and partly for diversion.

Some wag had it put in the royal brain
  To drop a visit at an old chateau,
Quite unexpected, with his courtly train ;
  The monarch lik'd it,—but it happened so,
That Death had got before them by a post,
And they were "reckoning without their *host*,"

Who died exactly as a child should die,
  Without a groan or a convulsive breath
Closing without one pang his quiet eye,
  Sliding composedly from sleep—to death ;
A corpse so placid ne'er adorn'd a bed,
He had seem'd not quite—but only rather dead.

All night the widow'd Baroness contriv'd
 To shed a widow's tears; but on the morrow
Some news of such unusual sort arriv'd,
 There came strange alteration in her sorrow ;
From mouth to mouth it pass'd, one common humming
Throughout the house—the King ! the King is coming.

The Baroness, with all her soul and heart,
 A loyal woman, (now called ultra royal,)
Soon thrust all funeral concerns apart,
 And only thought about a banquet royal ;
In short, by aid of earnest preparation,
The visit quite dismiss'd the visitation.

And, spite of all her grief for the ex-mate,
 There was a secret hope she could not smother,
That some one, early, might replace " the late '—
 It was too soon to think about another ;
Yet let her minutes of despair be reckon'd
Against her hope, which was but for a *second.*

She almost thought that being thus bereft
 Just then, was one of time's propitious touches ;
A thread in such a nick so nick'd, it left
 Free opportunity to be a duchess ;
Thus all her care was only to look pleasant,
But as for tears—she dropp'd them—for the present.

Her household, as good servants ought to try,
 Look'd like their lady—anything but sad,
And giggled even that they might not cry,
 To damp fine company; in truth they had
No time to mourn, thro' choking turkeys' throttles,
Scouring old laces, and reviewing bottles.

Oh what a hubbub for the house of woe !
　All, resolute to one irresolution,
Kept tearing, swearing, plunging to and fro
　Just like another French mob revolution.
There lay the corpse that could not stir a muscle,
But all the rest seem'd Chaos in a bustle.

The Monarch came: oh ! who could ever guess
　The Baroness had been so late a weeper !
The kingly grace and more than graciousness,
　Buried the poor defunct some fathoms deeper.—
Could he have had a glance—alas poor Being !
Seeing would certainly have led to *D*—ing.

For casting round about her eyes to find
　Some one to whom her chattels to endorse,
The comfortable dame at last inclin'd
　To choose the cheerful Master of the Horse ;
He was so gay,—so tender,—the complete
Nice man,—the sweetest of the monarch's suite.

He saw at once and enter'd in the lists—
　Glance unto glance made amorous replies ;
They talk'd together like two egotists,
　In conversation all made up of *eyes:*
No couple ever got so right consort-ish
Within two hours—a courtship rather shortish.

At last, some sleepy, some by wine opprest,
　The courtly company began "nid noddin ;"
The King first sought his chamber, and the rest
　Instanter followed by the course he trod in.
I shall not please the scandalous by showing
The order, or disorder of their going.

The old Chateau, before that night, had never
   Held half so many underneath its roof,
It task'd the Baroness's best endeavour,
   And put her best contrivance to the proof,
To give them chambers up and down the stairs,
In twos and threes, by singles, and by pairs

She had just lodging for the whole—yet barely;
   And some, that were both broad of back and tall,
Lay on spare beds that served them very sparely:
   However, there were beds enough for all;
But living bodies occupied so many
She could not let the dead one take up any.

The act was, certainly, not over decent:
   Some small respect, e'en after death, she ow'd him,
Considering his death had been so recent:
   However, by command, her servants stow'd him,
(I am asham'd to think how he was slubber'd,)
Stuck bolt upright within a corner cupboard!

And there he slept as soundly as a post,
   With no more pillow than an oaken shelf,
Just like a kind accommodating host,
   Taking all inconvenience on himself.
None else slept in that room, except a stranger,
A decent man, a sort of Forest Ranger.

Who, whether he had gone too soon to bed,
   Or dreamt himself into an appetite,
Howbeit he took a longing to be fed,
   About the hungry middle of the night;
So getting forth, he sought some scrap to eat,
Hopeful of some stray pasty, or cold meat.

The casual glances of the midnight moon,
  Bright'ning some antique ornaments of brass,
Guided his gropings to that corner soon,
  Just where it stood, the coffin-safe, alas !
He tried the door—then shook it—and in course
Of time it open'd to a little force.

He put one hand in, and began to grope ;
  The place was very deep and quite as dark as
The middle night ;—when lo ! beyond his hope,
  He felt a something cold, in fact, the carcase ;
Right overjoy'd, he laugh'd, and blest his luck
At finding, as he thought, this haunch of buck !

Then striding back for his couteau de chasse,
  Determined on a little midnight lunching,
He came again and prob'd about the mass,
  As if to find the fattest bit for munching ;
Not meaning wastefully to cut it all up,
But only to abstract a little collop.

But just as he had struck one greedy stroke,
  His hand fell down quite powerless and weak ;
For when he cut the haunch it plainly spoke
  As haunch of ven'son never ought to speak ;
No wonder that his hand could go no further—
Whose could?—to carve cold meat that bellow'd, "murther !"

Down came the Body with a bounce, and down
  The Ranger sprang, a staircase at a spring,
And bawl'd enough to waken up a town ;
  Some thought that *they* were murder'd, some, the King,
And, like Macduff, did nothing for a season,
But stand upon the spot and bellow, "Treason !"

A hundred nightcaps gather'd in a mob,
  Torches drew torches, swords brought swords together,
It seem'd so dark and perilous a job ;
  The Baroness came trembling like a feather
Just in the rear, as pallid as a corse,
Leaning against the Master of the Horse.

A dozen of the bravest up the stair,
  Well lighted and well watch'd, began to clamber ;
They sought the door—they found it—they were there,
  A dozen heads went poking in the chamber ;
And lo ! with one hand planted on his hurt,
There stood the body bleeding thro' his shirt,—

No passive corse—but like a duellist
  Just smarting from a scratch—in fierce position,
One hand advanced, and ready to resist ;
  In fact, the Baron doff'd the apparition,
Swearing those oaths the French delight in most,
And for the second time "gave up the ghost !"

A living miracle !—for why?—the knife
  That cuts so many off from grave gray hairs,
Had only carv'd him kindly into life :
  How soon it chang'd the posture of affairs !
The difference one person more or less
Will make in families, is past all guess.

There stood the Baroness—no widow yet ;
  Here stood the Baron—"in the body" still ;
There stood the Horses' Master in a pet,
  Choking with disappointment's bitter pill,
To see the hope of his reversion fail,
Like that of riding on a donkey's tail.

The Baron liv'd—'twas nothing but a trance :
 The lady died—'twas nothing but a death :
The cupboard-cut serv'd only to enhance
 This postscript to the old Baronial breath :
He soon forgave, for the revival's sake,
A little *chop* intended for a *steak!*

ELEGY ON DAVID LAING, ESQ.,[*]

BLACKSMITH AND JOINER (WITHOUT LICENCE) AT GRETNA GREEN.

AH me ! what causes such complaining breath,
 Such female moans, and flooding tears to flow?
It is to chide with stern, remorseless Death,
  For laying Laing low !
From Prospect House there comes a sound of woe—
A shrill and persevering loud lament,
Echoed by Mrs. J.'s Establishment
  " For Six Young Ladies,
In a retired and healthy part of Kent."
 All weeping, Mr. L—— gone down to Hades !
Thoughtful of grates, and convents, and the veil !
  Surrey takes up the tale,
And all the nineteen scholars of Miss Jones
With the two parlour-boarders and th' apprentice—
So universal this mis-timed event is—
  Are joining sobs and groans !
The shock confounds all hymeneal planners
 And drives the sweetest from their sweet behaviours ;
The girls at Manor House forget their manners,
  And utter sighs like paviours !

---

[*] On the 3d inst., died in Springfield, near Gretna Green, David Laing, aged seventy-two, who had for thirty-five years officiated as high-priest at Gretna Green. He caught cold on his way to Lancaster, to give evidence on the trial of the Wakefields, from the effects of which he never recovered.—*Newspapers, July* 1827.

Down—down through Devon and the distant shires
  Travels the news of Death's remorseless crime ;
And in all hearts, at once, all hope expires
    Of *matches* against time !

    Along the northern route
The road is water'd by postilions' eyes ;
  The topboot paces pensively about,
And yellow jackets are all strained with sighs ;
There is a sound of grieving at the Ship,
And sorry hands are ringing at the Bell,
    In aid of David's knell.
The postboy's heart is cracking—not his whip—
  To gaze upon those useless empty collars
His way-worn horses seem so glad to slip—
  And think upon the dollars
That used to urge his gallop—quicker! quicker!
    All hope is fled,
    For Laing is dead—
Vicar of Wakefield—Edward Gibbon's vicar!
    The barristers shed tears
Enough to feed a snipe (snipes live on suction),
  To think in after years
No suits will come of Gretna Green abduction,
    Nor knaves inveigle
Young heiresses in marriage scrapes or legal.
    The dull reporters
Look truly sad and seriously solemn
    To lose the future column
On Hymen-Smithy and its fond resorters !
  But grave Miss Daulby and the teaching brood
Rejoice at quenching the clandestine flambeau—
  That never real beau of flesh and blood
Will henceforth lure young ladies from their *Chambaud.*

    Sleep—David Laing—sleep
In peace, though angry governesses spurn thee !
Over thy grave a thousand maidens weep,
    And honest postboys mourn thee !

Sleep, David !—safely and serenely sleep,
    Be-wept of many a learnëd legal eye !
To see the mould above thee in a heap
    Drowns many a lid that heretofore was dry !—
Especially of those that, plunging deep
    In love, would "ride and tie !"—
Had I command, thou shouldst have gone thy ways
In chaise and pair—and lain in Père-la-Chaise !

———

SONNET.

WRITTEN IN A VOLUME OF SHAKSPEARE.

How bravely Autumn paints upon the sky
The gorgeous fame of Summer which is fled !
Hues of all flow'rs, that in their ashes lie,
Trophied in that fair light whereon they fed,—
Tulip, and hyacinth, and sweet rose red,—
Like exhalations from the leafy mould,
Look here how honour glorifies the dead,
And warms their scutcheons with a glance of gold !—
Such is the memory of poets old,
Who on Parnassus-hill have bloom'd elate ;
Now they are laid under their marbles cold,
And turn'd to clay, whereof they were create ;
But god Apollo hath them all enroll'd,
And blazon'd on the very clouds of Fate !

———

A RETROSPECTIVE REVIEW.

Oh, when I was a tiny boy,
My days and nights were full of joy,
    My mates were blithe and kind !—
No wonder that I sometimes sigh,
And dash the tear-drop from my eye,
    To cast a look behind !

Q

A hoop was an eternal round
Of pleasure.   In those days I found
  A top a joyous thing ;—
But now those past delights I drop,
My head, alas! is all my top,
  And careful thoughts the string !

My marbles—once my bag was stored,—
Now I must play with Elgin's lord,
  With Theseus for a taw !
My playful horse has slipt his string.
Forgotten all his capering,
  And harness'd to the law !

My kite—how fast and far it flew !
Whilst I, a sort of Franklin, drew
  My pleasure from the sky !
'Twas paper'd o'er with studious themes,
The tasks I wrote—my present dreams
  Will never soar so high !

My joys are wingless all and dead ;
My dumps are made of more than lead ;
  My flights soon find a fall ;
My fears prevail, my fancies droop,
Joy never cometh with a hoop,
  And seldom with a call !

My football's laid upon the shelf ;
I am a shuttlecock myself
  The world knocks to and fro ;—
My archery is all unlearn'd,
And grief against myself has turn'd
  My arrows and my bow !

No more in noontide sun I bask;
My authorship's an endless task,
    My head's ne'er out of school :
My heart is pain'd with scorn and slight;
I have too many foes to fight,
    And friends grown strangely cool !

The very chum that shared my cake
Holds out so cold a hand to shake,
    It makes me shrink and sigh :—
On this I will not dwell and hang,—
The changeling would not feel a pang
    Though these should meet his eye !

No skies so blue or so serene
As then ;—no leaves look half so green
    As clothed the playground tree !
All things I loved are alter'd so,
Nor does it ease my heart to know
    That change resides in me !

Oh for the garb that mark'd the boy,
The trousers made of corduroy,
    Well ink'd with black and red ;
The crownless hat, ne'er deem'd an ill—
It only let the sunshine still
    Repose upon my head !

Oh for the riband round the neck !
The careless dogs'-ears apt to deck
    My book and collar both !
How can this formal man be styled
Merely an Alexandrine child,
    A boy of larger growth ?

Oh for that small, small beer anew!
And (heaven's own type) that mild sky-blue
   That wash'd my sweet meals down;
The master even!—and that small Turk
That fagg'd me!—worse is now my work—
   A fag for all the town!

Oh for the lessons learn'd by heart!
Ay, though the very birch's smart
   Should mark those hours again;
I'd "kiss the rod," and be resign'd
Beneath the stroke, and even find
   Some sugar in the cane!

The Arabian Nights rehearsed in bed!
The Fairy Tales in school-time read,
   By stealth, 'twixt verb and noun!
The angel form that always walk'd
In all my dreams, and look'd and talk'd
   Exactly like Miss Brown!

The *omne bene*—Christmas come!
The prize of merit, won for home—
   Merit had prizes then!
But now I write for days and days,
For fame—a deal of empty praise,
   Without the silver pen!

Then "home, sweet home!" the crowded coach—'
The joyous shout—the loud approach—
   The winding horns like rams'!
The meeting sweet that made me thrill,
The sweetmeats, almost sweeter still,
   No "satis" to the "jams!"—

When that I was a tiny boy
My days and nights were full of joy,
    My mates were blithe and kind!
No wonder that I sometimes sigh,
And dash the tear-drop from my eye,
    To cast a look behind!

THE LADY'S DREAM.

The lady lay in her bed,
　Her couch so warm and soft,
But her sleep was restless and broken still :
　For turning often and oft
From side to side, she mutter'd and moan'd.
　And toss'd her arms aloft.

At last she startled up,
　And gazed on the vacant air,
With a look of awe, as if she saw
　Some dreadful phantom there—
And then in the pillow she buried her face
　From visions ill to bear.

The very curtain shook,
　Her terror was so extreme ;
And the light that fell on the broider'd quilt
　Kept a tremulous gleam ;
And her voice was hollow, and shook as she cried :—
　"Oh me! that awful dream !

"That weary, weary walk,
    In the churchyard's dismal ground !
And those horrible things, with shady wings,
    That came and flitted round,—
Death, death, and nothing but death,
    In every sight and sound !

"And oh ! those maidens young,
    Who wrought in that dreary room,
With figures drooping and spectres thin,
    And cheeks without a bloom ;
And the Voice that cried, 'For the pomp of pride,
    We haste to an early tomb !

"'For the pomp and pleasure of Pride,
    We toil like Afric slaves,
And only to earn a home at last,
    Where yonder cypress waves ; '—
And then they pointed—I never saw
    A ground so full of graves !

"And still the coffins came,
    With their sorrowful trains and slow;
Coffin after coffin still,
    A sad and sickening show ;
From grief exempt, I never had dreamt
    Of such a World of Woe !

"Of the hearts that daily break,
    Of the tears that hourly fall,
Of the many, many troubles of life,
    That grieve this earthly ball—
Disease and Hunger, and Pain, and Want,
    But now I dreamt of them all !

"For the blind and the cripple were there,
   And the babe that pined for bread,
And the houseless man, and the widow poor
   Who begged—to bury the dead;
The naked, alas, that I might have clad,
   The famish'd I might have fed!

"The sorrow I might have sooth'd,
   And the unregarded tears;
For many a thronging shape was there,
   From long forgotten years,
Ay, even the poor rejected Moor,
   Who raised my childish fears!

"Each pleading look, that long ago
   I scann'd with a heedless eye,
Each face was gazing as plainly there,
   As when I pass'd it by:
Woe, woe for me if the past should be
   Thus present when I die!

"No need of sulphurous lake,
   No need of fiery coal,
But only that crowd of human kind
   Who wanted pity and dole—
In everlasting retrospect—
   Will wring my sinful soul!

"Alas! I have walk'd through life
   Too heedless where I trod;
Nay, helping to trample my fellow worm,
   And fill the burial sod—
Forgetting that even the sparrow falls
   Not unmark'd of God!

"I drank the richest draughts;
    And ate whatever is good—
Fish, and flesh, and fowl, and fruit,
    Supplied my hungry mood;
But I never remember'd the wretched ones
    That starve for want of food!

"I dress'd as the noble dress,
    In cloth of silver and gold,
With silk, and satin, and costly furs,
    In many an ample fold;
But I never remembered the naked limb
    That froze with winter's cold.

"The wounds I might have heal'd!
    The human sorrow and smart!
And yet it never was in my soul
    To play so ill a part:
But evil is wrought by want of Thought,
    As well as want of Heart!"

She clasp'd her fervent hands,
    And tears began to stream;
Large, and bitter, and fast they fell,
    Remorse was so extreme:
And yet, oh yet, that many a Dame
    Would dream the Lady's Dream!

———

DEATH'S RAMBLE.

ONE day the dreary old King of Death
    Inclined for some sport with the carnal,

So he tied a pack of darts on his back,
    And quietly stole from his charnel.

His head was bald of flesh and of hair,
    His body was lean and lank,
His joints at each stir made a crack, and the cur
    Took a gnaw, by the way, at his shank.

And what did he do with his deadly darts,
    This goblin of grisly bone?
He dabbled and spill'd man's blood, and he kill'd
    Like a butcher that kills his own.

The first he slaughter'd it made him laugh
    (For the man was a coffin-maker)
To think how the mutes, and men in black suits,
    Would mourn for an undertaker.

Death saw two Quakers sitting at church:
    Quoth he, " We shall not differ."
And he let them alone, like figures of stone.
    For he could not make them stiffer.

He saw two duellists going to fight,
    In fear they could not smother;
And he shot one through at once—for he knew
    They never would shoot each other.

He saw a watchman fast in his box,
    And he gave a snore infernal;
Said Death, " He may keep his breath, for his sleep
    Can never be more eternal."

He met a coachman driving his coach
  So slow, that his fare grew sick ;
But he let him stray on his tedious way,
  For Death only wars on the *quick.*

Death saw a toll-man taking a toll,
  In the spirit of his fraternity ;
But he knew that sort of man would extort,
  Though summon'd to all eternity.

He found an author writing his life,
  But he let him write no further ;
For Death, who strikes whenever he likes,
  Is jealous of all self-murther !

Death saw a patient that pulled out his purse,
  And a doctor that took the sum ;
But he let them be—for he knew that the "fee"
  Was a prelude to "faw" and "fum."

He met a dustman ringing a bell,
  And he gave him a mortal thrust ;
For himself, by law, since Adam's flaw,
  Is contractor for all our dust.

He saw a sailor mixing his grog,
  And he mark'd him out for slaughter :
For on water he scarcely had cared for Death,
  And never on rum-and-water.

Death saw two players playing at cards,
  But the game wasn't worth a dump,
For he quickly laid them flat with a spade,
  To wait for the final trump !

BALLAD.

It was not in the Winter
  Our loving lot was cast ;
It was the Time of Roses,—
  We pluck'd them as we pass'd ;

That churlish season never frown'd
  On early lovers yet :—
Oh, no—the world was newly crown'd
  With flowers when first we met !

'Twas twilight, and I bade you go,
  But still you held me fast ;
It was the Time of Roses,—
  We pluck'd them as we pass'd.—

What else could peer thy glowing cheek.
  That tears began to stud !
And when I ask'd the like of Love,
  You snatched a damask bud ;

And oped it to the dainty core,
  Still glowing to the last.—
It was the Time of Roses,—
  We pluck'd them as we pass'd !

AUTUMN.

The Autumn is old,
The sere leaves are flying :
He hath gather'd up gold,
And now he is dying ;
Old Age, begin sighing !

The vintage is ripe,
The harvest is heaping ;—
But some that have sow'd
Have no riches for reaping ;—
Poor wretch, fall a-weeping !

The year's in the wane,
There is nothing adorning,
The night has no eve,
And the day has no morning ;—
Cold winter gives warning.

The rivers run chill,
The red sun is sinking,
And I am grown old,
And life is fast shrinking ;—
Here's enow for sad thinking !

TO HOPE.

OH ! take, young seraph, take thy harp,
 And play to me so cheerily ;
For grief is dark, and care is sharp,
 And life wears on so wearily.
  Oh ! take thy harp !
Oh ! sing as thou were wont to do,
 When, all youth's sunny season long,
 I sat and listen'd to thy song,
And yet 'twas ever, ever new,
With magic in its heaven-tuned string—
 The future bliss thy constant theme,
Oh ! then each little woe took wing
 Away, like phantoms of a dream ;
   As if each sound
   That fluttered round
 Had floated over Lethe's stream !

By all those bright and happy hours
We spent in life's sweet eastern bow'rs,
Where thou wouldst sit and smile, and show,
Ere buds were come, where flowers would grow,
And oft anticipate the rise
Of life's warm sun that scaled the skies;
By many a story of love and glory,
And friendships promised oft to me;
By all the faith I lent to thee,—
Oh! take, young seraph, take thy harp,
    And play to me so cheerily;
For grief is dark, and care is sharp,
    And life wears on so wearily,
        Oh! take thy harp!

Perchance the strings will sound less clear,
    That long have lain neglected by
In sorrow's misty atmosphere;
It ne'er may speak as it has spoken
    Such joyous notes so brisk and high;
But are its golden chords all broken?
Are there not some, though weak and low,
To play a lullaby to woe?
But thou canst sing of love no more,
    For Celia show'd that dream was vain;
And many a fancied bliss is o'er,
    That comes not e'en in dreams again.
        Alas! alas!
        How pleasures pass,
And leave thee now no subject, save
The peace and bliss beyond the grave!

Then be thy flight among the skies:
    Take, then, oh! take the skylark's wing.
And leave dull earth, and heavenward rise
    O'er all its tearful clouds, and sing
        On skylark's wing!
Another life-spring there adorns
    Another youth, without the dread

Of cruel care, whose crown of thorns
   Is here for manhood's aching head.
Oh! there are realms of welcome day,
A world where tears are wiped away!
Then be thy flight among the skies :
   Take, then, oh ! take the skylark's wing,
And leave dull earth, and heavenward rise
   O'er all its tearful clouds and sing
     On skylark's wing !

TO CELIA.

OLD fictions say that Love hath eyes
Yet sees, unhappy boy! with none ;
Blind as the night ! but fiction lies,
For Love doth always see with one.

To one our graces all unveil,
To one our flaws are all exposed ;
But when with tenderness we hail,
He smiles, and keeps the critic closed.

But when he's scorned, abused, estranged,
He opes the eye of evil ken,
And all his angel friends are changed
To demons—and are hated then !

Yet once it happ'd that, semi-blind,
He met thee on a summer day,
And took thee for his mother kind,
And frown'd as he was push'd away.

But still he saw thee shine the same,
Though he had oped his evil eye,

And found that nothing but her shame
Was left to know his mother by !

And ever since that morning sun
He thinks of thee, and blesses Fate
That he can look with both on one
Who hath no ugliness to hate.

———

THE SEA OF DEATH.

A FRAGMENT.

————Methought I saw
Life swiftly treading over endless space ;
And, at her foot-print, but a bygone pace,
The ocean Past, which, with increasing wave,
Swallow'd her steps like a pursuing grave.

Sad were my thoughts that anchor'd silently
On the dead waters of that passionless sea,
Unstirr'd by any touch of living breath :
Silence hung over it, and drowsy Death,
Like a gorged sea-bird, slept with folded wings
On crowded carcases—sad passive things
That wore the thin grey surface, like a veil
Over the calmness of their features pale.

And there were spring-faced cherubs that did sleep
Like water-lilies on that motionless deep,
How beautiful ! with bright unruffled hair
On sleek unfretted brows, and eyes that were
Buried in marble tombs, a pale eclipse !
And smile-bedimpled cheeks, and pleasant lips,
Meekly apart, as if the soul intense
Spake out in dreams of its own innocence :
And so they lay in loveliness, and kept
The birth-night of their peace, that Life e'en wept
With very envy of their happy fronts ;

For there were neighbour brows scarr'd by the brunts
Of strife and sorrowing—where Care had set
His crooked autograph, and marr'd the jet
Of glossy locks, with hollow eyes forlorn,
And lips that curl'd in bitterness and scorn—
Wretched,—as they had breathed of this world's pain
And so bequeathed it to the world again,
Through the beholder's heart in heavy sighs.
So lay they garmented in torpid light,
Under the pall of a transparent night,
Like solemn apparitions lull'd sublime
To everlasting rest,—and with them Time
Slept, as he sleeps upon the silent face
Of a dark dial in a sunless place.

TO AN ABSENTEE.

O'ER hill, and dale, and distant sea,
Through all the miles that stretch between,
My thought must fly to rest on thee,
And would—though worlds should intervene.

Nay, thou art now so dear, methinks
The farther we are forced apart,
Affection's firm elastic links
But bind thee closer round the heart.

For now we sever each from each,
I learn what I have lost in thee ;
Alas, that nothing else could teach
How great indeed my love should be !

Farewell ! I did not know thy worth;
But thou art gone, and now 'tis prized ;
So angels walked unknown on earth,
But when they flew were recognised !

R

THE DEATHBED.

WE watch'd her breathing through the night,
   Her breathing soft and low,
As in her breast the wave of life
   Kept heaving to and fro.

So silently we seem'd to speak,
   So slowly moved about,
As we had lent her half our powers
   To eke her living out.

Our very hopes belied our fears,
   Our fears our hopes belied—
We thought her dying when she slept,
   And sleeping when she died.

For when the morn came dim and sad,
   And chill with early showers,
Her quiet eyelids closed—she had
   Another morn than ours.

TO MY WIFE.

STILL glides the gentle streamlet on,
   With shifting current new and strange ;
The water, that was here, is gone,
   But those green shadows never change.

Serene or ruffled by the storm,
   On present waves, as on the past,
The mirror'd grove retains its form,
   The self-same trees their semblance cast.

The hue each fleeting globule wears,
That drop bequeaths it to the next ;
One picture still the surface bears,
To illustrate the murmur'd text.

So, love, however time may flow,
Fresh hours pursuing those that flee,
One constant image still shall show
My tide of life is true to thee.

- - - - - -

SONG.

THERE is dew for the flow'ret
    And honey for the bee,
And bowers for the wild bird,
    And love for you and me.

There are tears for the many
    And pleasures for the few ;
But let the world pass on, dear,
    There's love for me and you.

There is care that will not leave us
    And pain that will not flee ;
But on our hearth unalter'd
    Sits Love—'tween you and me.

Our love it ne'er was reckon'd,
    Yet good it is and true,
It's *half* the world to me, dear,
    It's *all* the world to you.

I REMEMBER, I REMEMBER.

I REMEMBER, I remember,
The house where I was born,
The little window where the sun
Came peeping in at morn ;
He never came a wink too soon,
Nor brought too long a day,
But now, I often wish the night
Had borne my breath away!

I remember, I remember,
The roses, red and white,
The violets, and the lily-cups,
Those flowers made of light !
The lilacs where the robin built,
And where my brother set
The laburnum on his birth-day,—
The tree is living yet !

I remember, I remember,
Where I was used to swing,
And thought the air must rush as fresh
To swallows on the wing ;
My spirit flew in feathers then,
That is so heavy now,
And summer pools could hardly cool
The fever on my brow !

I remember, I remember,
The fir trees dark and high ;
I used to think their slender tops
Were close against the sky :
It was a childish ignorance,
But now 'tis little joy
To know I'm farther off from Heav'n
Than when I was a boy.

* From " Friendship's Offering," 1826.

THE POET'S PORTION.

WHAT is a mine—a treasury—a dower—
A magic talisman of mighty power?
A poet's wide possession of the earth.
He has th' enjoyment of a flower's birth
Before its budding—ere the first red streaks,
And Winter cannot rob him of their cheeks.

Look—if his dawn be not as other men's!
Twenty bright flushes—ere another kens
The first of sunlight is abroad—he sees
Its golden 'lection of the topmost trees,
And opes the splendid fissures of the morn.

When do his fruits delay, when doth his corn
Linger for harvesting?   Before the leaf
Is commonly abroad, in his pil'd sheaf
The flagging poppies lose their ancient flame.

No sweet there is, no pleasure I can name,
But he will sip it first—before the lees.
'Tis his to taste rich honey,—ere the bees
Are busy with the brooms.   He may forestall
June's rosy advent for his coronal;
Before th' expectant buds upon the bough,
Twining his thoughts to bloom upon his brow.

Oh! blest to see the flower in its seed,
Before its leafy presence; for indeed
Leaves are but wings on which the summer flies
And each thing perishable fades and dies,
Escap'd in thought; but his rich thinkings be
Like overflows of immortality:
So that what there is steep'd shall perish never,
But live and bloom, and be a joy for ever.

ODE TO THE CAMELEOPARD.

WELCOME to Freedom's birth-place—and a den !
    Great Anti-climax, hail !
So very lofty in thy front—but then,
      So dwindling at the tail !—
In truth, thou hast the most unequal legs !
Has one pair gallop'd, whilst the other trotted,
Along with other brethren, leopard-spotted,
O'er Afric sand, where ostriches lay eggs?
Sure thou wert caught in some hard uphill chase,
Those hinder heels still keeping thee in check !
      And yet thou seem'st prepared in any case,
      Tho' they had lost the race,
        To win it by a neck !

That lengthy neck—how like a crane's it looks !
Art thou the overseer of all the brutes?
Or dost thou browze on tip-top leaves or fruits—
Or go a bird-nesting amongst the rooks?
How kindly nature caters for all wants ;
Thus giving unto thee a neck that stretches,
      And high food fetches—
To some a long nose, like the elephant's !

Oh ! had'st thou any organ to thy bellows,
To turn thy breath to speech in human style,
      What secrets thou might'st tell us,
Where now our scientific guesses fail ;
      For instance of the Nile,
Whether those Seven Mouths have any tail—
      Mayhap thy luck too,
From that high head, as from a lofty hill,
Has let thee see the marvellous Timbuctoo—
Or drink of Niger at its infant rill ;
What were the travels of our Major Denham,
      Or Clapperton, to thine
      In that same line,
If thou could'st only squat thee down and pen 'em !

Strange sights, indeed, thou must have overlook'd,
With eyes held ever in such vantage-stations!
Hast seen, perchance, unhappy white folks cook'd,
And then made free of negro corporations?
Poor wretches saved from cast away three-deckers—
 By sooty wreckers—
From hungry waves to have a loss still drearier,
To far exceed the utmost aim of Park—
And find themselves, alas! beyond the mark,
In the *insides* of Africa's Interior!

Live on, Giraffe! genteelest of raff kind!
Admir'd by noble, and by royal tongues!
 May no pernicious wind,
Or English fog, blight thy exotic lungs!
Live on in happy peace, altho' a rarity,
Nor envy thy poor cousin's more outrageous
 Parisian popularity;
Whose very leopard-rash is grown contagious,
And worn on gloves and ribbons all about,
 Alas! they'll wear him out!
So thou shalt take thy sweet diurnal feeds—
When he is stuff'd with undigested straw,
Sad food that never visited his jaw!
And staring round him with a brace of beads!

JOHN TROT.

A BALLAD.

I.

John Trot he was as tall a lad
 As York did ever rear—
As his dear Granny used to say,
 He'd make a grenadier.

II.

A serjeant soon came down to York,
  With ribbons and a frill ;
My lads, said he, let broadcast be,
  And come away to drill.

III.

But when he wanted John to 'list,
  In war he saw no fun,
Where what is call'd a raw recruit,
  Gets often over-done.

IV.

Let others carry guns, said he,
  And go to war's alarms,
But I have got a shoulder-knot
  Impos'd upon my arms.

V.

For John he had a footman's place
  To wait on Lady Wye—
She was a dumpy woman, tho'
  Her family was high.

VI.

Now when two years had past away,
  Her Lord took very ill,
And left her to her widowhood,
  Of course more dumpy still.

VII.

Said John, I am a proper man,
  And very tall to see ;
Who knows, but now her Lord is low,
  She may look up to me ?

VIII.

A cunning woman told me once,
  Such fortune would turn up ;
She was a kind of sorceress,
  But studied in a cup !

IX.

So he walk'd up to Lady Wye,
  And took her quite amazed,—
She thought, tho' John was tall enough,
  He wanted to be raised.

X.

But John—for why? she was a dame
  Of such a dwarfish sort—
Had only come to bid her make
  Her mourning very short.

XI.

Said he, your Lord is dead and cold,
  You only cry in vain ;
Not all the Cries of London now,
  Could call him back again !

XII.

You'll soon have many a noble beau,
  To dry your noble tears—
But just consider this, that I
  Have follow'd you for years.

XIII.

And tho' you are above me far,
  What matters high degree,
When you are only four foot nine.
  And I am six foot three?

XIV.

For tho' you are of lofty race,
   And I'm a low-born elf ;
Yet none among your friends could say,
   You matched beneath yourself.

XV.

Said she, such insolence as this
   Can be no common case ;
Tho' you are in my service, sir,
   Your love is out of place.

XVI.

O Lady Wye ! O Lady Wye !
   Consider what you do ;
How can you be so short with me,
   I am not so with you !

XVII.

Then ringing for her serving men,
   They show'd him to the door :
Said they, you turn out better now,
   Why didn't you before ?

XVIII.

They stripp'd his coat, and gave him kicks
   For all his wages due ;
And off, instead of green and gold,
   He went in black and blue.

XIX.

No family would take him in,
   Because of this discharge ;
So he made up his mind to serve
   The country all at large.

XX.

Huzza ! the Serjeant cried, and put
  The money in his hand,
And with a shilling cut him off
  From his paternal land.

XXI.

For when his regiment went to fight
  At Saragossa town,
A Frenchman thought he look'd too tall
  And so he cut him down !

THE WIDOW.

ONE widow at a grave will sob
A little while, and weep, and sigh!
If two should meet on such a job,
They'll have a gossip by and by.
If three should come together—why,
Three widows are good company!
If four should meet by any chance,
Four is a number very nice,
To have a rubber in a trice—
But five will up and have a dance!

Poor Mrs. C——— (why should I not
Declare her name?—her name was Cross)
Was one of those the "common lot"
Had left to weep "no common loss;"-
For she had lately buried then
A man, the "very best of men,"
A lingering truth, discover'd first
Whenever men "are at the worst."
To take the measure of her woe,
It was some dozen inches deep—
I mean in crape, and hung so low,
It hid the drops she did *not* weep:

In fact, what human life appears,
It was a perfect "veil of tears."
Though ever since she lost "her prop
And stay,"—alas ! he wouldn't stay—
She never had a tear to mop,
Except one little angry drop,
From Passion's eye, as Moore would say;
Because, when Mister Cross took flight,
It looked so very like a spite—
He died upon a washing-day !

Still Widow Cross went twice a week,
As if "to wet a widow's cheek,"
And soothe his grave with sorrow's gravy,—
'Twas nothing but a make-believe,
She might as well have hoped to grieve
Enough of brine to float a navy ;
And yet she often seem'd to raise
A cambric kerchief to her eye—
A *duster* ought to be the phrase,
Its work was all so very dry.
The springs were lock'd that ought to flow—
In England or in widow-woman—
As those that watch the weather know,
Such "backward Springs" are not uncommon.

But why did Widow Cross take pains,
To call upon the "dear remains,"—
Remains that could not tell a jot,
Whether she ever wept or not,
Or how his relict took her losses ?
Oh ! my black ink turns red for shame —
But still the naughty world must learn,
There was a little German came
To shed a tear in "Anna's Urn,"
At the next grave to Mr. Cross's !
For there an angel's virtues slept,
"Too soon did Heaven assert its claim !"

But still her painted face he kept,
"Encompass'd in an angel's frame."

He look'd quite sad and quite deprived,
His head was nothing but a hat-band;
He look'd so lone, and so *un*wived,
That soon the Widow Cross contrived
To fall in love with even *that* band ;
And all at once the brackish juices
Came gushing out thro' sorrow's sluices—
Tear after tear too fast to wipe,
Tho' sopp'd, and sopp'd, and sopp'd again—
No leak in sorrow's private pipe,
But like a bursting on the main !
Whoe'er has watch'd the window-pane—
I mean to say in showery weather—
Has seen two little drops of rain,
Like lovers very fond and fain,
At one another creeping, creeping,
Till both, at last, embrace together:
So far'd it with that couple's weeping !
The principle was quite as active—
  Tear unto tear,
  Kept drawing near,
Their very blacks became attractive.
To cut a shortish story shorter,
Conceive them sitting tête à tête—
Two cups,—hot muffins on a plate,—
With "Anna's Urn" to hold hot water !
The brazen vessel for a while,
Had lectured in an easy song,
Like Abernethy—on the bile—
The scalded herb was getting strong ;
All seem'd as smooth as smooth could be,
To have a cosey cup of tea ;
Alas ! how often human sippers
With unexpected bitters meet,
And buds, the sweetest of the sweet,
Like sugar, only meet the nippers !

The Widow Cross, I should have told,
Had seen three husbands to the mould ;
She never sought an Indian pyre,
Like Hindoo wives that lose their loves,
But with a proper sense of fire,
Put up, instead, with "three removes :'
Thus, when with any tender words
Or tears she spoke about her loss,
The dear departed, Mr. Cross,
Came in for nothing but his thirds ;
For, as all widows love too well,
She liked upon the list to dwell,
And oft ripp'd up the old disasters—
She might, indeed, have been supposed
A great *ship* owner, for she prosed
Eternally of her Three Masters !

Thus, foolish woman ! while she nursed
Her mild souchong, she talk'd and reckon'd
What had been left her by her first,
And by her last, and by her second.
Alas ! not all her annual rents
Could then entice the little German,—
Not Mr. Cross's Three Per Cents,
Or Consols, ever make him *her* man ;
He liked her cash, he liked her houses,
But not that dismal bit of land
She always settled on her spouses.
So taking up his hat and band,
Said he " You'll think·my conduct odd—
But here my hopes no more may linger ;
I thought you had a wedding-finger,
But oh !—it is a curtain-rod ! "

"DON'T YOU SMELL FIRE?"

I.

RUN!—run for St. Clements's engine!
  For the Pawnbroker's all in a blaze,
And the pledges are frying and singing—
  Oh! how the poor pawners will craze!
Now where can the turncock be drinking?
  Was there ever so thirsty an elf?—
But he still may tope on, for I'm thinking
  That the plugs are as dry as himself.

II.

The engines!—I hear them come rumbling;
  There's the Phœnix! the Globe! and the Sun!
What a row there will be, and a grumbling
  When the water don't start for a run!
See! there they come racing and tearing,
  All the street with loud voices is fill'd;
Oh! it's only the firemen a-swearing
  At a man they've run over and kill'd!

III.

How sweetly the sparks fly away now,
  And twinkle like stars in the sky;
It's a wonder the engines don't play now,
  But I never saw water so shy!
Why there isn't enough for a snipe,
  And the fire it is fiercer, alas!
Oh! instead of the New River pipe,
  They have gone—that they have—to the gas!

IV.

Only look at the poor little P——'s
  On the roof—is there anything sadder?

My dears, keep fast hold, if you please,
    And they won't be an hour with the ladder!
But if any one's hot in their feet,
    And in very great haste to be saved,
Here's a nice easy bit in the street,
    That M'Adam has lately unpaved!

V.

There is some one—I see a dark shape
    At that window, the hottest of all,—
My good woman, why don't you escape?
    Never think of your bonnet and shawl:
If your dress isn't perfect, what is it
    For once in a way to your hurt?
When your husband is paying a visit
    There, at Number Fourteen, in his shirt!

VI.

Only see how she throws out her *chaney!*
    Her basons, and teapots, and all
The most brittle of *her* goods—or any,
    But they all break in breaking their fall:
Such things are not surely the best
    From a two-story window to throw—
She might save a good iron-bound chest,
    For there's plenty of people below!

VII.

O dear! what a beautiful flash!
    How it shone thro' the window and door;
We shall soon hear a scream and a crash,
    When the woman falls thro' with the floor!
There! there! what a volley of flame,
    And then suddenly all is obscured!—
Well—I'm glad in my heart that I came;—
    But I hope the poor man is insured!

S

THE VOLUNTEER.

" The clashing of my armour in my ears
  Sounds like a passing bell ; my buckler puts me
  In mind of a bier ; this, my broadsword, a pickaxe
  To dig my grave."   THE LOVER'S PROGRESS.

I.

'TWAS in that memorable year
France threaten'd to put off in
Flat-bottom'd boats, intending each
To be a British coffin,
To make sad widows of our wives,
And every babe an orphan :—

II.

When coats were made of scarlet cloaks,
And heads were dredg'd with flour,
I listed in the Lawyers' Corps,
Against the battle hour ;
A perfect Volunteer—for why?
I brought my "will and pow'r."

III.

One dreary day—a day of dread,
Like Cato's, over-cast—
About the hour of six, (the morn
And I were breaking fast,)
There came a loud and sudden sound,
That struck me all aghast !

IV.

A dismal sort of morning roll,
That was not to be eaten :
Although it was no skin of mine,
But parchment that was beaten,
I felt tattoo'd through all my flesh,
Like any Otaheitan.

V

My jaws with utter dread enclosed
The morsel I was munching,
And terror lock'd them up so tight,
My very teeth went crunching
All through my bread and tongue at once,
Like sandwich made at lunching.

VI.

My hand that held the tea-pot fast,
Stiffen'd, but yet unsteady,
Kept pouring, pouring, pouring o'er
The cup in one long eddy,
Till both my hose were mark'd with *tea,*
As they were mark'd already.

VII.

I felt my visage turn from red
To white—from cold to hot;
But it was nothing wonderful
My colour changed, I wot,
For, like some variable silks,
I felt that I was shot.

VIII.

And looking forth with anxious eye,
From my snug upper story,
I saw our melancholy corps,
Going to beds all gory;
The pioneers seem'd very loth
To axe their way to glory.

IX.

The captain march'd as mourners march,
The ensign too seem'd lagging.

And many more, although they were
No ensigns, took to flagging—
Like corpses in the Serpentine,
Methought they wanted dragging.

X.

But while I watch'd, the thought of death
Came like a chilly gust,
And lo! I shut the window down,
With very little lust
To join so many marching men,
That soon might be March dust.

XI.

Quoth I, "since Fate ordains it so,
Our foe the coast must land on;"—
I felt so warm beside the fire
I cared not to abandon;
Our hearths and homes are always things
That patriots make a stand on.

XII.

"The fools that fight abroad for home,"
Thought I, "may get a wrong one;
Let those that have no homes at all,
Go battle for a long one."
The mirror here confirm'd me this
Reflection, by a strong one.

XIII.

For there, where I was wont to shave,
And deck me like Adonis,
There stood the leader of our foes,
With vultures for his cronies—
No Corsican, but Death himself,
The Bony of all Bonies.

XIV.

A horrid sight it was, and sad
To see the grisly chap
Put on my crimson livery,
And then begin to clap
My helmet on—ah me! it felt
Like any felon's cap.

XV.

My plume seem'd borrow'd from a hearse.
An undertaker's crest ;
My epaulettes like coffin-plates ;
My belt so heavy press'd,
Four pipeclay cross-roads seem'd to lie
At once upon my breast.

XVI.

My brazen breast-plate only lack'd
A little heap of salt,
To make me like a corpse full dress'd,
Preparing for the vault—
To set up what the Poet calls
My everlasting halt.

XVII.

This funeral show inclined me quite
To peace :—and here I am !
Whilst better lions go to war,
Enjoying with the lamb
A lengthen'd life, that might have been
A martial epigram.

THE WEE MAN.

A ROMANCE.

IT was a merry company,
  And they were just afloat,
When lo! a man, of dwarfish span,
  Came up and hail'd the boat.

"Good morrow to ye, gentle folks,
  And will you let me in?—
A slender space will serve my case,
  For I am small and thin."

They saw he was a dwarfish man,
  And very small and thin;
Not seven such would matter much,
  And so they took him in.

They laugh'd to see his little hat,
  With such a narrow brim;
They laugh'd to note his dapper coat
  With skirts so scant and trim.

But narely had they gone a mile,
  When, gravely, one and all,
At once began to think the man
  Was not so very small.

His coat had got a broader skirt,
  His hat a broader brim,
His leg grew stout, and soon plump'd out
  A very proper limb.

Still on they went, and as they went,
   More rough the billows grew,—
And rose and fell, a greater swell,
   And he was swelling too !

And lo ! where room had been for seven,
   For six there scarce was space !
For five !—for four !—for three !—not more
   Than two could find a place !

There was not even room for one !
   They crowded by degrees—
Aye—closer yet, till elbows met,
   And knees were jogging knees.

"Good sir, you must not sit a-stern,
   The wave will else come in !"
Without a word he gravely stirr'd,
   Another seat to win.

"Good sir, the boat has lost her trim,
   You must not sit a-lee !"
With smiling face, and courteous grace,
   The middle seat took he.

But still, by constant quiet growth,
   His back became so wide,
Each neighbour wight, to left and right,
   Was thrust against the side.

Lord ! how they chided with themselves,
   That they had let him in ;
To see him grow so monstrous now,
   That came so small and thin.

On every brow a dew-drop stood,
   They grew so scared and hot,—
"I' the name of all that's great and tall,
   Who are ye, sir, and what?"

Loud laugh'd the Gogmagog, a laugh
   As loud as giant's roar—
"When first I came, my proper name
   Was Little—now I'm *Moore!*"

———

"THE LAST MAN."

'Twas in the year two thousand and one,
A pleasant morning of May,
I sat on the gallows-tree all alone,
A-chaunting a merry lay,—
To think how the pest had spared my life,
To sing with the larks that day!

When up the heath came a jolly knave,
Like a scarecrow, all in rags:
It made me crow to see his old duds
All abroad in the wind, like flags :—
So up he came to the timbers' foot
And pitch'd down his greasy bags.—

Good Lord ! how blithe the old beggar was !
At pulling out his scraps,—
The very sight of his broken orts
Made a work in his wrinkled chaps :
"Come down," says he, "you Newgate-bird,
And have a taste of my snaps !"——

Then down the rope, like a tar from the mast,
I slided, and by him stood ;
But I wished myself on the gallows again
When I smelt that beggar's food,
A foul beef-bone and a mouldy crust ;
"Oh !" quoth he, "the heavens are good !"

Then after this grace he cast him down :
Says I, "You'll get sweeter air
A pace or two off, on the windward side,"
For the felons' bones lay there.
But he only laugh'd at the empty skulls,
And offered them part of his fare.

"I never harm'd *them*, and they won't harm me :
Let the proud and the rich be cravens !"
I did not like that strange beggar man,
He look'd so up at the heavens.
Anon he shook out his empty old poke ;
"There's the crumbs," saith he, "for the ravens !"

It made me angry to see his face,
It had such a jesting look ;
But while I made up my mind to speak,
A small case-bottle he took :
Quoth he, "though I gather the green water-cress
My drink is not of the brook !"

Full manners-like he tender'd the dram ;
Oh, it came of a dainty cask !
But, whenever it came to his turn to pull,
"Your leave, good Sir, I must ask ;
But I always wipe the brim with my sleeve,
When a hangman sups at my flask !"

And then he laugh'd so loudly and long,
The churl was quite out of breath ;
I thought the very Old One was come
To mock me before my death,
And wish'd I had buried the dead men's bones
That were lying about the heath !

But the beggar gave me a jolly clap—
"Come, let us pledge each other,
For all the wide world is dead beside,
And we are brother and brother—
I've a yearning for thee in my heart,
As if we had come of one mother.

"I've a yearning for thee in my heart
That almost makes me weep,
For as I pass'd from town to town
The folks were all stone-asleep,—
But when I saw thee sitting aloft,
It made me both laugh and leap !"

Now a curse (I thought) be on his love,
And a curse upon his mirth,—
An' it were not for that beggar man
I'd be the King of the earth,—
But I promis'd myself an hour should come
To make him rue his birth—

So down we sat and bous'd again
Till the sun was in mid-sky,
When, just as the gentle west-wind came,
We hearken'd a dismal cry ;
"Up, up, on the tree," quoth the beggar man.
"Till these horrible dogs go by !"

And, lo ! from the forest's far-off skirts,
They came all yelling for gore,
A hundred hounds pursuing at once,
And a panting hart before,
Till he sunk adown at the gallows' foot,
And there his haunches they tore !

IIis haunches they tore, without a horn
To tell when the chase was done ;
And there was not a single scarlet coat
To flaunt it in the sun !—
I turn'd, and look'd at the beggar man,
And his tears dropt one by one !

And with curses sore he chid at the hounds.
Till the last dropt out of sight,
Anon, saith he, "let's down again,
And ramble for our delight,
For the world's all free, and we may choose
A right cozie barn for to-night !"

With that, he set up his staff on end,
And it fell with the point due West ;
So we far'd that way to a city great,
Where the folks had died of the pest--
It was fine to enter in house and hall,
Wherever it liked me best ;

For the porters all were stiff and cold,
And could not lift their heads ;
And when we came where their masters lay,
The rats leapt out of the beds ;
The grandest palaces in the land
Were as free as workhouse sheds.

But the beggar man made a mumping face,
And knock'd at every gate :
It made me curse to hear how he whin'd,
So our fellowship turn'd to hate,
And I bade him walk the world by himself,
For I scorn'd so humble a mate !

So *he* turn'd right and *I* turn'd left,
As if we had never met ;
And I chose a fair stone house for myself,
For the city was all to let ;
And for three brave holydays drank my fill
Of the choicest that I could get.

And because my jerkin was coarse and worn,
I got me a properer vest ;
It was purple velvet, stitch'd o'er with gold,
And a shining star at the breast !—
'Twas enough to fetch old Joan from her grave
To see me so purely drest !—

But Joan was dead and under the mould,
And every buxom lass ;
In vain I watch'd, at the window pane,
For a Christian soul to pass !
But sheep and kine wander'd up the street,
And browz'd on the new-come grass.—

When lo ! I spied the old beggar man,
And lustily he did sing !—
His rags were lapp'd in a scarlet cloak,
And a crown he had like a King ;
So he stept right up before my gate
And danc'd me a saucy fling !

Heaven mend us all.!—but, within my mind,
I had kill'd him then and there ;
To see him lording so braggart-like
That was born to his beggar's fare ;
And how he had stol'n the royal crown
His betters were meant to wear,

But God forbid that a thief should die
Without his share of the laws !
So I nimbly whipt my tackle out,
And soon tied up his claws,—
I was judge myself, and jury, and all,
And solemnly tried the cause.

But the beggar man would not plead, but cried
Like a babe without its corals,
For he knew how hard it is apt to go,
When the law and a thief have quarrels,—
There was not a Christian soul alive
To speak a word for his morals.

Oh, how gaily I doff'd my costly gear,
And put on my work-day clothes ;
I was tired of such a long Sunday life,—
And never was one of the sloths ;
But the beggar man grumbled a weary deal,
And made many crooked mouths.

So I haul'd him off to the gallows' foot,
And blinded him in his bags ;
'Twas a weary job to heave him up,
For a doom'd man always lags ;
But by ten of the clock he was off his legs
In the wind, and airing his rags !

So there he hung, and there I stood,
The LAST MAN left alive,
To have my own will of all the earth :
Quoth I, now I shall thrive !
But when was ever honey made
With one bee in a hive !

My conscience began to gnaw my heart,
Before the day was done,
For other men's lives had all gone out,
Like candles in the sun !—
But it seem'd as if I had broke, at last,
A thousand necks in one !

So I went and cut his body down
To bury it decentlie ;
God send there were any good soul alive
To do the like by me !
But the wild dogs came with terrible speed,
And bay'd me up the tree !

My sight was like a drunkard's sight,
And my head began to swim,
To see their jaws all white with foam,
Like the ravenous ocean brim ;—
But when the wild dogs trotted away
Their jaws were bloody and grim !

Their jaws were bloody and grim, good Lord !
But the beggar man, where was he?—
There was nought of him but some ribbons of rags
Below the gallows' tree !—
I know the Devil, when I am dead,
Will send his hounds for me !—

I've buried my babies one by one,
And dug the deep hole for Joan,
And cover'd the faces of kith and kin,
And felt the old churchyard stone
Go cold to my heart, full many a time,
But I never felt so lone !

For the lion and Adam were company,
And the tiger him beguil'd ;
But the simple kine are foes to my life,
And the household brutes are wild.
If the veriest cur would lick my hand,
I could love it like a child !

And the beggar man's ghost besets my dream,
At night to make me madder,—
And my wretched conscience within my breast,
Is like a stinging adder :—
I sigh when I pass the gallows' foot,
And look at the rope and ladder !—

For hanging looks sweet,— but alas ! in vain
My desperate fancy begs,—
I must turn my cup of sorrows quite up,
And drink it to the dregs,—
For there's not another man alive,
In the world, to pull my legs !

BACKING THE FAVOURITE.

Oh a pistol, or a knife!
For I'm weary of my life,—
    My cup has nothing sweet left to flavour it ;
My estate is out at nurse,
And my heart is like my purse—
    And all through-backing of the Favourite!

At dear O'Neil's first start,
I sported all my heart,—
    Oh, Becher, he never marr'd a braver hit !
For he cross'd her in her race,
And made her lose her place,
    And there was an end of that Favourite !

Anon, to mend my chance,
For the Goddess of the Dance *

---

* The late favourite of the King's Theatre, who left the pas seul of life, for a
perpetual *Ball.* Is not that her effigy now commonly borne about by the Italian
image vendors—an ethereal form holding a wreath with both hands above her
head—and her husband, in emblem, beneath her foot?

I pin'd and told my enslaver it ;
But she wedded in a canter,
And made me a Levanter,
   In foreign lands to sigh for the Favourite !

Then next Miss M. A. Tree
I adored, so sweetly she
   Could warble like a nightingale and quaver it ;
But she left that course of life
To be Mr. Bradshaw's wife,
   And all the world lost on the Favourite !

But out of sorrow's surf
Soon I leap'd upon the turf,
   Where fortune loves to wanton it and waver it ;
But standing on the pet,
" Oh my bonny, bonny Bet !"
   Black and yellow pull'd short up with the Favourite !

Thus flung by all the crack,
I resolv'd to cut the pack,—
   The second-raters seem'd then a safer hit !
So I laid my little odds
Against Memnon ! Oh, ye Gods !
   Am I always to be floored by the Favourite !

THE BALLAD OF

"SALLY BROWN, AND BEN THE CARPENTER."

I HAVE never been vainer of any verses than of my part in the
following Ballad. Dr. Watts, amongst evangelical nurses, has an
enviable renown—and Campbell's Ballads enjoy a snug genteel
popularity. "Sally Brown" has been favoured, perhaps, with as
wide a patronage as the Moral Songs, though its circle may not
have been of so select a class as the friends of "Hohenlinden."

But I do not desire to see it amongst what are called Elegant Extracts. The lamented Emery, drest as Tom Tug, sang it at his last mortal Benefit at Covent Garden ;—and, ever since, it has been a great favourite with the watermen of Thames, who time their oars to it, as the wherry-men of Venice time theirs to the lines of Tasso. With the watermen, it went naturally to Vauxhall :—and, over land, to Sadler's Wells. The Guards, not the mail coach, but the Life Guards,—picked it out from a fluttering hundred of others—all going to one air—against the dead wall at Knightsbridge. Cheap Printers of Shoe Lane, and Cowcross, (all pirates !) disputed about the Copyright, and published their own editions,—and, in the meantime, the Authors, to have made bread of their song, (it was poor old Homer's hard ancient case !)must have sung it about the streets. Such is the lot of Literature ! the profits of "Sally Brown" were divided by the Ballad Mongers :—it has cost, but has never brought me, a half-penny.

FAITHLESS SALLY BROWN.

AN OLD BALLAD.

I.

Young Ben he was a nice young man,
    A carpenter by trade ;
And he fell in love with Sally Brown,
    That was a lady's maid.

II.

But as they fetch'd a walk one day,
    They met a press-gang crew ;
And Sally she did faint away,
    While Ben he was brought to.

III.

The Boatswain swore with wicked words,
    Enough to shock a saint,
That though she did seem in a fit,
    'Twas nothing but a feint.

IV.

"Come, girl," said he, "hold up your head,
  He'll be as good as me ;
For when your swain is in our boat,
  A boatswain he will be."

V.

So when they'd made their game of her,
  And taken off her elf,
She rous'd, and found she only was
  A coming to herself.

VI.

"And is he gone, and is he gone ?"
  She cried, and wept outright :
"Then I will to the water side,
  And see him out of sight."

VII.

A waterman came up to her,—
  "Now, young woman," said he,
"If you weep on so, you will make
  Eye-water in the sea."

VIII.

"Alas ! they've taken my beau Ben
  To sail with old Benbow ;"
And her woe began to run afresh,
  As if she'd said, Gee woe !

IX.

Says he, "they've only taken him
  To the Tender-ship, you see ; "

"The Tender-ship," cried Sally Brown,
  "What a hard-ship that must be !

X.

"Oh ! would I were a mermaid now
  For then I'd follow him ;
But oh !—I'm not a fish-woman,
  And so I cannot swim.

XI.

"Alas ! I was not born beneath
  The virgin and the scales,
So I must curse my cruel stars,
  And walk about in Wales."

XII.

Now Ben had sail'd to many a place
  That's underneath the world ;
But in two years the ship came home
  And all her sails were furl'd.

XIII.

But when he call'd on Sally Brown,
  To see how she got on,
He found she'd got another Ben,
  Whose Christian-name was John.

XIV.

"O Sally Brown, O Sally Brown,
  How could you serve me so ?
I've met with many a breeze before,
  But never such a blow !"

Then reading on his 'bacco box,
    He heav'd a bitter sigh,
And then began to eye his pipe,
    And then to pipe his eye.

XVI.

And then he tried to sing "All's Well,"
    But could not though he tried ;
His head was turn'd and so he chew'd
    His pigtail till he died.

XVII.

His death, which happen'd in his birth,
    At forty-odd befell :
They went and told the sexton, and
    The sexton toll'd the bell.

———

A VALENTINE.

I.

Oh ! cruel heart ! ere these posthumous papers
    Have met thine eyes, I shall be out of breath ;
Those cruel eyes, like two funereal tapers
    Have only lighted me the way to death.
Perchance, thou wilt extinguish them in vapours,
    When I am gone, and green grass covereth
Thy lover, lost ; but it will be in vain—
It will not bring the vital spark again.

II.

Ah ! when those eyes, like tapers, burn'd so blue,
    It seemed an omen that we must expect

The sprites of lovers; and it boded true,
  For I am half a sprite—a ghost elect;
Wherefore I write to thee this last adieu,
  With my last pen—before that I effect
My exit from the stage; just stopp'd before
The tombstone steps that lead us to death's door.

III.

Full soon those living eyes, now liquid bright,
  Will turn dead dull, and wear no radiance, save
They shed a dreary and inhuman light,
  Illum'd within by glow-worms of the grave;
These ruddy cheeks, so pleasant to the sight,
  These lusty legs, and all the limbs I have,
Will keep Death's carnival, and, foul or fresh,
Must bid farewell, a long farewell, to flesh!

IV.

Yea, and this very heart, that dies for thee,
  As broken victuals to the worms will go;
And all the world will dine again but me—
  For I shall have no stomach;—and I know.
When I am ghostly, thou wilt sprightly be
  As now thou art: but will not tears of woe
Water thy spirits, with remorse adjunct,
When thou dost pause, and think of the defunct?

V.

And when thy soul is buried in a sleep,
  In midnight solitude, and little dreaming
Of such a spectre—what, if I should creep
  Within thy presence in such dismal seeming?
Thine eyes will stare themselves awake, and weep,
  And thou wilt cross thyself with treble screaming,
And pray with mingled penitence and dread
That I were less alive—or not so dead.

VI.

Then will thy heart confess thee, and reprove
 This wilful homicide which thou hast done:
And the sad epitaph of so much love
 Will eat into my heart, as if in stone:
And all the lovers that around thee move,
 Will read my fate, and tremble for their own;
And strike upon their heartless breasts, and sigh,
"Man, born of woman, must of woman die!"

VII.

Mine eyes grow dropsical—I can no more—
 And what is written thou may'st scorn to read,
Shutting thy tearless eyes.—'Tis done—'tis o'er—
 My hand is destin'd for another deed.
But one last word wrung from its aching core,
 And my lone heart in silentness will bleed;
Alas! it ought to take a life to tell
That one last word—that fare—fare—fare thee well.

"PLEASE TO RING THE BELLE."

I.

I'll tell you a story that's not in Tom Moore:—
Young Love likes to knock at a pretty girl's door:
So he call'd upon Lucy—'twas just ten o'clock—
Like a spruce single man, with a smart double knock.

II.

Now a hand-maid, whatever her fingers be at,
Will run like a puss when she hears a *rat*-tat:
So Lucy ran up—and in two seconds more
Had question'd the stranger and answer'd the door.

III.

The meeting was bliss; but the parting was woe;
For the moment will come when such comers must go:
So she kiss'd him, and whisper'd—poor innocent thing—
"The next time you come, love, pray come with a ring."

LOVE.

O Love! what art thou, Love? the ace of hearts,
   Trumping earth's kings and queens, and all its suits;
A player, masquerading many parts
   In life's odd carnival;—a boy that shoots,
From ladies' eyes, such mortal woundy darts;
   A gardener, pulling heart's-ease up by the roots;
The Puck of Passion—partly false—part real—
A marriageable maiden's "beau ideal."

O Love! what art thou, Love? a wicked thing,
   Making green misses spoil their work at school;
A melancholy man, cross-gartering?
   Grave ripe-fac'd wisdom made an April fool?
A youngster, tilting at a wedding ring?
   A sinner, sitting on a cutty stool?
A Ferdinand de Something in a hovel,
Helping Matilda Rose to make a novel?

O Love! what art thou, Love? one that is bad
   With palpitations of the heart—like mine—
A poor bewilder'd maid, making so sad
   A necklace of her garters—fell design!
A poet, gone unreasonably mad,
   Ending his sonnets with a hempen line?
O Love!—but whither, now? forgive me, pray;
I'm not the first that Love hath led astray.

A RECIPE—FOR CIVILIZATION.

THE following Poem—is from the pen of DOCTOR KITCHENER !
—the most heterogeneous of authors, but at the same time—in the
Sporting Latin of Mr. Egan,—a real Homo-*genius* or a Genius of a
Man ! In the Poem, his CULINARY ENTHUSIASM, as usual——*boils
over!* and makes it seem written, as he describes himself (see The
Cook's Oracle)—with the Spit in one hand !—and the Frying Pan
in the other,—while in the style of the rhymes it is Hudibrastic,——
as if in the ingredients of Versification, he had been assisted by his
BUTLER !

As a Head Cook, Optician—Physician, Music Master—Domestic
Economist and Death-bed Attorney !—I have celebrated The Author elsewhere with approbation ;—and cannot now place him upon
the Table *as a Poet*,——without still being his LAUDER, a phrase
which those persons whose course of classical reading recalls the
INFAMOUS FORGERY on *the Immortal Bard of Eden!*——will find
easy to understand.

> SURELY, those sages err who teach
> That man is known from brutes by speech,
> Which hardly severs man from woman,
> But not th' inhuman from the human, —
> Or else might parrots claim affinity,
> And dogs be doctors by latinity,—
> Not t' insist, (as might be shown)
> That beasts have gibberish of their own,
> Which once was no dead tongue, tho' we
> Since Æsop's days have lost the key;
> Nor yet to hint dumb men,—and, still, not
> Beasts that could gossip though they will not,
> But play at dummy like the monkeys,
> For fear mankind should make them flunkies.
> Neither can man be known by feature
> Or form, because so like a creature,
> That some grave men could never shape
> Which is the aped and which the ape,
> Nor by his gait, nor by his height,
> Nor yet because he's black or white,

But *rational*,—for so we call
The only COOKING ANIMAL!
The only one who brings his bit
Of dinner to the pot or spit,
For where's the lion e'er was hasty,
To put his ven'son in a pasty?
Ergo, by logic, we repute,
That he who cooks is not a brute,—
But Equus brutum est, which means,
If a horse had sense he'd boil his beans,
Nay, no one but a horse would forage
On naked oats instead of porridge,
Which proves, if brutes and Scotchmen vary,
The difference is culinary.
Further, as man is known by feeding
From brutes,—so men from men, in breeding,
Are still distinguished as they eat,
And raw in manners, raw in meat,—
Look at the polish'd nations hight,
The civilized—the most polite
Is that which bears the praise of nations
For dressing eggs two hundred fashions,
Whereas, at savage feeders look,—
The less refined the less they cook;
From Tartar grooms that merely straddle
Across a steak and warm their saddle,
Down to the Abyssinian squaw,
That bolts her chops and collops raw,
And, like a wild beast, cares as little
To dress her person as her victual,—
For gowns, and gloves, and caps, and tippets,
Are beauty's sauces, spice, and sippets,
And not by shamble bodies put on,
But those who roast and boil their mutton;
So Eve and Adam wore no dresses
Because they lived on water-cresses,
And till they learn'd to cook their crudities,
Went blind as beetles to their nudities.
For niceness comes from th' inner side
(As an ox is drest before his hide),
And when the entrail loathes vulgarity

The outward man will soon cull rarity,
For 'tis th' effect of what we eat
To make a man look like his meat,
As insects show their food's complexions :
Thus foplings' clothes are like confections.
But who to feed a jaunty coxcomb,
Would have an Abyssinian ox come ?—
Or serve a dish of fricassees,
To clodpoles in a coat of frieze ?
Whereas a black would call for buffalo
Alive—and, no doubt, eat the offal too
Now, (this premised) it follows then
That certain culinary men
Should first go forth with pans and spits
To bring the heathens to their wits,
(For all wise Scotchmen of our century
Know that first steps are alimentary ;
And, as we have prov'd, flesh pots and saucepans
Must pave the way for Wilberforce plans ;)
But Bunyan err'd to think the near gate
To take man's soul, was battering Ear gate,
When reason should have work'd her course
As men of war do—when their force
Can't take a town by open courage,
They steal an entry with its forage.
What reverend bishop, for example,
Could preach horn'd Apis from his temple ?
Whereas a cook would soon unseat him,
And make his own churchwardens eat him.
Not Irving could convert those vermin
Th' Anthropophages, by a sermon ;
Whereas your Osborne,* in a trice,
Would "take a shin of beef and spice,"—
And raise them such a savoury smother,
No Negro would devour his brother,
But turn his stomach round as loth
As Persians, to the old black broth,—
For knowledge oftenest makes an entry,
As well as true love, thro' the pantry,

* Cook to the late Sir Joseph Banks.

Where beaux that came at first for feeding
Grow gallant men and get good breeding ;—
Exempli gratia—in the West,
Ship-traders say there swims a nest
Lin'd with black natives, like a rookery,
But coarse as carrion crows at cookery.—
This race, though now call'd O. Y. E. men,
(To show they are more than A. B. C. men.)
Was once so ignorant of our knacks
They laid their mats upon their backs,
And grew their quartern loaves for luncheon
On trees that baked them in the sunshine.
As for their bodies, they were coated,
(For painted things are so denoted ;)
But, the naked truth is, stark primevals,
That said their prayers to timber devils,
Allow'd polygamy—dwelt in wig-wams,—
And, when they meant a feast, ate big yams.—
And why?—because their savage nook
Had ne'er been visited by Cook,—
And so they fared till our great chief
Brought them, not methodists, but beef,
In tubs,—and taught them how to live,
Knowing it was too soon to give,-
Just then, a homily on their sins,
(For cooking ends ere grace begins)
Or hand his tracts to the untractable
Till they could keep a more exact table—
For nature has her proper courses,
And wild men must be back'd like horses,
Which, jockeys know, are never fit
For riding till they've had a bit
I' the mouth ; but then, with proper tackle,
You may trot them to a tabernacle ;
Ergo (I say) he first made changes
In the heathen modes, by kitchen ranges,
And taught the king's cook, by convincing
Process, that chewing was not mincing,
And in her black fist thrust a bundle
Of tracts abridg'd from Glasse and Rundell,
Where, ere she had read beyond Welsh rabbits.

She saw the spareness of her habits,
And round her loins put on a striped
Towel, where fingers might be wiped,
And then her breast clothed like her ribs,
(For aprons lead of course to bibs)
And, by the time she had got a meat-
Screen, veil'd her back, too, from the heat—
As for her gravies and her sauces,
(Tho' they reform'd the royal fauces,)
Her forcemeats and ragouts,—I praise not,
Because the legend further says not,
Except, she kept each Christian high-day,
And once upon a fat good Fry-day
Ran short of logs, and told the Pagan,
That turn'd the spit, to chop up Dagon !—

————

THE MERMAID OF MARGATE.

"Alas ! what perils do inviron
'That man who meddles with a siren !"
                    HUDIBRAS.

On Margate beach, where the sick one roams,
   And the sentimental reads ;
Where the maiden flirts, and the widow comes—
   Like the ocean—to cast her weeds ;—

Where urchins wander to pick up shells,
   And the Cit to spy at the ships,—
Like the water gala at Sadler's Wells,—
   And the Chandler for watery dips ;—

There's a maiden sits by the ocean brim,
   As lovely and fair as sin !
But woe, deep water and woe to him
   That she snareth like Peter Fin !

Her head is crown'd with pretty sea-wares,
   And her locks are golden and loose ;
And seek to her feet, like other folk's heirs,
   To stand, of course, in her shoes !

And, all day long, she combeth them well,
   With a sea-shark's prickly jaw ;
And her mouth is just like a rose-lipp'd shell,
   The fairest that man e'er saw !

And the Fishmonger, humble as love may be,
   Hath planted his seat by her side ;
"Good even, fair maid ! Is thy lover at sea,
   To make thee so watch the tide ?"

She turn'd about with her pearly brows,
   And clasped him by the hand :—
"Come, love, with me ; I've a bonny house
   On the golden Goodwin Sand."

And then she gave him a siren kiss,
   No honeycomb e'er was sweeter :
Poor wretch ! how little he dreamt for this
   That Peter should be salt-Peter !

And away with her prize to the wave she leapt,
   Not walking, as damsels do,
With toe and heel, as she ought to have stept,
   But she hopt like a Kangaroo !

One plunge, and then the victim was blind,
   Whilst they gallop'd across the tide ;
At last, on the bank he waked in his mind,
   And the Beauty was by his side.

One half on the sand, and half in the sea,
　　But his hair all began to stiffen ;
For when he look'd where her feet should be,
　　She had no more feet than Miss Biffen !

But a scaly tail, of a dolphin's growth,
　　In the dabbling brine did soak :
At last she open'd her pearly mouth,
　　Like an oyster, and thus she spoke :—

'You crimpt my father, who was a skate ;—
　　And my sister you sold—a maid ;
So here remain for a fishlike fate,
　　For lost you are, and betray'd ! "

And away she went, with a seagull's scream,
　　And a splash of her saucy tail ;
In a moment he lost the silvery gleam
　　That shone on her splendid mail !

The sun went down with a blood-red flame,
　　And the sky grew cloudy and black,
And the tumbling billows like leap-frog came,
　　Each over the other's back !

Ah, me ! it had been a beautiful scene,
　　With the safe terra-firma round ;
But the green water-hillocks all seem'd to him,
　　Like those in a church-yard ground ;

And Christians love in the turf to lie,
　　Not in watery graves to be ;
Nay, the very fishes will sooner die
　　On the land than in the sea.

And whilst he stood, the watery strife
    Encroached on every hand,
And the ground decreas'd—his moments of life
    Seem'd measur'd, like Time's, by sand ;

And still the waters foam'd in, like ale,
    In front, and on either flank,
He knew that Goodwin and Co. must fail,
    There was such a run on the bank.

A little more, and a little more,
    The surges came tumbling in ;
He sang the evening hymn twice o'er.
    And thought of every sin !

Each flounder and plaice lay cold at his heart,
    As cold as his marble slab ;
And he thought he felt, in every part,
    The pincers of scalded crab.

The squealing lobsters that he had boil'd,
    And the little potted shrimps,
All the horny prawns, he had ever spoil'd.
    Gnaw'd into his soul, like imps !

And the billows were wandering to and fro,
    And the glorious sun was sunk,
And Day, getting black in the face, as tho'
    Of the night-shade she had drunk !

Had there been but a smuggler's cargo adrift.
    One tub, or keg, to be seen,
It might have given his spirits a lift
    Or an *anker* where *Hope* might lean !

But there was not a box or a beam afloat,
    To raft him from that sad place;
Not a skiff, not a yawl, or a mackarel boat,
    Nor a smack upon Neptune's face.

At last, his lingering hopes to buoy,
    He saw a sail and a mast,
And called "Ahoy!"—but it was not a hoy,
    And so the vessel went past.

And with saucy wing that flapp'd in his face,
    The wild bird about him flew,
With a shrilly scream, that twitted his case,
    "Why, thou art a sea-gull too!"

And lo! the tide was over his feet;
    Oh! his heart began to freeze,
And slowly to pulse:—in another beat
    The wave was up to his knees!

He was deafen'd amidst the mountain-tops,
    And the salt spray blinded his eyes,
And wash'd away the other salt-drops
    That grief had caused to arise:—

But just as his body was all afloat,
    And the surges above him broke,
He was saved from the hungry deep by a boat,
    Of Deal—(but builded of oak).

The skipper gave him a dram, as he lay,
    And chafed his shivering skin;
And the Angel return'd that was flying away
    With the spirit of Peter Fin!

U

AS IT FELL UPON A DAY.

Oh ! what's befallen Bessy Brown,
    She stands so squalling in the street ;
She's let her pitcher tumble down,
    And all the water's at her feet !

The little school-boys stood about,
    And laughed to see her pumping, pumping ;
Now with a curtsey to the spout,
    And then upon her tiptoes jumping.

Long time she waited for her neighbours,
    To have their turns :—but she must lose
The watery wages of her labours,—
    Except a little in her shoes !

Witnout a voice to tell her tale,
    And ugly transport in her face ;
All like a jugless nightingale,
    She thinks of her bereaved case.

At last she sobs—she cries—she screams !—
    And pours her flood of sorrows out,
From eyes and mouth, in mingled streams,
    Just like the lion on the spout.

For well poor Bessy knows her mother
    Must lose her tea, for water's lack,
That Sukey burns—and baby-brother
    Must be dry-rubb'd with huck-a-back !

RUTH.

SHE stood breast high amid the corn
Clasp'd by the golden light of morn,
Like the sweetheart of the sun,
Who many a glowing kiss had won.

On her cheek an autumn flush,
Deeply ripen'd ;—such a blush
In the midst of brown was born,
Like red poppies grown with corn.

Round her eyes her tresses fell,
Which were blackest none could tell,
But long lashes veil'd a light,
That had else been all too bright.

And her hat, with shady brim,
Made her tressy forehead dim ;—
Thus he stood amid the stooks,
Praising God with sweetest looks:—

Sure, I said, Heav'n did not mean,
Where I reap thou shouldst but glean,
Lay thy sheaf adown and come,
Share my harvest and my home.

A FAIRY TALE.

On Hounslow heath—and close beside the road,
  As western travellers may oft have seen,—
A little house some years ago there stood,
      A minikin abode;
And built like Mr. Birkbeck's, all of wood:
The walls of white, the window shutters green;—
Four wheels it had at North, South, East, and West.
      (Tho' now at rest)
On which it used to wander to and fro',
Because its master ne'er maintain'd a rider,
    Like those who trade in Paternoster Row;
But made his business travel for itself,
      Till he had made his pelf,
And then retired—if one may call it so,
      Of a roadsider.

Perchance, the very race and constant riot
Of stages, long and short, which thereby ran,
Made him more relish the repose and quiet
      Of his now sedentary caravan;
Perchance, he lov'd the ground because 'twas common,
    And so he might impale a strip of soil,
      That furnish'd, by his toil,
Some dusty greens, for him and his old woman ;—
And five tall hollyhocks, in dingy flower:
Howbeit, the thoroughfare did no ways spoil
His peace, unless, in some unlucky hour,
A stray horse came and gobbled up his bow'r!

But tired of always looking at the coaches,
The same to come,—when they had seen them one day !
   And, used to brisker life, both man and wife
Began to suffer N U E's approaches,
And feel retirement like a long wet Sunday:—
So, having had some quarters of school breeding,
They turn'd themselves, like other folks, to reading ;
But setting out where others nigh have done,
   And being ripen'd in the seventh stage,
     The childhood of old age,
Began, as other children have begun,—
Not with the pastorals of Mr. Pope,
   Or Bard of Hope,
Or Paley ethical, or learned Porson,—
But spelt, on Sabbaths, in St. Mark, or John,
And then relax'd themselves with Whittington,
   Or Valentine and Orson—·
But chiefly fairy tales they loved to con,
And being easily melted in their dotage,
   Slobber'd,—and kept
   Reading,—and wept
Over the white Cat, in their wooden cottage.

   Thus reading on—the longer
They read, of course, their childish faith grew stronger
In Gnomes, and Hags, and Elves, and Giants grim,—
If talking Trees and Birds reveal'd to him,
She saw the flight of Fairyland's fly-waggons,
   And magic-fishes swim
In puddle ponds, and took old crows for dragons.—
Both were quite drunk from the enchanted flagons ;
When, as it fell upon a summer's day,
   As the old man sat a feeding
     On the old babe-reading,
Beside his open street-and-parlour door,
   A hideous roar
Proclaim'd a drove of beasts was coming by the way.

Long-horn'd, and short, of many a different breed,

Tall, tawny brutes, from famous Lincoln-levels
          Or Durham feed ;
With some of those unquiet black dwarf devils
          From nether side of Tweed,
          Or Firth of Forth ;
Looking half wild with joy to leave the North,—
With dusty hides, all mobbing on together,—
When,—whether from a fly's malicious comment
Upon his tender flank, from which he shrank ;
          Or whether
Only in some enthusiastic moment,—
However, one brown monster, in a frisk,
Giving his tail a perpendicular whisk,
Kick'd out a passage thro' the beastly rabble ;
And after a pas seul,—or, if you will, a
Horn-pipe before the Basket-maker's villa,
          Leapt o'er the tiny pale,—
Back'd his beef-steaks against the wooden gable,
And thrust his brawny bell-rope of a tail
          Right o'er the page,
          Wherein the sage
Just then was spelling some romantic fable.

The old man, half a scholar, half a dunce,
Could not peruse,—who could?—two tales at once ;
          And being huff'd
At what he knew was none of Riquet's Tuft,
          Bang'd-to the door,
But most unluckily enclosed a morsel
Of the intruding tail, and all the tassel :—
          The monster gave a roar,
And bolting off with speed, increased by pain,
The little house became a coach once more,
And, like Macheath, "took to the road " again !

Just then, by fortune's whimsical decree,
The ancient woman stooping with her crupper
Towards sweet home, or where sweet home should be,
Was getting up some household herbs for supper ;

Thoughtful of Cinderella, in the tale,
And quaintly wondering if magic shifts
Could o'er a common pumpkin so prevail,
To turn it to a coach;—what pretty gifts
Might come of cabbages, and curly kale;
Meanwhile she never heard her old man's wail,
Nor turn'd, till home had turn'd a corner, quite
        Gone out of sight!

At last, conceive her, rising from the ground,
Weary of sitting on her russet clothing;
        And looking round
        Where rest was to be found,
There was no house—no villa there—no nothing!
        No house!
        The change was quite amazing;
It made her senses stagger for a minute,
The riddle's explication seem'd to harden;
But soon her superannuated *nous*
Explained the horrid mystery;—and raising
Her hand to heaven, with the cabbage in it,
        On which she meant to sup,—
"Well! this *is* Fairy Work! I'll bet a farden,
Little Prince Silverwings has ketch'd me up,
And set me down in some one else's garden!"

THE FALL OF THE DEER.

[FROM AN OLD MS.]

Now the loud Crye is up, and harke!
The barkye Trees give back the Bark;
The House Wife heares the merrie rout,
And runnes,—and lets the beere run out,
Leaving her Babes to weepe,—for why?
She likes to heare the Deer Dogges crye,
And see the wild Stag how he stretches
The naturall Buck-skin of his Breeches,

Running like one of Human kind
Dogged by fleet Bailiffes close behind—
As if he had not payde his Bill •
For Ven'son, or was owing still
For his two Hornes, and soe did get
Over his Head and Ears in Debt ;—
Wherefore he strives to paye his Waye
With his long Legges the while he maye: —
But he is chased, like Silver Dish,
As well as anye Hart may wish
Except that one whose Heart doth beat
So faste it hasteneth his feet ;—
And runninge soe, he holdeth Death
Four Feet from him,—till his Breath
Faileth, and slacking Pace at last,
From runninge slow he standeth faste,
With hornie Bayonettes at baye,
To baying Dogges around, and they
Pushing him sore, he pusheth sore,
And goreth them that seeke his Gore,
Whatever Dogge his Horne doth rive
Is dead—as sure as he's alive !
Soe that courageous Hart doth fight
With Fate, and calleth up his might,
And standeth stout that he maye fall
Bravelye, and be avenged of all,
Nor like a Craven yeeld his Breath
Under the Jawes of Dogges and Death !

————

DECEMBER AND MAY.

"Crabbed Age and Youth cannot live together."

SHAKSPEARE.

I.

SAID Nestor, to his pretty wife, quite sorrowful one day,
"Why, dearest, will you shed in pearls those lovely eyes away?
You ought to be more fortified ;" "Ah, brute, be quiet, do,
I know I'm not so fortyfied, nor fiftyfied as you !

II.

Oh, men are vile deceivers all, as I have ever heard,
You'd die for me you swore, and I—I took you at your word.
I was a tradesman's widow then—a pretty change I've made ;
To live, and die the wife of one, a widower by trade !"

III.

"Come, come, my dear, these flighty airs declare, in sober truth,
You want as much in age, indeed, as I can want in youth ;
Besides, you said you liked old men, though now at me you huff."
"Why, yes," she said, " and so I do—but you're not old enough !''

IV.

"Come, come, my dear, let's make it up, and have a quiet hive ;
I'll be the best of men,—I mean,—I'll be the best *alive!*
Your grieving so will kill me, for it cuts me to the core."—
" I thank ye, Sir, for telling me—for now I'll grieve the more !"

A WINTER NOSEGAY.

O, WITHER'D winter Blossoms,
Dowager-flowers,—the December vanity.
In antiquated visages and bosoms,—
What are ye plann'd for,
Unless to stand for
Emblems, and peevish morals of humanity?

There is my Quaker Aunt,
A Paper-flower,—with a formal border
No breeze could e'er disorder,
Pouting at that old beau—the Winter Cherry,
A pucker'd berry ;

And Box, like tough-liv'd annuitant,—
    Verdant alway—
From quarter-day even to quarter-day;
And poor old Honesty, as thin as want,
    Well named—God-wot ;
Under the baptism of the water-pot,
The very apparition of a plant ;
    And why,
Dost hold thy head so high,
    Old Winter-Daisy ;—
Because thy virtue never was infirm,
    Howe'er thy stalk be crazy?
That never wanton fly, or blighted worm,
Made holes in thy most perfect indentation?
    'Tis likely that sour leaf,
    To garden thief,
Forcepp'd or wing'd, was never a temptation ;—
Well,—still uphold thy wintry reputation ;
Still shalt thou frown upon all lovers' trial :
And when, like Grecian maids, young maids of ours
    Converse with flow'rs,
Then thou shalt be the token of denial.

    Away ! dull weeds,
Born without beneficial use or needs !
Fit only to deck out cold winding-sheets ;
And then not for the milkmaid's funeral bloom,
    Or fair Fidele's tomb——
    To tantalise,—vile cheats !
Some prodigal bee, with hope of after-sweets,
    Frigid, and rigid,
    As if ye never knew
    One drop of dew,
    Or the warm sun resplendent ;
Indifferent of culture and of care,
Giving no sweets back to the fostering air,
    Churlishly independent—
    I hate ye, of all breeds!
Yea, all that live so selfishly—to self,
And not by interchange of kindly deeds—
    Hence !—from my shelf !

EQUESTRIAN COURTSHIP.

I.

It was a young maiden went forth to ride,
And there was a wooer to pace by her side ;
His horse was so little, and hers so high,
He thought his angel was up in the sky.

II.

His love was great tho' his wit was small ;
He bade her ride easy—and that was all.
The very horses began to neigh,—
Because their betters had nought to say.

III.

They rode by elm, and they rode by oak,
They rode by a church-yard, and then he spoke :—
" My pretty maiden, if you'll agree
You shall always amble through life with me."

IV.

The damsel answer'd him never a word,
But kick'd the gray mare, and away she spurr'd.
The wooer still follow'd behind the jade,
And enjoy'd– like a wooer—the dust she made.

V.

They rode thro' moss, and they rode thro' moor,—
The gallant behind and the lass before :—
At last they came to a miry place,
And there the sad wooer gave up the chase.

VI.

Quoth he, " If my nag were better to ride,
I'd follow her over the world so wide.
Oh, it is not my love that begins to fail,
But I've lost the last glimpse of the gray mare's tail ! "

A TRUE STORY

Of all our pains, since man was curst,
I mean of body, not the mental,
To name the worst, among the worst,
The dental sure is transcendental ;
Some bit of masticating bone,
That ought to help to clear a shelf,
But let its proper work alone,
And only seems to gnaw itself ;
In fact, of any grave attack
On victual there is little danger,
'Tis so like coming to the *rack*,
As well as going to the manger.

Old Hunks—it seem'd a fit retort
Of justice on his grinding ways—
Possess'd a grinder of the sort,
That troubled all his latter days.
The best of friends fall out, and so
His teeth had done some years ago,
Save some old stumps with ragged root,
And they took turn about to shoot ;
If he drank any chilly liquor,
They made it quite a point to throb ;
But if he warm'd it on the hob,
Why then they only twitch'd the quicker.

One tooth—I wonder such a tooth
Had never kill'd him in his youth—

One tooth he had with many fangs,
That shot at once as many pangs,
It had an universal sting ;
One touch of that ecstatic stump
Could jerk his limbs, and make him jump,
Just like a puppet on a string ;
And what was worse than all, it had
A way of making others bad.
There is, as many know, a knack,
With certain farming undertakers,
And this same tooth pursued their track,
By adding *achers* still to *achers !*

One way there is, that has been judg'd
A certain cure, but Hunks was loth
To pay the fee, and quite begrudg'd
To lose his tooth and money both ;
In fact, a dentist and the wheel
Of Fortune are a kindred cast,
For after all is drawn, you feel
It's paying for a blank at last ;
So Hunks went on from week to week,
And kept his torment in his cheek ;
Oh ! how it sometimes set him rocking,
With that perpetual gnaw—gnaw—gnaw,
His moans and groans were truly shocking
And loud,—altho' he held his jaw.
Many a tug he gave his gum,
And tooth, but still it would not come,
Tho' tied by string to some firm thing.
He could not draw it, do his best,
By draw'rs, altho' he tried a chest.

At last, but after much debating,
He joined a score of mouths in waiting,
Like his, to have their troubles out.
Sad sight it was to look about
At twenty faces making faces,
With many a rampant trick and antic,

For all were very horrid cases,
And made their owners nearly frantic.
A little wicket now and then
Took one of these unhapy men,
And out again the victim rush'd,
While eyes and mouth together gush'd ;
At last arrived our hero's turn,
Who plunged his hands in both his pockets,
And down he sat, prepared to learn
How teeth are charm'd to quit their sockets.

Those who have felt such operations,
Alone can guess the sort of ache,
When his old tooth began to break
The thread of old associations ;
It touch'd a string in every part,
It had so many tender ties ;
One chord seem'd wrenching at his heart,
And two were tugging at his eyes ;
"Bone of his bone," he felt of course,
As husbands do in such divorce ;
At last the fangs gave way a little,
Hunks gave his head a backward jerk,
And lo ! the cause of all this work,
Went—where it used to send his victual !

The monstrous pain of this proceeding
Had not so numb'd his miser wit,
But in this slip he saw a hit
To save, at least, his purse from bleeding ;
So when the dentist sought his fees,
Quoth Hunks, " Let's finish, if you please."
" How, finish ! why it's out ! "—"Oh ! no—
'Tis you are out, to argue so ;
I'm none of your before-hand tippers,
My tooth is in my head no doubt,
But as you say you pull'd it out,
Of course it's there—between your nippers."

"Zounds ! sir, d'ye think I'd sell the truth
To get a fee? no, wretch, I scorn it."
But Hunks still ask'd to see the tooth,
And swore by gum ! he had not drawn it.

His end obtain'd, he took his leave,
A secret chuckle in his sleeve ;
The joke was worthy to produce one,
To think, by favour of his wit,
How well a dentist had been bit
By one old stump, and that a loose one !
The thing was worth a laugh, but mirth
Is still the frailest thing on earth :
Alas ! how often when a joke
Seems in our sleeve, and safe enough,
There comes some unexpected stroke,
And hangs a weeper on the cuff !

Hunks had not whistled half a mile,
When, planted right against a stile,
There stood his foeman, Mike Mahoney,
A vagrant reaper, Irish-born,
That help'd to reap our miser's corn,
But had not help'd to reap his money,
A fact that Hunks remembered quickly ;
His whistle all at once was quell'd,
And when he saw how Michael held
His sickle, he felt rather sickly.

Nine souls in ten, with half his fright,
Would soon have paid the bill at sight,
But misers (let observers watch it)
Will never part with their delight
Till well demanded by a hatchet—
They live hard—and they die to match it.
Thus Hunks prepared for Mike's attacking,

Resolved not yet to pay the debt,
But let him take it out in hacking;
However Mike began to stickle
In words before he used the sickle;
But mercy was not long attendant:
From words at last he took to blows,
And aim'd a cut at Hunks's nose;
That made it what some folks are not—
A member very independent.

Heaven knows how far this cruel trick
Might still have led, but for a tramper
That came in danger's very nick,
To put Mahoney to the scamper.
But still compassion met a damper;
There lay the sever'd nose, Alas!
Beside the daisies on the grass,
"Wee, crimson-tipt!" as well as they,
According to the poet's lay:
And there stood Hunks, no sight for laughter:
Away ran Hodge to get assistance,
With nose in hand, which Hunks ran after,
But somewhat at unusual distance.
In many a little country place
It is a very common case
To have but one residing doctor,
Whose practice rather seems to be
No practice, but a rule of three,
Physician—surgeon—drug-decoctor;
Thus Hunks was forced to go once more
Where he had ta'en his tooth before.
His mere name made the learn'd man hot,–
"What! Hunks again within my door!
"I'll pull his nose;" quoth Hunks, "you cannot."

The doctor look'd and saw the case
Plain as the nose *not* on his face.
"O! hum—ha—yes—I understand."
But then arose a long demur,

For not a finger would he stir
Till he was paid his fee in hand ;
That matter settled, there they were,
With Hunks well strapp'd upon his chair.

The opening of a surgeon's job—
His tools, a chestful or a drawful—
Are always something very awful,
And give the heart the strangest throb ;
But never patient in his funks
Look'd half so like a ghost as Hunks,
Or surgeon half so like a devil
Prepared for some infernal revel :
His huge black eye kept rolling, rolling,
Just like a bolus in a box :
His fury seem'd above controlling,
He bellow'd like a hunted ox :
"Now, swindling wretch, I'll show thee how
We treat such cheating knaves as thou ;
Oh ! sweet is this revenge to sup ;
I have thee by the nose—it's now
My turn—and I will turn it up."

Guess how the miser liked the scurvy
And cruel way of venting passion ;
The snubbing folks in this new fashion
Seem'd quite to turn him topsy turvy ;
He utter'd pray'rs, and groans, and curses,
For things had often gone amiss
And wrong with him before, but this
Would be the worst of all *reverses!*
In fancy he beheld his snout
Turn'd upward like a pitcher's spout ;
There was another grievance yet,
And fancy did not fail to show it,
That he must throw a summerset,
Or stand upon his head to blow it.

X

And was there then no argument
To change the doctor's vile intent,
And move his pity?—yes, in truth,
And that was—paying for the tooth.
"Zounds! pay for such a stump! I'd rather—"
But here the menace went no farther,
For with his other ways of pinching,
Hunks had a miser's love of snuff,
A recollection strong enough
To cause a very serious flinching;
In short he paid and had the feature
Replaced as it was meant by nature;
For tho' by this 'twas cold to handle,
(No corpse's could have felt more horrid,)
And white just like an end of candle,
The doctor deem'd and proved it too,
That noses from the nose will do
As well as noses from the forehead;
So, fix'd by dint of rag and lint,
The part was bandag'd up and muffled.
The chair unfasten'd, Hunks arose,
And shuffled out, for once unshuffled;
And as he went, these words he snuffled—
"Well, this *is* 'paying thro' the nose.'"

TIM TURPIN,

A PATHETIC BALLAD.

I.

TIM TURPIN he was gravel blind,
  And ne'er had seen the skies:
For Nature, when his head was made,
  Forgot to dot his eyes.

II.

So, like a Christmas pedagogue,
  Poor Tim was forc'd to do—

Look out for pupils, for he had
  A vacancy for two.

III.

There's some have specs to help their sight
  Of objects dim and small :
But Tim had *specs* within his eyes,
  And could not see at all.

IV.

Now Tim he woo'd a servant maid,
  And took her to his arms ;
For he, like Pyramus, had cast
  A wall-eye on her charms.

V.

By day she led him up and down
  Where'er he wish'd to jog,
A happy wife, altho' she led
  The life of any dog.

VI.

But just when Tim had liv'd a month
  In honey with his wife,
A surgeon ope'd his Milton eyes,
  Like oysters, with a knife.

VII.

But when his eyes were open'd thus,
  He wish'd them dark again :
For when he look'd upon his wife,
  He saw her very plain.

VIII.

Her face was bad, her figure worse,
  He couldn't bear to eat :
For she was any thing but like
  A Grace before his meat.

IX.

Now Tim he was a feeling man:
  For when his sight was thick,
It made him feel for everything—
  But that was with a stick.

X.

So with a cudgel in his hand—
  It was not light or slim—
He knock'd at his wife's head until
  It open'd unto him.

XI.

And when the corpse was stiff and cold
  He took his slaughter'd spouse,
And laid her in a heap with all
  The ashes of her house.

XII.

But like a wicked murderer,
  He liv'd in constant fear
From day to day, and so he cut
  His throat from ear to ear.

XIII.

The neighbours fetch'd a doctor in :
  Said he, this wound I dread

Can hardly be sow'd up—his life
   Is hanging on a thread.

XIV.

But when another week was gone,
   He gave him stronger hope—
Instead of hanging on a thread,
   Of hanging on a rope.

XV.

Ah! when he hid his bloody work,
   In ashes round about,
How little he supposed the truth
   Would soon be sifted out.

XVI.

But when the parish dustman came,
   His rubbish to withdraw,
He found more dust within the heap,
   Than he contracted for !

XVII.

A dozen men to try the fact,
   Were sworn that very day ;
But tho' they all were jurors, yet
   No conjurors were they.

XVIII.

Said Tim unto those jurymen,
   You need not waste your breath,
For I confess myself at once,
   The author of her death.

XIX.

And, oh! when I reflect upon
   The blood that I have spilt,
Just like a button is my soul,
   Inscrib'd with double *guilt!*

XX.

Then turning round his head again,
   He saw before his eyes,
A great judge, and a little judge,
   The judges of a-size!

XXI.

The great judge took his judgment cap,
   And put it on his head,
And sentenc'd Tim by law to hang,
   Till he was three times dead.

XXII.

So he was tried, and he was hung
   (Fit punishment for such)
On Horsham-drop, and none can say
   It was a drop too much.

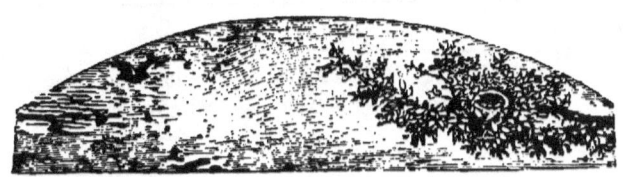

THE MONKEY-MARTYR.

A FABLE.

"God help thee, said I, but I'll let thee out, cost what it will: so I turned about the cage to get to the door."—STERNE.

'TIS strange, what awkward figures and odd capers
Folks cut, who seek their doctrine from the papers;
But there are many shallow politicians,
Who take their bias from bewilder'd journals—
    Turn state-physicians,
And make themselves fools'-caps of the diurnals.
One of this kind, not human, but a monkey,
Had read himself at last to this sour creed—
That he was nothing but Oppression's flunkey,
And man a tyrant over all his breed.
    He could not read
Of niggers whipt, or over-trampled weavers,
But he applied their wrongs to his own seed,
And nourish'd thoughts that threw him into fevers;
His very dreams were full of martial beavers,
And drilling Pugs, for liberty pugnacious,
    To sever chains vexations:
In fact, he thought that all his injur'd line
Should take up pikes in hand, and never drop 'em

Till they had cleared a road to Freedom's shrine,—
Unless perchance the turn-pike men should stop 'em.

Full of this rancour,
Pacing one day beside St. Clement Danes,
It came into his brains
To give a look in at the Crown and Anchor;
Where certain solemn sages of the nation
Were at that moment in deliberation
How to relieve the wide world of its chains,
Pluck despots down,
And thereby crown
Whitee- as well as blackee-man-cipation.
Pug heard the speeches with great approbation,
And gaz'd with pride upon the Liberators;
To see mere coal-heavers
Such perfect Bolivars—
Waiters of inns sublim'd to innovators,
And slaters dignified as legislators—
Small publicans demanding (such their high sense
Of liberty) an universal license—
And pattern-makers easing Freedom's clogs—
The whole thing seem'd
So fine, he deem'd
The smallest demagogues as great as Gogs!

Pug, with some curious notions in his noddle,
Walk'd out at last, and turn'd into the Strand,
To the left hand,
Conning some portions of the previous twaddle,
And striding with a step that seem'd design'd
To represent the mighty March of Mind,
Instead of that slow waddle
Of thought, to which our ancestors inclin'd—
No wonder, then, that he should quickly find
He stood in front of that intrusive pile,
Where Cross keeps many a kind
Of bird confin'd,

And free-born animal, in durance vile—
A thought that stirr'd up all the monkey-bile!

The window stood ajar—
It was not far,
Nor, like Parnassus, very hard to climb—
The hour was verging on the supper-time,
And many a growl was sent through many a bar.
Meanwhile Pug scrambled upward like a tar,
And soon crept in,
Unnotic'd in the din
Of tuneless throats, that made the attics ring
With all the harshest notes that they could bring;
For like the Jews,
Wild beasts refuse,
In midst of their captivity—to sing.

Lord! how it made him chafe,
Full of his new emancipating zeal,
To look around upon this brute-bastille,
And see the king of creatures in—a safe!
The desert's denizen in one small den,
Swallowing slavery's most bitter pills—
A bear in bars unbearable.   And then
The fretful porcupine, with all its quills
Imprison'd in a pen!
A tiger limited to four feet ten;
And, still worse lot,
A leopard to one spot!
An elephant enlarg'd,
But not discharg'd;
(It was before the elephant was shot;)
A doleful wanderoo, that wandered not;
An ounce much disproportion'd to his pound.
Pug's wrath wax'd hot
To gaze upon these captive creature's round;
Whose claws—all scratching—gave him full assurance
They found their durance vile of vile endurance.

He went above—a solitary mounter
Up gloomy stairs—and saw a pensive group
  Of hapless fowls—
  Cranes, vultures, owls,
In fact, it was a sort of Poultry-Compter,
Where feather'd prisoners were doom'd to droop:
Here sat an eagle, forc'd to make a stoop,
Not from the skies, but his impending roof;
  And there aloof,
A pining ostrich, moping in a coop;
With other samples of the bird creation,
All cag'd against their powers and their wills,
And cramp'd in such a space, the longest bills
Were plainly bills of least accommodation.
In truth, it was a very ugly scene
To fall to any liberator's share,
To see those winged fowls, that once had been
Free as the wind, no freer than fixed air.

  His temper little mended,
Pug from this Bird-cage Walk at last descended
  Unto the lion and the elephant,
  His bosom in a pant
To see all nature's Free List thus suspended,
And beasts depriv'd of what she had intended.
  They could not even prey
  In their own way;
A hardship always reckon'd quite prodigious.
  Thus he revolv'd—
  And soon resolv'd
To give them freedom, civil and religious.

That night there were no country cousins, raw
From Wales, to view the lion and his kin:
The keeper's eyes were fix'd upon a saw;
The saw was fix'd upon a bullock's shin:
  Meanwhile with stealthy paw,
  Pug hastened to withdraw

The bolt that kept the king of brutes within.
Now, monarch of the forest! thou shalt win
Precious enfranchisement—thy bolts are undone ;
Thou art no longer a degraded creature,
But loose to roam with liberty and nature ;
And free of all the jungles about London—
All Hampstead's heathy desert lies before thee !
Methinks I see thee bound from Cross's ark,
Full of the native instinct that comes o'er thee,
   And turn a ranger
Of Hounslow Forest, and the Regent's Park—
Thin Rhodes's cows—the mail-coach steeds endanger,
And gobble parish watchman after dark :—
Methinks I see thee, with the early lark,
Stealing to Merlin's cave—(*thy* cave.)—Alas,
That such bright visions should not come to pass !
Alas, for freedom, and for freedom's hero !
  Alas, for liberty of life and limb !
For Pug had only half unbolted Nero,
  When Nero *bolted him !*

CRANIOLOGY.

'TIS strange how like a very dunce,
Man—with his bumps upon his sconce,
Has lived so long, and yet no knowledge he
Has had, till lately, of Phrenology—
A science that by simple dint of
Head-combing he should find a hint of,
When scratching o'er those little pole-hills,
The faculties throw up like mole-hills ;—
A science that, in very spite
Of all his teeth, ne'er came to light,
For though he knew his skull had *grinders*,
Still there turn'd up no *organ* finders,
Still sages wrote, and ages fled,
And no man's head came in his head—
Not even the pate of Erra Pater,
Knew aught about its pia mater.

At last great Dr. Gall bestirs him—
I don't know but it might be Spurzheim—
Tho' native of a dull and slow land,
And makes partition of our Poll-land,
At our Acquisitiveness guesses,
And all those necessary *nesses*
Indicative of human habits,
All burrowing in the head like rabbits.
Thus Veneration, he made known,
Had got a lodging at the Crown :
And Music (see Deville's example)
A set of chambers in the Temple :
That Language taught the tongues close by.
And took in pupils thro' the eye,
Close by his neighbour Computation,
Who taught the eyebrows numeration.

The science thus—to speak in fit
Terms—having struggled from its nit,
Was seiz'd on by a swarm of Scotchmen
Those scientifical hotch-potch men,
Who have at least a penny dip
And wallop in all doctorship,
Just as in making broth they smatter
By bobbing twenty things in water :
These men, I say, make quick appliance
And close, to phrenologic science ;
For of all learned themes whatever,
That schools and colleges deliver,
There's none they love so near the bodles,
As analyzing their own noddles ;
Thus in a trice each northern blockhead
Had got his fingers in his shock head,
And of his bumps was babbling yet worse
Than poor Miss Capulet's dry wet-nurse ;
Till having been sufficient rangers
Of their own heads, they took to strangers',
And found in Presbyterians' polls
The things they hated in their souls ;
For Presbyterians hear with passion

Of organs join'd with veneration.
No kind there was of human pumpkin,
But at its bumps it had a bumpkin;
Down to the very lowest gullion,
And oiliest scull of oily scullion.
No great man died but this they *did* do,
They begg'd his cranium of his widow:
No murderer died by law disaster,
But they took off his sconce in plaster;
For thereon they could show depending,
" The head and front of his offending,"
How that his philanthropic bump
Was master'd by a baser lump;
For every bump (these wags insist)
Has its direct antagonist,
Each striving stoutly to prevail,
Like horses knotted tail to tail;
And many a stiff and sturdy battle
Occurs between these adverse cattle,
The secret cause, beyond all question,
Of aches ascribed to indigestion,—
Whereas 'tis but two knobby rivals
Tugging together like sheer devils,
Till one gets mastery good or sinister,
And comes in like a new prime-minister.

Each bias in some master node is :—
What takes M'Adam where a road is,
To hammer little pebbles less?
His organ of destructiveness.
What makes great Joseph so encumber
Debate? a lumping lump of Number:
Or Malthus rail at babies so?
The smallness of his Philopro—
What severs man and wife? a simple
Defect of the Adhesive pimple:
Or makes weak women go astray?
Their bumps are more in fault than they.

These facts being found and set in order

By grave M.D.'s beyond the Border,
To make them for some months eternal,
Were enter'd monthly in a journal,
That many a northern sage still writes in,
And throws his little Northern Lights in,
And proves and proves about the phrenos,
A great deal more than I or he knows.
How Music suffers, *par exemple,*
By wearing tight hats round the temple ;
What ills great boxers have to fear
From blisters put behind the ear:
And how a porter's Veneration
Is hurt by porter's occupation :
Whether shillelaghs in reality
May deaden Individuality :
Or tongs and poker be creative
Of alterations in th' Amative :
If falls from scaffolds make us less
Inclin'd to all Constructiveness :
With more such matters, all applying
To heads—and therefore *head*ifying.

A PARTHIAN GLANCE.

"Sweet Memory, wafted by thy gentle gale,
Oft up the stream of time I turn my sail."
ROGERS.

I.

COME, my Crony, let's think upon far-away days,
And lift up a little Oblivion's veil ;
Let's consider the past with a lingering gaze,
Like a peacock whose eyes are inclined to his tail.

II.

Ay, come, let us turn our attention behind,
Like those critics whose heads are so heavy, I fear,

That they cannot keep up with the march of the mind,
   And so turn face about for reviewing the rear.

III.

Looking over Time's crupper and over his tail,
   Oh, what ages and pages there are to revise !
And as farther our back-searching glances prevail,
   Like the emmets, "how little we are in our eyes !"

IV.

What a sweet pretty innocent, half-a-yard long,
   On a dimity lap of true nursery make !
I can fancy I hear the old lullaby song
   That was meant to compose me, but kept me awake.

ı

V

Methinks I still suffer the infantine throes,
   When my flesh was a cushion for any long pin—
Whilst they patted my body to comfort my woes,
   Oh ! how little they dreamt they were driving them in !

VI.

Infant sorrows are strong—infant pleasures as weak—
   But no grief was allow'd to indulge in its note ;
Did you ever attempt a small "bubble and squeak,"
   Thro' the Dalby's Carminative down in your throat?

VII.

Did you ever go up to the roof with a bounce ?
   Did you ever come down to the floor with the same?
Oh! I can't but agree with both ends, and pronounce
   "Head or tails" with a child, an unpleasantish game !

VIII.

Then an urchin—I see myself urchin, indeed,
  With a smooth Sunday face for a mother's delight ;
Why should weeks have an end?—I am sure there was need
  Of a Sabbath, to follow each Saturday-night.

IX.

Was your face ever sent to the housemaid to scrub?
  Have you ever felt huckaback soften'd with sand?
Had you ever your nose towell'd up to a snub,
  And your eyes knuckled out with the back of the hand?

X.

Then a school-boy—my tailor was nothing in fault,
  For an urchin will grow to a lad by degrees,—
But how well I remember that "pepper and salt"
  That was down to the elbows, and up to the knees !

XI.

What a figure it cut when as Norval I spoke !
  With a lanky right leg duly planted before ;
Whilst I told of the chief that was kill'd by my stroke,
  And extended *my* arms as "the arms that he wore !"

XII.

Next a Lover—Oh ! say, were you ever in love?
  With a lady too cold—and your bosom too hot !
Have you bow'd to a shoe-tie, and knelt to a glove?
  Like a *beau* that desired to be tied in a knot ?

XIII.

With the Bride all in white, and your body in blue,
  Did you walk up the aisle—the genteelest of men?

When I think of that beautiful vision anew,
  Oh ! I seem but the *biffin* of what I was then !

XIV.

I am wither'd and worn by a premature care,
  And my wrinkles confess the decline of my days ;
Old Time's busy hand has made free with my hair,
  And I'm seeking to hide it—by writing for bays !

———:

A SAILOR'S APOLOGY FOR BOW-LEGS.

THERE'S some is born with their straight legs by natur—
And some is born with bow-legs from the first—
And some that should have grow'd a good deal straighter,
    But they were badly nurs'd,
And set, you see, like Bacchus, with their pegs
    Astride of casks and kegs :
I've got myself a sort of bow to larboard,
    And starboard,
And this is what it was that warp'd my legs.—

'Twas all along of Poll, as I may say,
That foul'd my cable when I ought to slip ;
    But on the tenth of May,
    When I gets under weigh,
Down there in Hartfordshire, to join my ship,
    I sees the mail
    Get under sail,
The only one there was to make the trip.
    Well—I gives chase,
    But as she run
    Two knots to one,
There warn't no use in keeping on the race !

Y

Well—casting round about, what next to try on,
    And how to spin,
I spies an ensign with a Bloody Lion,
And bears away to leeward for the inn,
    Beats round the gable,
And fetches up before the coach-horse stable :
Well—there they stand, four kickers in a row,
    And so
I just makes free to cut a brown 'un's cable.
But riding isn't in a seaman's natur—
So I whips out a toughish end of yarn,
And gets a kind of sort of a land-waiter
    To splice me, heel to heel,
    Under the she-mare's keel,
And off I goes, and leaves the inn a-starn !

    My eyes ! how she did pitch !
And wouldn't keep her own to go in no line,
Tho' I kept bowsing, bowsing at her bow-line,
But always making lee-way to the ditch,
And yaw'd her head about all sorts of ways.
    The devil sink the craft !
And wasn't she trimendus slack in stays!
We couldn't, no how, keep the inn abaft !
    Well—I suppose
We hadn't run a knot—or much beyond—
(What will you have on it ?)—but off she goes,
Up to her bends in a fresh-water pond !
    There I am !—all a-back !
So I looks forward for her bridle-gears,
To heave her head round on the t'other tack ;
    But when I starts,
    The leather parts,
And goes away right over by the ears !

    What could a fellow do,
Whose legs, like mine, you know, were in the bilboes,
But trim myself upright for bringing-to,

And square his yard-arms, and brace up his elbows,
      In rig all snug and clever,
Just while his craft was taking in her water?
I didn't like my burth tho', howsomdever,
Because the yarn, you see, kept getting taughter,—
Says I—I wish this job was rayther shorter!
      The chase had gain'd a mile
A-head, and still the she-mare stood a-drinking:
      Now, all the while
Her body didn't take of course to shrinking.
Says I, she's letting out her reefs, I'm thinking—
      And so she swell'd, and swell'd,
      And yet the tackle held,
'Till both my legs began to bend like winkin.
My eyes! but she took in enough to founder!
And there's my timbers straining every bit,
      Ready to split,
And her tarnation hull a-growing rounder!

      Well, there—off Hartford Ness,
We lay both lash'd and water-logg'd together,
      And can't contrive a signal of distress;
Thinks I, we must ride out this here foul weather,
Tho' sick of riding out—and nothing less;
When, looking round, I sees a man a-starn:—
Hollo! says I, come underneath her quarter!—
And hands him out my knife to cut the yarn.
So I gets off, and lands upon the road,
And leaves the she-mare to her own concarn,
      A-standing by the water.
If I get on another, I'll be blow'd!—
And that's the way, you see, my legs got bow'd!

THE STAG-EYED LADY.

A MOORISH TALE.

Scheherazade immediately began the following story.

Ali Ben Ali (did you never read
  His wond'rous acts that chronicles relate,—
How there was one in pity might exceed
  The sack of Troy?) Magnificent he sate
Upon the throne of greatness—great indeed,
  For those that he had under him were great—
The horse he rode on, shod with silver nails,
Was a Bashaw—Bashaws have horses' tails.

Ali was cruel—a most cruel one !
  'Tis rumour'd he had strangled his own mother—
Howbeit such deeds of darkness he had done,
  'Tis thought he would have slain his elder brother
And sister too—but happily that none
  Did live within *harm's* length of one another,
Else he had sent the Sun in all its blaze
To endless night, and shorten'd the Moon's days.

Despotic power, that mars a weak man's wit,
  And makes a bad man—absolutely bad,
Made Ali wicked—to a fault :—'tis fit
  Monarchs should have some check-strings; but he had
No curb upon his will—no not a *bit*—
  Wherefore he did not reign well—and full glad
His slaves had been to hang him—but they falter'd,
And let him live unhang'd—and still unalter'd,

Until he got a sage-bush of a beard,
  Wherein an Attic owl might roost—a trail
Of bristly hair—that, honour'd and unshear'd,
  Grew downward like old women and cow's tail :

Being a sign of age—some gray appear'd,
   Mingling with duskier brown its warnings pale;
But yet not so poetic as when Time
Comes like Jack Frost, and whitens it in rime.

Ben Ali took the hint, and much did vex
   His royal bosom that he had no son,
No living child of the more noble sex,
   To stand in his Morocco shoes—not one
To make a negro-pollard—or tread necks
   When he was gone—doom'd, when his days were done,
To leave the very city of his fame
Without an Ali to keep up his name.

Therefore he chose a lady for his love,
   Singling from out the herd one stag-eyed dear
So call'd, because her lustrous eyes, above
   All eyes, were dark, and timorous, and clear;
Then, through his Muftis piously he strove,
   And drumm'd with proxy-prayers Mohammed's ear,
Knowing a boy for certain must come of it,
Or else he was not praying to his *Profit.*

Beer will grow *mothery*, and ladies fair
Will grow like beer; so did that stag-eyed dame:
Ben Ali, hoping for a son and heir,
   Boy'd up his hopes, and even chose a name
Of mighty hero that his child should bear;
   He made so certain ere his chicken came:
But oh! all worldly wit is little worth,
Nor knoweth what to-morrow will bring forth.

To-morrow came, and with to-morrow's sun
   A little daughter to this world of sins;—
Miss-fortunes never come alone—so one
   Brought on another, like a pair of twins:

Twins ! female twins !—it was enough to stun
   Their little wits and scare them from their skins
To hear their father stamp, and curse and swear,
Pulling his beard because he had no heir.

Then strove their stag-eyed mother to calm down
   This his paternal rage, and thus addrest
"O ! Most Serene ! why dost thou stamp and frown,
   And box the compass of the royal chest ?
Ah ! thou wilt mar that portly trunk, I own
   I love to gaze on !—Pr'ythee, thou hadst best
Pocket thy fists.   Nay, love, if you so thin
Your beard, you'll want a wig upon your chin ! "

But not her words, nor e'en her tears, could slack
   The quicklime of his rage, that hotter grew :
He called his slaves to bring an ample sack
   Wherein a woman might be *poked*— a few
Dark grimly men felt pity and look'd black
   At this sad order ; but their slaveships knew
When any dared demur, his sword so bending
Cut off the "head and front of their offending."

For Ali had a sword, much like himself,
   A crooked blade, guilty of human gore—
The trophies it had lopp'd from many an elf
   Were stuck at his *head*-quarters by the score—·
Nor yet in peace he laid it on the shelf,
   But jested with it, and his wit cut sore ;
So that (as they of Public Houses speak)
He often did his dozen *butts* a week.

Therefore his slaves, with most obedient fears,
   Came with the sack the lady to enclose ;
In vain from her stag-eyes "the big round tears
   Coursed one another down her innocent nose;"

In vain her tongue wept sorrow in their ears ;
  Though there were some felt willing to oppose,
Yet when their heads came in their heads, that minute,
Though 'twas a piteous *case*, they put her in it.

And when the sack was tied, some two or three
  Of these black undertakers slowly brought her
To a kind of Moorish Serpentine ; for she
  Was doom'd to have *a winding sheet of water*.
Then farewell, earth—farewell to the green tree—
  Farewell, the sun—the moon—each little daughter !
She's shot from off the shoulders of a black,
Like a bag of Wall's-End from a coalman's back.

The waters oped, and the wide sack full-fill'd
  All that the waters oped, as down it fell ;
Then closed the wave, and then the surface rill'd
  A ring above her, like a water-knell ;
A moment more, and all its face was still'd,
  And not a guilty heave was left to tell
That underneath its calm and blue transparence
A dame lay drowned in her sack, like Clarence.

But Heaven beheld, and awful witness bore,
  The moon in black eclipse deceased that night,
Like Desdemona smother'd by the Moor—
  The lady's natal star with pale affright
Fainted and fell—and what were stars before,
  Turn'd comets as the tale was brought to light,
And all look'd downward on the fatal wave,
And made their own reflections on her grave.

Next night, a head—a little lady head,
  Push'd through the waters a most glassy face,
With weedy tresses, thrown apart and spread,
  Comb'd by 'live ivory, to show the space

Of a pale forehead, and two eyes that shed
　A soft blue mist, breathing a bloomy grace
Over their sleepy lids—and so she rais'd
　Her *aqua*line nose above the stream, and gazed.

She oped her lips—lips of a gentle blush,
　So pale it seem'd near drowned to a white,—
She oped her lips, and forth their sprang a gush
　Of music bubbling through the surface light ;
The leaves are motionless, the breezes hush
　To listen to the air—and through the night
There come these words of a most plaintive ditty,
Sobbing as they would break all hearts with pity :

THE WATER PERI'S SONG.

Farewell, farewell, to my mother's own daughter,
　The child that she wet-nursed is lapp'd in the wave ;
The *Mussul*-man coming to fish in this water,
　Adds a tear to the flood that weeps over her grave.

This sack is her coffin, this water's her bier,
　This greyish *bath* cloak is her funeral pall ;'
And, stranger, O stranger ! this song that you hear
　Is her epitaph, elegy, dirges, and all !

Farewell, farewell, to the child of Al Hassan,
　My mother's own daughter—the last of her race—
She's a corpse, the poor body ! and lies in this basin,
　And sleeps in the water that washes her face.

REMONSTRATORY ODE,

FROM THE ELEPHANT AT EXETER CHANGE, TO MR. MATHEWS AT THE ENGLISH OPERA-HOUSE.

"——See with what courteous action,
He beckons you to a more removed ground."—*Hamlet.*

[WRITTEN BY A FRIEND.]

OH, Mr. Mathews ! Sir !
(If a plain elephant may speak his mind,
And that I have a mind to speak I find
    By my inward stir)
I long have thought, and wished to say, that we
Mar our well-merited prosperity
    By being such near neighbours,
My keeper now hath lent me pen and ink,
Shov'd in my truss of lunch, and tub of drink,
    And left me to my labours.
The whole menagerie is in repose,
The Coatamundi is in his Sunday clothes,
Watching the Lynx's most unnatural doze ;
The Panther is asleep, and the Macaw ;
The Lion is engaged on something raw ;
    The white Bear cools his chin
    'Gainst the wet tin ;
And the confined old Monkey's in the straw :
All the nine little Lionets are lying
Slumbering in milk, and sighing ;
    Miss Cross is sipping ox-tail soup,
    In her front coop,
So here's the happy mid-day moment ;—yes,
I seize it, Mr. Mathews, to address
    A word or two
      To you
On the subject of the ruin which must come
By both being in the Strand, and both at home
  On the same nights ; two treats
    So very near each other,
    As, oh my brother !
To play old gooseberry with both receipts.

When you begin
Your summer fun, three times a week, at eight,
   And carriages roll up, and cits roll in,
   I feel a change in Exeter 'Change's change.
And, dash my trunk ! I hate
To ring my bell, when you ring yours, and go,
With a diminish'd glory through *my* show !
      It is most strange ;
But crowds that meant to see me eat a stack,
And sip a water-butt or so, and crack
    A root of mangel-wurzel with my foot,
    Eat little children's fruit,
    Pick from the floor small coins,
And then turn slowly round and show my India-rubber
    loins :
   'Tis strange—most strange, but true,
   That these same crowds seek *you !*
   Pass *my* abode and pay at *your* next door !
    It makes me roar
With anguish when I think of this ; I go
With sad severity my nightly rounds
    Before one poor front row,
    My fatal funny foe !
And when I stoop, as duty bids, I sigh
And feel that, while poor elephantine I,
   Pick up a sixpence, you pick up the pounds !

      Could you not go ?
Could you not take the Cobourg or the Surrey ?
Or Sadler's Wells,—(I am not in a hurry,
I never am !) for the next season ?—oh !
     Woe ! woe ! woe !
To both of us, if we remain ; for not
In silence will I bear my altered lot,
To have you merry, sir, at my expense ;
     No man of any sense,
No true great person (and we both are great
In our own ways) would tempt another's fate.
    I would myself depart
    In Mr. Cross's cart ;

But, like Othello, "am not easily moved."
There's a nice house in Tottenham Court, they say,
Fit for a single gentleman's small play;
  And more conveniently near your home;
  You'll easily go and come.
Or get a room in the City—in some street—
Coachmakers' Hall, or the Paul's Head,
  Catcaton Street;
Any large place, in short, in which to get your bread;
  But do not stay, and get
  Me into the Gazette!

  Ah! The Gazette!
I press my forehead with my trunk, and wet
My tender cheek with elephantine tears,
  Shed of a walnut size
  From my wise eyes,
To think of ruin after prosperous years.
  What a dread case would be
  For me—large me!
To meet at Basinghall Street, the first and seventh
  And the eleventh!
  To undergo (D————n!)
  My last examination!
  To cringe, and to surrender,
  Like a criminal offender,
All my effects—my bell-pull, and my bell,
My bolt, my stock of hay, my new deal cell.
  To *post* my ivory, Sir!
And have some curious commissioner
Very irreverently search my trunk;
  'Sdeath! I should die
With rage, to find a tiger in possession
 Of my abode; up to his yellow knees
In my old straw; and my profound profession
 Entrusted to two beasts of assignees!

The truth is simply this,—if you *will* stay
  Under my very nose,

Filling your rows
Just at my feeding time, to see *your* play,
      My mind's made up,
      No more at nine I sup,
Except on Tuesdays, Wednesdays, Fridays. Sundays,
      From eight to eleven,
      As I hope for heaven,
On Thursdays, and on Saturdays, and Mondays,
   I'll squeak and roar, and grunt without cessation,
   And utterly confound your recitation.
And, mark me ! all my friends of the furry snout
      Shall join a chorus shout :
   We will be heard—we'll spoil
   Your wicked ruination toil.
      Insolvency must ensue
      To you, Sir, you ;
   Unless you move your opposition shop,
      And let me stop.

I have no more to say :—I do not write
   In anger, but in sorrow ; I must look,
However, to my interests every night,
   And they detest your " Memorandum-book."
If we could join our forces—I should like it ;
      You do the dialogue, and I the songs.
      A voice to me belongs ;
(The Editors of the Globe and Traveller ring
With praises of it, when I hourly sing
      God save the King.)
If such a bargain could be schemed, I'd strike it !
   I think, too, I could do the Welch old man
   In the Youthful Days, if dress'd upon your plan ;
And the attorney in your Paris trip,—
      I'm large about the hip !
Now think of this !—for we cannot go on
   As next door rivals, that my mind declares :
I must be pennyless, or you be gone !
We must live separate, or else have shares.

I am a friend or foe
As you take this ;
Let me your profitable hubbub miss,
Or be it "Mathews, Elephant, and Co. !"

———

FAITHLESS NELLY GRAY.

A PATHETIC BALLAD.

I.

BEN BATTLE was a soldier bold,
And used to war's alarms :
But a cannon-ball took off his legs,
So he laid down his arms !

II.

Now as they bore him off the field,
Said he, " Let others shoot,
For here I leave my second leg,
And the Forty-second Foot ! "

III.

The army-surgeons made him limbs :
Said he,—" They're only pegs :
But there's as wooden members quite,
As represent my legs ! "

IV.

Now Ben he loved a pretty maid,
Her name was Nelly Gray ;
So he went to pay her his devours,
When he'd devoured his pay !

V.

But when he called on Nelly Gray,
    She made him quite a scoff;
And when she saw his wooden legs,
    Began to take them off!

VI.

"O, Nelly Gray! O, Nelly Gray!
    Is this your love so warm?
The love that loves a scarlet coat,
    Should be more uniform!"

VII.

Said she, "I loved a soldier once,
    For he was blythe and brave;
But I will never have a man
    With both legs in the grave!

VIII.

"Before you had those timber toes,
    Your love I did allow,
But then, you know, you stand upon
    Another footing now!"

IX.

"O, Nelly Gray! O, Nelly Gray!
    For all your jeering speeches,
At duty's call, I left my legs
    In Badajos's *breaches!*"

X.

"Why, then," said she, "you've lost the feet
    Of legs in war's alarms,

And now you cannot wear your shoes
  Upon your feats of arms !"

XI.

"O, false and fickle Nelly Gray!
  I know why you refuse :—
Though I've no feet—some other man
  ·Is standing in my shoes !

XII.

I wish I ne'er had seen your face ;
  But, now, a long farewell !
For you will be my death ;—alas !
  You will not be my *Nell!*"

XIII.

Now when he went from Nelly Gray,
  His heart so heavy got—
And life was such a burthen grown,
  It made him take a knot !

XIV.

So round his melancholy neck,
  A rope he did entwine,
And, for his second time in life,
  Enlisted in the Line !

XV.

One end he tied around a beam,
  And then removed his pegs,
And, as his legs were off,—of course.
  He soon was off his legs !

XVI.

And there he hung, till he was dead
  As any nail in town,—
For though distress had cut him up,
  It could not cut him down !

XVII.

A dozen men sat on his corpse,
  To find out why he died—
And they buried Ben in four cross-reads,
  With a *stake* in his inside !

THE DREAM OF EUGENE ARAM.

'TWAS in the prime of summer time,
  An evening calm and cool,
And four-and-twenty happy boys
  Came bounding out of school :
There were some that ran and some that leapt,
  Like troutlets in a pool.

Away they sped with gamesome minds,
  And souls untouch'd by sin ;
To a level mead they came, and there
  They drave the wickets in :
Pleasantly shone the setting sun
  Over the town of Lynn.

Like sportive deer they coursed about,
  And shouted as they ran,—
Turning to mirth all things of earth,
  As only boyhood can ;
But the Usher sat remote from all
  A melancholy man !

His hat was off, his vest apart,
　　To catch heaven's blessed breeze ;
For a burning thought was in his brow,
　　And his bosom ill at ease :
So he lean'd his head on his hands, and read
　　The book between his knees !

Leaf after leaf he turn'd it o'er,
　　Nor ever glanced aside,
For the peace of his soul he read that book
　. In the golden eventide :
Much study had made him very lean,
　　And pale, and leaden-eyed.

At last he shut the ponderous tome,
　　With a fast and fervent grasp
He strain'd the dusky covers close,
　　And fix'd the brazen hasp :
"Oh, God ! could I so close my mind,
　　And clasp it with a clasp !"

Then leaping on his feet upright,
　　Some moody turns he took,—
Now up the mead, then down the mead,
　　And past a shady nook,—
And, lo ! he saw a little boy
　　That pored upon a book !

"My gentle lad, what is't you read—
　　Romance or fairy fable ?
Or is it some historic page,
　　Of kings and crowns unstable ?"
The young boy gave an upward glance,—
　　"It is 'The Death of Abel.'"

The Usher took six hasty strides,
  As smit with sudden pain,—
Six hasty strides beyond the place,
  Then slowly back again;
And down he sat beside the lad,
  And talk'd with him of Cain;

And, long since then, of bloody men,
  Whose deeds tradition saves;
Of lonely folk cut off unseen,
  And hid in sudden graves;
Of horrid stabs, in groves forlorn,
  And murders done in caves;

And how the sprites of injured men
  Shriek upward from the sod,—
Aye, how the ghostly hand will point
  To show the burial clod;
And unknown facts of guilty acts
  Are seen in dreams from God!

He told how murderers walk the earth
  Beneath the curse of Cain—
With crimson clouds before their eyes,
  And flames about their brain:
For blood has left upon their souls
  Its everlasting stain!

"And well," quoth he, "I know, for truth,
  Their pangs must be extreme,—
Woe, woe, unutterable woe,—
  Who spill life's sacred stream!
For why? Methought, last night, I wrought
  A murder, in my dream!

"One that had never done me wrong—
  A feeble man, and old;
I led him to a lonely field,—
  The moon shone clear and cold:
Now here, said I, this man shall die,
  And I will have his gold!

"Two sudden blows with a ragged stick,
  And one with a heavy stone,
One hurried gash with a hasty knife,—
  And then the deed was done:
There was nothing lying at my foot
  But lifeless flesh and bone!

"Nothing but lifeless flesh and bone,
  That could not do me ill;
And yet I fear'd him all the more,
  For lying there so still:
There was a manhood in his look,
  That murder could not kill!

"And, lo! the universal air
  Seem'd lit with ghastly flame;—
Ten thousand thousand dreadful eyes
  Were looking down in blame:
I took the dead man by his hand,
  And call'd upon his name!

"Oh, God! it made me quake to see
  Such sense within the slain!
But when I touch'd the lifeless clay,
  The blood gush'd out amain!
For every clot, a burning spot
  Was scorching in my brain!

"My head was like an ardent coal,
　My heart as solid ice ;
My wretched, wretched soul, I knew,
　Was at the Devil's price ;
A dozen times I groan'd ; the dead
　Had never groan'd but twice !

"And now, from forth the frowning sky,
　From the heaven's topmost height,
I heard a voice—the awful voice
　Of the blood-avenging Sprite :—
'Thou guilty man ! take up thy dead
　And hide it from my sight !'

"I took the dreary body up,
　And cast it in a stream,—
A sluggish water, black as ink,
　The depth was so extreme:—
My gentle boy, remember this
　Is nothing but a dream !

"Down went the corse with a hollow plunge,
　And vanish'd in the pool !
Anon I cleansed my bloody hands,
　And wash'd my forehead cool,
And sat among the urchins young,
　That evening in the school.

"Oh, heaven ! to think of their white souls,
　And mine so black and grim !
I could not share in childish prayer,
　Nor join in Evening Hymn :
Like a Devil of the Pit I seem'd
　'Mid holy Cherubim !

" And peace went with them, one and all,
　　And each calm pillow spread;
But Guilt was my grim chamberlain
　　That lighted me to bed;
And drew my midnight curtains round,
　　With fingers bloody red!

" All night I lay in agony,
　　In anguish dark and deep;
My fever'd eyes I dared not close,
　　But stared aghast at Sleep:
For Sin had render'd unto her
　　The keys of Hell to keep!

" All night I lay in agony,
　　From weary chime to chime,
With one besetting horrid hint,
　　That rack'd me all the time;
A mighty yearning, like the first
　　Fierce impulse unto crime!

" One stern tyrannic thought, that made
　　All other thoughts its slave;
Stronger and stronger every pulse
　　Did that temptation crave,—
Still urging me to go and see
　　The Dead Man in his grave!

" Heavily I rose up, as soon
　　As light was in the sky,
And sought the black accursed pool
　　With a wild misgiving eye;
And I saw the Dead in the river bed,
　　For the faithless stream was dry.

" Merrily rose the lark, and shook
    The dew-drop from its wing ;
But I never mark'd its morning flight,
    I never heard it sing:
For I was stooping once again
    Under the horrid thing.

" With breathless speed, like a soul in chase,
    I took him up and ran ;—
There was no time to dig a grave
    Before the day began :
In a lonesome wood, with heaps of leaves,
    I hid the murder'd man !

" And all that day I read in school,
    But my thought was other-where ;
As soon as the mid-day task was done,
    In secret I was there :
And a mighty wind had swept the leaves,
    And still the corse was bare !

" Then down I cast me on my face,
    And first began to weep,
For I knew my secret then was one
    That earth refused to keep :
Or land or sea, though he should be
    Ten thousand fathoms deep.

" So wills the fierce avenging Sprite,
    Till blood for blood atones !
Ay, though he's buried in a cave,
    And trodden down with stones,
And years have rotted off his flesh,—
    The world shall see his bones !

" Oh, God ! that horrid, horrid dream
    Besets me now awake !
Again—again, with dizzy brain,
    The human life I take ;
And my red right hand grows raging hot.
    Like Cranmer's at the stake.

" And still no peace for the restless clay,
    Will wave or mould allow ;
The horrid thing pursues my soul,—
    It stands before me now !"
The fearful Boy look'd up and saw
    Huge drops upon his brow.

That very night, while gentle sleep
    The urchin eyelids kiss'd,
Two stern-faced men set out from Lynn,
    Through the cold and heavy mist ;
And Eugene Aram walk'd between,
    With gyves upon his wrist.

THE SEA-SPELL.

> "*Cauld, cauld,* he lies beneath the deep."
>   *Old Scotch Ballad.*

I.

IT was a jolly mariner !
The tallest man of three,—
He loosed his sail against the wind,
And turned his boat to sea :
The ink-black sky told every eye,
A storm was soon to be !

II.

But still that jolly mariner
Took in no reef at all,
For, in his pouch, confidingly,
He wore a baby's caul ;
A thing, as gossip-nurses know,
That always brings a squall !

III.

His hat was knew, or, newly glazed,
Shone brightly in the sun ;
His jacket, like a mariner's,
True blue as e'er was spun ;
His ample trowsers, like Saint Paul,
Bore forty stripes save one.

IV.

And now the fretting foaming tide
He steer'd away to cross ;
The bounding pinnance play'd a game
Of dreary pitch and toss ;
A game that, on the good dry land,
Is apt to bring a loss !

V.

Good Heaven befriend that little boat,
And guide her on her way !
A boat, they say, has canvas wings,
But cannot fly away !
Though, like a merry singing-bird,
She sits upon the spray !

VI.

Still east by south the little boat,
With tawny sail, kept beating :

Now out of sight, between two waves,
Now o'er th' horizon fleeting :
Like greedy swine that feed on mast,—
The waves her mast seem'd eating !

VII.

The sullen sky grew black above,
The wave as black beneath ;
Each roaring billow show'd full soon
A white and foamy wreath ;
Like angry dogs that snarl at first,
And then display their teeth.

VIII

The boatman looked against the wind,
The mast began to creak,
The wave, per saltum, came and dried,
In salt, upon his cheek !
The pointed wave against him rear'd,
As if it own'd a pique !

IX.

Nor rushing wind, nor gushing wave,
That boatman could alarm,
But still he stood away to sea,
And trusted in his charm ;
He thought by purchase he was safe,
And arm'd against all harm !

X.

Now thick and fast and far aslant,
The stormy rain came pouring,
He heard, upon the sandy bank,
The distant breakers roaring,—
A groaning intermitting sound,
Like Gog and Magog snoring !

XI.

The sea-fowl shriek'd around the mast,
Ahead the grampus tumbled,
And far off, from a copper cloud,
The hollow thunder rumbled ;
It would have quail'd another heart,
But his was never humbled.

XII.

For why? he had that infant's caul ;
And wherefore should he dread ?
Alas ! alas ! he little thought,
Before the ebb-tide sped,—
That like that infant, he should die,
And with a watery head !

XIII.

The rushing brine flow'd in apace ;
His boat had ne'er a deck ;
Fate seem'd to call him on, and he
Attended to her beck ;
And so he went, still trusting on,
Though reckless—to his wreck !

XIV.

For as he left his helm, to heave
The ballast-bags a-weather,
Three monstrous seas came roaring on,
Like lions leagued together.
The two first waves the little boat
Swam over like a feather.—

XV.

The two first waves were past and gone,
And sinking in her wake ;

The hugest still came leaping on,
And hissing like a snake ;
Now helm a-lee ! for through the midst,
The monster he must take !

XVI.

Ah, me ! it was a dreary mount !
Its base as black as night,
Its top of pale and livid green,
Its crest of awful white,
Like Neptune with a leprosy, —
And so it rear'd upright !

XVII.

With quaking sails, the little boat
Climb'd up the foaming heap ;
With quaking sails it paused awhile,
At balance on the steep ;
Then rushing down the nether slope,
Plunged with a dizzy sweep !

XVIII.

Look, how a horse, made mad with fear,
Disdains his careful guide ;
So now the headlong headstrong boat,
Unmanaged, turns aside,
And straight presents her reeling flank
Against the swelling tide !

XIX.

The gusty wind assaults the sail ;
Her ballast lies a-lee !
The sheet's to windward taught and stiff !
Oh ! the Lively—where is she?
Her capsiz'd keel is in the foam,
Her pennon's in the sea !

The wild gull, sailing overhead,
Three times beheld emerge
The head of that bold mariner,
And then she screamed his dirge!
For he had sunk within his grave,
Lapp'd in a shroud of surge!

XXL

The ensuing wave, with horrid foam,
Rush'd o'er and cover'd all, —
The jolly boatman's drowning scream
Was smother'd by the squall, —
Heaven never heard his cry, nor did
The ocean heed his *caul*.

———

MORAL REFLECTIONS ON THE CROSS OF ST. PAUL'S.

THE man that pays his pence, and goes
    Up to thy lofty cross, St. Paul,
Looks over London's naked nose,
        Women and men :
        The world is all beneath his ken,
    He sits above the *Ball*.
He seems on Mount Olympus' top,
Among the Gods, by Jupiter! and lets drop
    His eyes from the empyreal clouds
        On mortal crowds.

Seen from these skies,
How small those emmets in our eyes!
    Some carry little sticks—and one
His eggs—to warm them in the sun :
        Dear! what a hustle,
            And bustle!

And there's my aunt. I know her by her waist,
　　So long and thin,
　　And so pinch'd in,
　　Just in the pismire taste.

Oh! what are men?—Beings so small,
　　That, should I fall
Upon their little heads, I must
Crush them by hundreds into dust!

And what is life? and all its ages—
　　There's seven stages!
Turnham Green! Chelsea! Putney! Fulham!
　　Brentford! and Kew!
　　And Tooting, too!
And oh! what very little nags to pull 'em.
　　Yet each would seem a horse indeed,
If here at Paul's tip-top we'd got 'em;
　　Although, like Cinderella's breed,
They're mice at bottom.
　　Then let me not despise a horse,
　　Though he looks small from Paul's high cross!
Since he would be,—as near the sky,
　　—Fourteen hands high.

What is this world with London in its lap?
　　Mogg's Map.
The Thames, that ebbs and flows in its broad channel?
　　A *tidy* kennel.
The bridges stretching from its banks?
　　Stone planks.
Oh me! hence could I read an admonition
　　To mad Ambition!
But that he would not listen to my call,
Though I should stand upon the cross, and *ball!*

THE DEMON-SHIP.

'Twas off the Wash—the sun went down—the sea looked black
    and grim,
For stormy clouds, with murky fleece, were mustering at the brim ;
Titanic shades ! enormous gloom !—as if the solid night
Of Erebus rose suddenly to seize upon the light !
It was a time for mariners to bear a wary eye,
With such a dark conspiracy between the sea and sky !

Down went my helm—close reef'd—the tack held freely in my
    hand—
With ballast snug—I put about, and scudded for the land.
Loud hiss'd the sea beneath her lee—my little boat flew fast,
But faster still the rushing storm came borne upon the blast.
Lord ! what a roaring hurricane beset the straining sail !
What furious sleet, with level drift, and fierce assaults of hail !
What darksome caverns yawn'd before ! what jagged steeps be-
    hind !
Like battle-steeds, with foamy manes, wild tossing in the wind.
Each after each sank down astern, exhausted in the chase,
But where it sank another rose and gallop'd in its place ;
As black as night—they turned to white, and cast against the
    cloud
A snowy sheet, as if each surge upturn'd a sailor's shroud :—
Still flew my boat ; alas ! alas ! her course was nearly run !
Behold yon fatal billow rise—ten billows heap'd in one !
With fearful speed the dreary mass came rolling, rolling, fast,
As if the scooping sea contain'd one only wave at last !
Still on it came, with horrid roar, a swift pursuing grave ;
It seem'd as though some cloud had turn'd its hugeness to a wave !
Its briny sleet began to beat beforehand in my face—
I felt the rearward keel begin to climb its swelling base !
I saw its alpine hoary head impending over mine !
Another pulse—and down it rush'd—an avalanche of brine !
Brief pause had I, on God to cry, or think of wife and home ;
The waters closed—and when I shriek'd, I shriek'd below the
    foam !

Beyond that rush I have no hint of any after deed—
For I was tossing on the waste, as senseless as a weed.

  . . .   .

"Where am I? in the breathing world, or in the world of death?"
With sharp and sudden pang I drew another birth of breath;
My eyes drank in a doubtful light, my ears a doubtful sound—
And was that ship a *real* ship whose tackle seem'd around?
A moon, as if the earthly moon, was shining up aloft;
But were those beams the very beams that I had seen so oft?
A face, that mock'd the human face, before me watch'd alone;
But were those eyes the eyes of man that look'd against my own?

Oh! never may the moon again disclose me such a sight
As met my gaze, when first I look'd, on that accursed night!
I've seen a thousand horrid shapes begot of fierce extremes
Of fever; and most frightful things have haunted in my dreams—
Hyenas—cats—blood-loving bats—and apes with hateful stare—
Pernicious snakes, and shaggy bulls—the lion, and she-bear—
Strong enemies, with Judas looks, of treachery and spite—
Detested features, hardly dimm'd and banish'd by the light!
Pale-sheeted ghosts, with gory locks, upstarting from their tombs—
All phantasies and images that flit in midnight glooms—
Hags, goblins, demons, lemures, have made me all aghast,—
But nothing like that GRIMLY ONE who stood beside the mast!

His cheek was black—his brow was black—his eyes and hair as
  dark:
His hand was black, and where it touch'd, it left a sable mark;
His throat was black, his vest the same, and when I look'd beneath,
His breast was black—all, all was black, except his grinning teeth.
His sooty crew were like in hue, as black as Afric slaves!
Oh, horror! e'en the ship was black that plough'd the inky waves!

"Alas!" I cried, "for love of truth and blessed mercy's sake,
Where am I? in what dreadful ship? upon what dreadful lake?

What shape is that, so very grim, and black as any coal?
It is Mahound, the Evil One, and he has gain'd my soul!
Oh, mother dear! my tender nurse! dear meadows that beguil'd
My happy days, when I was yet a little sinless child,—
My mother dear—my native fields, I never more shall see:
I'm sailing in the Devil's Ship, upon the Devil's Sea!"

Loud laugh'd that SABLE MARINER, and loudly in return
His sooty crew sent forth a laugh that rang from stem to stern—
A dozen pair of grimly cheeks were crumpled on the nonce—
As many sets of grinning teeth came shining out at once:
A dozen gloomy shapes at once enjoy'd the merry fit,
With shriek and yell, and oaths as well, like Demons of the Pit.
They crow'd their fill, and then the Chief made answer for the
    whole;—
"Our skins," said he, "are black ye see, because we carry coal;
You'll find your mother sure enough, and see your native fields—
For this here ship has pick'd you up—the Mary Ann of Shields!"

MARY'S GHOST.

A PATHETIC BALLAD.

I.

'TWAS in the middle of the night,
  To sleep young William tried,
When Mary's ghost came stealing in,
  And stood at his bed-side.

II.

O William dear! O William dear!
  My rest eternal ceases;
Alas! my everlasting peace
  Is broken into pieces.

III.

I thought the last of all my cares
  Would end with my last minute ;
But tho' I went to my long home,
  I didn't stay long in it.

IV.

The body-snatchers they have come,
  And made a snatch at me ;
It's very hard them kind of men
  Won't let a body be !

V.

You thought that I was buried deep,
  Quite decent like and chary,
But from her grave in Mary-bone
  They've come and bon'd your Mary.

VI.

The arm that used to take your arm
  Is took to Dr. Vyse ;
And both my legs are gone to walk
  The hospital at Guy's.

VII.

I vow'd that you should have my hand,
  But fate gives us denial ;
You'll find it there, at Doctor Bell's,
  In spirits and a phial.

VIII.

As for my feet, the little feet
  You used to call so pretty,
There's one, I know, in Bedford Row,
  The t'other's in the city.

IX.

I can't tell where my head is gone,
  But Doctor Carpue can :
As for my trunk, it's all pack'd up
  To go by Pickford's van.

X.

I wish you'd go to Mr. P.
  And save me such a ride ;
I don't half like the outside place,
  They've took for my inside.

XI.

The cock it crows—I must be gone !
  My William, we must part !
But I'll be your's in death, altho'
  Sir Astley has my heart.

XII.

Don't go to weep upon my grave,
  And think that there I be ;
They haven't left an atom there
  Of my anatomie.

THE PROGRESS OF ART.

I.

O HAPPY time ! Art's early days !
When o'er each deed, with sweet self-praise,
  Narcissus-like I hung !
When great Rembrandt but little seem'd,
And such Old Masters all were deem'd
  As nothing to the young !

II.

Some scratchy strokes—abrupt and few,
So easily and swift I drew,
    Suffic'd for my design ;
My sketchy, superficial hand,
Drew solids at a dash—and spann'd
    A surface with a line.

III.

Not long my eye was thus content.
But grew more critical—my bent
    Essay'd a higher walk ;
I copied leaden eyes in lead—
Rheumatic hands in white and red,
    And gouty feet—in chalk.

IV

Anon my studious art for days
Kept making faces—happy phrase.
    For faces such as mine !
Accomplish'd in the details then,
I left the minor parts of men,
    And drew the form divine.

V.

Old Gods and Heroes—Trojan—Greek,
Figures—long after the antique,
    Great Ajax justly fear'd ;
Hectors, of whom at night I dreamt.
And Nestor, fringed enough to tempt
    Bird-nesters to his beard.

VI.

A Bacchus, leering on a bowl,
A Pallas, that out-stared her owl,

A Vulcan—very lame,
A Dian stuck about with stars,
With my right hand I murder'd Mars—
    (One Williams did the same.)

VII.

But tired of this dry work at last,
Crayon and chalk aside I cast,
    And gave my brush a drink !
Dipping—" as when a painter dips
In gloom of earthquake and eclipse,"—
    That is—in Indian ink.

VIII.

Oh then, what black Mont Blancs arose,
Crested with soot, and not with snows :
    What clouds of dingy hue !
In spite of what the bard has penn'd,
I fear the distance did not "lend
    Enchantment to the view."

IX.

Not Radclyffe's brush did e'er design
Black Forests, half so black as mine,
    Or lakes so like a pall ;
The Chinese cake dispers'd a ray
Of darkness, like the light of Day
    And Martin over all.

X.

Yet urchin pride sustain'd me still,
I gaz'd on all with right good wiil,
    And spread the dingy tint ;
"No holy Luke help'd me to paint,
The devil surely, not a Saint,
    Had any finger in't !"

XI.

But colours came !—like morning light,
With gorgeous hues displacing night,
    Or Spring's enliven'd scene :
At once the sable shades withdrew ;
My skies got very, very blue ;
    My trees extremely green.

XII.

And wash'd by my cosmetic brush,
How Beauty's cheek began to blush
    With lock of auburn stain—
(Not Goldsmith's Auburn)—nut-brown hair,
That made her loveliest of the fair ;
    Not "loveliest of the plain !"

XIII.

Her lips were of vermilion hue ;
Love in her eyes, and Prussian blue,
    Set all my heart in flame !
A young Pygmalion, I ador'd
The maids I made—but time was stor'd
    With evil—and it came !

XIV.

Perspective dawn'd—and soon I saw
My houses stand against its law ;
    And "keeping" all unkept !
My beauties were no longer things
For love and fond imaginings ;
    But horrors to be wept !

XV.

Ah ! why did knowledge ope my eyes ?
Why did I get more artist-wise ?

It only serves to hint,
What grave defects and wants are mine ;
That I'm no Hilton in design—
  In nature no Dewint !

XVI.

Thrice happy time !—Art's early days !
When o'er each deed, with sweet self-praise,
    Narcissus-like I hung !
When great Rembrandt but little seem'd.
And such Old Masters all were deem'd
    As nothing to the young !

ODE TO M. BRUNEL.

"Well said, old Mole! canst work i' the dark so fast? a worthy pioneer!"
HAMLET.

WELL !——Monsieur Brunel,
How prospers now thy mighty undertaking,
To join by a hollow way the Bankside friends
Of Rotherhithe, and Wapping,—
　　　　Never be stopping,
But poking, groping, in the dark keep making
An archway, underneath the Dabs and Gudgeons,
For Collier men and pitchy old Curmudgeons,
To cross the water in inverse proportion,
Walk under steam-boats under the keel's ridge,
To keep down all extortion,
And without sculls to diddle London Bridge !
In a fresh hunt, a new Great Bore to worry,
Thou didst to earth thy human terriers follow,
Hopeful at last from Middlesex to Surrey,
　　To give us the "View hollow."
In short it was thy aim, right north and south,
To put a pipe into old Thames's mouth ;
Alas! half-way thou hadst proceeded, when
Old Thames, through roof, not water-proof,
Came, like "a tide in the affairs of men ;"

And with a mighty stormy kind of roar,
  Reproachful of thy wrong,
  Burst out in that old song
Of Incledon's, beginning "Cease, rude Bore"—
Sad is it, worthy of one's tears,
 Just when one seems the most successful,
To find one's self o'er head and ears
 In difficulties most distressful !
Other great speculations have been nursed,
 Till want of proceeds laid them on a shelf ;
But thy concern was at the worst,
 When it began to *liquidate* itself !
But now Dame Fortune has her false face hidden,
And languishes thy Tunnel,—so to paint,
Under a slow incurable complaint,
  Bed-ridden !
Why, when thus Thames—bed-bother'd—why repine !
Do try a spare bed at the Serpentine !
Yet let none think thee daz'd, or craz'd, or stupid ;
 And sunk beneath thy own and Thames's craft ;
Let them not style thee some Mechanic Cupid
 Pining and pouting o'er a broken shaft !
I'll tell thee with thy tunnel what to do ;
Light up thy boxes, build a bin or two,
The wine does better than such water trades :
 Stick up a sign—the sign of the Bore's Head ;
 I've drawn it ready for thee in black lead,
And make thy cellar subterrane,—Thy Shades ?

ANACREONTIC.

FOR THE NEW YEAR.

COME, fill up the Bowl, for if ever the glass
 Found a proper excuse or fit season,
For toasts to be honour'd, or pledges to pass,
 Sure, this hour brings an exquisite reason :
For hark ! the last chime of the dial has ceased,

And Old Time, who his leisure to cozen,
Had finish'd the Months, like the flasks at a feast,
Is preparing to tap a fresh dozen !
           Hip ! Hip ! and Hurrah !

Then fill, all ye Happy and Free, unto whom
  The past Year has been pleasant and sunny;
Its months each as sweet as if made of the bloom
  Of the *thyme* whence the bee gathers honey—
Days usher'd by dew-drops, instead of the tears,
  May be wrung from some wretcheder cousin-
Then fill, and with gratitude join in the cheers
  That triumphantly hail a fresh dozen !
           Hip ! Hip ! and Hurrah !

And ye, who have met with Adversity's blast,
  And been bow'd to the earth by its fury;
To whom the Twelve Months, that have recently pass'd,
  Were as harsh as a prejudiced jury,—
Still, fill to the Future ! and join in our chime,
  The regrets of remembrance to cozen,
And having obtained a New Trial of Time,
  Shout in hopes of a kindlier dozen !
           Hip ! Hip ! and Hurrah !

A WATERLOO BALLAD.

To Waterloo, with sad ado,
  And many a sigh and groan,
Amongst the dead, came Patty Head,
  To look for Peter Stone.

"O prithee tell, good sentinel,
  If I shall find him here?
I'm come to weep upon his corse,
  My Ninety-Second dear !

'Into our town a sergeant came
 With ribands all so fine,
A·flaunting in his cap—alas
 His bow enlisted mine!

"They taught him how to turn his toes,
 And stand as stiff as starch;
I thought that it was love and May,
 But it was love and March!

"A sorry March indeed to leave
 The friends he might have kep',—
No March of Intellect it was,
 But quite a foolish step.

"O prithee tell, good sentinel,
 If hereabout he lies?
I want a corpse with reddish hair,
 And very sweet blue eyes."

Her sorrow on the sentinel
 Appear'd to deeply strike:—
"Walk in," he said, "among the dead,
 And pick out which you like."

And soon she pick'd out Peter Stone,
 Half turn'd into a corse;
A cannon was his bolster, and
 His mattrass was a horse.

"O Peter Stone, O Peter Stone,
 Lord here has been a skrimmage!
What have they done to your poor breast,
 That used to hold my image?"

"O Patty Head, O Patty Head,
  You're come to my last kissing,
Before I'm set in the Gazette
  As wounded, dead, and missing!

" Alas ! a splinter of a shell
  Right in my stomach sticks ;
French mortars don't agree so well
  With stomachs as French bricks.

" This very night a merry dance
  At Brussels was to be ;—
Instead of opening a ball,
  A ball has opened me.

" Its billet every bullet has,
  And well it does fulfil it ;—
I wish mine hadn't come so straight,
  But been a 'crooked billet.'

" And then there came a cuirassier
  And cut me on the chest ;—
He had no pity in his heart,
  For he had *steel'd his breast.*

" Next thing a lancer, with his lance,
  Began to thrust away;
I call'd for quarter, but, alas !
  It was not Quarter-day.

" He ran his spear right through my arm,
  Just here above the joint :—
O Patty dear, it was no joke,
  Although it had a point.

"With loss of blood I fainted off,
　As dead as women do—
But soon by charging over me,
　The *Coldstream* brought me to.

　With kicks and cuts, and bans and blows,
　　I throb and ache all over;
　I'm quite convinc'd the field of Mars
　　Is not a field of clover!

"O why did I a soldier turn
　For any royal Guelph?
I might have been a butcher, and
　In business for myself!

"O why did I the bounty take
　(And here he gasp'd for breath)
My shillingsworth of 'list is nail'd
　Upon the door of death!

"Without a coffin I shall lie
　And sleep my sleep eternal:
Not ev'n a *shell*—my only chance
　Of being made a *Kernel!*

"O Patty dear, our wedding bells
　Will never ring at Chester!
Here I must lie in Honour's bed,
　That isn't worth a *tester!*

"Farewell, my regimental mates,
　With whom I used to dress!
My corps is changed, and I am now,
　In quite another mess.

"Farewell, my Patty dear, I have
   No dying consolations,
Except, when I am dead, you'll go
   And see th' Illuminations."

COCKLE v. CACKLE.

THOSE who much read advertisements and bills
   Must have seen puffs of Cockle's Pills,
     Call'd Anti-bilious—
Which some Physicians sneer at, supercilious,
But which we are assured, if timely taken,
   May save your liver and bacon;
Whether or not they really give one ease,
    I, who have never tried,
    Will not decide ;
But no two things in union go like these—
Viz.—Quacks and Pills—save Ducks and Pease.
Now Mrs. W. was getting sallow,
Her lilies not of the white kind, but yellow,
And friends portended was preparing for
    A human Pâté Périgord ;
She was, indeed, so very far from well,
Her Son, in filial fear, procured a box
Of those said pellets to resist Bile's shocks,
And—tho' upon the ear it strangely knocks—
To save her by a Cockle from a shell !
But Mrs. W., just like Macbeth,
Who very vehemently bids us "throw
Bark to the Bow-wows," hated physic so,
It seem'd to share "the bitterness of Death :"
Rhubarb—Magnesia—Jalap, and the kind—
Senna—Steel—Assa-fœtida, and Squills—
Powder or Draught—but least her throat inclined
To give a course to Boluses or Pills ;
No—not to save her life, in lung or lobe,
For all her lights' or all her liver's sake,
Would her convulsive thorax undertake,
Only one little uncelestial globe !

'Tis not to wonder at, in such a case,
If she put by the pill-box in a place
For linen rather than for drugs intended—
Yet for the credit of the pills let's say
　　After they thus were stow'd away,
　　Some of the linen mended ;
But Mrs. W. by disease's dint,
Kept getting still more yellow in her tint,
When lo ! her second son, like elder brother,
Marking the hue on the parental gills,
Brought a new charge of Anti-tumeric Pills,
To bleach the jaundiced visage of his Mother—
Who took them—in her cupboard—like the other.

"Deeper and deeper, still," of course,
　　The fatal colour daily grew in force ;
Till daughter W. newly come from Rome,
Acting the self-same filial, pillial, part,
To cure Mamma, another dose brought home
Of Cockles ;—not the Cockles of her heart !
　　These going where the others went before,
　　Of course she had a very pretty store ,
And then—some hue of health her cheek adorning,
　　The Medicine so good must be,
　　They brought her dose on dose, when she
Gave to the up-stairs cupboard, "night and morning."
Till wanting room at last, for other stocks,
Out of the window one fine day she pitch'd
The pillage of each box, and quite enrich'd
The feed of Mister Burrell's hens and cocks,—
　　A little Barber of a by-gone day,
　　　　Over the way
Whose stock in trade, to keep the least of shops,
Was one great head of Kemble,—that is, John,
Staring in plaster, with a *Brutus* on,
And twenty little Bantam fowls—with *crops*.
Little Dame W. thought when through the sash
　　She gave the physic wings,
　　To find the very things
So good for bile, so bad for chicken rash,

For thoughtless cock, and unreflecting pullet !
But while they gather'd up the nauseous nubbles,
Each peck'd itself into a peck of troubles,
And brought the hand of Death upon its gullet.
They might as well have addled been, or ratted,
For long before the night—ah woe betide
The Pills ! each suicidal Bantam died
         Unfatted !

     Think of poor Burrell's shock,
Of Nature's debt to see his hens all payers,
And laid in death as Everlasting Layers,
With Bantam's small Ex-Emperor, the Cock,
In ruffled plumage and funereal hackle,
Giving, undone by Cockle, a last Cackle !
To see as stiff as stone, his un'live stock.
It really was enough to move his block.
Down on the floor he dash'd, with horror big,
Mr. Beh's third wife's mother's coachman's wig ;
And with a tragic stare like his own Kemble,
Burst out with natural emphasis enough,
     And voice that grief made tremble,
Into that very speech of sad Macduff—
" What !—all my pretty chickens and their dam,
     At one fell swoop !—
     Just when I'd bought a coop
To see the poor lamented creatures cram !

     After a little of this mood,
     And brooding over the departed brood,
With razor he began to ope each craw,
Already turning black, as black as coals ;
When lo ! the undigested cause he saw—
     " Pison'd by goles !"

To Mrs. W.'s luck a contradiction,
Her window still stood open to conviction ;
And by short course of circumstantial labour,
He fixed the guilt upon his adverse neighbour ;—

Lord! how he rail'd at her: declaring now,
He'd bring an action ere next Term of Hilary,
Then, in another moment, swore a vow,
He'd make her do pill-penance in the pillory!
She, meanwhile distant from the dimmest dream
Of combating with guilt, yard-arm or arm-yard,
Lapp'd in a paradise of tea and cream;
When up ran Betty with a dismal scream—
"Here's Mr. Burrell, ma'am, with all his farm-yard!"
Straight in he came, unbowing and unbending,
    With all the warmth that iron and a barber
        Can harbour;
To dress the head and front of her offending,
The fuming phial of his wrath uncorking;
In short, he made her pay him altogether,
In hard cash, very *hard*, for ev'ry feather,
Charging of course, each Bantam as a Dorking;
Nothing could move him, nothing make him supple,
So the sad dame unpocketing her loss,
Had nothing left but to sit hands across,
And see her poultry "going down ten couple."

Now birds by poison slain,
As venom'd dart from Indian's hollow cane,
Are edible; and Mrs. W.'s thrift,—
She had a thrifty vein,—
Destined one pair for supper to make shift,—
Supper as usual at the hour of ten:
But ten o'clock arrived and quickly pass'd,
Eleven—twelve—and one o'clock at last,
Without a sign of supper even then!
At length the speed of cookery to quicken,
Betty was call'd, and with reluctant feet,
    Came up at a white heat—
"Well, never I see chicken like them chicken!
My saucepans, they have been a pretty while in 'em!
Enough to stew them, if it comes to that,
To flesh and bones, and perfect rags; but drat
Those Anti-biling Pills! there is no bile in 'em!"

ODE ON A DISTANT PROSPECT OF CLAPHAM ACADEMY *

Ah me ! those old familiar bounds !
That classic house, those classic grounds
  My pensive thought recalls !
What tender urchins now confine
What little captives now repine.
  Within yon irksome walls ?

Ay, that's the very house ! I know
Its ugly windows, ten a-row !
  Its chimneys in the rear !
And there's the iron rod so high,
That drew the thunder from the sky
  And turn'd our table-beer !

There I was birch'd ! there I was bred !
There like a little Adam fed
  From Learning's woeful tree !
The weary tasks I used to con !—
The hopeless leaves I wept upon !—
  Most fruitless leaves to me !—

The summon'd class !—the awful bow !—
I wonder who is master now
  And wholesome anguish sheds !
How many ushers now employs,
How many maids to see the boys
  Have nothing in their heads !

And Mrs. S——?—Doth she abet
(Like Pallas in the parlour) yet
  Some favour'd two or three,—
The little Crichtons of the hour,
Her muffin-medals that devour,
  And swill her prize—bohea ?

* No connection with any other Ode.

Ay, there's the playground! there's the lime,
Beneath whose shade in summer's prime
  So wildly I have read!—
Who sits there *now*, and skims the cream
Of young Romance, and weaves a dream
Of Love and Cottage-bread?

Who struts the Randall of the walk?
Who models tiny heads in chalk?
  Who scoops the light canoe?
What early genius buds apace?
Where's Poynter? Harris? Bowers? Chase?
  Hal Baylis? blithe Carew?

Alack! they're gone—a thousand ways!
And some are serving in "the Greys,"
  And some have perish'd young!—
Jack Harris weds his second wife;
Hal Baylis drives the *wane* of life;
  And blithe Carew—is hung!

Grave Bowers teaches A B C
To savages at Owhyee!
  Poor Chase is with the worms!—
All, all are gone—the olden breed!—
New crops of mushroom boys succeed,
  "And push us from our *forms!*"

Lo! where they scramble forth, and shout,
And leap, and skip, and mob about,
  At play where we have play'd!
Some hop, some run, (some fall,) some twine
Their crony arms; some in the shine,—
  And some are in the shade!

Lo there what mix'd conditions run!
The orphan lad; the widow's son;

And Fortune's favour'd care—
The wealthy-born, for whom she hath
Mac-Adamised the future path—
   The Nabob's pamper'd heir !

Some brightly starr'd—some evil born,—
For honour some, and some for scorn,—
   For fair or foul renown !
Good, bad, indiff'rent—none may lack !
Look, here's a White, and there's a Black
   And there's a Creole brown !

Some laugh and sing, some mope and weep,
And wish *their* "frugal sires would keep
   Their only sons at home ; "—
Some tease the future tense, and plan
The full-grown doings of the man,
   And pant for years to come !

A foolish wish !   There's one at hoop;
And four at *fives !* and five who stoop
   The marble taw to speed !
And one that curvets in and out,
Reining his fellow Cob about,—
   Would I were in his *steed !*

Yet he would gladly halt and drop
That boyish harness off, to swop
   With this world's heavy van—'
To toil, to tug.   O little fool !
While thou canst be a horse at school,
   To wish to be a man !

Perchance thou deem'st it were a thing
To wear a crown,—to be a king !
   And sleep on regal down !
Alas ! thou know'st not kingly cares ;

Far happier is thy head that wears
  That hat without a crown !

And dost thou think that years acquire
New added joys? Dost think thy sire
  More happy than his son?
That manhood's mirth?—Oh, go thy ways
To Drury-lane when ———* *plays,*
  And see how *forced* our fun !

Thy taws are brave !—thy tops are rare !—
Our tops are spun with coils of care,
  Our *dumps* are no delight !—
The Elgin marbles are but tame,
And 'tis at best a sorry game
  To fly the Muse's kite !

Our hearts are dough, our heels are lead,
Our topmost joys fall dull and dead
  Like balls with no rebound !
And often with a faded eye
We look behind, and send a sigh
  Towards that merry ground !

Then be contented. Thou hast got
The most of heaven in thy young lot ;
  There's sky-blue in thy cup !
Thou'lt find thy Manhood all too fast—
Soon come, soon gone ! and Age at last
  A sorry *breaking-up!*

---

* This blank exists in the original.

PLAYING AT SOLDIERS.

"WHO'LL SERVE THE KING?"

AN ILLUSTRATION.

WHAT little urchin is there never
Hath had that early scarlet fever,
  Of martial trappings caught ?
Trappings well call'd—because they trap
And catch full many a country chap
  To go where fields are fought !

What little urchin with a rag
Hath never made a little flag,
  (Our plate will show the manner,)
And wooed each tiny neighbour still,
Tommy or Harry, Dick or Will,
  To come beneath the banner !

Just like that ancient shape of mist,
In Hamlet, crying, " 'List, O 'list !"
  Come, who will serve the king,
And strike frog-eating Frenchmen dead
And cut off Boneyparty's head?—
  And all that sort of thing.

So used I, when I was a boy,
To march with military toy,
  And ape the soldier's life ;—
And with a whistle or a hum,
I thought myself a Duke of Drum
  At least, or Earl of Fife.

With gun of tin and sword of lath,
Lord ! how I walk'd in glory's path
  With regimental mates,
By sound of trump and rub-a-dubs—

To 'siege the washhouse—charge the tubs—
 Or storm the garden gates.

Ah me! my retrospective soul!
As over memory's muster-roll
 I cast my eyes anew,
My former comrades all the while
Rise up before me, rank and file,
 And form in dim review.

Ay, there they stand, and dress in line,
Lubbock, and Fenn, and David Vine,
 And dark "Jamacky Forde!"
And limping Wood, and "Cockey Hawes,"
Our captain always made, because
 He had a *real* sword!

Long Lawrence, Natty Smart, and Soame,
Who said he had a gun at home,
 But that was all a brag;
Ned Ryder, too, that used to sham
A prancing horse, and big Sam Lamb
 That *would* hold up the flag!

Tom Anderson, and "Dunny White,"
Who never right-abouted right,
 For he was deaf and dumb;
Jack Pike, Jem Crack, and Sandy Gray
And Dickey Bird, that wouldn't play
 Unless he had the drum.

And Peter Holt, and Charley Jepp,
A chap that never kept the step—
 No more did "Surly Hugh;"
Bob Harrington, and "Fighting Jim"—
We often had to halt for him,
 To let him tie his shoe.

" Quarrelsome Scott," and Martin Dick,
That kill'd the bantam cock, to stick
    The plumes within his hat ;
Bill Hook, and little Tommy Grout
That got so thump'd for calling out
    " Eyes right !" to " Squinting Matt."

Dan Simpson, that, with Peter Dodd,
Was always in the awkward squad,
    And those two greedy Blakes,
That took our money to the fair
To buy the corps a trumpet there,
    And laid it out in cakes.

Where are they now?—an open war
With open mouth declaring for ?—
    Or fall'n in bloody fray?
Compell'd to tell the truth I am,
Their fights all ended with the sham,—
    Their soldiership in play.

Brave Soame sends cheeses out in trucks,
And Martin sells the cock he plucks,
    And Jepp now deals in wine ;
Harrington bears a lawyer's bag,
And warlike Lamb retains his flag,
    But on a tavern sign.

They tell me Cocky Hawes's sword
Is seen upon a broker's board :
    And as for " Fighting Jim,"
In Bishopsgate, last Whitsuntide,
His unresisting cheek I spied
    Beneath a quaker brim !

Quarrelsome Scott is in the church,
For Ryder now your eye must search

The marts of silk and lace—
Bird's drums are filled with figs, and mute,
And I—I've got a substitute
To Soldier in my place !

———

"NAPOLEON'S MIDNIGHT REVIEW."

A NEW VERSION.

In his bed, bolt upright,
In the dead of the night,
The French Emperor starts like a ghost !
By a dream held in charm,
He uplifts his right arm,
For he dreams of reviewing his host.

To the stable he glides,
For the charger he rides ;
And he mounts him, still under the spell ;
Then, with echoing tramp,
They proceed through the camp,
All intent on a task he loves well

Such a sight soon alarms,
And the guards present arms,
As he glides to the posts that they keep ;
Then he gives the brief word,
And the bugle is heard,
Like a hound giving tongue in its sleep.

Next the drums they arouse,
But with dull row-de-dows,
And they give but a somnolent sound ;
Whilst the foot and horse, both,
Very slowly and loth,
Begin drowsily mustering round.

To the right and left hand,
They fall in, by command,
In a line that might better be dress'd;
Whilst the steeds blink and nod,
And the lancers think odd
To be rous'd like the spears from their rest.

With their mouths of wide shape,
Mortars seem all·agape,
Heavy guns look more heavy with sleep;
And, whatever their bore,
Seem to think it one more
In the night such a field day to keep.

Then the arms, christened small,
Fire no volley at all,
But go off, like the rest, in a doze;
And the eagles, poor things,
Tuck their heads 'neath their wings,
And the band ends in tunes through the nose.

Till each pupil of Mars
Takes a wink like the stars—
Open order no eye can obey:
If the plumes in their heads
Were the feathers of beds,
Never top could be sounder than they!

So, just wishing good night,
Bows Napoleon, polite;
But instead of a loyal endeavour
To reply with a cheer;
Not a sound met his ear,
Though each face seem'd to say, *"Nap* for ever!"

QUEEN MAB.

A LITTLE fairy comes at night,
　Her eyes are blue, her hair is brown,
With silver spots upon her wings,
　And from the moon she flutters down.

She has a little silver wand,
　And when a good child goes to bed
She waves her wand from right to left,
　And makes a circle round its head.

And then it dreams of pleasant things,
　Of fountains filled with fairy fish,
And trees that bear delicious fruit,
　And bow their branches at a wish:

Of arbours filled with dainty scents
　From lovely flowers that never fade;
Bright flies that glitter in the sun,
　And glow-worms shining in the shade:

And talking birds with gifted tongues,
  For singing songs and telling tales,
And pretty dwarfs to show the way
  Through fairy hills and fairy dales.

But when a bad child goes to bed,
  From left to right she weaves her rings,
And then it dreams all through the night
  Of only ugly horrid things!

Then lions come with glaring eyes,
  And tigers growl, a dreadful noise,
And ogres draw their cruel knives,
  To shed the blood of girls and boys.

Then stormy waves rush on to drown,'
  Or raging flames come scorching round,
Fierce dragons hover in the air,
  And serpents crawl along the ground.

Then wicked children wake and weep,
  And wish the long black gloom away;
But good ones love the dark, and find
  The night as pleasant as the day.

———

ODE TO DR. KITCHENER.

YE Muses nine inspire
And stir up my poetic fire;
Teach my burning soul to speak
With a bubble and a squeak!
Of Dr. Kitchener I fain would sing,
Till pots, and pans, and mighty kettles ring.

O culinary sage !
(I do not mean the herb in use,
That always goes along with goose)
   How have I feasted on thy page :
    " When like a lobster boil'd the morn
    From black to red began to turn,"
Till midnight, when I went to bed,
And clapt my tewah-diddle on my head.

Who is there cannot tell,
Thou leadest a life of living well ?
" What baron, or squire, or knight of the shire
Lives half so well as a holy Fry—er ? "
In doing well thou must be reckon'd
The first,—and Mrs. Fry the second ;
And twice ↄ Job,—for, in thy fev'rish toils,
Thou wast all over roasts—as well as boils.

  Thou wast indeed no dunce,
  To treat thy subjects and thyself at once ;
Many a hungry poet eats
    His brains like thee,
    But few there be
Could live so long on their receipts.
  What living soul or sinner
  Would slight thy invitation to a dinner,
Ought with the Danaïdes to dwell,
    Draw gravy in a cullender, and hear
    For ever in his ear
The pleasant tinkling of thy dinner bell.

  Immortal Kitchener ! thy fame
  Shall keep itself when Time makes game
Of other men's—yea, it shall keep, all weathers,
And thou shalt be upheld by thy pen feathers.
Yea, by the sauce of Michael Kelly !
    Thy name shall perish never,
    But be magnified for ever—
—By all whose eyes are bigger than their belly.

Yea, till the world is done—
—To a turn—and Time puts out the sun,
Shall live the endless echo of thy name.
But, as for thy more fleshy frame,
Ah ! Death's carnivorous teeth will tittle
Thee out of breath, and eat it for cold victual ;
But still thy fame shall be among the nations
Preserved to the last course of generations.

Ah me, my soul is touch'd with sorrow !
To think how flesh must pass away—
So mutton, that is warm to-day,
Is cold, and turn'd to hashes, on the morrow !
Farewell ! I would say more, but I
Have other fish to fry.

THE CIGAR.

SOME sigh for this and that ;
My wishes don't go far ;
The world may wag at will,
So I have my cigar.

Some fret themselves to death
With Whig and Tory jar,
I don't care which is in,
So I have my cigar.

Sir John requests my vote,
And so does Mr. Marr ;
I don't care how it goes,
So I have my cigar.

Some want a German row,
   Some wish a Russian war;
I care not—I'm at peace,
   So I have my cigar.

I never see the Post,
   I seldom read the Star;
The Globe I scarcely heed,
   So I have my cigar.

They tell me that Bank Stock
   Is sunk much under par;
It's all the same to me,
   So I have my cigar.

Honours have come to men
   My juniors at the Bar;
No matter—I can wait,
   So I have my cigar.

Ambition frets me not;
   A cab or glory's car
Are just the same to me,
   So I have my cigar.

I worship no vain gods,
   But serve the household Lar;
I'm sure to be at home,
   So I have my cigar.

I do not seek for fame,
   A General with a scar;
A private let me be,
   So I have my cigar.

To have my choice among
　　The toys of life's bazaar,
The deuce may take them al'
　　So I have mv cigar.

Some minds are often tost
　　By tempests like a tar;
I always seem in port,
　　So I have my cigar.

The ardent flame of love
　　My bosom cannot char,
I smoke, but do not burn,
　　So I have my cigar.

They tell me Nancy Low
　　Has married Mr. R.;
The jilt! but I can l've,
　　So I have my cigar.

THE END.